THE ITALIAN

Shukri Mabkhout was born in Tunis in 1962. He holds a state doctorate in Literature from the Arts College of Manouba, Tunisia, and is head of the Manouba University. He is the author of several works of literary criticism. *The Italian* is his first novel.

Miled Faiza is a Tunisian-American poet and translator. Among his translations are the Booker Prize-shortlisted novel *Autumn*, and *Winter* by Ali Smith. He teaches Arabic at Brown University.

Karen McNeil has translated poems and short stories for *Banipal* and *World Literature Today*. *The Italian* is her first novel translation. She was a revising editor of the *Oxford Arabic Dictionary* (2014) and is currently completing a Ph.D. in Arabic linguistics at Georgetown University.

Shukri Mabkhout

THE ITALIAN

*Translated from the Arabic
by Karen McNeil and Miled Faiza*

Europa
editions

Europa Editions
8 Blackstock Mews
London N4 2BT
www.europaeditions.co.uk

Translation by Karen McNeil and Miled Faiza
Original title: *al Talyānī*
Translation copyright © 2021 by Europa Editions

A catalogue record for this title is available from the British Library
ISBN 978-1-78770-317-9

Mabkhout, Shukri
The Italian

Book design by Emanuele Ragnisco
www.mekkanografici.com

Cover image: iStock

Prepress by Grafica Punto Print – Rome

Printed and bound in Great Britain by Clays Ltd, Elcograf S.p.A.

CONTENTS

1

No one at the cemetery that day could understand why Abdel Nasser had lashed out so violently. Yes, the death of his father, Hajj Mahmoud, had been a shock, but that didn't fully explain it.

The general sentiment was that "fire had brought forth ash," as the saying goes. On the one hand, you had the poised and dignified Hajj Mahmoud, equally elegant in his cream-colored Tunisian *jebba* and Turkish fez as in his Western suit and fedora. And on the other, you had his slovenly son, in jeans and a chambray shirt with unkempt hair and beard. He was handsome—a mix of Andalusian origins on his mother's and grandmother's side and marks of Turkish beauty on his father's and grandfather's—but his good looks were spoiled by his behavior, which made him look more like a dockworker or ignorant local thug.

Jellaz Cemetery was stone silent. You could hear nothing throughout but the Quranic readers reciting surahs, and the soft refrain of *Allahu akbar*. The size of the funeral procession left no doubt about the respect the community had for Hajj Mahmoud and his family. For in the end, even the dead aren't equal: a man's funeral reflects not only his bank account but also his social currency.

Among the mourners were the extended family, the neighbors (both from their quartier and the residents of the surrounding areas) and other regular people. But there were also artists, intellectuals, academics, journalists, and even some politicians and government ministers. Most of them were friends of Abdel Nasser and his brother Salah Eddine, the esteemed academic and international finance expert.

The funeral was held in the cemetery's large courtyard. Silence reigned over the scene as the men formed rows to pray. I had been with Abdel Nasser ever since I first heard the news and had not left his side for more than a few hours. A group of our friends had gathered with us. We stood on the right side of the courtyard next to a column, waiting for the funeral prayer to end so we, along with some other men, could escort the *hajj* to his final resting place. Tawfiq, Abdel Nasser's uncle, came over, and I heard him whispering to Abdel Nasser, urging him to join the men standing for the prayer: "Shame on you! What will people say? Go join your brother in the front row—the least you could do is behave appropriately at your father's burial!"

Abdel Nasser snapped back, annoyed, "You know as well as they do that I don't fast and I don't pray."

The crowd followed the hearse toward the road leading to the shrine of Sidi Abi Belhassan Chedly, with Abdel Nasser in the front of the procession. He glanced back and glimpsed the imam, a portly man wearing a burgundy *jebba*. As he stared at him to be sure, their eyes met. The imam lowered his eyes, flustered. Abdel Nasser kept glancing at the imam as he walked with us in the procession behind the hearse.

When we arrived at the gravesite, the calls of *Allahu akbar* rose on all sides. The coffin was placed next to the grave, and the Fatiha and other prayers were recited. Unlike the rest of the group around the grave and the coffin, Abdel Nasser didn't raise his palms in supplication during the recitation of the Fatiha and prayers; instead I saw him staring at his neighbor, the imam. The man avoided his gaze, reciting the Quran and the prayers, his turban drooping low over his closed eyes.

Abdel Nasser seemed agitated. His uncle patted his shoulder, and when Salah Eddine noticed his younger brother's distress, he hugged him. At that, tears rolled down Abdel Nasser's cheeks. He closed his eyes and wiped them away. When he opened them again, he saw the imam on his left, standing in the grave to receive the body and lay it to rest.

No one in the large crowd around the grave knew why the imam was suddenly screaming. No one saw what happened except those in the front rows.

"You hypocritical son of a bitch! Despicable piece of shit! Get out of there, you motherfu****. . ."

The imam was groaning in pain, and his mouth was bleeding. Blood stained his white shirt and vest, and flecks of blood marked his socks. He was nearly unconscious and moaning.

A babble of voices drowned each other out in the din that followed:

The imam is covered in blood! . . . Abdel Nasser el-Talyani attacked the imam! . . . Hajj Mahmoud's poor son has gone crazy! . . . I don't know what happened, all I can see is the imam bleeding from the mouth . . . El-Talyani's screaming and swearing at the imam! . . . The hajj's *son is hysterical! . . . How could this be happening at a funeral?! . . . God forgive us, I never thought I'd live to see the day! . . . God protect us!*

Those of us who were in the front row surrounding the grave saw what happened: as Imam Sheikh Allala was preparing to lay down the body of Hajj Mahmoud, Abdel Nasser—in a rage and screaming the most vulgar curses imaginable— smashed his heavy military boots into the imam's face so forcefully you could hear the thud. As if that weren't enough, he then jumped on him and probably would have beaten him to death or strangled him if I hadn't intervened and, with the help of some friends, dragged him away forcibly. He was foaming at the mouth, screaming, cursing, and making threats until he lost consciousness.

The group hurried to bury Hajj Mahmoud, and no one in

the family stood to receive condolences. The shock distracted everyone—Salah Eddine, their uncle Tawfiq, and the family elders, in addition to the crowd—and kept them from finishing the condolence rituals.

All of this happened in late June or early July 1990, on the day of Hajj Mahmoud's death. Those in attendance that day witnessed the first scandal in the neighborhood, maybe even the country, to have a dead man as its victim.

2

While Salah Eddine expressed his sorrow with silence, the rest of the family—especially the women—lambasted Abdel Nasser mercilessly.

His older sister Jweeda (divorced for several years after a marriage that lasted no more than a week) blamed the corrupt books that Abdel Nasser had been reading since he was a child. Books that called for blasphemy and corruption, *God help us*.

His mother Hajja Zeinab, the iron lady of the house, blamed the bad influence of his university classmates. He would bring these vagrants to his room on the top floor, and they would fill it with heavy smoke and discussions, sometimes in whispers and sometimes in loud voices on the verge of a fight. In the midst of her angry commentary, she muttered, "Bastards like him bring nothing but shame."

His youngest sister, Yosser, who had a special place in his heart, insisted that they should sympathize with Abdel Nasser, especially after his failed marriage. She would say, in the form of some unwise words of wisdom: "Forgive Abdel Nasser— every man has his circumstances."

His middle sisters kept quiet, content to express their displeasure with everything they heard with a slight movement of lips and eyebrows, turning their faces toward the offenders and looking at them askance. Sakeena, for instance, after hearing Jweeda's explanation for Abdel Nasser's actions, observed, ". . . that's clear from your prayers and worship. You should've paid more attention to your *own* behavior." She was whispering to Baiya, who was two years older than her. Baiya whispered back, leaning in with a sarcastic comment on her mother's words, "And who's the mother of that 'bastard'?"

His uncle Tawfiq, who had only recently become devout, attributed the problem to a deep-rooted corruption of el-Talyani's morals, as displayed not only by his clothes and appearance but also by his drinking and hedonistic lifestyle.

Neighbors, for their part, expressed their sympathy for the venerable family, explaining the incident away with the proverb that every family has its black sheep.

The only person smiling—a mysterious smile, full of satisfaction and malice—was Lella Jnayna, the imam's wife and the family's neighbor in the same alley. She told them, "Abdel Nasser is right. If I were him, I'd have done that and more!"

People were shocked at this and turned their faces away. Though she was only in her early forties, people had considered Jnayna a bit senile and feeble-minded for years. She spent too much time with the neighborhood children, they thought, to compensate for her own childlessness. But the larger proof was that she wore the *hijab* and was an imam's wife, yet was not observant. Even her husband, Imam Sheikh Allala, had given up on her, asking God every day, morning and evening, in prayer and outside of prayer, to guide her to the right path.

But all of that was just outward appearances. What happened was surely a terrible thing, and many questions remained unanswered. Some of our mutual friends were questioning me, and at that time I couldn't find the courage to answer them: *Why did Abdel Nasser do what he did? Supposing he had good reason for beating up Sheikh Allala, why did he pick the day of his father's funeral? How'd he get so hysterical that he wound up in a mental hospital where they had to sedate him? Shouldn't someone in their thirties be past this kind of reckless behavior?*

Even now, no one—not the neighbors, or the funeral attendees, or the visitors who came to offer condolences during the first two days of mourning, or those who came to provide comfort at the memorial on the final day—no one understood the truth of the matter.

No one but Lella Jnayna. It seemed she knew something, but she didn't breathe a word of it, just tucked the matter away with the other secrets in her collection.

1

All the rituals were finished, and the secret remained a piece of cud that the family chewed over and over on their visits. The women of the neighborhood recited the story on the front steps of their houses, and the young men rehashed it over beers. Yet no one dared talk to Abdel Nasser. He had clearly had some kind of breakdown after what happened and seemed to be descending toward death, from what they could see. His face had become pale, and the sparkle was gone from his eyes. He was thin and sickly, drowning himself in drink, cigarettes, and isolation. At least, that's the meagre information they were able to glean from the terse reports from his sister Yosser, the only one he would suffer to see. He had given her the keys to the two houses that he lived in, and some time ago had assigned her the task of finding some domestic help from the neighborhood and supervising their cleaning. He had heaped money on her ever since he got a job as a journalist in the government newspaper. He opened up a checking account so she could deposit all her money in it. When she protested that it was too much, he answered, "I want you to go buy yourself the best trousseau there is, while you still can. Because you know in a week some young man will come, asking for your hand."

She laughed and joked with him, "A whole week? No, no, I can't wait. I want my groom tomorrow!"

She would hold his head between her hands and kiss his forehead, her eyes filled with tears. But the last time they had replayed this record, when he was in the middle of his divorce from Zeina, she said to him, trying to lift his spirits, "But where could I ever find a man as good as you?"

He answered her coldly and quietly, with a tone of warning, "God forbid he should be like me."

"Don't say that! You're a prince among men. She just wasn't for you—she wasn't good enough for you."

He smiled wanly, his voice filled with a sadness she'd never heard before when he answered her, "I'm the one who wasn't good enough. Believe it: I'm hopeless."

2

Hajja Zeinab asked Salah Eddine to do his duty as eldest brother and at least reprimand Abdel Nasser, or find out the reason behind the scandal. She spoke from the position of the strong matriarch who controlled the entire family—from her recently departed husband all the way down to her youngest daughter, Yosser—and none had ever dared defy her, save Abdel Nasser. He had strayed from the flock, as far as she was concerned. He was the rotten black seed on her threshing floor. She charged Salah Eddine with putting out the flame that the "bastard" had lit and restoring the honor of his late father and the entire family. He had made them the laughing-stock of the neighborhood, after all their years of respect and high position.

Salah Eddine listened to her, feigning interaction and agreement and his intent to perform this crucial mission, until he had almost convinced his mother that she'd reclaimed the family's honor. She told him, "I'd give my life to find out why he did what he did."

Jweeda was also playing her usual role, pouring fuel on the fire. Salah Eddine was stuck between the pincers of two sharp tongues.

In reality, what Abdel Nasser had done seemed disgraceful to Salah Eddine. But he was pragmatic and did not really care to know all the details—it seemed to him that the matter was finished and there was no use going back to it. His youngest brother had chosen a different style of life years ago and had planned for himself a personal path that was markedly different from the family conventions. What on earth good could he do with him now, when he was a grown man in his thirties? He was no longer that child or teenager that you could punish or advise or reform. The best thing to do was to try and understand him, and let him be.

There was nothing for Salah Eddine to do but appear to severely condemn Abdel Nasser in front of his mother and older sister, to put them off until he returned home to Switzerland in a day or two. His ties to his country had been severed years ago, and he didn't much like to return to his family and its never-ending drama. During the summer holidays, Salah Eddine often came to Tunisia with his wife Carla, to spend his vacation on the beaches of Djerba or Tabarka or Sousse or Hammamet, without telling his family and without having to see any of them—except Abdel Nasser, if the chance presented itself. He only visited them when he was participating in a conference at this university or that, or when he came to Tunisia as a visiting professor or part of an international delegation to confer with Tunisian authorities on economic matters. He was a major expert in the field and was relied upon by many people involved with the economies of the Maghreb and Africa and their financial policy. He had bought an apartment in the Ennasr district and outfitted it with the finest furnishings, but he only stayed there a few days a year. That was why he asked Abdel Nasser, after his divorce from Zeina, to live there.

3

Early in the morning the day of his return to Switzerland, Salah Eddine took a bouquet of flowers and went to say good-bye to his brother. Yosser set up the meeting, after checking with Abdel Nasser. He was still exhausted but hadn't yet entered complete isolation. He refused to see anyone who asked to see him—except his older brother.

It was clear that Abdel Nasser didn't want to talk about anything. But he harbored great respect for his brother and was proud of him for both his intellect and his international success. And he couldn't forget his brother's generosity to him during his university days and after his graduation in 1986. If not for all that, Abdel Nasser would have refused to see his brother, too.

He considered himself the complete opposite of his brother, but when his friends, or the businessmen or journalists or politicians he happened to meet, asked him about Salah Eddine and their relationship, he would respond simply: "He's my older brother." He called him "the pasha" and always mentioned his work ethic, modesty, expertise, and integrity, in addition to the self-reliance it took for him to reach the highest ranks.

In reality, their relationship was complicated. Salah Eddine, on account of his university rank and international position, would defend his younger brother whenever anyone compared them. He would say that Abdel Nasser was a free person, with his own way of thinking. Maybe his way of life just wasn't appropriate for a conservative society like Tunisia that respected neither personal freedom nor individual choice. If he himself hadn't moved to Switzerland, maybe he would have been like Abdel Nasser.

Nonetheless, this mutual respect between the brothers came belatedly. In the early eighties, when Abdel Nasser was still a student studying law (or, you could say, studying politics!) at the university, there were some sharp discussions between them during the few visits that Salah Eddine made to his family in Tunisia. They were discussions that left both of them tense, and Salah Eddine quickly put an end to many of them, anticipating the inevitable unpleasantness to come. The younger brother was virulently opposed to the current international financial policy and especially the World Bank and the IMF. He considered structural reform of the Tunisian economy—which, in his words, was on the verge of bankruptcy—to be an imperial impingement on its sovereignty: it prevented the national economy from being built up and laid the foundations for neocolonial dependency and a brutal neo-liberal policy.

Salah Eddine, on the other hand, viewed the issue with the logic of an economist and a well-informed expert on the international economy. He argued that it was related to specific choices in the economic sphere, in particular to the Tunisian economy's relationship with the European ones, chiefly those of France and Germany. He stressed that the past social and economic policy was mere populism, and that it had led to crises like the Tunisian General Labor Union strike of 1978 and the Bread Riots of 1984.

They were intractable debates: it was impossible for a law student to convince an economist. Conversely, the academic defender of market economies was unable to curb the intensity of the young man whose head was full of socialist revolutions and the Marxist books he had consumed. These discussions generally ended with the student being accused of leftist extremism based on total ignorance of economic principles and the economist being accused of not knowing Karl Marx's *Capital* and not understanding the fundamental contradiction between the forces and relations of production, leading him (consciously or unconsciously) to be complicit with the parasites sucking the blood of the people.

What neither of them confessed, however, was how much they admired each other. Salah Eddine admired his brother's enthusiasm: he saw that his political consciousness had matured and that he was a committed young man, still forming his opinions. He was impressed by his brother's audacity and eloquence and his ability to express his views so strongly. As for Abdel Nasser, he was struck by his brother's precise knowledge, especially when he presented economic facts that Abdel Nasser had never heard before, either in his many readings or at the university. Or when he provided statistics (local, regional, and international) to support his words. But what Abdel Nasser liked most was his brother's calmness during these discussions, his imperturbability, and his clear vision of things, despite the drastic differences between them.

4

Si Mahmoud, God rest his soul, would interfere from time to time on the side of his older son. He would accuse his younger son of going too far and tell him to show some respect when speaking to Salah Eddine, his elder.

Abdel Nasser was always impressed at how his brother defended him when responding to their father: "Let him speak, he has some important points" or "It's not disrespectful of him to be passionate about defending his opinion" or "Please, Father, it's just his opinion." At this, the father would fall into a defeated silence. Abdel Nasser saw that his brother—though his political adversary—was a chivalrous intellectual warrior who respected his opponent. So his great respect for his brother grew, though he never considered him a role model.

One particular incident stood out in his memory, the words still ringing in his ears. The family was gathered in the courtyard, the summer breeze carrying the fragrance of porcelain-flowers. Gradually the discussion between Abdel Nasser and Salah Eddine—about politics or the economy or something like that—became heated. Abdel Nasser started raising his voice, despite Salah Eddine maintaining his composure. Their father came out into the courtyard after the *'isha* prayer, and everyone's attention was fixed on the two brothers; they didn't really understand what was going on, though, other than that Abdel Nasser was upset. Si Mahmoud yelled at his younger son, "When are you going to stop being so insolent when you're speaking to your older brother and *sayyid*?"

Abdel Nasser responded, irritated, "My *sayyid*? I don't have a 'master,' and I'm no one's slave. I'll leave the slave morality to you all."

"Shut your mouth, you little shit," his father answered, his hands visibly itching to strike his insolent son. Abdel Nasser leapt up in response to such a bald public insult, and Salah Eddine grabbed him and held him back as he struggled to get free. Once he had managed to calm his younger brother, he turned to his father and said, "Hajj, you should be proud of your son—other people wish they had one like him. He's much more cultured and experienced than I was at his age, and a deeper thinker. Don't be so hard on him. I'm telling you: I can't have discussions this sophisticated with any of my students, or even my colleagues, in Switzerland."

The father stood rooted to his spot, mouth agape. He saw that Sakeena and Baiya's eyes were red with held-back tears. Hajja Zeinab—who, at that time, hadn't made the pilgrimage and so was not yet a *hajja*—stayed where she was, silent. Salah Eddine's praise likely did not please her, but there was nothing she could do about it. Jweeda flashed a wide, fake smile, no doubt to flatter the older brother. As for Yosser, she gently patted Abdel Nasser's shoulder, and Salah Eddine embraced him affectionately.

The moody youth's gaze roved over the people around him seated on floor cushions and carpets and then, with a final challenging smile for his father, headed for the room leading outside. Later, Yosser told him what was discussed after he left: Salah Eddine had reproached them for what they thought about Abdel Nasser and changed everyone's minds about him. And so Abdel Nasser's stock in the family rose.

5

Salah Eddine waited in front of the intercom for some time before Abdel Nasser buzzed him into the building. He was wearing a grey tracksuit, and his face looked pale; he was even thinner than what Yosser had described. He had a thermos of coffee in front of him, and cartoons were playing on the television. The clock hands pointed to 10:00 A.M.

Abdel Nasser asked him the usual questions about how he was doing and his health. He thanked him for the flowers. He poured him a cup of coffee, then said, taking a long look at the flowers, "You're always the best, even in the flowers you choose."

Salah Eddine didn't wait long before broaching the subject. He spoke to Abdel Nasser frankly about the family's confusion and their astonishment at what had happened. He told him about the pressure coming from their domineering mother but assured him that he hadn't come to do what he'd been asked, just to check on his brother and friend.

He added, "I don't know why you did it. But I'm sure you have your reasons. I won't lie—I would feel better if I knew, but I don't want to upset you. I'm only worried about you, not about what you did."

"I'm not okay. I'm not going to *be* okay. I wasn't okay before."

"Why all this pessimism, Abdu?"

"I know you're a realist, and you're smart, so I'll be straight with you. You've got to know I'm no good. I'm a failure; I just didn't want to admit it to myself."

"You're just seeing the glass half empty—that's natural, given your current situation."

"No, the glass shattered a long time ago. And I can't repair the cracks—I used to think I could, but I was just kidding myself."

Given the painful turn the conversation was taking, Salah Eddine thought that Abdel Nasser had fallen into depression. So he asked him about his work and about the foreign newspaper he had become a correspondent for. Abdel Nasser smiled and said, "This isn't a nervous breakdown, like you're thinking. My health and my mental health are fine. I'm just seeing things clearly. I always have, whatever people think."

He lit a second cigarette from the one he'd just taken out of his mouth and went on, "Know why this isn't a nervous breakdown?"

"No . . ."

"Because I've been living a double life, ever since I was young. All the obscenity and vices people see me indulging in: Abdel Nasser the undisciplined hedonist, the renegade. I knew the family wasn't a fan of my life, but they were living their own big lie."

Salah Eddine interrupted, "They don't think that badly of you!"

"How many years have you been gone? At this point, you're just a guest in your country, and even in your own family. Don't try and cheer me up. I'm just telling you this because I know you don't think like these miserable lying idiots in Tunisia."

He stared off into space for a moment, took a few drags on his cigarette, then said, "What saved me from a nervous breakdown was somebody else, somebody inside me. It's not my soul or a guilty conscience. It's a completely rational person, cold, unfeeling, razor-sharp. He's the one who guides me when the road gets mixed up. If it weren't for him, I would've become completely deviant and criminal, or I'd have wasted away and killed myself."

Salah Eddine watched him while he talked, keeping his face neutral. But he noticed that, for the first time, Abdel Nasser was speaking calmly, tranquilly. His enthusiasm had gone, and his passion and tension had faded away, though his mental sharpness was intact.

Abruptly, Abdel Nasser asked Salah Eddine to look him in the eye. He was startled, but he did. "Why did you run away to France and leave Jnayna?" Abdel Nasser asked.

The question took him aback. He was silent a moment, trying to figure out what was behind it. Finally he said, "That's ancient history—why are you asking me about it now? And I didn't run away; I was awarded a merit scholarship."

"I know all that. But you left Jnayna alone, and that destroyed her."

"You were little, you didn't know the whole story."

"I know you were lovers, that you took her virginity and then didn't want to marry her."

"No—who told you that? It wasn't that simple."

"So you weren't lovers?"

"What kind of love could there be between a naive high school student and a spoiled girl whose father had ruined her? Who'd dropped out of school, so, young as she was, her father was already trying to find her a husband? Should I have to pay the price for that?"

"What price?"

"Listen, Abdel Nasser. Let's keep this between you and me, and not dig up the past—she's married now, so it doesn't do anybody any good." Abdel Nasser agreed, so he continued: "Jnayna looked older than her age. A grown woman, exciting and seductive. I heard that she was talking about me to the guys in the neighborhood, very admiringly. I was buried in my books; I couldn't even look at a girl without blushing. I didn't dare go near her, even though she used to come to the house all the time and Mother treated her like a daughter. I didn't dare, until the incident . . ."

He was silent a moment with his memories, then continued, "One summer she spent two days at our house . . . I remember that Hajj Shadhli had gone to Monastir with his Sufi singing group to sing in one of Bourguiba's birthday celebrations, so he left her with us. She snuck into my room during the afternoon *qailulah* when everybody was napping—it must have been the end of July or beginning of August. She stripped all her clothes off right in front of me. And what happened happened. It was the first time I had touched a girl. And as much as I liked it, you don't know how guilty I felt. It was more than you'd imagine, because she'd lost her mother, and I'd been brought up conservatively; I knew what I did would be considered a shame on the family. My guilt was partly relieved, though, because I knew that she was having affairs with other guys. Her maids encouraged her and were complicit in everything; they even joined her in some of her adventures. But, for me, that was the first time and the last time. Everyone knew what was going on, but it was all swept under the rug."

"I thought that whole story with her affairs happened after you left . . ."

"Why would I lie to you about something that happened so long ago? I'm talking to you friend to friend. Though I remember that Father wrote me a letter when I was in France to try to deal with the matter. He accused me of preying on women and threatened me with the divine punishment that comes to those who mess around with decent, motherless girls. I didn't respond to him at the time; I had already decided to stay in France during the summer to work in the grape fields or travel in Europe. I didn't come back to Tunisia until they lied to me and told me Father was on his deathbed, asking to see me. When I spoke to Father and denied the whole thing, he sat me down, against my will, with Hajj Shadhli ben Y. I repeated the story and accused his daughter of lying and moral corruption. I told him about the things going on under his nose that he had no idea about. He believed me. And after that, I learned that he'd died. Maybe he died of a broken heart, after hearing my story about what happened. I was just defending myself: they wanted me as a sacrifice on the altar of preserving the spotless Shadhli family honor, and his religious position and reputation. Maybe I was the reason she was married off to that *darwish* Alalla, or the reason for her father's death. But I had no intention of paying the price for Hajj Shadhli's brothel, not when so many before me had got in for free."

"Looks like I was the sucker who paid the price with his childhood."

"What do you mean?"

"Long story . . . Goes back to that shattered glass that I tried to fix but couldn't."

"Then maybe we should save it for my next visit? I might come back in November to teach at the Université de Sousse. Promise me we'll have a good long chat."

"Yeah, yeah, of course," Abdel Nasser said. "If I'm still alive."

"Don't say things like that. You're just at a crossroads: that pure mind that you were telling me about will lead you down the right path."

"It might have gotten bored of me standing at the crossroads so often."

"In any case, I'm leaving in a few hours, and I haven't packed yet. I'm proud of you, cracks and all."

They were heading toward the door when Salah Eddine suddenly smiled and asked el-Talyani, "Would you like to spend a few days with us in Switzerland? Angelika always asks about you, and remembers what the two of you had. She still hasn't married after her fiancé was killed."

He promised to think about it, though he immediately rejected it. So Salah Eddine hugged him in front of the door and said again, "I'm proud of my little brother. He's still a child who loves life."

At the doorway he told him, jokingly, "Is the misled idealist convinced yet of the triumph of capitalism, and the crushing defeat of the poverty and misery of socialism?"

Abdel Nasser laughed for the first time since Hajj Mahmoud's death and closed the door. To himself, he muttered, "I'm proud of you, too. If not for you, I wouldn't be here."

6

Abdel Nasser was not exaggerating when he connected his existence with that of his brother. He had always looked different from his siblings—he was better looking than the rest of them, ever since he was little. So much so that the women in the family were always asking his mother, "Where did you get him from?"

She would play them off with a joke that Abdel Nasser was "the last hurrah before the factory shut down."

Sometimes one of the bawdy women would be insistent and spoil the joke: "But you had Yosser after Abdel Nasser." So Zeinab would respond, in a half-joking, half-serious way that put an end to the discussion: "I'm talking about bearing boys. Girls—well, even cats can bear them."

But the women themselves came to a more rational conclusion: when Zeinab was pregnant with Abdel Nasser, she must have had a craving for one of the characters on the

Italian station, Rai Uno TV. That was the only foreign station they could pick up in Tunisia at the time, and Hajj Mahmoud was one of the first to have a television back then. So maybe it was a news announcer from the station, or one of the actors in the series they broadcast.

But then some of the other women would point out that this supposed pregnancy craving of Zeinab's didn't fit the timeline; Abdel Nasser was born in 1960, when the radio was still the only available means of entertainment. These women explained Abdel Nasser's Italian good looks by pointing out that Hajj Mahmoud was one of those open-minded men who didn't mind mixing with affluent French, Jewish, Italian, and Maltese people. He was a high-ranking employee in the finance ministry and the scion of an old Turkish family and was one of the few men you would see walking home carrying a French newspaper. He was also one of the few men who would take their wives to the movies. So maybe Zeinab had a craving for one of the foreigners she met with her husband. When this kind of talk would start to annoy Zeinab, she would suffice by saying, "maybe . . . ," "possibly . . . ," "could be . . . ," offering vague answers that appealed, ultimately, to the workings of divine providence.

7

I don't know when exactly everyone in the extended family and in the neighborhood began to call Abdel Nasser *el-Talyani*, "the Italian." However, his foreign Italian lineage became stronger and more entrenched day after day and showed ever more clearly. This was the first difference that distinguished Abdel Nasser within the family and drew attention to him, to the point that he became the center of attention even as a child.

A boy has a contradictory position in our Tunisians families. On the one hand, he is completely neglected and left to his own devices; no adult ever goes looking for him if he wants to be by himself, or to go out to play with the neighborhood kids, or to climb onto the roof, or to go into one of the rooms rifling through his siblings' or his parents' things. But on the other hand, he is the business of everyone who wants to play grown-up, all his teenage siblings who want to prove their strength by beating him up, convinced that it will make him better behaved. Or, at best, who want to play the role of disciplinarian by reprimanding him if he makes a mistake, or yelling at him, or treating him like a servant: "Bring me a glass of water," "Bring me my shoes from the other room," "Quick, go get two loaves of bread from the bakery."

One of the funniest stories about this that Abdel Nasser told was when the family was all getting ready to spend the summer in Hammam Lif. Zeinab found herself in an empty house—with no servants or children except him—just her and her husband, who was taking his usual *qailulah*. As Abdel Nasser remembered it, they were waiting for a car to take them and some of their belongings to the coastal town. Zeinab asked him to go to his grandmother's house, where his divorced aunt lived, about fifteen minutes away. His divorced aunt was also beautiful, with an Italian kind of beauty that she never lost, even in her old age.

"Tell your aunt: Give me a few *miswak* twigs to brighten my smile and keep this one with you." The boy, who was around ten years old at the time, hurried to do his mother's bidding. He ran the whole way, wanting to get to his aunt's house quickly so he could get back home quickly and join the others in Hammam Lif. He found his aunt chatting with a group of her neighbors in the center courtyard of the house. He repeated what his mother had said verbatim, like a student reciting a memorized lesson. He didn't understand at the time why the women all burst out laughing but stood dumbfounded, looking from one woman to the next. His aunt took him in her arms and started showering him with kisses. She detained him for what felt like forever, talking with him sweetly and stroking his hair, while he tried to extract himself so he could take the *miswak* and hurry home. Finally she set him free, saying, "Tell your mother: If the *miswak* are spicy, don't forget to save me some next time."

His aunt didn't give him anything to take back with him, and he didn't understand a word of what she said. The laughter of the women followed him as he headed toward the entryway to leave. He ran home and stood knocking for several minutes on the door, until he started to imagine that his mother and father had gone to the summer house and left him behind.

Many years later, as an adult, he remembered this incident and finally understood what had happened. I first heard it from him when he was telling his ex-wife Zeina, after she said how much she hated spicy *miswak*.

8

As a child, el-Talyani viewed anything connected with his older brother as an intriguing secret to be discovered. His room was the only room in the house that was locked; no one knew what was in there except the maid and his mother, who would intrude in her eldest child's room without knocking. He was the only one who was allowed to invite friends over, so they would meet in summer or in winter whenever he wanted, in his private space on the top floor. And he was the only one the father allowed to travel before graduating from high school, to France during the summer break.

It was true that Salah Eddine was always excellent in school, and well behaved, and didn't spend much time mixing

with his peers—he didn't even spend much time playing soccer with the neighborhood boys. He didn't smoke or cause
problems in the house. He was not a troublemaker and never
spoke out of turn, only saying "yes" if his mother asked him to
do something or when his father spoke to him. A perfect child
that the neighbors and their relatives envied them for.

Abdel Nasser, when he began to understand the world a bit,
thought it likely that Salah Eddine had been raised to be an
older brother that everyone in the house respected and, at the
same time, to be a mini replica of his father. He was certain that
this was the doing of his mother, Zeinab, the iron fist of the
house. Si Mahmoud assisted her in that role, in that he deliberately left space between himself and everyone else and only
spoke to them through her, with the exception of Abdel Nasser.

The father was not an ill-mannered brute; he never insulted
their mother or beat her, like in some other families. But everyone in the house knew that he was as regimented as the hands
of a clock. At exactly 12:20 P.M. he would enter the house to
find the table set and ready. He would eat lunch by himself,
and Zeinab would give him a detailed report of the morning's
events. Then he would go to his room to take his customary
rest, which demanded absolute silence in the house. Speech
became whispered; movement stopped entirely or was done
with soft footsteps in cases of absolute necessity. (And woe to
he who disturbed the king's rest!) In the winter, life did not
return to normal until around one-thirty; in the summer, the
household's hours were set around the schedule of the king's
qailulah, which usually extended until nearly four-thirty.

9

In 1966, at the age of eighteen, Salah Eddine went to
France to continue his studies. At the time, Abdel Nasser was

six years old and was a boy with zero supervision. No one remembered him except on the rare occasions when they sent him to fetch something they needed, if Baba Ali was not available. Baba Ali was a mysterious figure: he lived in one of the small rooms and was charged with serving the family. One of his tasks, once Abdel Nasser turned six, was to accompany him to school and back. Beyond this mission, Baba Ali would go to the market for whatever the mistress of the house needed or the family asked for. He would eat alone in his room. He never joined the rest of the family, not even once, though he frequented the local café after finishing his household duties.

Not much was known about him, just that he returned home to his village when Abdel Nasser was in fourth grade. Abdel Nasser was only aware of that because that was when, at around ten years old, he had to learn how to get to school and back by himself or with the other neighborhood kids.

But the meager information that he had, when he tried to organize it in his head as an adult, made him think that Baba Ali was one of the migrants who came from the east coast villages, a great number of whom had come to greet the leader Bourguiba in the port of La Goulette when he returned from exile on June 1, 1955. Abdel Nasser thought that Baba Ali must have been one of the thousand poor peasants the Constitutional Party gathered together to pad the attendance of their meetings, and possibly for protection or applause, or to undertake little missions in the service of the party.

Abdel Nasser guessed, based on the meager information and the thoughts that he constructed about Baba Ali's life, that he had lived homeless in the capital. The likes of him were not greedy: they asked for no more in life than enough cash to keep them breathing and buy cigarettes and coffee. Which they were given, in exchange for the sorts of services their well-to-do masters, and even those a rung or two below them on the ladder, refused to dirty their hands with. Abdel Nasser did not know, and he never asked, how Baba Ali came to their house or from where. He never heard that he had any family, until one day when he saw him carrying a small bag. He was told that he was going "back home," and they never heard from him again. He must be dead by now. Even back then he was older than Hajj Mahmoud, his age quite visible when he walked.

Baba Ali was, in the family's view, a person to be made an example of. Whenever el-Talyani went to bed without washing his feet, or was too lazy to wash his hands after eating, or came home with dirty clothes, or was found to have dirty knees from playing games in the street, Jweeda would wash him in the bath and would tell him, "You're as filthy as Baba Ali!"

When he was at university, he used to get a kick out of calling whatever student he saw who happened to be dirty "Baba Ali." None of his friends or acquaintances understood what he was talking about; he knew they didn't get the reference. But in spite of that, it affected some of his close friends, who took it in various ways, some as a compliment and some as an insult.

One of the funniest "Baba Ali" incidents began when Abdel Nasser was standing in a general meeting in the Faculté de Droit, listening to a speech by one of the fiery revolutionary orators at the university—one of the very few female ones at that time. She had riled up the students, who thought she was pretty in her jeans and grey wool vest and old-fashioned shirt, even though she wore no makeup, not even eyeliner or lip gloss. Looking at her in her short-sleeved shirt, Abdel Nasser noticed that her elbows were noticeably black and there were food stains on her trousers. So he whispered in the ear of his friend, a loyal fighter for Marxism and the son of a trader from far away, "Enjoy Baba Ali, with all her talk about freeing Palestine and uniting Arabs from the Gulf to the sea!"

After the meeting ended, when they were returning on the

designated students' bus (which they called the *spécial*), the Arab Marxist leaned over to whisper to Abdel Nasser, as though discussing the start date of a revolution against Bourguiba and trying to keep it from the police, "Comrade Baba Ali's speech was excellent, wasn't it?"

"Who?"

"The comrade whose code name you said was Baba Ali . . ."

Everyone on the bus turned to stare when Abdel Nasser burst out laughing so hard he almost fell off his seat, clutching his stomach. His friend grew angry at this inexplicable laughter and came close to hitting him. Only when Abdel Nasser's hysterics had died down could he tell him that that wasn't what he'd meant, that he wasn't laughing at anything he said but that he'd reminded him of a joke.

The Arab Marxist did not even crack a smile but looked at him with loathing, then responded (with the earnest stupidity of the true believers), "Jokes like that are vulgar and beneath us resistance fighters. That's the bullshit values of the petit-bourgeois."

10

When Salah Eddine left, his room stayed locked. But his mother would sometimes give the maid Yamina (whose real name was Ghzala) the key to it so she could air it out and dust, so that it would be clean in case of Salah Eddine's unexpected return. Seeing as how he was one of the most important men in all of Tunisia, it just wouldn't do for him to find his room in an unsuitable condition. Especially since the government (the *government*, you know) sent him to France (*France*). And in any case, Salah Eddine was the most important person in the family, and everyone knew his place in Zeinab's heart was even above that of her husband, Mahmoud, though no one dared say it out loud.

During one of his unplanned searches, Abdel Nasser discovered that the key to Salah Eddine's room was kept in a sugar bowl. It was made of glass and rimmed with silver, part of a set of decorative glasses called Tripoli glasses. There were larger glasses for green tea and smaller ones for black tea, all laid out tastefully on a silver tray. And it was his good luck that he happened to look at the tray, otherwise he would have never found the key. He tended to search on the insides of things—in the drawers, under the mattress, in the hidden corners—and he never would have imagined that he would find something so valuable so close by and easily accessible to anyone, in a set of tea glasses that he had never seen used. But he considered this a sign of his mother's cleverness in hiding what she wanted to keep hidden. She was an expert in the art of dissimulation and concealment; she had put the key at the very bottom of the sugar bowl, where it couldn't be seen through the glass.

With total calm, he slipped the key into his pocket and planned his storming of Fort Salah Eddine during the afternoon *qailulah*, when everyone would be sleeping or keeping quiet for fear of disturbing Si Mahmoud. As for el-Talyani himself, his mother used to describe him as "the *qailulah* devil" because he didn't, and couldn't be forced to, sleep during these hours. They were precious hours he had to himself, when he could do what he wanted without supervision.

Unfortunately, he was to be greatly disappointed. There were no secrets in the fort, other than what you could see when you went in normally. He opened the cabinets and looked everywhere that you could hide things: under the bed, behind the wardrobe, on top of it, in the suitcase, in the wallet, inside the desk drawers. Not a single surprise.

Nothing worthy of mention. A number of books, most of them in French, whose titles Abdel Nasser sounded out without understanding. Photographs and transparent nega-tives, yellowed and warped from the sunlight coming from the latticed *mashrabiya*, only their subjects' faces still clearly visible. He recognized some of the boys from the neighbor-hood in them, and guessed that the others were classmates.

But mostly Salah Eddine had papers, piles of papers writ-ten in French, in his pleasant, neat handwriting that resembled their father's. Old notebooks with tatty covers (the remnants of many years of school), a group of certificates of achievement arranged carefully in a glossy yellow folder, a group of maga-zines and folders full of newspaper stories and pictures of soc-cer players from Salah Eddine's favorite team, Club Africain.

Why go to the trouble of locking the door, then? Maybe the only explanation for the aura of mystery surrounding the fortress was the record collection: large and small records, as well as the player for these "plates," as the family called them. The player was in a position of pride where you couldn't miss seeing it, on a medium-sized table in one of the corners of the room, near the latticed *mashrabiya* and beside a rocking chair.

Despite his disappointment—disappointment at not dis-covering the important secret that he'd assumed was there—Abdel Nasser decided at the time that he should keep some small things to himself, as his own private knowledge. Perhaps he realized that people's secrets (like the banalities in his brother's room) didn't have value in and of themselves: rather their value came from being hidden from curious eyes like his own.

He understood later on, after he had grown up and spent time with his classmates in high school and university, that "storming the fort" had opened up a whole world of music and art for him. Listening to those recordings in his brother's room introduced him to types of music other people didn't know about. This was made possible by a historic agreement he made with the strict commander of the house, his mother

Zeinab. It had begun with a request from him, after he had gotten a bit older, to have the key for an hour or two to listen to records and enjoy them. He didn't like everything he heard, but he made himself sit on his brother's rocking chair and listen. What enjoyment he found in that chair, trying on the personality of his absent brother, imagining he was like him! During those sessions, listening to music and identifying with his brother, he loved jazz more than any other kind of music.

When Abdel Nasser was fourteen or fifteen years old, and everyone was certain that Salah Eddine would never return to his bedroom, the keys were surrendered to him, and he became its rightful master. The proprietress of the hammam had noticed, about a year before, that he had started to stare at the women bathing, stealing glances and listening to them as they played around and enjoyed themselves. So he was no longer welcome to accompany his mother and four sisters on Friday afternoons, the set time for their weekly purification.

Abdel Nasser was still a child in the eyes of his mother and sisters, but in the eyes of other women he was a teenager with raging hormones. He began to charm girls (and even older women) with his good looks and attractive build. He captivated them with his enchanting smile and eyes, not to mention his manhood, which the neighborhood women slyly called his "feather." The final verdict was "You can't leave the rooster wandering among the hens."

11

Zeinab decided that the boy should be independent in his brother's room on the top floor, with the four hens in the other two rooms on the ground floor. Abdel Nasser felt he had finally gained a measure of independence from his family. Prior to the new arrangement—which he had secretly and fervently hoped for—he had had to guard his secrets himself. He refused to let any of his sisters touch him or enter his room (to make his bed or dust or clean the floor) without knocking on the door first. Yamina alone, who, contrary to the rest of the family, he deliberately called "Ghzala," did all that in his presence. Before she started looking after these matters related to his room, for a short period it had been Lella Jnayna. As for his hammam, its appointed time had changed a year or two before to every Sunday, with Si Mahmoud.

His mother—the only one who would violate the sanctity of the room—did not abide either secrets or knocking on doors. She would burst in and yell, "Look at this mess! What a disaster!" Or "Pick up your clothes! How can you leave them on the floor like that!" Or "Why do I bother? You've become the heir of Baba Ali!" Or "What is this? Is it a coalman's pillow or the pillow of Si Mahmoud's son?" Or "Good lord, when will this swine become a human like everyone else?" Or "Salah Eddine's room has become a chicken coop—what a shame!" Zeinab would shout these along with other artful comments she'd come up with, then call for Si Mahmoud to come and bring his son into line.

The son, however, no longer stood for insults. As much as he was polite and respectful to his elders in the neighborhood and the family, he didn't hold back in the face of his mother's contempt. He was the first person in the house who dared to challenge her absolute rule, responding to her words with equal vitriol: "It's my room, and I can do what I want in it" or "I like my mess. Leave me alone, or I'll leave and not come back."

His mother understood, from her intuition and experience, that she was faced with a son who was cut from a different cloth. She resisted in the beginning, trying to preserve her threatened authority, then, after several unpleasant altercations, changed her strategy. She started avoiding direct confrontations with him and instead would set Si Mahmoud on him. He obliged, reluctantly, pretending to scold Abdel Nasser. But what he hid from his wife was that he had made a secret agreement with his son: Abdel Nasser would accept his father's scolding and harsh reprimand in front of his mother, enough to satisfy her of his obedience to his father. This secret agreement was made during one of their weekly trips to the hammam, though Abdel Nasser never understood why his father did that. He supposed that he was trying to walk the fine line between the role of a father and that of a friend.

The situation stayed this way for several years. At first, Abdel Nasser attributed it to his father's mentality, which leaned toward the Western model in child rearing. But eventually he realized that the real reason was that Si Mahmoud simply didn't see anything wrong with his son's behavior—despite his own fastidiousness and his efforts to maintain his elegance and good reputation as a government official and heir of a Turkish family. He saw two benefits to his father's position: on the one hand, there was the perverse pleasure of spiting his wife, who always stuck her nose into everything and expected everyone (including Si Mahmoud) to be under her command. And, on the other, there was the simple desire to avoid hassles and headaches, like any husband. So Abdel Nasser thought that this understanding between them allowed Si Mahmoud to avoid getting involved in the conflicts and gave his sole remaining son in the house the chance to grow and mature. Several times he heard his mother blame his father, sometimes sharply. "You're going to lose your son if you don't stand up to him and confront him."

And his father would answer, mildly, "He's still young, Zeinab. Force is useless; what's best is to guide him and give him friendly advice, as our Lord says in his holy book . . ."

He would then cite an *ayah* or proverb or a line of poetry, or any words bearing no clear relation to the topic of rearing children. And she would fall silent, defeated by this conclusive and unassailable argument.

His mother came to understand after these maneuvers and retreats that she was not going to gain control over the situation—neither through her direct attacks nor through the claws of her husband, the outsized housecat. Her final attempt was to play a game known among the women as "I'm talking to you (and the neighbor, too)." In other words, to say things intended for Abdel Nasser's ears in front of him, but speaking to someone else. But this game failed, as well, because of how little time Abdel Nasser spent with the family or any part of it. He had declared his independence to the extent that he had almost completely severed ties with them, including going to the hammam with his father on Sundays. And whenever his mother would take up her favorite hobby of scolding, advising, or indirectly criticizing him, el-Talyani would stand up, putting his hands in his pockets and humming a French song or whistling, and leave the house or go up to his room or call Yosser to come help him with something.

As the young hothead grew up, his mother realized that continuing down this path would threaten her prestige in her kingdom and, by all appearances, decided to relinquish the small princedom that had declared its independence. She would say to her daughters and the other women in the family, "I no longer care about that bastard." They found her opinion strange and would only answer her with prayers and platitudes: "May God guide him to the right path," "He's still young," "This is how kids behave nowadays," "Boys are always difficult." The conversation then always and predictably ended with mention of the good son, Salah Eddine, the neat and polite boy who honored the family with his genius and was working on his PhD, so it wouldn't be a surprise if he ended up one of Bourguiba's ministers.

And so there was no rocking of the boat or disruption of

the mapped-out stages—unless Khala Assiya was there. She would respond by snapping at her sister, "Bastard? How can you talk about Abdel Nasser like that? God save him from your arrogance. Pull yourself together, lady, and quit saying such nasty things, or I swear I'll never set foot in your house again."

As Khala Assiya stood and started to wind her *safseri* around herself, Zeinab would rush to change her sister's mind, trying to hide her weak position with her firm tone. "Sit, sit! Don't be silly, I was just kidding. You know how much I care about him. I know you love him more than Salah Eddine, but remember *I'm* his mother, and *I'm* the one who nursed him. Stay, take off your *safseri* . . . There's something I want tell you, and something else I want to ask your opinion on . . ."

Abdel Nasser overheard this exchange once. It was a summer evening, and the women in the family, along with some of the neighborhood women, had gathered in the center courtyard of the house, not realizing he was in his room and could hear them. He also heard the dirty jokes some of the other women told. He laughed most at the jokes told by Assiya, the aunt he loved more than he should. How he wished that Assiya was his mother!

12

Khala Assiya was not the only one who defended the strong-willed boy; he also had Jnayna. She was their neighbor but also lived with them for a while as part of the family, owing to the strife between her and her husband, Imam Allala. One day, after a period of daily fights, Jnayna came close to killing Allala Darwish, so Zeinab interceded and urged Hajj Mahmoud to ward off the scandal. A deal was struck between Hajj Mahmoud and Allala (though plotted by Zeinab), and although el-Talyani was not privy to the details, he saw the result: Lella Jnayna came to stay at Si Mahmoud's house while Allala remained in his home, the house of the late Hajj Shadhli. Peace was secured on the street and in the two houses.

The boy was the biggest winner in this deal. Jnayna became the one to take care of him, including bathing him and spoiling him, and therefore spared him his sister Jweeda's roughness. Jnayna would shower kisses on him, hug him, and hold him in her lap and play with him. She also covered up for him when he was naughty and conspired with him in his adventures. With her help, he would often steal chocolate or halvah or any of the other candies that Hajja Zeinab so carefully rationed as junk food. If his mother or one of his sisters found out about any of his plots or his violations of the strict house rules, he would take shelter with his new protector Jnayna to save him. And when the opprobrium of his mother, his sister, and the maid increased because of his negligence of basic hygiene in his room, Lella Jnayna became the only one allowed in to clean it. Abdel Nasser remembered that time as the best years of his life.

During those days, he started to recognize new scents, as he told me the day Hajj Mahmoud died. He especially came to know the scent of Jnayna, which he considered the essence of life itself. It all happened very naturally, imperceptibly, like water leaking from tiny cracks in a roof that grow wider and wider until the water is pouring in.

Abdel Nasser confided to me that she would sometimes sit and watch him while he was studying or doing his homework. She would look at him with eyes that were a bit sad at times, dreamy at others. She would smile at him. Her gaze would wander away, then return to him again. Abdel Nasser didn't understand at the time why she was doing that, but he liked it.

Sometimes she would suggest they play the game of doctor and patient. They made the pretend doctor's tools from whatever was at hand: a small rope nailed to pieces of cork for a stethoscope, a teaspoon to examine the tonsils for redness, a tablespoon to measure the pulse on the wrist. The doctor examines the patient. The patient submits to examination. They exchange roles.

When he was fourteen or fifteen years old, Lella Jnayna started to give him more hugs and kisses. In the beginning, she would kiss him the way she had since he was a child, on his cheeks and neck. But soon her lips when kissing him became two licks of flame stinging him sweetly. Then she was no longer satisfied with cold kisses but would suck his neck, gently sometimes and violently—which he liked—at others. And from time to time, she would touch his lips with her lips or her tongue, and he liked that. It aroused feelings he'd never experienced before, and he savored the drops of her saliva on his lips. Once he initiated a kiss on her lips using his tongue, and she accepted that with great satisfaction.

Their games of doctor become more serious. The doctor started to examine Lella Jnayna's full breasts, to touch the fruit and explore the soft flesh. He would flip her over on the bed to listen to her heartbeat, contemplating the warm marble of her back. As he passed his hand over the smooth marble or touched the soft fruit, goose bumps would ripple through her body, making his own body hot and tense. In the beginning he would blush, but his embarrassment vanished with the passage of time and repetition of the game.

Lella Jnayna herself became a very experienced doctor and explored areas that would never have occurred to him. Abdel Nasser noticed that what was between his legs began to get longer and bigger. He tried to hide it from Jnayna's eyes, but she quickly noticed. Once she took advantage of the chance to play and told him that this time his illness was in his "little soldier," as she called it. She began to all but devour his lips and rubbed her breasts over his burning body before planting his head between them. He watched as she licked every inch of his body, until a tremor went through him and he felt a shiver and a feeling like he had to pee. He wanted to stop, but it had already happened. She brought her face closer to his, smiling a smile that was half sly, half flirtatious.

He felt relaxed, but the trembling didn't stop. She held him close. He saw tears falling from her reddened eyes and asked her what was wrong. She hesitated, then fell silent.

From that day on, el-Talyani learned many different skills of the body at the hands of Lella Jnayna. She was a skilled teacher: she was never greedy and hid nothing from him. But sometimes he got sick of her insatiable appetite, especially when she would mistakenly call him "Salah" (meaning Salah Eddine). He didn't get angry, though, when she mixed up their names. He loved his brother, after all, and could see him in every corner of the room.

He realized after a while that Lella Jnayna, even after she went back home, was another inheritance that Salah Eddine had left for him, just as he had left the records and the record player, the various books, magazines, and notebooks, that rocking chair . . . and the room on the top floor.

13

Abdel Nasser had his own private kingdom now, from the comfort of which he declared his independence from the women of the house and their viciousness (all except Yosser, of course, who he loved and was close to). In the privacy of that room my own friendship with el-Talyani grew stronger. We were from the same neighborhood: we were brought together by school and playing games in the street, and our friendship strengthened as we shared secrets and explored life together. I admit that I was always a follower under Abdel

Nasser's leadership, since I generally preferred to observe silently rather than speak. I suppose I am still "passive" and "submissive," as Abdel Nasser used to say, but that has never bothered me. Even before I graduated from high school and enrolled at the Faculté 9 Avril to study philosophy, I had always had a somewhat philosophical way of looking at life. I was always content with what I had, never complaining about my circumstances, and I was never one to get excited about new and seductive things. That's how I was created; that's how I've lived my entire life.

Despite our different natures, Abdel Nasser took to me. He made me the keeper of his secrets and confided in me about everything. He confessed his fears to me and shared all of his tricks and ploys with me. He also let me in on all his plans— and he had so many plans! Looking back, I feel like he considered me putty in his hands, and a useful tool for honing his leadership instincts.

One summer when we were teenagers, he decided to set up an art and reading club in his room. This was to fill the long, boring days, since—while we could play soccer with the other kids in our neighborhood—we were too old to play with marbles or spinning tops.

There were four members of the club, and the party would start in the morning with music. Abdel Nasser would select one of the records that Salah Eddine left for him, a different record every day. Then we would listen to cassettes with the songs of Fairouz, Sheikh Imam, Léo Ferré, Jean Ferrat, Jacques Brel, and others, playing them on the cassette recorder that I used to sneak over from our house.

At first, we enjoyed reading Arabic and French poetry out loud in theatrical voices. Each of us would also choose selections from a favorite novel to discuss. But the following summer, there was a major change in the art and reading club at Hajj Mahmoud's house when Abdel Nasser brought us a novel entitled *Mother*, by a Russian writer we had never heard of at school.

El-Talyani suggested one day that we should become philosophers. And so the art and reading club became a young philosophers' circle. We had daily reading sessions throughout the summer, working together on a massive book (or, at least it seemed massive to us) by Georges Politzer. We had to summarize the most important points in a notebook and had essentially become pupils under Abdel Nasser, who was the most enthusiastic among us, as well as the most precise in his understanding.

I never argued with him, even though I didn't like a lot of what he said and couldn't bring myself to accept it. Sometimes I felt that his philosophy frightened me. So I thanked God that the school year was about to start and that the Abdel Nasser Academy of Philosophy would be closing (though we agreed to continue studying every Saturday evening).

After a while, el-Talyani confided in me that he used to get the strange books he shared with us from one of the French teachers at the high school. The teacher had noticed Abdel Nasser's natural propensity toward both learning and rebellion, and so had encouraged him outside of class and supplied him with those strange books. What Abdel Nasser hid from us was that Ustad Fathi K. was, himself, gathering students—among them Abdel Nasser—to talk about culture, literature, and politics at his house (which was near our neighborhood, in Bab Jedid). I later learned that Ustad Fathi was imprisoned after the events of January 26, 1978, in what was called the "*Echaab* newspaper case," after the Tunisian General Labor Union's underground publication. It was no stretch to suppose that it was he who recruited Abdel Nasser into the secret organization.

We went back to school, and the philosophers scattered after el-Talyani got busy with new friendships. While we continued to meet at school and on the way there, each of us chose a different path after graduation. In college, I chose philosophy mainly under his influence, but he betrayed me and chose to study law. He wanted to become a lawyer, despite Salah Eddine's urging to study management or business, and despite his father's desire for him to study medicine, since his grades gave him his choice of fields at any Tunisian university. But el-Talyani was like a swift, unstoppable river whose roaring water digs its own path.

1

After his meeting with the comrade lawyer, Abdel Nasser called an emergency meeting of the secret organization to discuss the matter. They were to meet at 8 P.M. at Najm Eddine's apartment, in the working-class neighborhood of El Zahrouni. There was no need to remind them of the precautions they needed to take on the way, given the current level of persecution by the authorities.

The attendees were the four most trusted members, the heart of the organization, with Abdel Nasser as the fifth. He outlined the situation for them, his conversation with Zeina on the one hand and his conversation with the movement's comrade theorist on the other. His speech was met with a gloomy silence, as the attendees thought about the issue, carefully examining it from every angle.

Nabeel was the first to break the silence, saying that Zeina was not their enemy and that what the comrade lawyer was asking for was like swatting a fly with a tank. Youssef spoke next, warning against falling into the muck of unfettered anarchism. Jaafar responded with his usual sarcasm: all members should follow in the footsteps of their great comrade the skilled lawyer and train with South Lebanon to eliminate Zeina—clearly.

The only one who did not speak, being shy by nature, was Comrade Redha. When Abdel Nasser directly asked him for his opinion, he tried to evade the question, saying, "You are my comrades and my friends. We're united by shared principles;

we've drunk water and broken bread together. I hope you will allow me to be excused from this issue."

But the group was not so easily dissuaded and kept pressing him. Finally, Redha explained that he and Zeina came from neighboring villages and had gone to high school together. Given how long he'd known her, he was afraid his opinion might not be very objective.

Jaafar jumped up, pointing at Redha and laughing, and said, "I swear on the name of Comrade Stalin, this boy's been in love with Zeina since elementary school!"

Everyone laughed. Redha blushed, at a loss for words. Finally he managed to mumble their well-worn but all-purpose reproach: "Be serious, Comrade."

Jaafar's comment had clearly embarrassed Redha. "It was just a joke," Abdel Nasser reassured him. "Jaafar doesn't mean anything." He didn't want to abandon the subject, though, so he approached it from a different angle. "I didn't know you knew Zeina," he began. "Tell us what you know about her."

2

At their small high school, and in its dormitories, Zeina was always the spearhead of student protests. She fascinated them with her speeches and always explained exactly what to do: when to start a protest and when to stop it. She was once suspended in the early eighties—for demanding a union for the school's students—but her intelligence and the high regard of all her teachers saved her from being expelled. She was also known for her tenacity when standing up for students' rights and for her protection of new students in the dormitory.

One of her most notable feats was her victory against the dorm master, a letch who had a habit of seducing the girls coming from the countryside. They were often naive and desperate to get married (especially to someone with a nice, secure job like dorm master). He took full advantage of their weakness and treated the high school girls in the dormitories like his own private harem. Zeina, who was neither naive nor desperate, tried at first to deal with the matter through the appropriate channels by reporting the dorm master's misconduct to the teachers' union and the principal. But rather than disciplining the dorm master, the principal threatened Zeina with expulsion if she continued to spread unfounded allegations. She let the matter lie for a while. When she saw that the teachers' union was not going to do anything, either, she spoke to the history and geography teacher—one of the honest members of the union. He used to give her books that she would devour, and magazines that she would read in the cafeteria and study room, even though they were against the rules. When questioned by the dorm monitors, she would provide the unassailable excuse that the history teacher had given them to her for a special research project.

One day, the dorm master summoned her to his office. He had heard that the students were refusing to eat and instead were banging their spoons and forks on the dishes, making an unbearable amount of noise. They were protesting the poor quality of the food: the stale bread, the tasteless "tagine" made of leftovers, the occasional presence of insects. The monitors accused Zeina of organizing these protests, as usual.

The dorm master asked her, "Why are you doing this?" But she lied to him, distancing herself from the protests and claiming that—unlike the other students—she was hungry and actually ate the food. "See?" she said, sticking out her tongue, stained with leftovers. He brought his head closer to verify, then, according to what Zeina related, seemed to get flustered, and a tremor ran through him. He stood up from his desk and, moving behind where she was sitting, slid both hands down to her breasts. She rose to the full extent of her slim stature and slapped him across the face. Then, nearly hysterical, she started yelling, accusing him of harassing her. The history and geography teacher rushed in, followed by several monitors who had been passing during the break between classes.

As the geography teacher worked on calming Zeina down, the monitors looked on in surprise, but with no doubt in their minds that Zeina was telling the truth. The dorm master kept his head down, powerless and incapable of extracting himself from the scandal. He knew he was trapped and that no one could save him. That was the last time the students saw him. Ever since that day, Zeina had been a hero in the school and her exploits a legend, every retelling embellished a little more.

After this incident, the principal and monitors began turning a blind eye to her actions, no longer daring even to reprimand her. She started smoking openly, getting her dose of nicotine without resorting to hiding in the bathrooms like the rest of the students. She would stand in a corner of the courtyard surrounded by her friends, both male and female, laughing and chatting with a cigarette in hand, as if she were one of the teachers.

Then she took to leaving the dorm, without permission from school officials or her parents, whenever she wanted and returning whenever she wanted. One day, the principal told her, "We are not a hotel. Abide by the rules, or we will expel you."

She answered calmly but quickly, as if shooting her words from a machine gun. "When you fix the broken windows that let in the wind and rain, when you clean the bathrooms so the hallways and bedrooms don't reek, when you take care of students' health instead of just dealing out aspirin from that hole you call a nurse's office, and when you get rid of the bugs in the food and serve us something decent, *then* you'll be a comfortable hotel—one your students won't run away from."

The principal, flabbergasted by her tone, replied, "You're an insolent girl, and I will expel you from both the dorm and the school."

Zeina met his threat with a stronger one. "What, you're going to avenge the dorm master, who went God knows where? I know you're *khwanji*; you hate women and the government like the rest of the Islamists."

It was a grave accusation, and he knew what it could lead to; the best-case scenario would be a demotion and a return to the classrooms he'd left behind years before. He swallowed his wounded pride.

But he didn't give up. He invited her father to his office. He was a peasant who worked on the farm during the season and spent the rest of his time hanging out in the village store, drinking tea and playing cards. Zeina's real guardian was her mother, who worked as a maid in a rich farmer's house from 6 A.M. until dark. The father said that Zeina was his daughter, and the principal had his permission to beat her or even kill her if he wanted. Personally, he had no control over her: she was the daughter of Bourguiba, who allowed women to challenge men, to defy their fathers and brothers. How could *he* reprimand the brilliant and educated Zeina when he couldn't even write his own name? He'd washed his hands of her; she hadn't spoken to him in years and no longer considered him her father. She'd even declared in front of the family that her mother was more of a man than he was, had called him a filthy and backwards drunk. If she hadn't had at least a modicum of shame left, she would have kicked him out of the house.

The principal understood that Zeina's family was not going to be any kind of deterrent to her and that he would risk his prestige and authority if he openly engaged in battle with her. So instead, he tried to use his political knowledge, the strategies he had used, successfully, when presiding over the local chapter of the Constitutional Party. So he invited her again to his office, and when she came, he saw for the first time that she was confident in herself and prepared to outmaneuver him.

He did not mention her father but rather spoke to her as a

THE ITALIAN · 53

peer. He confessed that he wasn't going to punish her: she was the top student in the school and he needed her to be the best, not only in her class grades but also in the national baccalaureate exam. He had no doubt that she was capable of it. He hinted that she would be free, for the rest of her junior and senior years, to do as she liked. But he asked her to show some discipline and respect for the school rules, for the benefit of the other students. They were not as smart or committed to their education as she was; they might become criminals rather than activists fighting for their rights. He made a deal with her: the administration would overlook her behavior and she would have her freedom. In exchange, and because she was so bright and serious about her academics, she would help her classmates prepare for the baccalaureate exam, making their school a model of hard work and success.

3

Redha's obvious admiration when speaking about Zeina was infectious. When he finished, the sarcastic Jaafar exclaimed, "I swear again on Comrade Stalin, if I were in Redha's shoes, I would have gotten down on my knees before her to declare my love!"

They all laughed, including Redha, dispelling the tension at the beginning of the meeting. Jaafar took the lead on the conversation, concluding that Zeina—despite the trouble she was causing among the student base with her criticism of the movement's theories—was a true fighter for the revolution. They might disagree with her, but she was not an enemy. They asked Abdel Nasser to convey this message to their comrade the lawyer.

His response, however, was baffling: "I'll level with you: I came to this meeting with something more important on my mind. I think we should completely break off our relationship with this comrade. I think he's sick in his head and considers us his pawns. And I'm not willing to be anyone's slave."

It was after 11 P.M. and they all had to wake up early the next morning. They had prepared a poster about the critical work that needed to be done for this next stage of the movement, and they needed to hang a copy at the law college and another at the liberal arts college in Manouba, arriving early enough to avoid being seen by the government spies on campus. They also needed to work on organizing the extraordinary 18th congress of the General Union of Tunisian Students, after the government party hijacked the Tunisian students' union elections in the early seventies. They all stayed the night at Najm Eddine and Redha's apartment, except for Abdel Nasser, who decided to return to his home in the suburb of Le Bardo.

4

El-Talyani met Zeina S. during the final years of his long tenure at the university. He married her under unusual circumstances, only to divorce two years later. Zeina was a decisive turning point in his life in many ways. If not for her, for instance, he would have continued his deliberate failure of many of his classes so that he could remain at the university and participate in the extraordinary 18th congress of the General Union of Tunisian Students in May 1988.

Zeina, whose real name was Anrouz, was from one of the Berber villages in the northwest. No one knew her Amazigh name but her very close friends like me and Abdel Nasser. Bourguiba had forced the Berbers to register their children in municipalities under Arab names, so their Berber names were used only at home with family members. The children grew up accustomed to hiding their names, to avoid any discrimination or exclusion, or to avoid being questioned and punished.

Anrouz was slim as a spear. She had a golden complexion and short, straight hair of a peculiar style, neither elegant from the hairdressers' ministrations nor neglected like the hair of most of the other female activists. (Abdel Nasser later found out that she achieved this particular shape herself by binding her hair in a ponytail when it had gotten too long, then chopping it off with a pair of scissors.) She rarely wore makeup. She was always dressed in jeans and athletic shoes, looking as if she was ready to climb and run at a moment's notice. But what most attracted attention was her green eyes, a shade of dark green made even brighter and more beautiful by their prominence. Her eyes were full of mystery; anyone who tried to focus on them would notice nuances of green that varied by the weather—one shade for sun, another for clouds—and by the openness of the space she was in.

With the mysterious charm of those eyes, she was able to captivate her debater and even her onlookers as she gave speeches at the Université de Tunis, either in the big courtyard of the Faculté 9 Avril or on Socrates' Rock at the Faculté de Droit. Hers was a lavish beauty that tried to negate its existence with its austerity. The beauty experts in our circle of friends were convinced that if she wore normal clothes (not too revealing, just normal) and some light, basic makeup and did her hair at any ordinary hairdresser's—in others words, if she made a modicum of effort to display her beauty and femininity—she would turn the world upside down. And perhaps this was why, from a frustrated desire for this out-of-reach beauty, the leftist students' opponents (Islamist and non-Islamist alike) were relentless in calling her "the proletarian revolution's whore" or "the cow of the revolutionary leadership."

They did not dare, of course, to say such things in the presence of her friends. But Abdel Nasser had his own ways of finding out that it was a particular Baathist student who was responsible for the epithets. He was a poet of the Arab Vanguard who would read at poetry events and concerts at the university. Abdel Nasser confronted him about it one day, relying on the trust he'd built for himself among other political parties, whose members respected him for his vast knowledge and his ability to negotiate and argue. The Baathist student denied it in the beginning, then confessed to him that he'd coined the names spontaneously, when he heard his comrades talking about Zeina's sexual relationships with other student leaders. He confessed that he was behind other well-known nicknames in the university, as well, which he'd come up with on the spur of the moment, in the context of a conversation or joke. He meant no offense; he was simply overcome by a poetic instinct. In his opinion, the ones at fault were the students who popularized the names.

He told him of another of his creations, nicknaming an Islamist leader "Al-Qadir bi-Allah Travolta," combining his Islamist affiliation and talk about the Islamic revolution with his appearance which (quite truthfully) resembled John Travolta. But he used this name because of the university girls' love for stars; they all said that this student's good looks didn't fit the grumpy, scowling image of Islamists. Again, he meant no offense. He also told him about nicknames that he had given his own comrades in the Arab Vanguard who he loved and whose views he shared. He mentioned specifically the "mule of Arab unity" (for an activist who didn't know the Baath ideology very well but was nonetheless ignorantly enthusiastic) and the "Mediterranean pig" (used often to describe Arab leaders).

Abdel Nasser tried to make the Baathist poet see that the matter was different with Zeina.

He explained to him that in our Arab societies, when a woman takes a stand in the public sphere (including in the student realm), she is often attacked for her values and behavior. This serves to weaken her position and dissuade her from participating in the fight for freedom and expressing her ideas on an equal footing with men. He spoke to him about the necessity of unity between men and women in their fight for freedom, and of supporting women in their struggle for equal rights.

The conversation in the law college cafeteria concluded with seemingly full agreement, but that didn't prevent the spreading of new epithets for student activists and syndicate members, both male and female. Abdel Nasser interpreted this as an intentional strategy by those who didn't believe in the student syndicate to defame its members. But he also knew that the efforts to hold the extraordinary 18th congress would continue, as would the necessity of fighting against the reactionaries. They were gaining ground in student councils and invading what were, historically, the most important strongholds of the left: the major universities. This had intensified since March 1986, after the Islamists held what they called "the Decisive Congress" and established the Tunisian General Union of Students as the student arm of the Islamic Tendency Movement.

5

Abdel Nasser didn't show any interest in Zeina S. during that period. He was pleased by some of her analyses—despite his disagreement with her—but he didn't talk to her. He didn't try to make a connection with her even at the political level. He was careful to separate his political life at the university from his personal life outside of it.

He had made that decision and stuck to it strictly since 1980, shortly after he entered the university, when he accepted (after negotiations with the organization's leadership) to prolong his studies as long as possible. He couldn't leave the university: the movement and his comrades needed him to support the temporary syndicate structure during these difficult political times.

Because of his age and seniority at the law college, he saw all
the students come and go as they were either expelled or graduated. And because of his leadership position in the temporary
syndicate structure, he was known by everyone not only at his
college but also by his comrades at other politically active colleges. He preserved his image as a tough and principled activist
in the organization when recruiting in the dorms and off-cam-
pus housing, as well as in high schools and colleges, in order to
strengthen the organization and buttress its position at the university. Recruiting was difficult, especially compared to the
Islamists, who could recognize their supporters as soon as they
gathered together to pray and could recruit them through ordinary meetings or financial aid. The left, on the other hand, had
to exert twice the effort to bring their supporters together politically and train them ideologically.

The few that came to the university from the left's ideological trainings—what they called their "summer universities"—
were not enough to stand up against oppression and persecution, nor to mobilize the students for political action. The
various summer universities around the country relied on
bringing in new baccalaureate holders through personal connections with people in families and neighborhoods. With their
secretiveness and the intensity of their discussions, they often
intimidated these new students who—happy with their success—were looking forward to starting a new life at university
and their opportunity to climb the social ladder.

Yet Abdel Nasser was one of the most skilled students of the
left in recruiting new members and supporters, owing to his
eloquence, knowledge, and enthusiasm in debates, as well as his
ability to listen and converse and his clear political vision.

He often told his comrades about his theory of the heart and
the circles: the firm student leadership was like a heart, pump-
ing blood into the struggle of student political activism. The circles, then, were the concentric rings that wrapped around the

heart of the student movement. In the innermost ring were the student fighters who sincerely believed in the movement. In the second circle were supporters who were physically strong and courageous. They were the "muscular arm of the movement"; they protected posters from those who thought about tearing them down and formed human shields when needed, for example in front of amphitheaters and classrooms when the leadership decided to strike. The third circle was made up of those Abdel Nasser called "interns," the large group of new comrades-in-training. The fourth circle was made up of those who received non-secretive training in the field of the syndicate work: the principles of the movement were explained to them, and they were lectured on the history of the General Union of Tunisian Students, the quantum leap after the Korba Congress, and the role of student movements in revolutionary change. As well as, of course, on the seminal February 1972 movement and its results, especially the organizational and political rift from the traitorous comprador regime.

Circles and rings continued outward from the beating heart of the student movement: to those who supported the movement without really being committing to it; then to the sympathizers who supported it from distance (most of their support was out of friendship); finally, they reached the student body whose interests the movement was meant to represent, while at the same time leading them and raising their awareness.

6

Zeina was not a member of the political syndicate movement that Abdel Nasser led at the Faculté de Droit. She wasn't even a law student. She came to it from the liberal arts college, the Faculté 9 Avril, where she was studying philosophy. She was an amazingly convincing orator, with a strong voice, able to project without yelling, though like all orators, she always looked tense. Most of her speeches were violent critiques of what she called "the students' deficient political conscious-ness." She decried the "fascist movements with their tyrannical religious projects," as well as both "the excessive centrality of the left" (which caused it to "drift away from the spontaneity of the movement") and "the cancerous fragmentation of the bureaucratic left." She completely rejected the professional par-tisans (among whose ranks she included Abdel Nasser!)

Zeina was opposed to the temporary syndicalist structure, believing that it co-opted the student movement and steered it toward a dead-end partisan path. She often mocked the orga-nizational and political rift that the left claimed; syndical work at its core, she said, was reform work requiring dialogue with the authorities. The student movement, then, was not the van-guard of the revolutionary movement but rather a fragile com-ponent of it. The leftists first tried to pigeonhole her in the reform movement, before beginning the exhausting process of trying to find a way to categorize her strange and volatile think-ing.

But most of what attracted Abdel Nasser to Zeina's speeches was her insistence on the role of intellectuals in analyzing real-ity. She accused the left of a lack of intellectual depth, of con-tentment with ready-made templates about the means of pro-duction and their talk of the main conflict and secondary conflicts. They were relying on Lenin and Mao Zedong's analy-ses of Russian and Chinese realities and projecting them on the Tunisian reality. She attributed this blunder to their ignorance of Marxism as a tool for historical–materialist social analysis, as well as an atrocious ignorance of the philosophical develop-ment of Marxism. She described the left as "an ignorant and blind dog, sniffing around in Leninism and Stalinism's rotting trash bin" (language that Abdel Nasser later learned was inspired by Lenin's criticism of Kautsky).

Listening to her speak, Abdel Nasser heard for the first time names and positions he had never encountered before. She glorified Kautsky, despite the fact that all of Lenin's writings attacked him. She talked in a scholarly way about Rosa Luxemburg, Pannekoek, and Karl Korsch and the Frankfurt School. She mentioned the names of Castoriadis and Edgar Morin. She said things about Althusser and Gramsci that were different from what he had heard or read about them. She cited council communism and boasted about the Tunisian Lafif Lakhdar who had produced the best Arabic translation of *The Communist Manifesto*. She delighted in mentioning some unusual analyses, eloquent and revolutionary expressions from the book of that other Tunisian, Mustapha Khayati, *On the Poverty of Student Life*. An eclectic mix of names, most of which meant nothing to Abdel Nasser. She threw his ideas into confusion, making him feel like he knew nothing, despite the fact that he was *the* expert in everything related to theory among his comrades.

Where had this crazy woman come from? There was clearly knowledge and legitimate criticism in what she said; he could feel it but didn't know how to reconcile it, which was something he didn't dare admit. Yet he had to respond: she had the potential of making his supporters and sympathizers leave the leftist political movement. Was it not enough that they had to deal with blow after blow from the Islamists, and their continued seizure of seats in the student council elections? Did he also have to deal with this leftist he couldn't even seem to categorize correctly?

Majority opinion settled on labeling her a Trotskyist. She told them, mockingly, in response to this "accusation," "Nope, guess again."

But all the comrades, from different schools of thought on the left, still insisted that she must be a Trotskyist. Or sometimes a councilist. They couldn't find, didn't know of any other place for her on the map of ideas. She only added to their confusion by saying, "Trotsky is just the losing side of the corrupt Bolshevik coin. The winning side was Stalin."

The conversation would be diverted to denouncing her description of the Bolsheviks—the architects of the greatest revolution in history—as wretched, as well as her grouping Trotsky and Stalin together. She then inflamed their anger by saying, "Stalin is the Soviet Union's Hitler."

The audience standing around her started yelling, and one of the toughs from the second circle (who loved Comrade Stalin more than his own father) tried to hit her. Yet she persisted in her mockery. "Fine, not Hitler. The Georgian with the moustache is the Soviet Union's Khomeini. They're all just local flavors of fascists."

In the clamor and din that erupted at moments like this, Zeina would leave them to seclude herself with her friends. She would light a cigarette and sip her coffee in the college cafeteria, or outside if the weather permitted.

Yet these faults—her hostile positions, her spread of vicious rumors about the sacred symbols of Marxism–Leninism—were ameliorated by the fact that she was a philosophy student and, for this reason, things that were forbidden to others were permissible for her. She was also a steadfast activist, found on the front lines during the most difficult times, like when they were confronting the police during protests, or when the state security forces raided the university. This was known about her at the Faculté 9 Avril and everywhere she visited, including the Faculté de Droit.

She was also one of the few people who were able to rebuke the students of the Islamic Tendency and beat them on their own playing field, Islamic identity. She was well-versed in Islamic history, *'ilm al-kalam*, the history of religion, the culture of Mesopotamia, and the Iranian philosophical thought that had developed in the Shi'a *hawzas* and contributed to a renewal of Islamic thought that diverged from the guardianship of the jurists. She mocked their discussions of "a dead identity" that they didn't really understand and their intellectual ignorance, telling them, "Your opinions are a naive mix of the Muslim Brotherhood's Islam, Wahhabism, and Shiite influences, and you can't tell the jewels from the droppings. Go read a little." She also warned them that "revolutions made out of fossilized ideas produce petty dictatorship." She mocked their intellectual sources: "You're consecrating the mummified ideas of your old Islamic studies teacher, who was either dim-witted or a country bumpkin from Egypt, but you don't consecrate the Creator. You're the children of an ignorance that's wrapped up in the search for an origin that never really existed."

This would make the leftists gloat over the Islamic Tendency students; they would gain a newfound respect for her and shower her with congratulations at the end of the discussion. But she didn't spare them: "You're not all that different. Each one of you has your own sacred ignorance and false origins." The leftists would cringe in shame, but her words would comfort the Islamist students, who sometimes attended the leftist discussion circles to listen without participating.

7

The echoes of these intellectual skirmishes reached one of the leaders of the political movement Abdel Nasser belonged to. He was a brilliant lawyer who had graduated almost ten years before and had been in prison and in exile for a while. He was known for his support of the syndicalists in the trials that followed the Tunisian Bread Riots of January 1984.

His elevated social status had not changed his ideas. He was a brilliant theorist and was behind many of the ideas and analyses that were still inspiring the student movement. A real luminary. He had passed many entrance exams (for the foreign affairs ministry, the prime minister's office, the judiciary) but was stymied by his criminal record. Although his official criminal record was clean, his security file at the interior ministry was black with ink and prevented him from securing government employment. Thus he was always eliminated from consideration, despite often being the highest-scoring applicant on the entrance exam. He was even deprived of his passport, notwithstanding the efforts of the Tunisian Order of Lawyers and the Tunisian Human Rights League to intercede on his behalf. The veto against him was firm and irrevocable.

The comrade lawyer invited Abdel Nasser to his office and asked him to do his best to stop Zeina the philosopher from spreading her philosophy, because it might seriously demoralize the students. Abdel Nasser took charge of the matter and decided to meet with her. He preferred not to meet her at the university and so asked me to set up the meeting for him. I arranged to meet them in the old medina of Tunis, in a cafe near the national library and the Zaytuna Mosque. It was impossible for me to refuse his request, as he was my best friend, and it was impossible for Zeina to refuse *my* request, as her classmate in the Philosophy Department for whom she had ties of both affection and gratitude. Being a native of the city, I had been there for her whenever she needed help navigating "the ruthless octopus," as she called Tunis. I also enjoyed a senior position at the university, owing to how many years I had had to repeat.

Abdel Nasser told her that he admired her broad knowledge, and he was humbled to tell her that he had learned a great deal from her. She had impelled him to look for the books of some theorists that she had mentioned in her discussions and that he still remembered. She was equally complimentary toward him, expressing her respect for his ability to listen and debate. Despite her differences in opinion from him, he was a skilled conversationalist who respected others and who responded to people's ideas in debates without ever attacking them personally. She ended her compliment saying, "Honestly, I'm not sure why you affiliate with that faction. You're one of its leaders and spokespeople, but your ideas are broader."

He was newly convinced of how dangerous this "philosopher" was: she had immediately put her finger on his major paradox. But he didn't want to divulge any of his secrets to her: his mission was clear.

He tried to explain to her that a person's political allegiance didn't always perfectly match their personal ideology. After all, the organization had a system for communal thinking that accepted diversity and difference from the very beginning. He wanted to strike the right chord to drive the point home for her, so he reminded her of Marx's statement that an individual is the sum total of his social relationships.

She agreed with part of his analysis but then started to challenge him. He asked her politely if they could leave the discussion of ideological and philosophical differences for another time. He explained that he'd asked to meet her because of another matter, an urgent one. When I seconded Abdel Nasser's opinion, she reluctantly accepted.

He was upfront in his request: he asked her to stop publicly criticizing Marxism–Leninism to avoid exacerbating the differences between the leftist parties and negatively affecting their fight against the Islamists. Abdel Nasser's hand movements were so agitated that he accidentally knocked over a cup of green tea that was on the table, spilling it on Zeina's jeans.

He had arrived at the crux of the matter. He told her, in a firm tone with a trace of accusation, "When you criticize the left so severely, your words play into the hands of our enemies, whether you like it or not and regardless of your intentions."

She responded, "I'm as free to criticize the left as I am the right."

"No one is disputing your freedom," he clarified. "That's not what I'm saying. I'm just warning you that the only real result your theoretical discussions have is to harm our work in the field."

"That's not my intention; I'm not aligned with any faction."

"That's the problem. It's not a matter of intentions, and I'm not asking you to become a member or to support our movement. You have great skills in debate and are a highly cultured thinker, the kind we need among our theorists, but your knowledge is politically ineffective."

"It is the cultured thinkers that criticize without political motivation," she retorted. "They criticize everything, fire at whatever moves. They lay out the crises through questioning and disrupt the status quo."

"That's fine—I'm not asking you to become a politician or give away your cultural role. I'm just asking you, plainly, to choose another podium for arguing and debate than public meetings and discussion circles."

"Then you're confiscating my right to free expression, same as Bourguiba's regime."

Abdel Nasser began to feel that the discussion had hit a dead end. He tried to rein in his emotions; he forced a smile and ended the discussion by saying, "I've made my request and explained the reasons behind it. You're free to do what you like; everyone bears the responsibility for their own actions."

He tried to leave, but I grabbed his hand, and he sat down again out of respect for me. He remained silent and did not look at Zeina. So I started chatting away, trying to clear the air of the tense silence that reigned. Zeina had turned her chair so that Abdel Nasser was out of her field of vision; she shifted her position and crossed her legs before lighting a cigarette.

Abdel Nasser wasn't paying attention to anything I was saying. He was, without a doubt, thinking about this stubborn philosopher and how he was going to deal with her. I imagined that he admired her stubbornness and her liberal positions but saw her as acting without a thought for the consequences.

For her part, Zeina was thinking about what he had asked from her. Doubtless she understood his request, but deep down she felt overwhelmingly gratified that her positions and discussions had made the dominant political group in the law college afraid of her influence on the students.

She told me, after the meeting, that she actually considered acquiescing to the handsome activist's request, for his sake rather than out of obedience to his organization's demands. But she quickly realized that the idiots in his faction would interpret this as a sign of their omnipotence and think they had cowed her. As she saw it, she was like the proletariat: she had nothing to lose, and they had everything to lose. She laughed at the delicious simile.

She decided to keep silent so as not to weaken in front of this guy with his Italian features and arrogant political faction. She wished he weren't a member of the organization so that she could explain to him her real position. She told me that, though my childhood friend carefully avoided speaking in the first person, she was certain he had a rich personality and intense emotions. He was clearly different from the rest of the "worn-out revolutionary proletariat," as she called the activists. She considered him an aristocrat of fine taste; his ascetic clothes couldn't hide his elegant bourgeois looks.

She quickly analyzed Abdel Nasser's personality based on his appearances: petit bourgeois with all the qualifications to become a full bourgeois. But one who chose instead to slum it with the ragged proletariat and the children of the "sack of potatoes," as Marx described the peasantry.

In all probability Zeina had a great respect for el-Talyani. And she was attracted to him even before I arranged that meeting in the café. But she ruled out the possibility of him being attracted to her: in addition to her masculine clothes and aversion to makeup and coiffure, there was the matter of the lingering village accent in her pronunciation of certain words. She saw herself as in a different category from him altogether. Better to beat him on the field of ideas and spread chaos in his beliefs and commitment to the organization. She wouldn't back off from exposing the lies of the fossilized Stalinist left, despite her respect for el-Talyani. That was what she resolved.

Abdel Nasser's parting words to Zeina, shaking her hand before leaving, were "Let's not let our disagreement upset our good relationship."

She responded to his compliment with a better one. "At the core, we don't disagree. I know you think like me; you just can't do like me."

He stared at her, saying nothing. He saw that she was still not rid of her desire to debate.

He left, his thoughts filled with this philosopher. He forgot the mission he'd been on in the meeting, and instead his mind wandered over the features of her face. He found her smile pretty; up close, her lips were fuller than they seemed from afar. He also noted the exquisite bosom buried in the turtleneck sweater, the slenderness of her long fingers, and the clarity of her skin. A natural woman without affect, but who overwhelmed you with a generous femininity when she spoke, in the movement of her hands and the sweep of her left index finger from right to left.

Abdel Nasser thought the intentional concealment of this generous femininity was abnormal and must have an explanation beyond her intellectual attitude or philosophical choices. There must be a secret behind it. El-Talyani's certainty grew as he thought about her stubbornness and her disposition toward arguing and demolishing the status quo.

8

These ideas were swirling through his head as he walked toward Boulevard Bab Bnet, on his way to the comrade lawyer's office to fill him in on the results of the mission he'd been charged with.

In the waiting room, after he had informed the lawyer's assistant of his arrival, he saw two well-known people—former political prisoners—leaving the office. The lawyer welcomed him in a hurry. Abdel Nasser informed him succinctly of the discussion with Zeina, confirming that she was insistent on what she felt was her personal freedom and her role as an unaffiliated intellectual.

The lawyer stood, putting on his jacket without looking at him. "You must act as the circumstances necessitate."

"That's what I've come for, to find out what I should do."

"She must be neutralized. Eliminated."

Abdel Nasser was stunned by what the lawyer had said and replied in astonishment, "What?"

"Just what I told you. Whoever stands as an obstacle in the way of the people's movement must be eliminated. Haven't you read the literature of revolutionary violence? Do you think it's just talk?"

"How exactly do we eliminate her? Assassinate her?"

"I am analyzing the situation and giving orders. How they're carried out is determined by the comrades."

"They'll refuse. That is murder, not revolutionary violence."

The lawyer sat down on the opposite chair, a contemptuous smile on his face. He pierced him with a venomous stare, barely concealing his anger. His teeth rattled as his words slipped past his lips, sharply violent despite their outward calm. He said, "When you were a babe in your mother's arms, I was fighting Zionists in the south of Lebanon. I am not a petit bourgeois like you, afraid of violence. Revolutionary action tolerates no hesitation; otherwise the enemy will devour us. You have to lunch on them before they dine on you. Why are you afraid? If you're afraid, you don't belong in this organization. Get out and let the true revolutionaries take your place. The whore must be taken out; if you can't do it, I will."

He stood up, took his briefcase, and headed toward the door. He walked ahead of Abdel Nasser, not saying a word. When he shook his hand in front of the building, he told him, "I'll be awaiting some happy news within a week at most."

Abdel Nasser left without answering. That day, he called his comrades from the university movement leadership to an urgent meeting.

9

Almost two weeks after the meeting in Najm Eddine's apartment and their break with the comrade lawyer, a new group emerged at the law college. Most of its members were from Abdel Nasser's "third circle," and all noted that most of the new faces were students from the Kairouan countryside—the same region the comrade lawyer came from. Students awoke to find posters signed with the new group's name, which was the same name as Abdel Nasser's faction with only the addition of the word "Radical" and the phrase "at the Faculté de Droit."

Some of the current members from the second circle wanted to physically interfere, to tear up the posters and teach the dissidents a lesson. Jaafar, who had been the first to initiate contact with the group, suggested that they bodily expel them from the school. Abdel Nasser, who was late to the meeting that day, arrived to find the new radical students—numbering not more than ten—standing ready to defend the posters and deal with any threat. Politicized students approached to read the posters, trying to figure out what this new faction was all about. Abdel Nasser was one of them, reading one of the posters closely, accompanied by four comrades on his sides and six behind him, just in case the students from the new faction tried anything. He read the poster once more, then laid out his conclusions to the group of leaders and comrades protecting him. He thought that the writing style was entirely that of the lawyer. The content was similar to their own faction's ideas with one exception: an insistence on the necessity of cleansing the students' movement of hidden opportunists and whoever sought to sabotage the rising revolutionary tide. Singled out in particular were the "petit bourgeois" and the "intellectual clergy" (an insulting term intended to demonize the activists who focused on theory and ideas).

Abdel Nasser asked his comrades not to interfere and not to touch the posters. Instead, he told them to monitor the situation and find out who was sympathetic or close to the new faction. He called on a group of students, members of the third circle, to open a discussion circle at noon to explain the views of the new faction. He lined up some other comrades to be ready to interfere if things went wrong.

At the discussion, Abdel Nasser saw that the lawyer's group was unable to explain the ideas of the faction, nor convince others of it. They exposed their weakness by repeatedly invoking the name of the comrade lawyer—Ustad Sahbi Karoui, whose last name derived from the name of the city of Kairouan—as a master theorist.

After almost an hour, the comrade lawyer entered the law college with a comrade on either side as bodyguards. All eyes were on him as news of his presence spread. He walked like a peacock toward Socrates' Rock, which incited the excited shouts of his supporters. "Sahbi! . . . Sahbi! . . . and *all* of us are Karoui!"

Students gathered out of curiosity, and Abdel Nasser and his comrades ran toward Socrates' Rock. The circle had grown larger, but it was still the voices of ten supporters or so repeating the same slogan. Ustad Sahbi stopped the chant with a gesture of his hand toward his supporters. Then they heard another voice, a student from Gabes, shouting, "Hey, Comrade! I'm Gabsi, not Karoui!"

Other voices followed, as if purposely arranged: "I'm Jendoubi," "I'm Kasserini," "I'm Kefi," "I'm Béji," "I'm Bouzidi," "I'm Djerbi," "I'm Sahli" . . .

The interjections came in quick succession, and a raucous laughter spread through the crowd. The lawyer, caught in the middle of this mayhem, was trying to start his speech over: "Students of the resistance . . . !" "Children of this fortress . . . !" "Comrades of the path . . ." But it was no use. It was impossible for him to start over because practically everyone was falling down laughing.

After about fifteen minutes of this, the lawyer descended from Socrates' Rock. He headed toward the main gate to leave, and at that moment they started chanting: "Bread, liberty, Tunisian dignity!" "Our movement marches on; we want Karoui gone!" "No government, no fascists, no Karoui or opportunists!"

Around one hundred students followed him to the gates of the school. Some started throwing rocks, but Abdel Nasser stopped them and told them to go back to the quad. That was the first day that the new faction appeared—and the last, for some time. But Abdel Nasser warned his comrades not to underestimate the lawyer's group. With Karoui's organizational skills, political cunning, and deviousness, the battle was far from over.

Abdel Nasser's warning was based on his extensive experience, but some intelligence supplied by a new comrade made him certain. This student, a freshman, was also from the Kairouan countryside and lived in the same dorm as the lawyer's cousin. The cousin tried to recruit him, holding meetings in his dorm room with others from the region to explain the faction's principles. He focused on their goal of eliminating opportunists and specifically mentioned Abdel Nasser, who the lawyer accused of launching a coup against the movement's principles. One of the biggest faults ascribed to him was that he was *beldi*—part of the old aristocracy in the capital—a despicable petit bourgeois who was willing to ally with Satan, including Constitutional Party supporters and Islamists, to maintain his leadership position.

The second name on the elimination list was Zeina, the philosophy student who, in discussion circles and public meetings, didn't hesitate to align herself with the Islamists by attacking Comrade "Youssef" Stalin, cursing the great leader Mao Zedong, and ridiculing the symbol of the Albanian revolution, Comrade Enver Hoxha. Worst of all, even the great revolutionary mind Vladimir Ilyich Ulyanov—Lenin!—didn't escape her vulgar attacks. This bourgeoise philosopher was destroying the symbols of the revolution and serving its enemies; she was no doubt a spy for the national security services, an infiltrator serving shady agendas. *It's all clear; we must act immediately. Here and now. To prevent the pandemic of opportunism and infiltration from spreading in the heart of the student resistance movement.*

The new comrade implored Abdel Nasser not to reveal his name to the other comrades, out of fear of the lawyer and the other students from his region. But he felt compelled to speak because of his debt of gratitude to Abdel Nasser. He hadn't forgotten how Abdel Nasser had helped him get a room in the dorm at Bab El Khadra at the beginning of the year, or how, before that, he'd found him lodging with some former comrades from the college.

10

Abdel Nasser hurried to arrange a second meeting with Zeina. He came to see me at the Faculté 9 Avril, but Zeina was absent from her morning class. I told him instead to meet her in the evening at the Charles de Gaulle Library near Avenue de Paris, in the heart of the capital. There was to be a 6:30 P.M.

screening of a documentary about the work of French sociologist Pierre Bourdieu, with a discussion following about the role of sociology in social unrest. Zeina had invited me to go with her as usual, but I had a dentist appointment scheduled and couldn't go. Abdel Nasser would be able to find her there.

Abdel Nasser watched the film and stayed for some of the discussion, but he was anxious to get Zeina somewhere they could talk freely. Zeina was not to be rushed, however, and insisted on staying and participating in the discussion. She spoke eloquently about several of Pierre Bourdieu's concepts that she considered ambiguous, more like rhetorical composition than scientific terms. She mentioned specifically his notions of *habitus* and *symbolic capital* as two terms that were vague. She then engaged in enthusiastic debate with some of Bourdieu's defenders.

Abdel Nasser listened, enthralled, to Zeina talking about Bourdieu—someone he had never heard of and whose work he had never read—and to her arguments with the sociologists. He was especially impressed by the pure French she spoke, as if she had just come from the Latin Quarter in Paris. If she dressed like a Parisian woman, it would be enough to fool anyone into thinking that she was a French, American, or German researcher rather than a philosophy student from the hinterlands of Tunisia. He was familiar with her ability to debate and her store of knowledge, but in that library she was another person: strongly argumentative, eloquent, and brilliant. His admiration for her became fascination.

It was around 8 P.M., and el-Talyani was torn between listening to this brilliant unleashed jinn, or warning her about the danger threatening her, until finally the end of the discussion about Bourdieu put an end to his dilemma. As they walked down the stairs together, discussants both Tunisian and foreign multiplied around her. She whispered to el-Talyani, "Stay close to me."

She surprised him by taking his arm. He put his hands in his jean pockets and stared at her while she continued her discussion with an old French man, who was expressing his admiration for her ideas and his desire for another opportunity to talk more deeply about Bourdieu and his work. Abdel Nasser gathered from their discussion that the man was a sociologist studying the way the Maghrebi national state dealt with the religious elite after independence. He was in Tunisia on a one-year fellowship with the Institut de Recherche sur le Maghreb Contemporain.

Zeina told him, "I will visit you at the institute, my friend, before you leave."

The French researcher acknowledged Abdel Nasser with a nod of his head, which Abdel Nasser reciprocated, then he and Zeina left. Outside, still holding his arm, she told him, "I need coffee and a cigarette; let's find a café."

They walked along Avenue de Paris toward Avenue Habib Bourguiba. He thought about making the coffee a dinner and the lone cigarette many; Salah Eddine had just that day sent him some money, unprompted. As if he knew he was going to meet Zeina. He asked her if she was hungry and suggested they go to a restaurant. She smiled at him and said, jokingly, "Are you trying to rope me into your political faction to contain me, O Comrade Leader?"

"Who can contain Zeina?" he responded. "It's you who contains entire colleges with your elegance, your knowledge, and your . . ."

She was waiting for the last word, but he didn't finish the sentence. "And your . . . what?" she prompted.

"Your Berber beauty."

"Is that *flirting*, Comrade Leader?"

El-Talyani looked at her, probing her green eyes. He saw a twinkle of coquetry that he didn't expect, and her pleased expression confirmed that, despite her appearance, she was as susceptible to flattery as other pretty girls. If they had been at the college, he would not have dared to say what he said next. "I was just describing you. If I'd wanted to flirt, there are other things I would say."

"Go on, then," she encouraged. "Give it your best shot."

"Answer my question first. Should we go to a restaurant? Or would that give you problems at your dorm?"

Zeina laughed coyly. "Don't you have a guest bed at your place?"

"My whole house belongs to the Berber princess. If all I had to my name was a single bed, it would still be all yours."

"The general can keep his bed. Private Zeina, number 7777, will stand watch for his comfort," she said, winking.

They both laughed. They turned off Avenue Habib Bourguiba after Librairie Al Kitab and onto Rue de Marseille. They found a small restaurant and began searching for a place. Luckily, there was a table in the corner that had some people paying their bill and about to leave.

They ordered fish. When he asked her what she wanted to drink, she answered, "red wine" without hesitation. When he reminded her that they had ordered fish, she told him that only red wine and gin and tonic got her tipsy and she didn't give a flip about the stupid French rules about white wine going with fish and red or rosé wine with meat. He started off drinking beer, then switched to what she was drinking.

"Why did you take my arm at the library just now?" he asked her.

"So they would assume I wasn't single and that you're my friend or boyfriend," she answered. "Men are like flies; they land on the first woman they see. Don't be fooled by the crowd there. Most of those guys were pretending to be erudite and cultured, but really they're on the hunt."

"Seriously?"

"I promise you, most of them have probably never read a single word by Bourdieu. But if you held a general meeting or a discussion circle tomorrow, you'd hear his name a hundred times."

"That's true," he admitted. "I've noticed that among some of the comrades."

"You can be sure it's common among the intellectuals and our professors at the university, as well."

"Where did you learn all this, Zeina?"

"What did you expect? A girl who never left her village, who never made it past the local high school?"

"But surely you're not saying that everyone from that world is like you?"

"I was voracious—I used to devour any scrap of writing I could get my hands on. I even read the sheets of newspaper that the groceries were wrapped in. We would get our textbooks from the local village authorities, as a donation for poor families, and I would read them immediately. And then I would reread them. Without following any curriculum or anything. I would ask the older students about difficult words and memorize them. Then I would ask to borrow *their* books and read those, too.'

"I was lucky," she continued. "When my mother discovered my interest, she started bringing me two newspapers every day from her employer's house. Then she discovered that they had a lot of French books and magazines in their basement; they'd been abandoned in the dust and damp for so long that some of the pages were stuck together and it was hard to separate them without tearing them. These books had been left by the colonizer Robert and his children, who used to live in the house where my mother worked. She would sneak me a book, and I would immediately devour it and long for the next one. I didn't understand everything, but I would write down the difficult words and hide them in an old backpack in the corner."

Most of the books were fiction, including some well-known works by Diderot, the Marquis de Sade, Stendhal, Balzac, and many other French writers. She found novels by Dostoevsky and plays by Chekov and Shakespeare. She thought that the nicest crime that the colonizer Robert had unwittingly committed were the philosophy books, works by Merleau-Ponty, Sartre, Rousseau, and others. According to her, she devoured the literature quickly, but the other books needed more time. Especially after she started keeping a small notebook that she would use to copy paragraphs. She found herself an unwitting philosopher while she was still in high school.

Her teachers first discovered her through her writing. When the effects of her reading first began to show in her elementary school writings, one of her teachers accused her of plagiarism. After insulting her in front of all her classmates, he took her to the principal and told her to confess. She was a shy, skinny child, poor and shabby looking, standing in front of the principal and her teacher with no idea of how to prove her innocence. She was shaking with fear and burst into tears as the principal sat her down. He asked her to read the essay she had written out loud, which she did with a smoothness that surprised him. Then he asked her to explain some of the difficult words she had used to him, which she also did. He smiled at the teacher: "Did you see that?"

She thought they were going to expel her or beat her, and she broke down again in bitter tears. The principal took her hand and patted her on her shoulders. Then he opened his desk drawer and gave her a fancy pen and a piece of candy. At first she couldn't believe it, but he assured her that he was serious. She looked at her teacher and saw that he was also smiling at her. He gave her a hug and a kiss on the cheek; she noticed that his eyes were watery.

The principal laid a blank piece of paper in front of her on the desk and asked her to write him two letters, one in French and one in Arabic, describing the pen he gave her and thanking him for the gift. She quickly filled the paper on both sides. They asked her to read what she had written out loud, and she had never seen either the principal or the teacher happier. The principal gathered all the teachers and students to introduce the school genius that God had seen fit to bless them with and swore to all of them that she would have a great future. Zeina became the talk of the village, and by freely writing letters for the village illiterates she took nearly all the business of the scrivener at Hajj Amar's little shop.

Zeina stopped talking. She looked at Abdel Nasser, whose fascination with her story was clear through his rapt attention and the look in his eyes. She told him, "Do you know this is the first time I've talked about all this? What did you put in this wine to unlock my memory chest for you like this?"

"I'm just listening to you," he responded. "Do you have an explanation?"

"Maybe because I like you . . . your personality . . . your good looks. You know—when I was holding your arm, I felt protected. I felt safe."

"Hey, is this how a woman flirts with a man?"

"Believe me, I only just realized that."

He laughed, then said, "Confession time for both of us, then. I liked it when you held my arm, too. It felt strange and exciting, refreshing in a way I can't quite put my finger on."

They both fell silent as they ate and considered what the other had said.

Zeina broke the silence. "You know, I'm happy now—very. I feel like maybe I've gained a friend."

Abdel Nasser responded with mock disapproval, "Just a *feeling* of *maybe* having gained a *friend*?"

"Don't blame me for being cautious," she retorted. "I'm sure you're different, but life has taught me to be cautious about rushing into happiness or getting overly excited about things. I'm strict with myself, and others—especially those I love and respect."

She stared off, her thoughts wandering for a moment, then resumed, "I'm sorry I was so stubborn during our last meeting. I may have been too harsh in my response. Our friend explained that to me, but I hadn't had the chance to apologize yet."

"My apologies, too. I might have surprised you with my request. But, like I said, it was based on my responsibilities; it wasn't personal."

"Never mind. I promise the great Comrade Leader that after this lovely dinner he's bought for me, I won't criticize his political movement."

Abdel Nasser smiled. Then he said, in a soft voice as he leaned in, "I actually asked to meet you today about something important. I don't want to bother you or scare you, but . . ."

He hesitated, and Zeina became serious. Her forehead wrinkled, and she leaned in closer to him to listen carefully. He told her everything about the lawyer and his relationship to him, the organization, and the faction. He assured her that he and his comrades would protect her whenever she was at the law college, but her being away from him at the Faculté 9 Avril was worrying him. He explained that they were both targets; these ignorant scum were motivated by regionalism and clannism, not values or principles. They were thugs who might do anything, pathetic but no less dangerous for it.

She asked him, calmly, about the possible dangers. He told her that it could be anything from a painful beating that would leave her black and blue, to a stabbing or bludgeoning. He tried to reassure her that these were just some possible scenarios, based on what he knew about an incident the lawyer was involved in at the Faculté des Lettres de la Manouba on March 30, 1982. But he also stressed that she should be cautious and reserved, so her final year at the university could pass without incident. He reminded her that there were only four months left in the academic year; she should restrict her activities severely.

She asked him what she had to do, the light sarcasm in her tone masking the fear just under the surface. He told her, "It's simple. Avoid appearing in the quad where they could find an opportunity. Try to always have two or three friends with you wherever you go to protect you. Be aware of your surroundings, of who is behind you. Don't get so involved in conversation that you become unaware of imminent danger. Avoid buses that are too crowded and always sit next to your friends. These are just some general precautions."

"So I have to put myself in a glass dome?"

"They're just precautions, Zeina. The days will pass by quickly, and it's better to be too cautious than to face possible catastrophe. You don't know these people . . ."

"And you? You've got me scared, but I have to say I'm worried about you, too. You're under just as much threat as I am."

"I'll be following the same advice I gave you," he reassured her. "The difference is that I can't leave the battlefield. But I'm not worried; I have a number of comrades who are tasked with noticing any unusual movement, inside the university and outside of it."

The waiter started clearing the empty dishes and asked if they wanted to order anything else, since the restaurant was about to close. El-Talyani paid the bill, and Zeina thanked him for the dinner, as well as for his concern and advice. She promised to do her best to strictly follow his instructions.

11

The road was nearly empty. The taxi charged up the road to Le Bardo, where Abdel Nasser was living with a friend of his. There were some police checkpoints at the edge of Le Jardin du Passage and the Bab Souika neighborhood, right before the tunnel in the Bab Saadoun district, but the taxi wasn't stopped.

The police trusted taxi drivers, especially at night. The Islamists were keeping the authorities in a state of alert—but in such circumstances, the smell of wine on a taxi passenger was enough to prove their innocence!

Zeina sat in the back seat of the taxi, and Abdel Nasser was next to the driver. The midnight news on the radio was reporting on tensions, attempted protests, and the police forces' decisive action to protect citizens' safety and confront the criminal gangs.

"God help us and our country," the driver commented.

Abdel Nasser responded to the driver's language in kind. "Amen."

Abdel Nasser didn't ask the driver to turn into Rue des Orangers but rather prolonged the trip by asking him to stop at the corner, in front of Café El Hajj. He walked the rest of the way with Zeina, often looking behind them and checking whenever they passed through a side street or alley. The street was empty when they arrived at his front door. Turning the key, he said, "Welcome to my humble abode—come on in."

She laughed and responded, "True! How humble compared to our castle in the village! How dare you bring me to this hovel, Comrade Leader?"

His roommate came out, and Abdel Nasser introduced him to Zeina. He welcomed her, then returned to his room. Abdel Nasser took Zeina to his room. She found it, unlike most students' rooms, tidy and clean, full of books and magazines. As she was perusing the book titles, he got her a pair of his pajamas and slippers and put them by the bed. He showed her the bathroom, and where the refrigerator was in the kitchen. He then took a wool blanket from the closet and a pillow from the bed and took them to the living room. When she came out of the bathroom, she found the bed ready and thanked him.

"The Berber princess can sleep like a queen now!"

"Goodnight, dear leader."

"Sweet dreams."

Zeina's dreams that night did turn out to be sweet. She'd discovered a kind, sophisticated person. She pictured his face as she fell asleep and thought back on some of the things he'd said.

Meanwhile, Abdel Nasser's mind drifted over the exceptional woman sleeping in his bed.

She thought: *That's the first time I've entered a man's house without waking up the animal in him. I wouldn't have minded a kiss, at least . . .*

He thought: *This is the first woman I've had over and haven't even thought about sleeping with, even though I want her. If she'd made a move or dropped a hint, I'd have given her the kind of passionate kiss she deserves.*

They confessed these thoughts to each other a few days later, after the incident in which they signed, with blood and kisses, a pact that changed their lives.

1

T ensions at the university reached their peak, and a general state of chaos reigned. Higher education minister Ibn Dhia revealed that, owing to the structural adjustment policy imposed by the World Bank and the IMF, the government would no longer be funding the university. This made for fertile ground for the Marxist–Leninists, who argued that this proved the dependency of the regime on global financial circles, its unpatriotic and unpopulist direction, and the clear return of the "savage economic liberalism," as Abdel Nasser liked to dub it in public meetings. The ministry re-enacted a 1973 law forbidding assembly without a permit and added new punishments on top of that.

The Islamic Tendency students escalated their confrontation with the regime. The university was besieged by security forces: there were arrests, conscriptions, and confrontations. The police surrounded and cut off some campuses.

The left, as far as Abdel Nasser could see, was being smothered between two conflicts: the regime in the front and the Islamists from behind. The leftist students no longer had any support and were forced to rely on themselves. Even the Tunisian General Labor Union was targeted, including Secretary General Achour, a scion of the Constitutional Party. But Abdel Nasser, in passionate oratory at public meetings, portrayed the current situation in the country as the throes of revolution: the regime, like its leader, was in its autumn, and a rain of blood would soon come to cleanse the country from the microbes infesting it. Impoverished workers and destitute peasants would demolish the regime of treasonous compradors and their feudal system and would establish a dictatorship of the proletariat. Now was the time for the students' movement and its revolutionary vanguards to raise their demands and intensify their protests to reach a true historical–political awareness of the working and peasant classes' mandates.

Abdel Nasser and Zeina happened to both be at the Université de la Manouba campus that day in April. He had gone there to coordinate a protest with some of his comrades. The protest, which was to take place at several different colleges during the reading period before final exams, was against the oppressive policy that the regime was pursuing, both inside universities and outside of them. It was also a protest to prove their existence: the conflict between the Islamists and the government had derailed the leftist student movement as the student arm of the Islamic Tendency fought the regime and forced concessions from it. Abdel Nasser was aware that the leadership of the Islamic student union had held meetings with several regime stakeholders, seeking legitimacy and legal recognition. The Islamists understood that this was their chance; they spread everywhere, grabbing most of the seats in much of the university, and also had strong logistic support. Meanwhile the left was divided into factions wrestling for power. Something had to be done.

Zeina, on the other hand, had only two months left until graduation and, as usual, was at the top of the student rankings. Her dream was to become a professor of philosophy, specifically political philosophy. She was ardently reading Hannah Arendt and believed that for Arabs and Muslims to achieve their freedom, they had to unshackle themselves from the concept of "the shepherd and his flock" and recognize the patriarchal underpinnings of their approach to government. She had gone to Manouba's Faculté des Lettres to visit the professor she had chosen to supervise her master's thesis once she completed her bachelor's degree.

They found themselves both riding the #4 bus and were happy at the coincidence. He was with four of his comrades, who, seeing their greeting, quickly understood that this rebel with a price on her head was more than a mere acquaintance. The classmate Zeina had been chatting with noticed the same. The bus was emptier than usual, but Abdel Nasser and Zeina seemed oblivious to the glances and smiles of those around them, who acted like they were watching a Nadia Lutfi and Abdel Halim Hafez romance. The pair were occupied with various topics, none of which had to do with love and passion, but their onlookers couldn't help but think they seemed made for each other.

When they entered the Faculté des Lettres, the atmosphere was tense. There were Islamist orators giving speeches one after another and a large number of attendees who, like them, came from different colleges. Heading to the cafeteria, they passed with difficulty through the crowd. One of the Manouba comrades accompanied Abdel Nasser and Zeina, leading them on a route that went behind the library and the French Department, coming into the cafeteria courtyard from the back entrance. He was asked to inform the comrades that Abdel Nasser was on campus and would be attending a meeting with them, as planned, in one of the classrooms at around one o'clock.

2

In the cafeteria, they heard occasional calls of "*Allahu akbar*" and people chanting from time to time. They learned that some courses had been canceled because of the strike and that the Islamic Tendency students had organized the public

meeting without abiding by Law 73 and without permission
from the dean. This was why so many of the students were
wearing masks.

She told him about her research and the supervisor she was
planning to meet. She didn't want to waste any time: she would
register her research subject in September and do her best to
finish it the following summer. It would be her first time teaching; she didn't know where she might be appointed, since she
had no high-level contacts who could help secure her a teaching post near the university and the capital, where the books
and libraries were. She was scanning and collecting as many
references as she could, and she had read all of Hannah
Arendt's writings; she was determined that her research would
be serious and well-documented.

She told him she was planning to complete her master's
degree only two years after graduating. One year to prepare
the research that would allow her to register in the master's
program and one year to prepare for the *agrégation* exam, con-
current with registering for the preparatory courses for the
Master of Advanced Studies. She had examined the research
subjects from previous years and read the syllabi and found
them within reach. She only needed to improve her German
writing and pronunciation. She'd made a plan to listen to the
one German radio station they could pick up and to reread
several philosophy books in German that she had originally
read in translation. It was just a matter of time—a year and a
half would be plenty to reach her goals.

She spoke passionately about her ambitions, and Abdel
Nasser listened attentively. Suddenly there was a loud distur-
bance: people screaming, shouting *"Allahu akbar,"* and the
sound of people running. Through the window, they saw
throngs of students jostling toward the door of the dormitory
behind the cafeteria. The door was small, and the crowd was
packed in tight. They saw some students jumping over the wall

and others—masked and unmasked—gathering stones and heading toward the center of the courtyard.

Zeina was tense, but Abdel Nasser was calm, or at least feigning it. The chaos spread to the cafeteria, and the students pushed and jostled to leave, but Abdel Nasser did not. He took Zeina's hand and retreated to the left corner of the cafeteria. He put her behind him and opened his arms, making a triangle with them in the corner. She clung to him, and he felt her breasts against his back. She buried her head between his shoulders, shielding from the approaching danger, terrified. But mixed with the fear was an overwhelming joy: "the meeting of Thanatos and Eros," as she later told him. She held tight to his belt and arms and laid her cheek on his back, as if on a pillow. She no longer heard the noise of the cafeteria and courtyard but was traveling through fields of golden wheat, spotted here and there with the red of poppies. In that moment, she saw the familiar landscape of her youth. But at the same time, with other eyes, she saw herself running through those fields with Abdel Nasser. They were running under a clear blue sky, illuminated by a bright and beautiful sun. When they grew tired, they lay down on the ground, disappearing among the stalks of wheat, and melted into feverish kisses and infinite dreams.

The arrival of the police officers, with their screaming and their truncheons, brought Zeina back to the courtyard. There was sharp pain as the truncheons struck her feet and shoulders, and she found herself thrown to the ground. Abdel Nasser was stretched out on top of her, his body protecting hers from the blows of the public order police, who they called *el-POP*, after the French abbreviation. Almost all the blows landed on him: his back, his feet, his buttocks. He covered his head with his hands while covering her head with his own. He screamed and cursed, and she saw drops of blood. She returned consciously to the dream, bringing him with her. She started kissing him on the neck, putting her hand on his head and pulling him to her. He didn't understand at first, but as they sank into a deep kiss, they forgot the pain of the truncheon blows. She heard nasty words pouring from the police officers, describing them in terms of prostitution and threatening her with rape and murder.

They were near the dean's office, in the wide hallway leading toward the exit, and they heard a man screaming, telling the police officers to stop their violence and let the couple go. They knew from the warning of one of the employees to the police officers that he was the dean of the college. They heard, while still lying on the ground like lovers, a hoarse voice giving orders to leave them alone and continue clearing the courtyard. The beatings stopped, and they opened their eyes. On the right was the dean and a group of other people: staff or professors. On the left, a group of police officers in riot gear and carrying tear gas moved forward toward the cafetcria. Abdel Nasser lifted his head a bit and saw a high-ranking officer with several stars and the motto of the Tunisian Republic on his shoulders. He was heavy, with a broad nose and a unibrow; he was pointing, indicating for the other officers to advance.

Abdel Nasser looked at Zeina. She smiled at him. She caressed his cheek, her long fingers wiping away the blood running down them. He smiled at her and was about to kiss her when two police officers without helmets or truncheons came. One held Abdel Nasser's arm and stood him up; the second held Zeina. He heard the high-ranking officer giving an order to put them in the police van. They walked slowly, Abdel Nasser staggering from the pain of the truncheon blows.

The police van was crammed with students. The police officers pushed them in with a flood of cursing and insults (*faggot, whore, bastard, pimp, slut, immoral trash*). Zeina was the only girl in the van. She clung to Abdel Nasser. She examined his bleeding head and found a small wound. She cleaned it with the Palestinian kaffiyeh that he was wearing around his neck. She continued treating the painful spots in spite of the lack of space in the van. It was clear that most of the people in the van were Islamists, along with a few ordinary students. He didn't see any of the comrades from the Faculté de la Manouba that he could recognize.

Zeina whispered in Abdel Nasser's ear, "If they put us in a cell together, I'd finish my research in a month and spend the rest of the time looking at you and smothering you in kisses."

He smiled. "Would you now?"

"Didn't the prophet say, 'May the kiss be a messenger between you'?"

Abdel Nasser burst out laughing, ignoring the pain shooting down his sides and back.

3

The van stopped at the El Gorjani police station. A new wave of cursing and insults began, with beating on their backs and kicks to the feet and buttocks.

Zeina, the only female in the van, got out before Abdel Nasser. He followed her closely to protect her from the officers, who had formed a wall on each side to prevent any detainees from escaping. As soon as one of them was about to kick Zeina, Abdel Nasser intercepted him with his own foot to protect her. The officers became agitated. After closing the van door, two officers attacked him, giving a sound beating. Abdel Nasser did not keep quiet but paid them back twofold in profanity and spitting, shielding his head from a potentially deadly kick. The officers of El Gorjani were not carrying truncheons or batons; most of them were wearing civilian clothes. They took him to a room with a large table. Next to it was a small table for the police officer taking notes, outfitted with an old typewriter that no doubt scratched and clanked with every keystroke. They sat him on a chair with one officer standing on each side, slapping and cursing at him from time to time. They took turns insulting him, cursing his mother, belittling his father, and accusing him of being a homosexual. Abdel Nasser, despite the handcuffs restraining his hands behind the chair, was also cursing and yelling, calling the officers dogs and cowards. This went on for no more than a few minutes. Then a well-dressed man, who Abdel Nasser estimated to be between thirty-five and forty, entered the room. He told the officers to stop and had them unbind Abdel Nasser's hands and take him into his office.

He offered him a cigarette. Using a disparaging term for the Islamists, he asked him, "Have you become *khwanji*, or was it fate that took you to Manouba today?"

Abdel Nasser protested the accusation, confidently rebutting him: "The principled don't change their principles."

The officer smiled. While pretending to busy himself with the paperwork on his desk, he blindsided him with, "You mean the children of Si Mahmoud don't change their roots."

Abdel Nasser's surprise was evident; he saw the officer watching him from behind the paper he was holding. He told him that they were from the same neighborhood, though he had left it a long time ago. He had brought him to his office in honor of that link, and because he knew that Abdel Nasser's presence at the El Gorjani police station must be a mistake. He asked him what he was doing in Manouba, given that he was one of the revolutionary leaders at the Faculté de Droit. Abdel Nasser, feeling that he could trust him, told him the truth. He asked him to release Zeina, explaining that she was simply waiting for the professor who was supervising her research. He discovered that the officer knew Zeina S., who he referred to as "that Trotskyite at the Faculté 9 Avril." He told Abdel

Nasser that she would be automatically released, since their mission was limited to arresting as many of the Islamic Tendency students as possible, because they were making trouble and plotting to bring down the state.

He gave Abdel Nasser a few newspapers to occupy himself with as he waited for them to finish the legal procedures. "One of our cars will take you to Le Bardo," he told him. "But if you're going to your family home in the neighborhood, I'll let you walk."

Abdel Nasser was now sure that they knew everything about him and that this officer was a member of the political police. The officer left the room, locking it with a key. Abdel Nasser started leafing through the newspapers quickly. There was nothing to read, as usual, except for the exploits of the Supreme Warrior, the activities of his ministers, and the obituary page. He found a report in *La Presse* about the structural amendment policy: all banalities, in Abdel Nasser's opinion, defending neocolonialism and the dominance of financial capital in the country. In *Assabah*, page 3, there were articles written by an Islamist leader in the student movement, demented with leadership, talking about the necessity of granting legitimacy to the *khwanji* student union and describing the state of the university from the Islamists' point of view. This was, in Abdel Nasser's view, evidence of the complicity of Mzali's cabinet with the Islamic Tendency and its old alliance in order to weaken the left and empty the university of any activism. The Islamist leader was begging the government to recognize the *khwanji* student union, which was splintering the student movements and had been ignoring the historical demand of the union, since February of '72, to hold the 18th congress and shore up the political and organizational break with the treasonous regime.

He went through the newspapers in just a few minutes, then looked at the desk and the papers on it. He turned to examine his surroundings. The office was on the upper floor of the building and had windows overlooking a large courtyard. He saw more students arriving in two new vans. He went to the door and assured that it was securely locked, with one lock in the middle and one at the top. His curiosity drew him to the papers on the desk, and he inspected them with caution, being careful not to rearrange them. There were search warrants, reports typed on very thin paper, newspaper cuttings, and fines for running red lights. He thought it noteworthy that the desk was so neat and organized.

Abdel Nasser thought this might be a good opportunity to find out how policemen think. The silence in the office encouraged him to open the desk drawers. There were three. The upper one was locked; the bottom two were not. In the unlocked drawers were blue and yellow manila folders. Some of them had labels, written in marker in French, with the all-caps initials of the Islamic Tendency. These folders had many papers, almost filling the entire first drawer, with the exception of a small folder beneath them. Abdel Nasser hesitated over this folder, trying to figure out if it was about the "Trotskyite Left" or the "Radical Left." He leafed through it quickly and saw a paper with the name of one of Zeina's friends—a member of the Council of Communist Students—which convinced him that it was the latter.

Abdel Nasser scanned the folders quickly, afraid that the officer might return at any moment. He was surprised to find a medium-sized folder for the political group he led at the law college. But the real surprise was when he found a typed sheet, devoid of any heading that would indicate the interior ministry or one of its divisions, with the word "Statement" written on top. Its subject was clear to Abdel Nasser:

A new political faction has appeared at the Faculté de Droit called _____. The person behind it is the lawyer S.K.

According to the information provided to us by the above-mentioned lawyer, this faction is in opposition to the leader A.A., who seized control of the original faction in the Faculté de Droit and other colleges in the university.

We have informed you of what we have, and yours is the final judgement.

Signed, N.N.

The content of the statement seemed ordinary, but Abdel Nasser was perplexed. What was the relationship between the lawyer and the person who wrote this statement? Either the lawyer was collaborating with the political police or the author of the statement was a political police infiltrator into the movement. He folded the piece of paper and tucked it into his underwear.

Leafing quickly through the rest of the folder, he found reports about the discussion circles, public meetings, and activities of the faction and its supporters. All the names were written with initials and organized based on the university division. He recognized most of them. Suddenly he heard footsteps approaching; by the time the key turned in one of the locks, he had already returned the folder to the drawer.

The officer stood near the door and indicated for Abdel Nasser to go. On the way out of the office, he said, "I want to talk to you about something that concerns you. Would you like to visit me here, or should we meet somewhere else?"

"Why should our paths cross?" Abdel Nasser asked. "What could a police officer serving the Constitutional Party have to do with a political union activist?"

"Never mind those cock-and-bull stories," he responded. "I'm protecting the country. Your problem is with the party, not with us."

"You're the tool it uses to govern and oppress the masses," Abdel Nasser responded.

"I thought you were more mature than that. Are the reports I have false, then?"

Abdel Nasser didn't respond. The officer added, "I prefer that you choose the time and place, so I'm not required to bring you in by force."

"I prefer to be brought in by force."

"Ah, you're worried about maintaining your activist image," said the officer. "Fine. But don't resist when the plain-clothes officers come get you."

Before leaving, Abdel Nasser asked about Zeina. The officer informed him that she'd been released immediately, two hours ago. He reminded him of the offer to drive him to Le Bardo, but Abdel Nasser refused. The officer gave him a small piece of paper with his phone number written on it to call if needed. Abdel Nasser hesitated for a moment before slipping it into his pocket.

4

It was almost seven o'clock, and darkness had started to spread over the city. Abdel Nasser breathed in the dewy air, a deep breath then a strong exhale, as if searching for oxygen to clear out the pain and tension and revive his nerves. He felt a bit dizzy, followed by a rush that made him forget the pain of the beating. He felt gingerly around the wound on his head; the blood was dry. He went to a nearby pharmacy to clean it. He wondered where he could find Zeina. It would be ignoble not to check on her. But last week she'd had a fight with her roommates and gone to live with some relatives in Jbal Lahmar—how would he find her?

He could see from the heavy police presence and multitude of checkpoints that the situation was still tense and the perse-cution of the Islamists was ongoing. They had killed an

Islamist student a day or two before, during a chase through one of the neighborhoods near Le Bardo. He'd found that out this morning, after asking why the Islamists were protesting. He didn't know, though, whether they had already organized protests in other colleges besides the Faculté des Lettres at the Université de la Manouba.

Lying on his bed in his room, listening to a pan flute piece by Gheorghe Zamfir, he wondered why the police officer from their neighborhood, Si Othman, wanted to meet with him. He'd been arrested several times yet had never seen the basement of the interior ministry—did he have Si Othman to thank for that? He quickly dismissed the idea: he had only been protesting, and he had never acted violently toward the police by throwing stones or Molotov cocktails or anything. The worst he could be accused of was belonging to an unauthorized organization plotting to overthrow the regime or something like that. But they all knew that the so-called secret organization was no more than a group of students playing politics at the university, passing out statements and hanging their ideas on the wall; it would be foolish to prosecute them. The temporary syndicate had become like a kitten imitating a lion's pounce. It was at death's door, riddled with contradictions; it had wizened just like Bourguiba. Everyone knew, but no one was willing to admit it.

5

Abdel Nasser had thought many times about taking the exam for the last elective certificate he needed to get his bachelor's degree in law. He'd thought many times about cutting his ties with the temporary syndicate and becoming just a grassroots activist in the second or third circle. Whenever these thoughts occurred to him, however, he couldn't escape the conclusion that to do so would mean the collapse of the leftist bastion and the fall of the law college into the hands of the Islamists. He wasn't sure if any of his colleagues could replace him, except maybe for Jaafar or Najm Eddine. But Jaafar's sarcastic nature sometimes got the best of him, making him undisciplined, whereas Najm Eddine was too rigid and impetuous in his decision-making, apt to use his fists rather than his tongue wherever possible. He trusted them and thought that their political and theoretical knowledge and their understanding of the movement literature was sufficient, but they weren't leadership material.

But at the same time, he wondered how long he could postpone his graduation. What did he gain from leading the movement? Several of the leaders who came before him, or started with him, had already begun their careers. Most were apprentices at law firms, or had already finished their training. Some of the others were in the finance ministry, the prime minister's office, or the École Nationale d'Administration, or they had passed the foreign affairs ministry exams. These former comrades forgot about the movement and became sympathizers from afar. They bragged about their great history of activism (even if it was sometimes a history of cowardice and evading responsibility), but they strove for a peaceful life: a wife, a car, a house if they could afford it. When he ran into them, they would ask, out of guilt, about the situation at the university and to what extent the Islamists' numbers were increasing and they were taking over. In their frozen university lexicon, they advised him to resist the fascist tide, as if trying to convince him (or themselves) that they were still resistance fighters, albeit in a different position. That the movement was in their hearts, and it was in the best interest of the revolution that the revolutionaries spread to all positions.

The only one who was honest with Abdel Nasser was our friend Taher C., who had enrolled at the École Nationale

d'Administration. He was a good student, who had chosen
from the beginning to just be a sympathizer with the movement.
He had gone to the same high school as us and had earned the
baccalaureate with distinction. It was he who had encouraged
Abdel Nasser to join the law college. His brother was a well-
known lawyer, and they had been friends for two years. They
used to sit at the same desk. Abdel Nasser didn't like school
then; he would come to class with only a notebook, which he
carried under his arm inside a newspaper, and rarely used to
take notes. But he loved books and reading: he read novels,
poetry, philosophy, history, everything. He would always tell
Taher that, with a few exceptions, the teachers were idiots who
hadn't read a quarter of what he had. "Have you heard the
nonsense they're spouting?"

The only teachers he liked were the French teacher and the
philosophy teacher, despite the fact that the latter's Standard
Arabic was broken; he was a francophone who found the Ara-
bization of philosophy unpalatable and didn't adhere to the
curriculum in the textbook. He always began the lesson with a
funny story that he had heard or had read in the newspaper. His
lesson was a game; the time passed without his students getting
bored. The teacher considered himself a facilitator for the deep
philosophical discussions springing from the students' spontaneous philosophy. So the textbook was nowhere to be found.
He always arrived late, with red and swollen eyes (from staying
up drinking, no doubt). But when the students left his class,
they felt that something in them had changed, despite the fact
that the teacher hadn't lectured them at all. He would propose
the topic of discussion and then let the students speak. But he
was skilled in remembering their ideas and, regardless of how
simple (and sometimes banal) they were, in reformulating them
in an amazing way. And that was the content of the lesson. His
motto in education, which he was fond of repeating, was "You
get back what you put in."

Taher told him one day, when they ran into each other on Avenue Habib Bourguiba, "Enough activism—finish your degree. How long are you going to live off your brother Salah Eddine? Don't you know that everybody's out for their own interests? Haven't you seen what your comrades have become? And those that are still with you: I bet half of them are idiots and the other half are informants who are writing reports about you. You've got everything you need: you're smart and intellectual, able to succeed at any international university and have a bright career. You'll live to regret this, Abdu, mark my words."

Abdel Nasser wasn't used to arguing with Taher. If not for him, he wouldn't have passed senior year. He hadn't been attending any of the classes before the exam, but Taher would copy all of his notes and lectures and confine Abdel Nasser to his house to study for the exam. Taher was always organized; his motto was "Never put off till tomorrow what you can do today." He would pretend not to understand a lesson or a judicial decision they had analyzed in the discussion session and would ask Abdel Nasser about it. Really he was just making sure his friend got it. So Abdel Nasser would pass with flying colors, usually even above Taher in the final rankings, but Taher would be the first to congratulate him and would invite him for a celebratory four bottles of wine—no more, no less— at Le Schilling, La Rotonde, or Café El Zunouj.

6

The next morning, I told Zeina that Abdel Nasser wanted to meet her at 6 P.M. He had called me the night before to let me know what had happened and to ask me to have her meet him in front of the Cinéma Africa. She told me how happy that made her, especially since she had waited for him by the

El Gorjani police station and was worried about him. Her eagerness in asking about him surprised me a little, and I couldn't resist commenting on it. "What's this? Has the wandering gazelle fallen into the hunter's trap?"

She laughed, masking a shyness and embarrassment I'd never seen in her before. She didn't answer my question, but I understood and was glad of it. In an hour she came back to me to talk about him, like a woman in love. She wanted to know more details about him and to tell me about her feeling of security and safety when she was with him, despite the police truncheons. She confessed that she'd held him and kissed him in front of the officers, under the blows of the truncheons.

Abdel Nasser woke up feeling sluggish. The intensity of the pain hadn't abated as he'd hoped, despite the hot compress and salt and the ice packs he'd applied with his roommate's help. He took two aspirins and decided to call Si Othman to make an appointment.

When he went into the college, his comrades gave him a battle hero's welcome. He found that they had hung a statement condemning the police prosecution and the kidnapping of their comrade activist and holding the treasonous state responsible for the consequences of this kidnapping. They called for protests demanding his unconditional release. Within half of an hour of them hanging the statement, Abdel Nasser arrived at the law college cafeteria. They took down the poster and replaced it with another, strongly condemning what had happened, promising to continue the fight until the traitor regime was brought down, and welcoming their returning comrade combatant. It was a text that Jaafar and Najm Eddine quickly composed on a table in the cafeteria without a draft and without consulting Abdel Nasser. They asked him to say something at noon, at a public meeting that would convey information and look into ways to condemn these oppressive practices.

He bowed out on the excuse of pain, but because they insisted that he take advantage of the opportunity to mobilize the student masses, he did end up speaking for a few minutes. He thanked the students for coming together around their strong union and for their support of activists, noting that he was and would remain ready to sacrifice for the salvation of his people. Then he quickly excused himself, on account of the pain.

7

It was 1:30 P.M. when Si Othman welcomed him into his office. Abdel Nasser was careful not to let anyone see him as he entered; he looked left, right, and behind him, then quickly strode into the building.

Si Othman was eating a sandwich; he asked if Abdel Nasser wanted to eat anything, then brought him a cup of coffee. He spoke with his mouth full of food: "Your speech today at the college was moderate. Why didn't you tell them you were treated differently from the others?"

"They had no right to even bring me here," Abdel Nasser responded.

"Still stubborn, okay," Othman said. "Then why didn't you tell them about the statement you stole from the folder?"

Abdel Nasser didn't say a word. Othman looked at him and said, "Of course, it would've been better for you not to touch the folders."

The silence continued. Si Othman laughed, then resumed, "Your problem—all of you—is that you think you're smarter than anybody else. You don't know the state, but you want to bring down the regime. You and the *khwanji* are both arrogant. Activism requires modesty and perseverance, but instead you're cocky."

"Did you invite me here to lecture me on activism? To dole out preaching and spiritual guidance?"

"If anyone else spoke to me here the way you have, I would have shown him real preaching and spiritual guidance," Othman said. "But I still appreciate our shared roots."

"Why did you ask to meet me?" Abdel Nasser asked.

"For your own good," Othman replied. "I know you come from an honorable family. You're loyal to your principles, but you move around with no clue about the imminent danger."

"What danger, aside from your oppression?"

"Give it a rest with the tough guy act. Why did you give up the bed in your room and sleep in the living room when you took Zeina to your house?"

"What?" sputtered Abdel Nasser. "Where did you get that?"

"Never mind, smart guy, what's important is whether or not my information is correct."

"You're spying on my private life," Abdel Nasser accused him. "You bugged my house."

"Again your intelligence fails you, but you still charge forward like a Spanish bull. Who do you think you are, that we would waste expensive equipment in your house? A minister? A president? Do you think you're a big threat to us? Do you fancy yourself Che Guevara?"

"How did you know, then?" Abdel Nasser asked.

The officer laughed arrogantly. Abdel Nasser was consumed in his thoughts, trying to figure out who could have sold this information to Si Othman. His first thought was of Zeina. He was torn between the accusation and his own defense of her. How could it be her, with all her knowledge and sharp political awareness and criticism of everything? Could she possibly be an informant intentionally placed in his path? Yes. She could. She wasn't politically or organizationally disciplined. The comrade lawyer was right. But this—this was unbelievable . . . But no, anything was possible in the world of politics. Was she just playing a role, making him think she was a sophisticated intellectual? And what about that kiss yesterday, that flood of tenderness in the heart of all that violence? It couldn't be Zeina; Si Othman was lying. He had to search his house and his room to find the listening devices.

Si Othman broke in, interrupting his thoughts: "I wanted to warn you about the students who defected from your faction. They want to hurt you and Zeina. They're a gang of riffraff, led by the person whose statement you stole. Our information is solid; they always carry knives. I've warned you; you make sure to warn Zeina. She's a girl who can't fight them, and we can't protect you."

"Thank you, I already know this. But how did you know about Zeina spending the night in my room?"

"First, I didn't say that she slept in your room," Othman said. "Second, I didn't ask for these kinds of personal details that don't interest us. I really am doubting your intelligence."

"Zeina informed you . . ." Abdel Nasser began.

"How smart you are!" Othman interrupted. "A girl and she tells me about herself and her private life!"

The name of Raeef, his roommate, suddenly occurred to him. Why didn't he think of it before? What kind of trusting fool was he?

Raeef was a student at the Institut Supérieur d'Administration from Kelibia. He was a calm young man, hardworking, clean; apolitical, but did not like the Islamists. He had a girlfriend from back home who studied the same concentration at a higher education institute in Carthage. A comrade who had become a lawyer introduced them; Raeef was a cousin of his looking for a place to live. He assured Abdel Nasser that Raeef was harmless. He was taciturn, from a respectable family; his father owned a number of fishing boats and was willing to rent him a house for himself but preferred that he live with someone a few years his senior, especially since he had never left Kelibia.

Abdel Nasser had agreed almost two years ago to share the house with him after seeing and talking to him. He thought that Raeef might be a useful cover for his political activism, although he didn't actually use the house for this purpose. Raeef was, after all, impossible to suspect. He seemed perfect. Within two days, a truck pulled up to the house with new bedroom furniture perfectly crafted by the carpenters of Kelibia, in addition to a big refrigerator filled with fish and seafood, an electric oven, living room furniture, carpets, and all the kitchen necessities, including dish soap. Raeef asked Abdel Nasser for permission to let in three maids to clean the house, including his bedroom. When el-Talyani came back, he found his room organized in a way he couldn't get used to, that reminded him of how his mother and sister Jweeda used to clean. He was sure he'd made a good choice. Raeef's conduct with him seemed to denote seriousness and a desire to provide good living conditions. They had a television in the house and a big cassette player and an electric stove in the kitchen. The maid (whose salary was paid by Raeef) came to the house three times a week, on Monday, Thursday, and Saturday. She would prepare whatever food she could and leave it in the refrigerator. On the days she didn't come, Raeef would cook.

As if Si Othman could tell that Abdel Nasser had no one left but Raeef to suspect, he told him, "Don't be unfair to Raeef. He has nothing to do with this."

"Who is it then? It's driving me crazy."

"You just need to know that we're stronger than you can imagine," Othman told him. "You cannot win." He laughed and added in a sarcastic tone, "You know they say that when a man and a woman are alone together, Satan makes three: we deal in Satans. Don't worry about it—just take precautions for yourself and your new girlfriend."

The meeting ended with Abdel Nasser still wondering, trying to think of who could have betrayed him. He shook Si Othman's hand, feeling defeated. When someone has information that you thought was private, it feels like they've stripped you naked and sat you down to mock your genitals.

Just as he reached the door and was about to leave the office, Si Othman told him in a firm voice, "Change the maid. Don't say anything to Raeef or Zeina."

Bitches! We defend them, and they sell us out. What can you expect from the ragged proletariat anyway? But despite all that, he felt an inner peace that calmed the storms that ravaged him. To him, Zeina was not a mere student who had entered his house, slept in his bed, and left like the other female students he'd had over. She had left her captivating scent on the sheets and the pillow and the pajamas she'd worn. Her apparition had started to visit him whenever he closed his eyes, and he would smell that scent, which had spread to the books, papers, and pens on his small table. The same scent that had filled his nose and possessed him yesterday, that was even stronger than the smell of the tear gas flooding the college cafeteria.

8

In front of Cinéma Africa, the street was crowded with people. He arrived half an hour early and bought two tickets. He was standing in front of the movie theater waiting, looking toward the Avenue Habib Bourguiba, when he suddenly felt soft hands cover his eyes from behind. Immediately, he knew it was Zeina. He was certain it was Zeina; he could smell her scent. She moved her hands to around his waist and pressed her chest against his back. Whenever he tried to turn, she turned with him.

When she finally released him and greeted him with a light

kiss on the lips, he noticed a change in her eyes. She had put black kohl around them, which brought out their vibrant green. He whispered, "I missed you . . ."

"I was going to visit you at your house if you hadn't contacted me," she responded. "I was so worried about you . . . I couldn't sleep at all."

They hugged. Then they heard the bell ringing, meaning that the movie was about to start. She told him she'd already seen *Amadeus* but that watching that crazy Mozart with a man who was starting to drive her crazy would give the film a new flavor. "Kissing under the dogs' barking and biting yesterday was creative madness. It will go down in student activist history!"

The theater was full of people. They held hands, and she put her head on his shoulder like a real lover.

She slept that night in his arms, and her scent filled him up to overflowing. He kept smelling her. He put his head in her short hair and between her beautiful breasts. He nuzzled her entire body. She was completely submissive, not moving or moaning or reacting in any visible way. He noticed this when, overwhelmed by pleasure, he looked at her to see the effect of his actions on her supple body. She seemed to him, with her eyes closed, as if she was wandering another world, separate from her body. He stopped and caressed her face. She kept her eyes closed. He saw a tear fall from one of her eyes. He lifted himself up, moving his upper body off of her, and asked her to open her eyes. They were filled with tears. He asked her what was the matter, and she pulled his head to her chest, caressing his beard with one hand and his hair with the other, and said, "Nothing . . . Tears of joy. I'm just feeling—so much."

Abdel Nasser believed her. He pressed his body against hers and put his head on her chest. They both wanted a cigarette and went into the living room. The light in Raeef's room was off. They went to sit at the kitchen table; he asked her if she wanted anything to eat, especially since she hadn't had much dinner, just a bit of grilled fish that Raeef had made. He offered her some seafood pasta. She said, mockingly, "The class warrior and student leader, eating shrimp and living like a bourgeois!"

"True," he responded. "But this is all from the fortune of the rich man's son I live with. I have no objections to living in comfort. Did you know that Lenin used to dream of bathrooms made of gold in the classless society?"

"You mean in the promised paradise of Communism?"

"Right now I'm exalting in *your* paradise: your extravagant spirit and bewitching eyes, the bliss of your body . . ."

"A class warrior *and* a romantic poet!" she laughed. "*Mmmmm*, delicious."

She sat on his lap and continued her meal. Then she turned to straddle his knees, putting her arms around his neck. She looked at him, smiling, examining his face as he stared into her eyes, mesmerized. He forgot the lingering pain in his body. He asked her whether she considered what was happening between them an adventure that would soon be over, or something else altogether. He just wanted things to be clear, he said. She answered him with a verse she attributed to Mahmoud Darwish: "Clarity is a crime; the ambiguity of your dead is the honest truth."

She explained that she didn't believe in what people called love, infatuation, passion, and all that. She thought love was the opium of the sleeping animal in the human heart, clipping its claws and taming its instincts. In her opinion, everything had to pass the test of the mind, and she found all the men who wanted her to be hypocrites, looking at her face while their minds worked out how to get at what was between her legs. She confessed that she'd made no exceptions for him; the only difference between him and them was his discipline.

He was a public figure at the university, used to being reserved and keeping his distance from things to avoid showing weakness or making himself vulnerable, lest he find himself in the grip of enemies, or those he might imagine are enemies.

Then she corrected herself, taking a drag from her cigarette and blowing it out in smoke rings that floated through the kitchen. She explained that she admired him for his ideas, in spite of their differences of opinion. She didn't deny that she found his personality attractive and strong, or that his rhetoric when he spoke made even the simplest, most ordinary ideas heart-piercing. But what had happened yesterday at the Faculté des Lettres in Manouba was beyond what she'd imagined, or could imagine. She told him what she'd dreamed about while pressed against his back in the cafeteria, and that the pleasure of that kiss under the truncheons was still running in her veins. Then, that the night she'd spent in his room had shown her how chivalrous and genuinely respectful he was with women—even though she'd wanted to kiss him to thank him for that night.

"That's when I knew," she said. "With you, I felt like I was under the protection of a lion, one that wanted to guard me, not harm me."

She surprised him by telling him that he was different from anyone else she'd ever known because he made her dream again. She hadn't dreamt in years. Not since her childhood. He took her back to the fields, before she had lost her memory of the wheat stalks and poppies. She felt, with him, that maybe what people called love was real, and not just an opiate. But she couldn't be sure of anything.

"I don't know—I'm not sure . . . I don't want to mislead you. Is what I'm feeling for you attraction, because of what happened yesterday, or is it love? I don't know. I don't know . . ."

Abdel Nasser told her, "Whatever it is, I feel . . . complete with you. It's a feeling I don't exactly have a name for, but I'm okay with calling it love. What else do you call it, longing for the other person, being afraid for her safety, spontaneously rushing to protect her, having her scent with you constantly, feeling joy when you see her, hearing her voice even in her absence . . . all of that. What do you want me to call it? Admiration? Attraction? I won't lose anything by calling it love, and I don't want to spoil how happy I am with you. If you *are* opium, you haven't clipped the claws of the animal inside me, you've sent it soaring. What could be wrong with that?

She stood up. She walked around the table. She sat on the chair across from him. She lit another cigarette. She sighed. Her expression was firm; her smile faded away, and she paled. "I'm not against the animal inside us," she began, "but I am afraid of it. It hurt me once and left a deep wound tattooed on my body that will never go away."

She put her arms on the table and hid her head between them. She started quietly sobbing. Abdel Nasser stood up and lifted her head from her hands and started to kiss her. He wiped away the tears and kohl running down her cheeks, not understanding what had put her in this strange state. He asked her why several times, but she just cried harder. He locked the kitchen door. He went to the window and opened it all the way, then took her hands and pulled her toward it for some fresh air. She went to the bathroom, and he heard the faucet running and her blowing her nose.

After a few minutes, Zeina came out of the bathroom and apologized. He held her close and led her back to the bedroom. "Why are you apologizing? You're my Berber princess, who led me into the wilds of passion."

She smiled, shaking her head with a mixture of scorn and sorrow. "You don't know anything about your princess and what she suffered at the hands of the Berbers."

"It doesn't matter to me what happened in the past. I only care about now and what will be. Did they betray you? Cheat you? Deceive you and take your virginity?"

"I wish that was all," she said, beginning to sob again. She pulled herself from his arms and moved away from him. She sat cross-legged on the far corner of the bed, rocking her head and sometimes her body back and forth as if trying to comfort herself. She brought her knees to her chest, wrapped her arms around them, and lay her head down on her knees. She was avoiding his eyes, though she glanced at him from time to time. He watched her, respecting her wishes. He put the pillow behind him, leaned against the headboard, and extended his legs, crossing one over the other. He was ready for the story, whenever she was ready to tell it. He projected calm and quiet.

9

It had all happened that summer. Everyone had heard about the marriage of Sidi Khalifa's older daughter. The wedding would last seven beautiful nights, of course, as was fitting for a spoiled beauty. She had studied French in college but had quit after only two years to marry her first cousin, a young man who was his parents' only child and who would inherit half of the land in the village. His scandals and trips outside the village had increased, and he traded in his cars as fast as he did his mistresses. When he was drunk, the whole village was on alert, not knowing what he might do. But no one dared to put an end to his carelessness; he imagined himself king of the world and all its people and thought he could violate the inviolable when he was drunk. No one young or old could stop him, considering the police were in his pocket, bought with the money and gifts his father showered them with.

One day he took the hunting gun and left to hunt boars in

the forests of Ain Darahim. Instead, he got drunk and shot chickens, dogs, cats, cows, everything that the poor people (and not so poor) owned. The village was in an uproar. The elders met to ask the father to stop his son's evil behavior, which had become unbearable. He was terrorizing them all, and they couldn't take it any more. The father dismissed them, throwing rolls of money at them as compensation for the losses. They refused the money and left lamenting. After about a month, the son went missing. His father sent some peasants to look for him. He'd been gone for more than thirty-six hours when they found him, bound and unconscious, at the edge of the woods near a river. On every inch of his body were marks of beatings with whips, sticks, and stones. His face was misshapen, his eyes barely visible under the swelling and bruises. It was clear they hadn't intended to kill him, but rather to teach him a lesson and make him rediscover whatever senses his father's money had spoiled. The peasants also found his fancy car, its windows broken and tires slashed, ditched in the valley. No one could figure out who had done it.

The police officers arrived. They interrogated the village's young men, torturing them in the process, but no one confessed. The police were soon convinced they were innocent. They expanded the scope of the investigation but couldn't find anyone to charge. The only possible conclusion was that it must have been revenge by people from another village; maybe he stained the honor of one of their daughters. Or maybe the people who attacked him—around six masked men, he remembered—were hired by someone to teach him a lesson. The young man couldn't remember exactly what had happened. He'd been driving back home, drunk, and had stopped to urinate at the edge of the woods. That's when the beating and kicking festival had started, continuing until he lost consciousness. Then they'd dunked his head in the brackish water until he nearly drowned. He came to briefly but wasn't able to move. He couldn't identify his attackers. The case was closed, and not even the money the rich father paid to spies, police officers, and the men of the village could uncover their identity. The truth was that everyone, including the police officers, were relieved to finally be free of the son's drunken revelry and mischief. The punishment had left him with a limp and a crooked jaw. He had also lost some teeth, which were soon replaced.

The father decided that the young man should get married. So Zeina's mother spent about ten days in the bride's house, helping with the preparations for the big day. Zeina's house became almost empty during the day, except during the afternoon *qailulah* and at night. Zeina was the only one in charge of everything in the house; she was so busy she didn't even have time to read. Her mother asked her to fill in for her and do a good job so that when her father and brother came back from the fields they would find the food ready.

10

The two men of the house would wake up at dawn, then come back home when the heat of the day got so intense that they had to rest before going back to work. The harvest season was at its peak. The new situation at the house had exhausted the young woman. It was almost a stretch to call it a house. The bed was a raised platform almost one and a half meters high. Underneath it were straw mats with clothes piled on them. The radio occupied one of the corners of the room, and in the opposite corner was a big old suitcase filled with various supplies and utensils. A small table sat in the middle of what was left. The room was no more than two meters in width and three meters in length. And that was the entire house. Next to this sleeping, dining, and sitting room, there was a lean-to with no door that was used for cooking, with a few dishes and a stove. Next to the lean-to was a clay oven for bread. Finally, there was an outhouse.

During the harvest season, the smell of wheat stalks and dry dirt filled the room. The scent, though reminiscent of strong decay, excited Zeina. She would breathe it in deeply, for reasons she herself did not understand. In all her life, she hadn't loved any smells except for this one—and olive oil. Her mother used to rub her body and hair with the oil and would tell her, "It makes your skin clear and soft, a gift from God to nourish the body—as food and drink, and even as moisturizer."

She was not shy of applying it even between Zeina's legs—front and back—saying, "When you grow up, you'll understand why I'm doing this, and you'll thank me for it."

Zeina didn't know why, but she continued the tradition on her own before going to sleep and didn't give up the habit until she went to boarding school.

One day she just completely ran out of energy. She had cooked, washed the clothes by hand, tidied up the house, ground some wheat and made bread with the flour, then gone to help her mother at Sidi Khalifa's house in the evening. She was so exhausted that she slept deeply until she woke up, terrified, just before dawn.

Her father and brother had fallen asleep up on the platform, snoring from physical fatigue and the effects of smoking. She was sleeping on the straw mat on the floor, facing the platform. She was awakened that night, at dawn or a little before, by a knife made of flesh stabbing her from behind, sometimes in her anus and other times in her vagina. The knife was slippery from the olive oil that she rubbed herself with, or from some other liquid that flowed directly from it. Or maybe it was the blood that came out of her and that she found on her clothes and on the mat when she got up. She couldn't believe what was happening; she wanted to look behind her, to scream, to move her body away—but the knife was hard and sharp, moving inside her like a saw. A hand on her mouth was suffocating her and keeping her from screaming, and the other was pushing her head against the wall of the platform, immobilizing her.

She knew that something shameful was happening. A scandal . . . Should she scream? But who was behind her, who was the person with the knife? Her father? Her brother? Someone else. But the smell was familiar, the smell of wheat stalks and dirt. The pain tore her in two. She went mute, felt hot tears on her cheeks, and lost consciousness from the shock.

When she came to, she was in a state of disbelief. Was it a nightmare or a waking dream? But the hand had pressed her head down so hard. And this blood. The sticky fluid she found. She didn't see anyone in the room. She surreptitiously looked up on the platform like a cat looking at a mouse. There was no one there. She cracked the door, then opened it all the way, slowly. The place was quiet, with no trace of movement save for the dog wagging his tail, surrendering to the dawn breeze.

She poked her head out of the door like a cautious thief, looked in every direction, then went to the kitchen. She took a bucket of water with her to the outhouse. She started rubbing her lower body, torn between crying and biting her lip so that she wouldn't make a sound. She went out to fill the bucket again and grabbed the sponge. She returned to the outhouse and scrubbed her thighs and privates as if trying to peel off her skin, scrape it off, rip it off. A feeling of filth made her fill and refill the bucket; even the dense green foam of the olive oil soap wasn't enough to rid her of the filth. The white skin of her body turned red. She scrubbed until she'd nearly split her rectum and left her vagina in tatters. It hurt, but it was nothing compared to the pain of being pierced by the knife.

She wished she could make a fire in the clay oven and sit on its opening, letting the fire cleanse her and help get rid of the filth. That it would burn away the slimy substance she could still feel dripping between her thighs, melting her skin, leaving nothing but the charred flesh. A fire beneath her and inside her, until she could feel the burning.

She vomited several times. Her stomach was empty, and a slimy liquid came out of her mouth, much like the one that flowed between her legs and clung to the fine pubic hair. Her eyes bulged, and the sense of suffocation and difficulty of voiding her stomach made the veins in her neck stand out. She dumped a bucket of water on her head and shivered. Her dress was wet, but she felt intense relief, as if the water had put out the fire spreading in her body.

She was dazed, didn't know what to do. She went to the kitchen and grabbed a knife, the big knife. She held it against her wrist. She thought about cutting her stomach open. Or her vagina, why not? She placed it against her neck and pictured the Eid lamb being slaughtered, vein to vein.

What if it was a nightmare? But there was blood on her legs, and that yellowish liquid. Who said it was her brother? Who said it was her father? They couldn't have done that. It must have been a stranger. But who? And that smell she knew so well. But that's not proof. The stranger could also have been a peasant carrying the field's scent. She hadn't been able to see him . . . she hadn't seen anyone. She had passed out. What would she say to her mother? Who would believe her? Maybe she had undressed while she was sleeping. Was it the first time she'd undressed without realizing it? Had her mother's presence been protecting her? But from who? From her father? From her brother?

Her ruminations were only interrupted when Khala Halima started calling, as usual, for the members of her sister's family from afar. She squatted in front of the room chatting, talking about the village news, about her son Salem, Zeina's cousin, who was working in Libya and wanted to marry Zeina. What would a fourteen-year-old girl do with school? Marriage is a young woman's destiny. Salem would come back soon and officially ask for her hand as soon as he finished building the house and saved up some money. She had told him to start choosing some golden jewelry for his bride Zeina, the village beauty.

She had heard this story many times, but was obliged to listen to the broken record. Khala Halima put her hand into her shirt and gave her a piece of chewing gum from Libya, *It's the tastiest chewing gum in the world! It freshens your mouth and fights bad smells, especially in the morning and after meals.*

Zeina started to hate herself. In spite of it all, she prepared the midday meal for her father and her brother. She couldn't look them in the eyes. She snuck glances at them, and they seemed normal. As if nothing had happened. She couldn't see any signs of turmoil in either of them; they just stared at her rudely, as usual. Her father told her to hurry and bring the water pitcher. Her brother asked her whether she'd fried some green peppers for the couscous, too, or if there were only the ones cooked in the sauce. Neither asked about her dark mood or her absent-mindedness. They asked her to hurry up and get the tea, while they belched like two bulls. She had peed in the couscous while she mixed it with the sauce, had spit in it with all her force. This was the beginning of her revenge on them. She could smell the pee when they burped.

She wanted to scream in their faces and release her hatred for them. She thought of taking the knife to stab them or killing one of them at least. She imagined using the big metal knife to cut off the knives of flesh hidden in their trousers. She saw the blood splatter and heard their screams while she laughed.

That day, Zeina became another person. Strange ideas occurred to her, and she started writing them down in a notebook.

In the notebooks, she found a refuge and a companion to talk to, spilling into it her silence and the feelings roiling in her chest. She got revenge on them every day, killing them in a page or two. She could only give voice to her resentment and describe her crimes in French, not in Arabic. No one would find what she was writing, but if they did, they wouldn't understand it. She learned pun and metaphor; she started calling the flesh knife "the opening of closures" and the vagina "the place of secrets"; the back opening was "the back of the paper." She named sadness "the preserved tablet" (like the one that fate is written on) and death "the antidote of grief." Things like that. So even if someone who knew French were to read it or if she put her words into action, no one would understand what she had planned.

11

She put her hand on el-Talyani's extended leg beside her. She pushed forcefully on his shin and cried, "Do you know what it means for a girl to be torn apart? Do you know how the oppression nests inside you, how you have to keep quiet out of fear and shame?"

"Yes . . . I do know," he answered. "On my honor, I do."

"You know nothing. You have a flesh knife, too, like all the others. You only draw them to slaughter dreams and slice hearts to shreds."

El-Talyani tried to get closer to her, to hug her. She withdrew again to herself and put her head between her knees. She wasn't crying, just staring blankly at the sheet. He didn't know what to do. He waited to see what she wanted and watched her, visibly emotional. He needed to stay with her; he wouldn't sleep until she did. She stayed in that position for almost an hour, then suddenly turned her face to him without looking at him. He moved to sit beside her. She looked like a small bird searching for the warmth of wings. She put her head on his shoulder, facing the door. She stayed that way until she said, almost whispering, "When I hold you, I feel strangely reassured. My mind clears, and it's like my body is pulsing. I forget the pain that hatched eight years ago and nested inside me."

"You have to put it behind you. That nightmare is over now."

"It's not some feeling or illusion I can get over. It's a shooting pain in the secret place, a sharp quill that tore up the back of the paper. My secret and paper were both violated . . . it was sickening . . . And that disgust is in the flesh—not the mind."

"Have you tried talking to a psychiatrist?"

"The pain's in my body, and it's incurable. I broke the silence with you; you're the only person I've ever opened up to about it. You must think I'm disgusting . . ."

"Don't say that!" he protested. "I'm with you. You're the victim, not the victimizer. The victimizers are the disgusting ones."

"You're just saying that out of sympathy, for the sake of the sexual proletariat."

"Where is this coming from? No disgust, no pity. I love you, and love is good and generous. We both have to rewrite the history of our bodies. We'll do it together, by the force of will, with our spiritual power. You're strong, Zeina. You've resisted, and I can see the horizon stretching into the distance. It's calling us."

"I don't know if I can even walk," she said. "I've been standing still for years, fighting my pain by trying to forget and repress, with books and school. I can't even look at my face in the mirror. I'm ashamed of my face, I hate my body."

He wanted to change the subject, to get her out of everything associated with that story and show her what she meant to him. He told her that he knew she'd had a fight with her roommates and gone to live at a relative's house. He suggested that she spend the two remaining months until graduation at his house. He would ensure that she was comfortable and would provide her with the best conditions to prepare for the exam. He asked if she had any objections. She said she didn't want to annoy him.

His response showed some anger, along with blame, at what she'd said. "How could you say that? I love you. And from a selfish point of view, you'll bring some joy to this boring house. You'll be a flower in the garden."

She smiled. "A flower that's lost some petals and smells like pain and repression and—"

"Why so dark? It's all over. You need a fresh beginning. With me. Together."

"You don't know what I look like when it gets bad. When I get sunk in my preserved tablet searching for the antidote to grief."

He stood up, taking the stance of an orator. "No more grief. The activist movement of love we're leading will resist the antidote of grief until victory is ours."

He raised his hand in the victory sign. Zeina smiled. She seemed somehow satisfied, and her silence showed that she accepted the idea. She kissed his forehead, then pulled his head to her chest and said, "I'll order up tonight's dream. And you'll be my dream sleeping next to me in the flesh."

SLOPES

1

That summer was tense. An oppressive heat the likes of which the country hadn't seen in years. There were protests almost every day, with arrests here and there. Conflict intensified between the wings of the presidential palace at Carthage. All the talk was about the succession of the Supreme Warrior, who had nothing left but the prestige of an old lion in his cage.

Zeina was preparing her portfolio for teaching high school. She did not go back to her village but rather stayed in the capital, between Charles de Gaulle Library, the National Library, and home. She began organizing her reading to better plan her research. She was racing against the clock because she knew that the first year of teaching would be exhausting. She would need to finish the syllabus (that she hadn't started), prepare her lessons and outlines, participate in professional development workshops and pedagogical training, and attend sample lessons. She realized she wouldn't have time for her research once school began but would have to rely on school breaks.

The first problem emerged after twenty days, when the interior ministry refused to grant her Form No. 3, the clearance document that would allow her to teach. She discovered that many student political activists, unionists, and participants in public meeting and discussion circles were having the same problem. There was no way to apply for and join the teaching profession without this ominous document. And no one in the police station or interior ministry would tell her why they were refusing to give it to her.

Abdel Nasser set out to help her. But how did you break into that frightening grey building, the castle of security secrets towering over Avenue Habib Bourguiba? He wouldn't get the certificate if he applied for it, either. He talked to a classmate from the École Normale Supérieure who'd graduated that year and had been bragging that he was able to get his clearance in three days, thanks to his brother-in-law. Abdel Nasser gave him the receipt number and date, and he assured him that he would take care of it. Abdel Nasser knew the weak point of the brother-in-law: his wife. They met, as agreed, after three days, and the man told Abdel Nasser he wasn't able to solve the problem. He was stuttering and seemed hesitant, as if he were hiding something. Abdel Nasser urged him to be frank with him and tell him if there was anything dangerous in the matter.

The classmate hesitated, then said, "To be honest, her file is full of reports. Form No. 2, which has all the intelligence information, is completely black. So it's hard to get her clearance— they've started blocking everything out of mere suspicion. Someone powerful, with authority, will have to intervene."

Zeina had already contacted her advising professor. He spoke honestly with her and told her that he couldn't do anything, but he arranged a meeting with the dean of the Faculté 9 Avril for her. The dean promised to do his best, especially since she was an excellent student and an honor to the university. He said he still didn't understand why she hadn't been awarded the President of the Republic prize on the Day of Knowledge. Her grade point average during the four years was above 15/20, an almost unheard-of exception in the Philosophy Department. He was frank with her. He took off his glasses and said, "I know that you're a union activist and a skilled orator, and this is an honor for you as well as us; the university is a space for critical thinking and seeks to graduate political cadres as well as scholars. They've started mixing everything up . . . Don't worry, my daughter; I'll speak to the minister."

The minister was not helpful. He was a minister in a police state threatened in daily protests with religious slogans. There were shouts of *"Allahu akbar,"* "God will blow away idols!," "Surrender to God, not government!," and a revision of the *shahada*, the oath that "there is no god but God and Muhammad is His prophet": "There is no god but God, and Bourguiba is his enemy!"

During one of their discussions of the matter, after she saw that all the attempts so far had failed and that other avenues would not be any more successful, Zeina told el-Talyani, "Never mind. I'll finish my research quickly, and in the meantime I'll support myself by writing articles for a francophone newspaper. I know the culture editor; he asked me during an event at Charles de Gaulle Library. Granted, he was one of those that I felt looked at my face while aiming for what's between my legs, but no matter. I know how to deal with that situation."

El-Talyani didn't comment. But two days later, he brought her Form No. 3; the problem had been solved. She asked him excitedly how he'd done it; her happiness confirmed for him that she was born to teach, and would succeed in it just as she had in her studies.

He told her about Si Othman, the old neighbor who now worked as a police officer. He was honest with her, though he hid from her what had happened the day they were arrested at the Faculté des Lettres de la Manouba. Si Othman was very kind when Abdel Nasser asked him for help solving the problem with Zeina's clearance. He didn't make the request look like a favor. He didn't talk to him about Form No. 2, despite the fact that Abdel Nasser had told him about it. He was reserved and explained that the state had its logic, which it didn't have to make clear to the people. He assured Abdel Nasser that he had helped Zeina because he knew how intelligent she was. The police couldn't destroy the future of the smart students; they were the future of the country. Abdel Nasser found Si Othman's words to be somewhat exaggerated, but he didn't argue with him. After all, he was the one asking for a favor. Si Othman told him, as he was leaving the office, "Tell Zeina not to worry about anything. What's in her file is just nonsense."

Then he added, in a fatherly tone that Abdel Nasser liked, "Consider Zeina carefully. Women like her are rare."

2

As soon as el-Talyani and Zeina were able to put the matter of the clearance behind them, a bigger issue emerged. The news came in early September like a thunderbolt: the education ministry had appointed Zeina to teach at a high school in Kebili, a desert governorate in the far south of Tunisia. El-Talyani went crazy; Zeina was leaving to go far away, and he would only be able to see her during school breaks. And what would she do during those breaks? Would she focus on her research, or would they quench their thirst for one another? And what would be left of the breaks, after the two days on the road to Tunis, two days back down to Kebili, and a short visit to her family in their remote village?

Zeina was torn between the job, which would secure her financial peace of mind, and her research, which necessitated being near the capital and its libraries. She made her decision: she would stay in Tunis and do what she'd agreed on with the cultural editor of the French newspaper. Her ambitions would not be limited to teaching high school; she was looking up to the college level. Even if she accepted the appointment in

Kebili and finished the master's thesis, she wouldn't be able to prepare for the *agrégation* exam or to attend the master's degree courses. She would have to forget her higher education forever. She would be consumed by teaching high school and forced to consider herself a failure.

By a favorable coincidence, Salah Eddine was in Tunis at the time, with a delegation of experts. They were preparing a report about connecting education with employment and the necessity of introducing reforms imposed by the IMF as part of their funding for education in Tunisia. There had been intensive meetings between the foreign delegation and the government delegation.

Abdel Nasser managed to meet his brother at the hotel where he was staying. He explained the situation and asked for his help. Salah Eddine ignored the issue of Zeina's appointment and instead started asking questions about her and Abdel Nasser. Was it merely an adventure, or a long-term relationship? He talked briefly about Abdel Nasser's status at the university. He made it clear to him that he would keep helping him, but Abdel Nasser needed to implement a structural reform policy for his own life if he intended to marry Zeina. Salah Eddine started describing her: she was a philosopher like his little brother, skillful in the art of debate and discussion. She was perfect for him and would take him to the very horizons of thought and firmaments of abstract concepts—all of which he liked, based on what Salah Eddine knew about him. He advised him, with the advice of a big brother, that while the most important thing in marriage was harmony in bed, the second most important was harmony in thought. He gave him a lesson in marriage, its limitations, its desires, and its pitfalls. He told him, summarizing his life experience, especially with women, "Live your life to the fullest, but don't forget that paradise—the great 'paradise of love'—is just a lie that makes the failure after it unbearably bitter."

Abdel Nasser was frank with him, trying to bring him back to the topic of securing Zeina's appointment at a high school in Tunis, or nearby at least. Salah Eddine only had two days left in Tunisia.

They met the next day, and Salah Eddine was angry at the country and its officials. He told him that the new minister, who was also the president's doctor, made the appointments personally. The education ministry was in a state of horror and dysfunction because of the arrogance of this minister, the dictator's doctor. He told him that the minister had burned all his bridges with the officials in secondary and higher education, with deans, principals, and inspectors. Nothing could please him.

On the day of Salah Eddine's departure, Abdel Nasser was with him at the airport to say goodbye. Salah Eddine gave him the business card of an executive director at the education ministry, along with a sealed envelope addressed to him. Attached to the envelope was Salah Eddine's business card, with his signature and a sentence in French: "With my sincere gratitude."

The sealed envelope and the business card were Zeina's lifeline, rescuing her from the sea of sand and a date palm gallows. Salvation had a price, though: their signatures on a marriage certificate.

The executive director—known for his sizable influence and his willingness to use that influence, for a price—recalled to Abdel Nasser everything Salah Eddine had said about the new minister and his arrogance. Abdel Nasser almost lost his chance; he was almost angered into insulting the director, beating him if need be, for not helping with such small matters except for a bribe. But he was sure the man was truthful, and this opened up a small window of opportunity to convince the minister. The director promised to do his best to keep Zeina with him in greater Tunis. He told Abdel Nasser about the policy of trying to appoint married people in the same area, for humanitarian reasons. He told him that this was his last chance; if it didn't succeed then there was no hope but to wait for the appointment of another, more open-minded, minister. Hence the marriage certificate.

3

Zeina was hesitant. It was not a simple matter, nor was it a mere piece of paper with her signature. What was growing between them was a plant that needed care—watering, pruning, and trimming—and she didn't think the soil was ready. This comment made Abdel Nasser angry, and he accused her of exaggerating or not wanting to be with him. He immediately jumped to the conclusion that she was comparing his situation as a student to hers as a new teacher. She assured him that that thought had never occurred to her; she was born poor and only went to school thanks to the support of philanthropists and public need-based scholarships, and she thought nothing of money or class differences. And if she *had* stooped so far as to play that dirty game, *she* was the poor peasant from the countryside, and *he* was the sophisticated urbanite with the Moorish and Turkish pedigree. She told him that she would never forget his support over the past few months. They had shared everything, both the sweet and the bitter—but mostly sweet. She felt like a princess in the palace of a knight in shining armor who made sure she was fed even before himself. She got very angry and broke down crying.

That was their first fight. She resolved it with tears, and he resolved it with an apology for what he said and an explanation that she'd taken his words the wrong way. The war of meanings and intentions ended quickly, though it left a small internal wound that did not completely heal. As a sign of her good intentions (and to make up for her misinterpretation of his words, or perhaps simply to avoid the headache), Zeina accepted Abdel Nasser's offer to marry him. She stipulated, though, that they keep it a secret until their life plans became clearer; then they could tell everyone. She also insisted that finishing her master's thesis and passing the *agrégation* exam were non-negotiable; he would need to share all the responsibilities and inconveniences involved in that and support her as she followed her dream of becoming a college professor. Abdel Nasser accepted these conditions with love. He had not forgotten what Si Othman had told him when he was leaving his office; he listened to his heart without hesitation.

In my opinion, she strengthened his attachment to her when she told him about being raped. It stirred his sympathy for the victims of society; he considered himself a champion of the wronged and the oppressed, so how could he not help this extraordinary woman? He would draw her out of her deep well of sadness and resurrect the part of her heart that had stopped in that moment of pure pain when the knife tore apart both flesh and soul.

El-Talyani insisted that his younger sister, Yosser (who had just turned twenty the month before), be the witness to the marriage and the one member of the family to know. Though of course he didn't forget to inform the financial circles in Switzerland (as he referred to his brother), so that he would understand the new situation and raise the monthly stipend he sent—a loan whose final installment date was unclear and that Abdel Nasser had no idea how to pay back.

I was Zeina's witness, at their request. They didn't trust anyone else, and I was both el-Talyani's childhood friend and a close college friend of Zeina's. To be honest, I found what they did to be courageous in a way I was incapable of. Despite studying philosophy and being what Zeina considered intelligent, I could never have shaken off my upbringing. My father, a schoolteacher, and my mother, with her excessive attention to me, were sacred. In defiance of Freud, I don't recall ever thinking of killing my father, metaphorically or literally—despite his harshness—and I never recall desiring my mother—despite her great care for me and her beauty, of which I inherited none. I'll admit that I used to have a crush on Zeina, but knowing my parents' scorn for peasants and their excessive pride in their urban roots, I never for a minute considered getting involved with her. My parents' opinion, which I fully understood, was that I should marry a woman from the city like me, not a country bumpkin from the middle of nowhere.

I attended the ceremony, signed as a witness, and wished them happiness. It was a duty that I performed for two friends, and once it was over, it was like it never happened. Deep inside, I felt like there was something wrong. But I didn't want to spend too long thinking about the problem; I was getting ready to move to one of the villages in Kairouan to teach. I had accepted the appointment happily; no one at home discussed whether I should stay in Tunis or go to the countryside. My mother was simply happy with her son—the high school teacher, the philosophy teacher—and gave me two pieces of advice. The first was to stop on the way and visit the mausoleum of Abu Zamaa Al Balawi, one of the companions of the prophet, and the second was to buy some *makroud*, the date and semolina pastry that Kairouan is famous for.

I committed to doing both for the three years I spent back and forth on the road to the Aghlabid city. I decided that philosophy and critical thinking did not conflict with visiting saints and enjoying the sweets that were spreading diabetes across the country. As a fan of anthropology and the philosophy of difference, I started applying such concepts to my mother's old-fashioned superstitions.

El-Talyani's plan, as suggested by the executive director, succeeded miraculously. Perhaps the minister was in a good mood, or maybe he was tired after a long day appointing teachers and considering transfers for special cases. The executive director assured Abdel Nasser that the minister had rejected ninety percent of the applications that crossed his desk. When the executive director asked for "a piece of the celebration cake," Abdel Nasser understood that he wanted a bribe. But instead he just kept thanking him for his help and reminding him that Salah Eddine sent him his best from Switzerland and promised to pay him a visit soon.

The interesting thing about all this is that signing the marriage license took Zeina by surprise; it wasn't something she'd planned for. But she soon became busy with her research and preparing her courses and had little time for el-Talyani. She would wake up early to teach in the suburb of Mohammadia, then come back home exhausted to refresh herself a bit before starting work on her research.

4

One day, Zeina came home around 4:00 P.M. to find a piece of cake and a bottle of soda on the living room table. She called el-Talyani, but he didn't answer. When she went into the bedroom, her husband came out of the kitchen holding two glasses. He seemed upset and asked her to come to the living room. She asked him what was going on and what he was upset about. He didn't answer her. He asked her to sit down. She sat, confused.

"Sorry . . ." he started. "I don't know . . . I'm sorry."

"What is it? Spit it out!"

"I don't know where to start. It's dangerous—the movement is under threat."

"How?" she asked. "What do you mean, 'under threat'?"

"Threat of extinction after their national leader is gone."

"Which one? Leader of what?"

"The comrade activist leader at the university."

"What are you talking about?" she demanded. "Answer me—what's the matter?"

El-Talyani stood up and looked at her, his eyes flashing angrily. "I took the elective certificate exam," he said. "And I . . . I . . . I passed."

She jumped off the couch as if she'd been stung, punching and kicking him playfully: "You scared the hell out of me!"

Then, "Congratulations! Congratulations, graduate!"

She gave him a hug and a kiss and started dancing something that looked like Lebanese *dabke*. Then she asked him, "Have you told your family?"

"You're the first person I've told. I'll call them and tell them."

"No, you should go and tell them in person. And don't forget your brother Salah Eddine, and Raeef, too."

El-Talyani was surprised by her eagerness to conform to social conventions; it didn't seem like her. They agreed to go out to celebrate that night after he got back from his family's house.

5

At the restaurant, they discussed el-Talyani's future plans. He told her briefly that he'd changed his mind; he didn't want to be a lawyer or a judge anymore. Instead he would wait for the entrance exams for the foreign affairs ministry, or any other ministry.

Mostly, though, he spoke about the movement and who might lead it at the university. He had rushed to take the final exams in the September retakes session without telling anyone, even Zeina. He assured her that he had been sure of passing—

his problem was that the new academic year was starting and would be heated, but there was no one to take up the mission. None of his comrades—including Jaafar, Redha, Najm Eddine, or Nabeel—was up to the challenge. The word "treason" slipped from his tongue as he described to her what he'd done. She tried to calm him down, reminding him that he would need to wait to hear about the entrance exams (both the written and oral parts), as well as the announcement of the final results and job appointments. He would have plenty of time to prepare his successor.

She thought his fear was excessive. She told him about Alain Touraine, a scholar of the events of May 1986, and his criticism of the class understanding of the revolutionary movement. "You're not a traitor unless you somehow imagine yourself as Jesus the savior."

She continued, "You talk about history, but you don't want to learn from it. Did the students participate in the French Revolution? The Bolshevik revolution? The Chinese revolution? Forget about their role in the Iranian revolution, which doesn't even recognize them. You've all built an illusion and imprisoned yourself in it. Revolution will happen because the people need it, not because the theory has been implanted in their minds. Didn't Marx teach you this historical–materialist lesson?"

She explained to him that student movements were a force of protest but couldn't be a revolutionary force. Universities were affected by what was happening around them, but the impact they made was with their frameworks and renewal of human capital. She pointed out that the rise of the Islamists as a powerful force at the university happened at the same time as their rise in society. Clearly, the students' positions were determined by their original class affiliations.

6

After the excitement of his success had died down and his revolutionary consciousness had diminished enough that the "treason" accusation lost its sting, el-Talyani's life began to change. It was a new life in a golden cage—a cage he had chosen without serious considerations of the consequences—and he'd dragged Zeina into it after him.

The first major change was the flight of Raeef from the cage. The academic year had begun, and, although seniors did not attend the first week, Raeef came back early, on the first day of the academic year. He spoke with Abdel Nasser in front of Zeina. He gave him a beautiful gift as a graduation present, an expensive bottle of cologne and a luxury watch. He also brought a golden necklace and a finely crafted gold watch as a present for the bride. He told them that it was a gift from his mother, as a token of her gratitude to Abdel Nasser for taking care of her son for the past three years, as well as a symbol of affection for the woman he loved. Zeina and Abdel Nasser both thought the gifts were too much and couldn't find the right words to express their gratitude.

Raeef brought, as usual, fish and other seafood and prepared them himself. He also brought bottles of whiskey and gin, and enough wine and beer for a full wedding reception. The truck driver brought in the fish, the produce, and the drinks.

At dinner, Raeef told them that the dinner he'd made was a special gift for them, to thank them for their friendship, and that he hoped their friendship would continue. He read a long laudatory poem about Abdel Nasser, his words about Zeina in the poem flirtatious to the point that Abdel Nasser jokingly warned him about them. While they were all still sitting at the table, he told them that he had found a new house near the École Nationale d'Administration—a small independent house inside a large villa—that would be a comfortable place to spend the academic year. He promised he would visit; he wouldn't forget Abdel Nasser's favors and support.

Raeef mentioned in passing that the new house was small and unfurnished, and Abdel Nasser got the hint. "I will rent a small truck tomorrow," Abdel Nasser told him, "to move the living room furniture, the refrigerator, and the rest of the furniture to your new house."

Zeina interrupted, jokingly, "Why rent a house? You should stay with us; you're our son, and we'll spoil you."

Raeef laughed, but Abdel Nasser seemed nervous. In a more serious tone, Zeina asked her husband why Raeef couldn't just stay with them during the academic year.

"I don't see a reason why not," he answered, "but it seems he might not be comfortable here."

Raeef tried to lighten the mood, saying jokingly, "Should I stay and hold the candle for the newlyweds?"

He told them that his girlfriend, being shy and reserved, wouldn't be comfortable with the idea. But he assured them that the change would not affect his friendship and affection for them.

Zeina understood then, as el-Talyani already had, that Raeef had made up his mind. Zeina didn't yet grasp the size of the approaching catastrophe; Abdel Nasser could see it coming, but couldn't stop it. The house was stripped bare, save the furniture in Abdel Nasser's bedroom, in addition to some glasses, cups, spoons, a frying pan, and a small pot that Raeef left. He left the house looking like a woman who had been unexpectedly undressed by force.

7

This was the young newlyweds' first financial problem. Abdel Nasser seemed annoyed by the situation; Zeina tried to calm him down, especially since they were still practically students. She would collect her back salary in a few months and would be able to take care of it. She didn't realize what was going on in Abdel Nasser's head: since Zeina's university stipend had ended four months ago, he was waiting on the next loan installment from the bank of Salah Eddine and had to somehow take care of Zeina's expenses in the meantime. He thought about telling her the truth but then thought better of it. The Arab man inside him, who felt he had to protect and support his women, woke up. What puzzled him was that Zeina didn't make any comment about the expenses. He blamed himself for letting her get used to being in charge of the money coming in and giving him just enough for his daily expenses. She hadn't asked for that, and he didn't consciously choose to do it that way; it was just what his father did with his mother at the beginning of each month.

The quality of their food began to deteriorate. It became a daily burden for Abdel Nasser, who had volunteered to prepare all the food to leave Zeina time for her research. He found out then the value of having a refrigerator. He also realized how high the electricity bill was, since the stove that Raeef had left them was electric. He discovered the high prices that he used to lecture about at the university but had not yet experienced firsthand.

Zeina's position was no better. Her expenses had increased because of transportation and needing to eat out between the morning and evening sessions and sometimes during the professional development workshops. They had also increased with her increased smoking: she was up to two packs of Cristal Lights a day.

Abdel Nasser asked her one day for more money; he was going somewhere that was not on the bus line and needed to take a taxi. They were sitting at the kitchen table, and she told him, "We only have 15 dinars left for the rest of the month."

"What? It's only the twelfth! Will that be enough to cover the rest of this month's expenses?"

Zeina didn't say anything. She lit a cigarette, visibly tense. She started biting her nails. Then she went to the bedroom and brought back her purse, opening it nervously. She handed him three 5-dinar notes. "There you go."

He didn't take them. He gave her a look, both annoyed and quizzical. He answered, "What do you mean?"

"You asked for your money, and I'm giving it to you."

"Why are you talking about my money and your money?"

"I don't have any money—this is your money. Why are you angry? I was just stating a fact. Isn't it your money?"

"That has nothing to do with anything."

"Why are you asking how we're going to manage the rest of the month, then? Aren't you accusing me of wasting money?"

"I didn't say anything like that! Have you gone crazy?"

"Yes, I'm crazy. They should put me in the Razi asylum."

"Calm down . . . Why are you being so dramatic? What does the Razi asylum and mental illness have to do with this?"

"I'll figure out my own business until I get my salary."

"I'm responsible for you!"

"Responsible for me? Protector and supporter!" she laughed. "You should know that I'm free; that paper I signed doesn't mean a thing to me."

"What?"

"Yes, I mean exactly what I'm saying. My dear Marxist–Leninist freedom fighter, don't think you're going to enslave me with this marriage license. It's not worth the paper it's printed on."

"If that's how you want it."

"That's how I want it. You're the one who pushed me to sign the thing in the first place."

El-Talyani looked at her, trying to calm down. He took the

pack of cigarettes and the lighter that were on the table and headed toward the front door. She heard it slam.

In the morning, while gathering her textbook and pens, she found a wad of cash in her purse: five 10-dinar bills. She thought about leaving them on the table, but decided not to escalate the situation any further. Abdel Nasser had not come home the night before until dawn, smelling strongly of wine.

Two days of oppressive silence hung over the house, but it didn't affect the daily routine, with the exception that Abdel Nasser started coming home late (from Café El Hajj, as she later learned). He would greet her, then go to bed. When he came home one night around 11:30 P.M., Zeina decided to break the ice. As he was changing his clothes in the bedroom, Zeina burst in on him in his underwear. "How long are you going to be mad at me?"

He didn't respond.

"Are you trying to punish me with your silence? Or taking it out on me? We were both angry."

"And we're both free to do what we want."

"You're my husband and the crown on my head."

"I forced you to put that crown on your head, and it's pretty clear now that you don't want it."

"Come on, stop being so stubborn. Are you going to base everything on something I said in anger? Fine then, my apologies to the resentful camel."

"Now I'm a resentful camel!"

"I've never seen you act this foolish before. And anyway, haven't you heard that poem, *I love her and she loves me and my camel loves her she-camel?*

She moved toward him flirtatiously and put her arms around him. She put her head on his chest and whispered, "This she-camel misses her mate."

The fire she lit melted the ice. She talked to him about a friend of his who taught with her and sent his greetings and congratulations to Abdel Nasser on his graduation. He had heard about his graduation and marriage from Najm Eddine, who had grown up in the same coastal village as him and remembered him. He told her about his political affiliation. She told Abel Nasser that he'd promised her to work with the union members at the high school to collect some money from their colleagues as a loan. Everyone faces these difficulties while waiting for their first paycheck to arrive. He had asked her not to tell Abdel Nasser, since he knew how his pride would take it, and insisted on keeping it a secret between them, whether she used the money or not. She expressed her appreciation to him, for the spirit of solidarity and class awareness that the unions displayed.

8

One day el-Talyani came to her with good news: his brother Salah Eddine had offered to buy them two plane tickets to Switzerland so they could come and spend Christmas with his wife Carla and her Italian family. He was looking forward to seeing his brother and sister-in-law, and to spending the holiday with two members of his own family in addition to Carla's. But Zeina was concerned about her research; she had planned to start writing during the winter break. She was afraid that any delay would derail the plan she'd made to finish her research in May and free up time for reviewing and editing after that.

Abdel Nasser explained that there was no contradiction between her plans and accepting his brother's invitation, especially since Salah Eddine helped financially to support her plans. In addition, this gift—from an economist who didn't calculate profit and loss when it came to his younger brother— couldn't possibly be refused.

She agreed reluctantly, saying, "I'll go with you, but my gut is telling me it's a mistake."

"Why such pessimism? When we get back, you'll see that your gut was wrong."

Zeina's gut wasn't wrong, and it didn't change its tune after their return from Switzerland.

Salah Eddine was waiting for them at the Geneva Airport. He looked at Zeina like a happy father meeting his daughter-in-law. He slipped some money into Abdel Nasser's pocket when Zeina wasn't looking, even though he'd already sent them about two thousand Tunisian dinars. They had bought some gifts with them, traditional Tunisian handicrafts from the town of Den Den that Zeina had chosen with care. They also brought small boxes of *deglet nour* dates and had used some of the foreign currency to buy a selection of the finest Tunisian wines—white, rosé, and red—from the duty-free shop in the Tunis–Carthage Airport. Hajja Zeinab was always reminding el-Talyani not to enter a house empty-handed, but he didn't need her to teach him to bring wine: no Christmas party would be complete without a bit of Jesus's blood (whatever the color).

Salah Eddine's house in Switzerland was a palace by Tunisian standards. It was an apartment, really, but in a neighborhood full of luxury apartment buildings. His Italian wife Carla was not actually from Italy, as Abdel Nasser had assumed for many years, but rather was from an Italian-speaking region of Switzerland. He was completely ignorant of Swiss history, though Carla's sister Angelika was trying to educate him. Angelika was a translator at one of the international NGOs and was a sparkling young woman of around el-Talyani's age. She had all the sweetness of the Italians but spoke French fluently, unlike her sister. She had a beautiful smile, with generous lips, a wide mouth, and straight white teeth like pearls on a necklace. When she laughed, she laughed out loud, and

when she smiled, her smile was magical. Even when she wasn't
laughing or smiling, her face looked happy.

He talked with her for a long time when they first met.
Carla and Angelika's father helped them, unintentionally, by
tying Zeina up in conversation. The old man spoke slowly, with
frequent silences, as he told her of his suffering during the second world war and his military experience. He had been a soldier in Mussolini's army: his Italian roots led him to leave his
family in Switzerland to join Il Duce's army. He'd gone to
Libya and Ethiopia during the war. He was an old man and, for
him, history had stopped with the defeat and execution of
Mussolini. It was the end of Italian greatness.

Abdel Nasser didn't hear a single war story because of his
attraction to Angelika. She took advantage of her father
monopolizing Zeina's attention, and when the old soldier finished talking, Carla, her mother, and her brother Paolo all took
turns talking to and fussing over Zeina. Salah Eddine watched
the scene from his armchair, smiling at his guests.

In bed that night, el-Talyani complained to Zeina about
Carla's wearisome sister who'd kept him away from his Berber
princess. Her constant chatter and trivial stories were incredibly annoying, he said. He told Zeina he'd been watching her
and saw her dissatisfaction with Carla's father's war stories,
too, and how everyone (with the exception of Salah Eddine)
was tripping over themselves to talk with her. "You were
right," he told her. "If the whole week is like this, I'll have to
admit that your gut was correct."

"Well," she replied, "tonight was all about social obligation,
but starting tomorrow I'm going to go back to my schedule,
working from morning to evening."

Zeina hadn't noticed when Salah Eddine pulled Abdel
Nasser aside into the big living room before everyone retired
for the evening. He whispered to him, "I know you're attracted
to Angelika, but try not to make Zeina jealous."

"I haven't done anything to make her jealous," el-Talyani protested, "I wasn't even really talking to her, just listening."

"There's no time to argue about this now. You looked delighted when you were listening to her, and Zeina kept looking over at you."

"Okay," Abdel Nasser told him. "I'll take care of it. Goodnight."

What Abdel Nasser didn't know was that Zeina *had* felt something strange in the way her husband was looking at Angelika. As well as the way that Angelika would move her hands, putting one on el-Talyani's knee or briefly touching his shoulder. Zeina didn't consider this suspicious behavior, but rather just a natural reaction during the conversation. This didn't mean that she didn't feel some jealousy—for the first time in her life—especially for a woman like Angelika who emptied the room she was in of oxygen with her energy and her resonant voice. What reassured her, though, was that el-Talyani was right: the topics the loud, engaging voice had touched on had all been trivial.

9

Salah Eddine had planned everything. He presented the plan at the breakfast table: in addition to the Christmas party at home and New Year's Eve at a fancy restaurant, it included visits to monuments, theaters, exhibits, and concerts. It encompassed all the important attractions in Geneva and the surrounding area, as well as an aerial tour on a cable car.

Zeina excused herself from participating in these plans rather bluntly. The people around the table were surprised by her words, but el-Talyani hurried to salvage the situation, explaining her commitments and her desire to take advantage of the break to work on her thesis. They all expressed understanding of her situation and wished her luck. Salah Eddine offered to let her use either his home office or his office at the university, as well as offering to help her find any books she might need.

After their return to Tunis, nothing of the trip remained in Zeina's memory save the joy of the pages she was able to write. She found Salah Eddine's office an ideal place to work, think, and write. She was also left, though, with a feeling that something had changed about Abdel Nasser. Something she couldn't quite put her finger on.

El-Talyani, on the other hand, returned from Switzerland with a new, indelible impression on his body and a different scent in his nose, a scent that would return to him whenever Zeina was sunk in the morass of Hannah Arendt.

10

It snowed heavily that night. They needed to add more logs to the fire, more than usual, to warm the room. Geneva's cold is harsh and merciless, especially at night. Abdel Nasser was astonished that Carla and her brother were wearing t-shirts in that unbearable cold. They stayed up late; it was two days before New Year's Eve, 1987. Everyone drank a toast to Angelika because it was her twenty-seventh birthday. No one knew about it ahead of time. Carla planned it as a surprise and made everyone, except her brother, stay up and drink a toast to her without giving her a present. Fortunately, Zeina had brought an olive-wood mortar and pestle from Tunisia, engraved with beautiful designs and painted colorfully, that she gave as a gift. She explained its importance to Tunisian heritage and the role it had in people's lives, both in the city and the countryside, as well as its different usages. She also explained the use of the pestle and hinted, jokingly, at the sexual connotations of *mehrasse*, the word for a mortar and pestle in Tunisian Arabic. Zeina saved the day with the mehrasse.

Thanks to this gift, the situation was reversed, and Zeina and her ingenuity became the star of the evening. No one said that, in so many words, but it was clear from the looks of admiration she received, as well as Carla's warm kisses, which belied both the cold weather and the Swiss people's reputation for coldness.

Following his brother's advice, Abdel Nasser stayed well away from where Angelika was sitting. But he'd already had the morning and evening walks to get to know her, as she explained the sights and told him stories and the history of this or that monument.

He found out on day one that she was living a tragedy and trying desperately to stay afloat. Her boyfriend—who she'd lived with for several years and planned to marry—had been kidnapped eight months prior. He was a young journalist chasing adventure and specializing in the Middle East, particularly Lebanon, which had gripped his attention since the Siege of Beirut in 1982. He'd gone there to film a televised report after four journalists were kidnapped. And . . . what else could you expect if you stuck your head in the crocodile's mouth? Was he dead? Did they kill him? Or was he taken hostage? And if so, why had no one presented any demands in order to free him?

Angelika was left in limbo, chewing on the bitterness of fidelity for a boyfriend who might be executed without reason. She told Abdel Nasser, "You always see me happy, but don't be fooled. This is my way of dealing with the pain . . . I'm no saint."

El-Talyani tried to change the subject, asking her again about the historical site under Saint Pierre church that he had visited that morning. He was sure that Angelika was attracted to him. It was hard to miss: she had complimented him on his "captivating Italian beauty" and told him he looked just like the dream lover of her teenage years, when she was trying to escape her fascist father's conservativism. It was definitely flirting, and not merely the frankness he'd expected from Western women, who he thought of as free minds in free bodies; surely, if she wanted something, she would just come out and say it.

But the language of the body, and growing desire, and tenderness when it fills the air a man and woman breathe . . . those things need no translation, no matter how different their two languages.

Zeina left the living room, leaving the rest of the evening to the night owls. She was hoping to get some rest, to be ready to immerse herself tomorrow in the kingdom of pure knowledge and philosophy. Carla's father had left before her. It was after midnight when everyone went back to their bedrooms, save Angelika, who continued her conversation with Abdel Nasser.

After everyone else had left, Angelika seemed happier and more comfortable. Her fast speech became slower, and it seemed to him that her vivacity and the liveliness in her hands started to flag every so often, replaced by absent mindedness or a touch of sadness on her face. Angelika was no longer Angelika. And Abdel Nasser hadn't been Abdel Nasser since she told him about her tragedy.

The truth was that he found himself, in some moments, comparing Zeina and Angelika. Zeina drowning in work in Salah Eddine's office, or sitting at the dinner table, or dazzling everyone with her smile as she chatted with the rest of the family at night. Compared to Angelika, his tour guide and companion, regaling him with stories and conversation. There was really no way to compare them; they each had their own charm and fascination. Though really, if forced to compare, Zeina was the more beautiful, sweeter, and more knowledgeable.

11

Everyone had left the living room except for Angelika and Abdel Nasser. They were sitting across from each other on two couches; then she came to sit next to him. She sat with her legs drawn into her chest, her chin resting on her knees. She looked into his eyes and asked if he wanted beer, another glass of champagne, some wine. He hesitated for a moment, then surrendered. She was being nice to him, even nicer than usual. Her voice, slowed down (by the alcohol, he presumed), took on a definite air of flirtation.

She was a bed of smoldering embers, an ashless fireplace filled with burning logs that sent off sparks that settled on every cell in his body. For days, he'd been frozen by Hannah Arendt and the harsh cold of Switzerland; now he was flooded with melting ice and warm femininity. Her lips tickled his body like an ostrich feather on the bottom of his feet or under his arms. Her tongue, at times like smooth cotton and others like a biting saw, made his body melt with pleasure wherever it touched. And a touch of violence, no doubt from the many months of abstinence, mixed with an authentic tenderness.

She played her role with enthusiasm, joy, pain, and pleasure. As if she was doing a duty that she was forced to do but enjoyed at the same time. He let her lead and did as he was directed. Today was her birthday, after all, and she was a skillful translator of feelings, of the body's vocabulary, expressions of pleasure, and the rhetoric of desire.

The book of her body was rich in meanings, and the meanings were full of shadows. It wasn't easy for him to analyze and annotate it in a single night, regardless of how long that night lasted, especially since his life's book was closed, sleeping in the other room, and might check in on them at any moment.

He had no idea how he slept that night after getting into bed. Zeina was sleeping like an angel. That's how he saw her that night. He could barely look at her, afraid that she might have seen him, embarrassed, or just being stupid. He hurried to turn off the bedside light and put his head under the covers.

It was what it was, and if anything was going to come of it, he would find out in the morning.

Nothing happened. He woke up early with Zeina when her alarm went off. He wouldn't let her leave the bed before he showered her with kisses and caresses in places he knew excited her. But her desire for writing and love of knowledge were stronger than her desire to be personally annotated, so he went back to sleep while she went off to her books. The important thing was that he was sure she had no idea about what had happened the previous night. He woke again at 10 A.M. to find Angelika as happy as a bride, full of liveliness and with no trace of sadness or absent-mindedness on her face. She kissed him, leaving some saliva on his lips, then whispered in his ear, "You were great. Thank you . . . so, so much."

He didn't respond. He made do with a wink, a message that no one could read but Angelika.

For the remaining three days, they weren't able to do anything but steal wild kisses wherever they could: in the coffee shop, in the museum, in an exhibit, in the elevator. Abdel Nasser got nervous after their first time passed without incident. Angelika knew the adventure had no future as long as Zeina was with him. They spoke honestly about the matter while sitting at a recently opened café called Black Cat Café (He liked it because it reminded him of the Naguib Mahfouz novel, *The Black Cat Pub*). Angelika was dealing with the matter in a surprisingly matter-of-fact way; she was an intelligent woman. She explained to him his conflicting feelings. And she told him that she was attracted to him but still faithful to her absent boyfriend. So the curtain closed on the story of el-Talyani and Angelika. He didn't see her again, and he didn't speak of her until that day that Salah Eddine mentioned her, after Hajj Mahmoud's passing and the incident at the cemetery.

12

The trip to Switzerland was the beginning of a crack that Zeina did not at first notice and whose consequences el-Talyani didn't fully comprehend. He considered telling her the truth one day, after feeling something like guilt. He admired her despite everything. She was luminous and intelligent, and she became sweeter in his eyes after signing the marriage certificate, even though she considered it a mere piece of paper while he viewed it as an eternal bond between them. He took advantage of a general conversation they were having about relationships between male and female teachers at the high school. The conversation meandered to include stories from her village, sexual behaviors with animals, homosexuality, cheating . . . all kinds of weird stories, some of which he was hearing about in detail for the first time, despite some vague awareness of them. The conversation moved to the motives and causes behind these things.

He was about to tell her about Lella Jnayna and Imam Sheikh Allala, but then a strange idea occurred to him. He asked her, hypothetically, what her reaction would be if he cheated on her.

She calmly told him her theory that men were hunters who would seize any opportunity to pounce on their prey. She considered it men's nature to monopolize money, status, women, and power. She then widened the circle of analysis to the original and inherent correlation between ownership, authority, and women's bodies. She surprised him by saying that polygamy was more appropriate for men than monogamy. She tried to remove the issue from its Islamic cultural framework, but he debated her on the issue of polygamy, the position of the Islamists, and their attacks on women's gains in society. She responded that he was misunderstanding her; the issue, in her opinion, had nothing to do with religion or the calls against gender equality. She clarified, citing anthropological evidence, that forms of ownership, and the movement of physical, sexual, and symbolic capital were diverse. In her opinion, it was necessary to strip the subject of ethical judgements, the *halal–haram* duality, and the historical weight of previous opinion in order to reevaluate the idea of polygamy. She went further by noting that, in Islamic jurisprudence, marriage contracts were included in the chapters on buying and selling. Marriage was a financial transaction, like buying slaves ("what the right hand possesses") or livestock, subject to distinctions based on the type of merchandise and the impact of human or business factors in determining its worth and economic function.

She asked him, "How is it you can't see this when you're a fan of Marx's *Capital* and the materialist conception of history?"

Abdel Nasser asked, "So does that mean you'd be okay with me taking a second wife?"

"Isn't your question about cheating, not polygamy?" she asked.

"I want to know your opinion on both issues," he responded.

"When we get married, I will refuse to share you with any other woman."

"The marriage certificate doesn't count?"

"Oh, we're back to that old story." She dismissed his question and moved on. "Let me tell you about infidelity."

He lowered his eyes, masking his anger, and tried to calm down. He was still listening to her, but his mind was floating around Salah Eddine's fireplace.

Meanwhile, the philosophy party had started. Infidelity was an adjective that was only applied to women, because they were synonymous with faithfulness whereas men were philanderers by nature. She examined the subject from all sides. She considered the observed tendency among women to search for pleasure outside the institutionalized relationship—or love relationship, whatever form it took—as a way for women to act like the male hunters. She singled out rural women in their behavior; she believed the villages enjoyed real equality, despite the ethics system and the long history of forced integration into larger societal values.

Throughout, Zeina denounced the "moralist" approach to these phenomena. She warned that women were originally condemned because they disrupted the dominant ideology, which was a phantasm created by men to protect their ownership of money, women's bodies, and power.

Abdel Nasser tried to bring her back down to earth. "So if I were to 'hunt' a woman, as you put it, how would you react?"

She didn't want to answer, saying the question was irrelevant because she was speaking objectively, not subjectively, like she said. He insisted on bringing the subject up again, pushing theory aside to talk about reality, leaving the abstract for the concrete. She avoided the topic and did not answer him. She said again, "Once we're married, you'll know my practical position."

Abdel Nasser lost his temper, and the conversation became an argument about what she'd been saying over and over: the marriage certificate was just a formality and not what she considered a real marriage. He argued the matter from a legal point of view; she tried to move the discussion to a general intellectual level. She went back to the story of love and ownership and the difference between marriage and free love. She stressed her maintenance of her freedom. She even considered him a voice, perhaps unwittingly, for the archaic social conventions and structures that forbade any relationship between men and women except marriage.

Abdel Nasser defended their marriage, accusing her of selfishness for not caring about his feelings and his devotion to their relationship. He asked her, "Is there someone else?"

She didn't know if the question was real or rhetorical, and laughed derisively. He repeated the question several times, until she was convinced that he meant it. So she answered "yes" just to spite him. She left him by himself in the kitchen (which also functioned as their living room) and closed the bedroom door behind her. After a moment, she heard the front door slam.

13

Without his awareness, the crack kept widening. He kept insisting on their relationship while she insisted on finishing her work. One day, he returned home soaked to the skin because of a flooding February rain that had come after several years of drought. Le Bardo was sunk in mud, and, as usual, its sewers flooded, and the drains spewed up everything inside them. He'd had a hard time getting home—when he'd left at noon, the only sign of the impending bad weather had been a drop in temperature.

He greeted Zeina without enthusiasm. She had her papers and books spread out on the kitchen table. He went to the bathroom, looking for their big towel, but couldn't find it. So he went into the bedroom and saw piles of shopping bags on the bed and floor. He noticed the women's clothing brands on the outside of the bags and opened them to take a look. Inside, he found two pairs of women's shoes, woolen jackets, trousers, two trouser suits, and a fancy dress.

After drying himself off and changing his clothes, he went to the kitchen and asked her, "Did you find buried treasure?"

"Beep, wrong answer. You get two more tries."

"Has the teachers' union comrade taken up another collection for you?"

"Last try."

"A gift from your other husband that you're cheating on me with?"

She laughed. "That's a terrible joke, and it's beneath you."

"I give up, then, what is it?"

"I finally got paid. Five months' salary all together. I'm one of the rich Arabs today."

He went over and kissed her head. "Congratulations," he said. "You're a fortune in and of yourself."

His romantic overtures went unnoticed; she remained wrapped up in her work as if nothing had happened. He brought a book from the bedroom (a novel by Philip Roth entitled *My Life as a Man*), but couldn't read more than a few pages. A barrage of thoughts was swirling around in his head, keeping him from focusing on the novel.

She wasn't responding to any of his romantic gestures anymore, even though he never let a chance to compliment her pass him by. Today, she had gone with Najla (a physical education teacher and her new friend, who lived close to them in Le Bardo) to buy clothes suitable for a philosophy teacher. Yet she didn't even think about buying him a shirt or a jacket or a pair of shoes as a gift? Didn't she know that he hadn't bought himself anything for a long time—that if it wasn't for Salah Eddine's gift during their Switzerland trip, he would still be in his old, worn-out clothes?

Why didn't she offer to take him out to a restaurant to celebrate her windfall? Couldn't she have postponed the research project for a few hours, or even a full day? She could even have brought home some take-out—something, anything that indicated that she had a partner at home to whom she was united by marriage, or even friendship, or whatever she wanted to call it. Didn't she know that he hadn't had a drop of wine bought with his own money for months? She knew he couldn't pay for his basic expenses anymore, much less the luxury goods. He'd been living like a king, thanks to the money Salah Eddine used to send him; his crisis only started when he began trusting every cent to her and making do with his pocket money. Couldn't she at least have bought a celebration cake, the way he did the day he graduated?

He remembered what his mother and sister Jweeda (and even Yosser) used to say about the rubes from the country. They warned him that they were impolite and ill-mannered; they lacked the kindness and traditions of city people.

His mother Zeinab used to always say, "A man born rich will give away his last few cents; a man born poor will hoard the millions he earns."

He remembered the women's conversations at home and their disdain for people who didn't live in the city. He used to mock those conversations; how could he give them credence now? There was something wrong with Zeina, some fault in her soul. It seemed to him that it didn't actually have to do with the research; after all, she'd found time to buy herself clothes. It didn't seem related to the lack of money either, since she'd just told him that she sent a money order to her mother, to make her happy and give her a taste of the harvest of many years of hard work, insults, humiliation, and oppression. She remembered this when he was reading the novel and mentioned it in passing, then buried her head again in her papers and books.

He thought about it for a long time, trying to get to the bottom of the issue. He couldn't find a satisfactory answer other than that she didn't love him the way he loved her and didn't treat him the way he treated her. He concluded that she was treating him like a neighbor living in the same house, taking advantage of his presence to protect her and using him to quench her sexual desire—although even that had been getting weaker and fading away. She used his money to get around, buy cigarettes, and pay for her daily expenses. She took advantage of his being home all the time to give her a hand (and even a foot if needed!) whenever she needed help rewriting a chapter, because Abdel Nasser's handwriting (which had often graced the posters at the university) was beautiful and clear.

14

There was something. He wanted to figure out what it was. At the same time, he was afraid to identify it precisely. He wasn't afraid of Zeina, but of himself. Reasonable and terrible ideas got mixed up in his head, multiplying while he pretended to read his book. Zeina didn't notice anything. Whenever he lifted his head he found her buried in papers, reading, writing, or thinking. He noticed a pack of expensive foreign cigarettes, Larks, on the table that he hadn't seen before. It had probably been covered with papers, or buried between books or under a dictionary, or in her bag. *Well, this is a leap*, he thought, *from the domestic Cristal Lights to American Larks. That clears things up.* He didn't want to comment and said nothing until she asked, "Is there anything to eat?"

He wasn't able to keep his thoughts silent. He gave her a calculating smile and answered, "I thought we would be eating out."

"What's the occasion?" she asked.

"We haven't eaten out, you and I, since the day of my graduation, if I recall. We used to do it just for fun."

She nodded but didn't say anything. He went on. "But today we have an excuse to go out to eat together."

"What excuse?" she asked.

"Buying new clothes," he responded.

"First of all, that's a normal thing to do," she told him. "And second, I can buy something with the money we would spend eating out."

He saw that she'd fallen into his trap, all the while pretending to be calm and reasonable while she answered his insinuations. He said, "What I mean is that I'm inviting you out. You save your money to buy something important. I'm a spender by nature; you're the one who's good with money, my love."

"Where did you get money from?" she asked. "All I have left that's yours is 30 dinars!"

El-Talyani didn't say anything, as he'd gotten what he needed through his hinting and provocation. He had wanted to see Zeina's attitude toward money. He smiled at her, then went back to pretending to read. It seemed that this problem of hers was a fault that was being exposed gradually over time; he couldn't force a new system on her as long as she was unwilling to change.

He waited for a few days to see if she would share in furnishing the house, with some small pieces at least. He didn't dare to dream of her buying living room furniture on a payment plan, or a refrigerator or washing machine. He was simply hoping for some of the small basics: some plates to eat on, or bath towels, things like that. But, apparently, good things don't come to those who wait.

15

Abdel Nasser had the habit of sitting at Café El Hajj, reading the newspaper, both to follow the news and to keep an eye out for any competitive entrance exams opening up. One day at the café, by happy coincidence, he met Aamm Hassan.

The man had noticed Abdel Nasser's annoyance with the newspaper ink blackening his hands. He started chatting with him, as people there do, even though he didn't know him. He was drinking coffee and smoking hookah; he started talking about the poor quality of Tunisian printing presses. He

compared them with what he'd seen in Germany, which he visited once for a training workshop. He also mentioned that the
newspaper he worked for was getting ready to buy a new press.
That day Abdel Nasser decided to let go of his fear of secret
police and trust his intuition that this was just a nice, ordinary
man starting a conversation with no ulterior motives. Aamm
Hassan asked about his profession, so he told him that he was
a recent graduate of the law college. He asked him about his
French fluency, since he saw the French novel sitting in front
of him and had seen him working on the crossword in the
newspaper. He told Abdel Nasser that his newspaper was
looking for competent proofreaders to work from 4 P.M. to 10
P.M., sometimes as late as midnight, depending on what was
happening in the news. He assured him that his chances of
being hired were very good, since the number of people (editors, journalists, and proofreaders) who had a solid mastery of
French had been decreasing. He and Abdel Nasser arranged a
time for him to meet with the editorial secretary. The test went
well: they gave him a long text full of mistakes, and he caught
every one of them. That day he started his new temporary job;
he'd not only saved himself the cost of buying his own newspaper, but also got to read the ministry and entrance exam
advertisements before they were published.

16

Abdel Nasser quickly became well known at the newspaper
for being the most consistent and perfectionist proofreader, a
fine sieve that caught all misconjugations of French verbs,
tense mistakes, and agreement problems. Once, in the editor-
in-chief's editorial, he found two egregious grammatical
errors that distorted the meaning (which was about the future
of the government and the head of state). Among the media

convention in Tunisia, this would be grounds to fire the editor, even if the mistake was unintentional.

Abdel Nasser was also able to witness, for the first time, how censorship worked at the government-owned newspapers. There was a person who read the newspaper front to back—not even the sports page or obituaries escaped his penetrating review. He was the most knowledgeable of the country's best interest and the most qualified to protect it. Often a paragraph would be deleted at the last minute, wasting all the effort it took to write it, proofread it, and set it. The journalist would not get to review what was written; rather, the matter was kept between the censor and the editorial manager. And the "Official for the Implementation of the Bourguiba Regime's Interests," as Abdel Nasser called him, always had the solution: put a piece of thick black tape through the offending paragraph, with a note warning against speeding, or advice for pedestrians, or an advisement of the dangers of smoking, or a call to conserve energy.

One day Abdel Nasser dared to correct an article written by the golden quill of the Tunisian francophone media, *sayyid* president of the whole company and the master editor-in-chief, as well. His articles were not usually corrected directly; rather, the corrections were suggested, leaving the final say to him. He would stay late to dictate the editorial, wait for its correction, then read it one last time before leaving the newspaper headquarters.

That day, the editorial had arrived after the rest of the newspaper was all prepared, and the golden quill's genius wasn't entirely clear. Abdel Nasser corrected the text, because that was his job and he had been chosen by Aamm Hassan and the editorial secretary to do it. He was about to leave when he heard the editorial secretary calling him angrily.

"What have you done?" he demanded. "Are you so pretentious that you think you can correct the texts of the most skilled pen in Tunisia?"

"What are you talking about?" Abdel Nasser asked.

"*Sayyid* the president wants to see you—you're about to have a very bad night. Don't argue with him; he's already in a foul mood after reading your corrections."

"I don't care," Abdel Nasser said. "Mistakes are mistakes."

"Come on, we're going to the second floor. Call Aamm Hassan; Abou Saoud H. and the president are waiting for us."

Abdel Nasser was not at all agitated. He said to himself, *The proletariat has nothing to lose. To hell with all of them.*

The three of them entered the office, led by the editorial secretary. The office was cloaked in an indignant silence. The censor, Abou Saoud, was speaking with the president, both of them in raised voices. Abdel Nasser heard the director say that "the baby bird is feeding the cock," and Abdel Nasser chuckled at the expression. He was one hundred percent sure of himself—he never corrected anything in editorials until he had double-checked the dictionary.

As soon as he saw him, the censor said, "That's him—brazen kid!"

The president approached Abdel Nasser, shaking his finger in his face and pointing at the text in front of him.

"Was it you who corrected the tense agreement in this sentence?"

Abdel Nasser tried to calm himself. He would have liked to break that pointing finger or kick him where it hurt. But he didn't; he chose a different kind of attack.

"A mistake is a mistake. Ask anyone who has mastered French."

The president exploded. "Are you saying that of Abou Saoud, the editorial secretary, and I, *none* of us knows French? Because we all agreed that what I wrote was correct before you went and distorted it."

"If you agreed, then fine. It's your text. I did my duty, but you have the final word. It's not like any of us are Molière."

"Are you mocking me?"

Abdel Nasser interrupted him. "No, not at all. You can either leave the text as is, or we can talk calmly, without insults."

The president gaped at him, as if wondering where this person could have come from, to dare to talk to him this way. Abdel Nasser sensed what he was thinking and said, jokingly, "If I'm wrong, I'll give you two months of my salary. And if I'm not, your censor and the editorial secretary will each give me a month of theirs. Agreed?"

The president smiled. "Clever boy. Why didn't you include me?"

"Because I wouldn't know what to do with your big money; it wouldn't fit in my pocket."

The president laughed, and the others tried to be serious but couldn't quite hide their smiles, shocked by the pure nerve they saw walking on two feet.

They discussed the sentence in question for fifteen minutes. They checked the meanings, the context, and the possible interpretations. Abdel Nasser brought a copy of Grevisse, one of the most trusted grammar references. The president spoke calmly (in contrast to the yelling when they had entered the office), and the young proofreader presented all his arguments. Finally he said, "That's what I think, anyway—the final call is yours."

The president, sitting at his desk, rested his head between his hands. Then he looked up at the censor and the editorial secretary and said, "You two can get an advance for next month; this boy is right."

17

After that, Abdel Nasser started going to the office around eight at night to write the editorial as the president dictated it to him. Eventually, the president started telling him the topic and asking him to write the next day's editorial himself, using the stiff, limpid prose befitting an editor-in-chief, and with his boss's byline. It was an easy exercise for Abdel Nasser, and a great service for the president.

A few days later the president asked him to write about national affairs under his own byline, but Abdel Nasser politely declined. Didn't he want to become a journalist, the president asked, but still Abdel Nasser demurred. He just wanted to help him increase his salary: the recompense for proofreading was meagre, and there was a limit to how many extra hours he could give him. But he was confident of his qualifications and that he could write better than any of the journalists at the paper.

The solution he found was to have Abdel Nasser write the sports pages, rewriting the important wire stories coming in from Tunis Afrique Presse. He did that for a few months, which helped increase his income. But before long there was a problem when Abdel Nasser published scandalous news about Baganda, a soccer player from his neighborhood he had known well and who was playing for a major team. Si Abdel Hamid knew how to get Abdel Nasser out of trouble. Since he was no longer welcome in the sports pages after that, he asked him to write about social issues under a pseudonym; his pay would be based on the number of articles he wrote.

One day, the censor blocked an article he had written about how fruits and vegetables were distributed, and that system's role in price increases. He boiled with rage and asked the president, while he was writing an editorial for him, to move him to the culture section. The president explained that the censor had the upper hand; he couldn't contradict any of his decisions (no matter how arbitrary) because he was supported by a wing of the presidential palace.

18

The wait for entrance exams to open was long. The country was in a grave economic crisis: it was on the brink of bankruptcy, and there were conflicts between different wings of the palace (whose leader spent only an hour or two awake per day). Abdel Nasser considered the matter carefully: a bird in the hand was better than a thousand in the sky. Especially in the overcast, stormy skies of Tunisia, where birds couldn't even fly properly. There were no birds and no entrance exams, so he should take the president up on his offer and become a journalist at a government newspaper.

In a surprisingly short amount of time, the president had everything arranged. He was an intellectual who had joined the Constitutional Party later in life. After some time, he confided in Abdel Nasser that he liked the smart leftists and harbored a visceral hatred for the Islamists, who were a threat to the modernist legacy of the country. He mentioned that he had been at the Korba Congress in 1971 and was one of the party members who opposed the coup on the leftist wing of the General Union of Tunisian Students. He felt nostalgia for that time and was sorry about what had happened. He deeply regretted the time that the country and its universities had wasted on an easily solved crisis.

Abdel Nasser's relationship with the president became stronger once the latter recognized his intelligence, as well as his editing abilities and distinguished style. The president also came to like him because of his honesty and the clarity of his position. He would sometimes invite him to his office to discuss what was happening in the country and to hear his analysis and opinions; he found that his newest journalist had great familiarity with even small details of important matters and a sharp political conscience. He liked that Abdel Nasser made no attempt to disguise his leftism: perhaps opposing Islamists brought them together. For his part, Abdel Nasser liked the president because he was not a loyal member of the Constitutional Party but rather—as he disclosed to him one day—had been someone who was close to the democrats inside the party. But the country was narrow-minded, and the so-called democracy wasn't sound. He also confessed, in a rare moment of honesty, that he hadn't chosen the Constitutional Party but that it had been forced on him. Otherwise, his position would have been given to someone less qualified. He was of a generation that considered itself Bourguibist, but he thought that Bourguibism was lacking in democracy. He counted himself among the distinguished elite that had founded the francophone magazine *Dialogue*, aiming to improve journalism by increasing both professionalism and freedom of expression. But the situation within the country had aborted that experiment.

Gradually, the kindness and mutual respect between them became an affection that time and friendship only increased. Abdel Nasser would never have imagined that he would find this human depth in a man who, regardless of what he was hiding in his heart, was one of the most loyal to the regime. Had he known him a year before, he would have considered him one of the watchdogs, a counterfeiter of the public consciousness and defender of a corrupt and ramshackle regime. But in their private meetings, after the president started taking him along to a fancy restaurant in the suburb of Gammarth, he would tell him about the novels he was addicted to. He told him about the great Russian novelists and about Latin American writers and American novels. He would tell him, "Don't waste your time; the real novels are the Russian novels." Or he would say, "The novel today is undisputedly American. It's the only novel that tells the truth about modern man."

He talked about international novels with the knowledge of an insatiable reader. If he particularly liked a novel that he'd read, he would give it to Abdel Nasser. He would ask Abdel

Nasser if he had read such-and-such a writer from Europe or Japan. If the answer was no—which it usually was—in a day or two he would bring him a novel or play or poetry collection by the writer he had mentioned.

One thing Abdel Nasser did not understand was Si Abdel Hamid's hatred for poetry, despite his great knowledge of it. He asked him about it once.

"Poetry is a rhetorical exercise," the president responded, "whereas the novel is the mother of deep truths."

Abel Nasser debated with him a lot, but insisted on his own opinion. What surprised him was Si Abdel Hamid's disdain for *le film d'auteur* and his love for commercially successful block-busters. Abdel Nasser didn't understand it, so he explained: "*A film d'auteur* is like a lover sleeping in his beloved's bed while she's absent, imagining her with him. Whereas the real movie actually recreates that dream. It tells the story in a far superior way to those stupid films of Godard and the like."

19

In their meetings, Si Abdel Hamid divulged the palace's secrets and the latest conflicts taking place in it, as well as the positions of different political parties and their scandals, deals, and two-faced speeches. He told him in detail about the governing party and its clandestine dealings: the secrets of every minister and official, who supported them, who was fighting with whom, who was sleeping with whose wife, and who was leaking whose secrets.

A rotten world, filled with cheating, profanity, and greed. He didn't confess his part in all of this, but he hinted that it was impossible for people in positions like his to escape the corruption of the system. Anyone who managed not to sink in it still got drenched by its spray.

He told Abdel Nasser that anyone who held a position in the current government was like a tightrope walker. He might be knocked off the wire with just the flap of a butterfly's wings to find crocodiles with their jaws gaping waiting for him below.

He seemed pleased when he told him for the first time his opinion on the young journalist Abdel Nasser: "I am certain that you'll make a great journalist. You didn't study at the Institut de Presse, and you don't need to. Truly great journalists don't come from those miserable places. Journalism is wielding a facile pen, intelligence, insightfulness, prior knowledge, and fast reflexes. The rules of journalism are learned by reading what the masters write, by training and attention. I've known you were a master since I read your first scribbles."

But then he leaned his head in toward el-Talyani and whispered, "But the real journalist is the one who has connections with the interior ministry, with the higher-ranking officials there. He gets the inside information and knows which way the wind is blowing. He needs these connections inside the decision-making circles, but he can't become a snitch or slanderer, or the faucet of secrets will be turned off. And he can't become a sycophantic kiss-ass, or he'll be kicked out of the circle."

1

Abdel Nasser's life had changed, in its rhythms, paths, and pleasures.

He now woke up late, after Zeina had already left the house to go teach. Even on Saturday, which the philosophy teachers had off, she would go to the National Library or the university library, or to meet with her research supervisor or her pedagogy advisor for philosophy. He would not see her until she returned home in the evening.

They never really saw each other except on Sunday mornings. She liked to laze around on Sundays and eat a real breakfast: extra virgin olive oil, Gruyère cheese, smoked beef salami, and boiled eggs. She would fry tomatoes, green peppers, and onions. She didn't like milk, so she would buy juice. She had started this ritual when she began receiving her monthly pay like the other high school teachers. This was the only day that she prepared breakfast herself. She would sit across from Abdel Nasser and summarize her weekly activities and goings-on: the pedagogy advisor visits, the situation in the high school, the stories she'd heard, echoes of the troubles happening in the country. When she got to her progress with her research, she would complain about not having enough time and express her fear of wasting the year without finishing her work and defending it. This fear had haunted her since her graduation the previous summer. Abdel Nasser used to try to lift her spirits, to encourage her to work and make her comfortable. After a while, though, the broken record became grating, and he stopped commenting on anything. He would just listen to her and remain neutral.

He no longer even tried to get romantic with her on those special weekly occasions. She focused on her research and seemed not to remember him, even though he usually returned home late, when she was already sleeping. By then he would have gulped down what he could with Si Abdel Hamid or with some journalists in the bars near the office, or at the home of one of his new friends. He would no longer ask about her meals. He could see from the discarded wrappers and some leftovers that she had gotten in the habit of eating fast food from one of the places on Avenue de Bourguiba in Le Bardo or on one of the side streets. He would find some cold pizza, smelling of sour tomatoes, or a leftover tuna or turkey or salami sandwich; sometimes he would find a crust of red cheese or Gruyère and bread. She wouldn't clean up those leftovers but rather would leave them on the kitchen counter, like a young woman who had never been taught manners. Abdel Nasser would sweep them up in the morning as he prepared his coffee, getting ready to smoke his cigarette and use the bathroom (where he spent a long time, reading a book or magazine), all the while cursing laziness, research, and bad manners.

Their marriage had become mere cohabitation, between a journalist taking his first steps in the world of press and its baseness (and, truth be told, these first steps were huge) and a Wise Woman who was still a high school teacher-in-training and a student conducting research that would open up the empire of college teaching for her (a rare, high-quality student who resembled a reading and editing machine, programmed to become a great doctor).

Were it not for the occasional romance and caresses in bed before sleeping when Abdel Nasser came home unusually early, their cohabitation could have been a strictly platonic one between strangers. And if not for this incendiary longing and explosion of lust and desire in the few times they chanced to come together, like lovers reuniting after a long separation, each would have taken their own path.

There was, after all, something tying them together other than the marriage certificate, which had been the accidental product of special circumstances. At times Abdel Nasser didn't know how his opinion of Zeina had changed. He had come to see her as a pure mind, incapable of anything but playing with concepts, hovering in abstracts, deconstructing terminology, debunking ideas, planting seeds of doubt in constants, and shaking paradoxes. Yet when el-Talyani's lips tasted the saliva of that "thinking reed" and his hands started to explore its soft skin's topography, this pure mind would become a jelly-like substance shaped to his whims, fantasies, and whatever shapes came to mind, some of which were never mentioned in the *Kama Sutra*. The reed became a tender green branch, shivering when touched by the wind of desire. The wicked plant was astonishing, moodily changing its shape. He saw her as a dry branch and solid trunk most of the time, sometimes a reed like a flute that emitted jostling and entrancing ideas. But at other times, she was a tender and blossoming branch, its perfume renewing senses that had grown dull from familiarity and habit.

That is perhaps part of what made them take separate paths on most days, but they still sometimes met in these rare moments, which were mysterious even to them.

The truth was that Zeina was feeling the same way, based on what she told me after her divorce. She saw Abdel Nasser as an organized and rational man who controlled everything, even his feelings and the pulses of his body. A strict man who planned everything, a great strategist who put in place tactical plans with no escape routes for whoever was with him. That bothered her a lot. But the paradox (that I cautioned her of and she admitted) was that at the same time he made her feel secure and protected. She lived with a responsible man who respected her and didn't sabotage her, but instead cleared her path of rocks (no matter how big) so that she could continue her journey.

Zeina admitted that she could see this New Organon (as she referred to Abdel Nasser) in his moments of anger, like the inferno of Dante or the fall of Orpheus. But in moments of desire, she saw in him an Indian lover ready to die for love or an exhilarating verse of erotic Arabic poetry. He was like a copy of *The Perfumed Garden of Sensual Delight* in the hands of a curious teenager. He was a timebomb of lust, and you never knew when he would explode, leaving no part of the body untouched by burns of ecstasy or deadly shrapnel, the kind that killed with pleasure.

Zeina didn't share her thoughts on the topic with Abdel Nasser; nor did he share his with her. But there was something deep and delicate in the issue that she couldn't understand. She used to feel, at the beginning, a kind of drunkenness mixed with tremors, as if she were in a state of ecstasy, melting into Abdel Nasser's body and completely fusing with him. His body was a beautiful magnetic field, hypnotizing the senses and stirring them up at the same time. It would shut down the mind, anesthetizing all her limbs, making her feel an intolerable pain and an unbearable pleasure at the same time. So she would surrender to the successive arrows of pain and pleasure, starvation and lust. But when she finally returned to her normal state, she was left with a sharp and terrifying pain below her belly, at the level of her pubic hair, as if large-gauge needles were eating away at her from the inside, wielded by a hidden hand that kept digging nonstop. Zeina never understood that, not at the beginning nor through the whole period of her marriage to Abdel Nasser. It wasn't that she didn't like him, his beauty, or the sublimity of the pleasure he gave her. But she limited herself to the minimum of all that because she always remembered, before finding herself in his arms, those terrifying pains that remained after their bodies separated. She would be seduced sometimes by his scent—the scent of rain when he got wet, or the compressed sweat under his arms, even the smell of his feet in his sneakers or military-style boots—but would hold herself back when she talked to him or touched him, trying to resist the magnetic field. She was fighting, and he had no idea.

Zeina told me, after visiting France a few times to see a psychiatrist, that the doctor told her the issue came down to a memory of the day she was penetrated by the flesh knife. She admitted that she felt better shortly after that, because it turned out the pain was psychological and not physical, despite its clear physical symptoms.

With the exception of these unplanned moments, the cohabitors on Rue des Orangers in Le Bardo were drifting apart, each on a different path.

2

Aamm Hassan advised Abdel Nasser to befriend Hammadi, the newspaper designer, if he wanted to learn the most important part of the newspaper industry. He already knew that journalism wasn't limited to writing articles. The stages that followed editing were also important. So he wanted to learn how to design and print a newspaper. Hammadi was an artist and an alcoholic, living by himself after his wife deserted him (for unknown reasons, he claimed). He refused to divorce her. Many stories were woven around his life that Abdel Nasser had heard from journalists and technicians at the press. All said that only he could make the newspaper come off the press in a polished form—if he wanted—or else an unsuitable one. He was, as Aamm Hassan said, moody and didn't care for gossip. He always carried a bottle of Boukha spirits in the pocket of his dirty jacket, sipping from it while he worked. All feared him and loved him, either out of pity or in recognition of his skill and impressive artistry.

El-Talyani later found out that he was a graduate of the Institut Supérieur des Beaux-Arts de Tunis or, rather, that he had studied there for two years before leaving after a disagreement with one of the art professors. Hammadi was known for his skill and rare talent. He could picture a face or a position or situation quickly and could pour it onto the paper in one sitting, and it always came out identical to the original. He could take one look at a face, close his eyes for a moment, take a pencil—or anything that could draw lines and circles, even just a piece of coal—and transfer the image in his mind to the paper with precision.

The art professor had been jealous of him and always tried to demean his work. The students were aware of it. While grading, the professor gave one of Hammadi's third-year exam sketches—which he finished in five minutes, though the allotted time was four hours—a failing grade. Hammadi did not lose his temper, but spoke with the professor calmly, requesting an explanation. The professor told him, "I am not obliged to justify the grades I give."

Hammadi went to the director, but he stood by the professor on the grounds of academic freedom and the authority of the professor, whose only judge and censor can be their conscience. Hammadi asked him to look at the sketch and grade it, as he had been a professor at the institute before becoming director. The suggestion was rejected. He asked to request the opinion of the department chair; the director refused again. He asked for a committee of other professors chosen by the director but was refused. So he burst into the exam room, finding the professor leaning over a female student from the back on the pretext of correcting her sketch. She was a student that everyone knew was guaranteed to pass her exams, even if she drew the sketch in the air or with her lipstick. Hammadi grabbed the professor by his shoulder and told him exactly what he thought of him. He spat in his face, then punched him hard enough to blacken his right eye. Then he calmly sauntered from the classroom.

Contrary to his nature, Hammadi took to Abdel Nasser from their first meeting. After almost a week of Abdel Nasser sitting with him, learning about what to do with the articles before laying them out on the large newspaper sheet, Hammadi began to teach him the secrets of the profession. He proceeded step by step. He warned Abdel Nasser to follow the steps and not try to jump ahead too quickly. He should not simply imitate Hammadi; everyone had their own style. Design, as he explained, was a taste and an art, not rigid rules. He told him that he would teach him the rules of designing this insipid newspaper, but he would also teach him visual possibilities not represented in Tunisian newspapers. He told him about papers like *Libération*, *Le Monde*, and *Le Figaro*: "Every newspaper has its own personality in terms of fonts and colors and the way it plays with white space over the sections and articles. They all talk about *Libération*, but they haven't discovered the beauty of the other two."

He started by teaching him how to quantify the articles and their sizes, simple rules that could be used even before the article was typed. "The average number of words in the line multiplied by the number of lines gives you an idea about size. You'll eventually understand the differences caused by font size and number of columns. This is how spaces should be calculated between columns and the top and bottom margins, and the way papers are prepared before you even start thinking about the visual content of a page. You'll learn from experience which are the permanent columns and which pages don't change, as well as which pages vary in content but not design, with rare exceptions. What we do is like laying tracks for the railroad, except that the designer also has to place the trains and organize the timetables."

Within a short period of time, Abdel Nasser had started to master the secrets of the newspaper pages, titles, and columns, the general distribution of content and the different maneuvering tricks. Hammadi was surprised by his intelligence and how quickly he learned. He started dividing up the pages with him, starting with the service and obituary pages, then the ad pages, and then the sports and culture pages. When he was certain of Abdel Nasser's mastery, he gave him the front page and back page. No one was able to distinguish between Abdel Nasser's designs and Hammadi's.

After almost a month, their relationship had grown strong. Abdel Nasser was like a studious pupil, and Hammadi decided to teach him some other things that "our insipid newspapers," as he called them, did not use. They were working together so seamlessly that Hammadi would prepare the day's paper in the ordinary design, with astonishing speed, while Abdel Nasser would prepare the same content in the style of *Le Figaro* one day, *Le Monde* another, and *Libération* another.

Abdel Nasser surprised his new friend and mentor one day with a new design he hadn't thought of before. Hammadi had left him alone, working in a corner, and when Abdel Nasser finished his work, he showed it to him. Hammadi's eyes sparkled, and he asked, "Is this something you saw or your own creation?"

"I followed the design of a German newspaper," Abdel Nasser responded.

"Great," he said, patting his shoulder and smiling like a teacher seeing his favorite student excel. "I hope one day you'll be able to launch a newspaper and keep artistry and skill from dying in this country, in spite of the philistines."

Aamm Hassan, to whom Hammadi expressed his admiration for Abdel Nasser, endeavored to show him the rest of the publication process. He was respected by all the newspaper employees, considered a kind of protective father. He defended them against the journalists' arrogance and the management's oppression; he was the one who always made sure they were paid for their extra hours and that they received what they were due. They had no need for a union: Aamm Hassan was union, Constitutional Party branch, and Technical Department head all rolled into one. A strange mix given all the different missions, but functioning in absolute harmony.

One day, he told Abdel Nasser, "I heard that you don't like the party. Well, I don't like it either, but I won't abandon it to the bootlickers and collaborators. I took this leadership role to protect my workers, but I know I'll never get anything out of it. These politicians want to ride on our coattails to better positions, and what do we ever have to show for it? I don't go to their meetings, and even the membership dues are paid by the management." He chuckled, "So we get protection without wasting a penny. Suckers."

3

The president and editor-in-chief had long dreamed of launching a weekly cultural and literary supplement but had never found the right person. Until Abdel Nasser. He sold him the idea by telling him that the conflict with the reactionaries was not only at the security level but also on the level of enlightenment and openness to international thought and literature. Abdel Nasser asked him if this idea had come from the party or the palace and Si Abdel Hamid scoffed. He told him that the palace, the entourage, and the party didn't care about anything but the front page and the ministers' activities. If they found the time, they might sometimes read the social news and skim through the pages looking for news that might cause trouble, like the bad news about Baganda on the sports page. As far as the officials were concerned, the newspaper consisted of only two pages: the front page—the section at the top the most important, as it was designated for the Supreme Warrior's glorious activities—and the editorial, which reflected government policy; the rest was just filling. No, he explained to him, this supplement was his own passion project, born of a love for literature and a desire to properly make use of Abdel Nasser's skills. Also out of his faith that our intellectuals and academics deserved their own pages, to get them out of the rut of over-used language. He asked him to make the supplement rich, serious, and unabashedly high-brow.

Abdel Nasser felt the weight of the responsibility. Where would he get the time to prepare the concept and start gathering the necessary content? Their conversation took place in late May 1987, with the supplement due to be launched shortly before the start of the new academic year; they agreed on the beginning of September.

Abdel Nasser bought many foreign newspapers, almost all the ones that were available in Tunisia, as well as the available French literary magazines. He chose black and blue as the two permanent colors in the supplement, especially the blue that would distinguish the name of the supplement—*Literary Notebooks*—and he chose the logo, which Hammadi had designed with a magical touch. He determined the different kinds of headlines and pull quotes to insert to break up the text in the absence of photos, to attract readers' attention to the essentials. He consulted Aamm Hassan about the fonts available for primary and secondary headlines and for emphasized text and the main body of the supplement. He chose a distinctive font, different from the main paper's: he wanted to make it a newspaper within a newspaper. He worked hard for an entire month.

He was focused on the artistic personality of his supplement; at the same time, he relied on his network of acquaintances among journalists, francophone writers, and academics whose research he had covered to select good articles. He made an agreement with Si Abdel Hamid that writers would be paid for their contributions to the supplement and that, for the house journalists, it would be considered extra work, with special compensation that he had negotiated with the editor-in-chief. Abdel Nasser himself would receive special pay of 200 dinars for every supplement he published.

The offer was profitable, as far as Abdel Nasser was concerned, and there was nothing left but to start working on it. He prepared the sample edition in mid-July as a prototype for the editor-in-chief to look at. Si Abdel Hamid was impressed with the tasteful and beautiful design and the high quality of the content. He knew that Abdel Nasser had, as expected, come up with the editorial policy and artistic design of the supplement, as well as executing it, all by himself. He started flipping through the four pages of the supplement, as if wanting more. He moved the large double paper away and opened the middle two pages on his desk. He looked carefully at them, then returned to the front and back. He noted the symmetry and parallelism that Abdel Nasser had added to the design, as well as some dynamic elements. Suddenly, he exclaimed to Abdel Nasser, "I'm not going to publish it like this!"

He was silent for a moment—that seemed an eternity for Abdel Nasser—before laughing and continuing, "I want a permanent quarter-page column on the right side of the last page entitled 'Mirrors of Ink,' a title I'm borrowing from a book I quite like."

Abdel Nasser acceded. "The editorial that deals with a

current literary issue, in Tunisia or elsewhere, is also yours. I will suggest the topic, and it will be under your name."

"No," Si Abdel Hamid responded. "My future is behind me; this is your project. It was my idea, but I want to highlight your work—your byline on the editorial is more important than mine."

"That's very generous."

"It's nothing. I don't want to steal the credit for all your effort. You'll write the editorial in your own name, and at the bottom of the back page you'll put 'Supplement prepared by Abdel Nasser A.'"

"But that will upset the editorial secretary and my other colleagues. It might create problems we don't need."

"To hell with them—let them drink sea water. They complain about censorship and about Abou Saoud, but they don't realize that there are many openings; the cracks in the building are wide."

4

During this period, Zeina finished writing her thesis. Her advisor read it and was impressed. There was nothing left but the introduction and the conclusion. So she finished her thesis, and he finished his supplement, and there was nothing left for them but the printing.

Zeina's new friend Najla had a cousin who was working as a secretary at a law office; she was a nice girl and a skilled typist. The office wasn't open in the afternoon during the summer, but the young secretary would return to the office in the evenings, with the lawyer's permission, to type up documents on the office's modern IBM electric typewriter. She made a deal with Zeina to type the thesis transcript for 500 millimes per page, a pittance considering her level of mastery and how few typos she made. She did it for the sake of her cousin Najla and to save up some extra money. She hadn't done typing for anyone but the lawyer, so she hoped it would be an opportunity to bring in more typing projects on the side. She was typing between eight and twelve pages a day and so was able to finish the project before the end of July. Abdel Nasser had suggested hiring one of the typists at the newspaper, but Zeina preferred Najla's cousin. He didn't argue with her, even though Aamm Hassan could have gathered a team of five typists and had the work finished in a few days. In truth, he was glad that Zeina relied on herself because she was under a lot of pressure and would have held him responsible for any typographical errors.

Because of the stress she was under and her unrealistic expectations of perfection, Zeina's never-ending editing, revising, additions, and corrections led to an argument with Najla's cousin. She had asked her to retype some pages in their entirety, on account of a paragraph she wanted to add or delete or rewrite while revising the work. The typist asked her to identify all the changes she wanted and mark them on the pages in a different color, so that she could correct them all at once. Zeina blew up and treated the girl like some kind of typing slave who had nothing to do in life but type up this great research that would change the history of philosophy. Abdel Nasser saw that she was foundering but left her alone since she hadn't asked for help. But in the second half of August, after the house became an interminable mass of nerves, he took the manuscript from her and promised to bring it back fully ready in three days.

Abdel Nasser fulfilled his promise, but Zeina's anxiety did not abate. The stage of making enough copies of the research had arrived. She was required to submit five copies, but she wanted ten. Then she brought up the matter of the cover. Abdel Nasser took care of it, preparing a hardback cover that was beyond anything she could have dreamed up. He designed it himself and supervised the bookbinding. She did not feel at ease until she submitted her thesis in August. Then she was anxious again, waiting for the defense. She was like a woman who had just given birth trying to come to terms with the void in her womb, touching her abdomen and feeling its distension but troubled by the raw emptiness.

5

On Thursday, September 3, 1987, the newspaper came out with the first *Literary Notebooks* supplement inside it, confirming that the young man with the Italian features, who had started as just a proofreader and writer working by the article, was now a journalist capable of overseeing an entire supplement. Malicious tongues immediately began to wag about "the editor-in-chief's friend." *It's obvious he's a relative of so-and-so minister and the minister of information was asked to take care of him . . . So the government newspapers have finally been reduced to granting concessions to left-wing extremists,* c'est la vie *. . . Literature and novels, blah blah blah, just what our journalism needs. What a waste of space. This supplement is only good for wrapping vegetables and fish; the design is showy, but the content is vacuous.*

All this gossip reached Si Abdel Hamid, and he made a show of laughing at it in front of Abdel Nasser and the rest of the attendees of a dinner party that included the editorial secretary and some of the writers who had contributed to the first issue. The party was in honor of Abdel Nasser and everyone who had participated in the supplement. He repeated what he had heard—sometimes through hints and sometimes directly—and concluded, "All of this just confirms the success of the supplement and your personal success. You know that in Tunisia we're very good at destroying beautiful things, at chopping down any stem that dares to rise too high. Isn't that right, Si Lotfi?"

He had addressed his remark to all of the attendees but directed the last part to Lotfi S., the editorial secretary. Si Lotfi answered him with a nod of approval, of course. The next time the editor-in-chief and Abdel Nasser happened to meet, he told him that he had deliberately singled out Lotfi with his remark because he was the one who had called him a left-wing extremist. And he would report him to those responsible for showing loyalty and reporting all they heard. He reassured Abdel Nasser that they were all cowards and that he shouldn't care what they said. He explained that they were jealous not only because of his success, but because they knew they themselves were incapable of doing what he did, especially in such a short period of time. "I wouldn't put anything past them," he told him, "but I know you're smart and will outwit their schemes and conspiracies."

A few weeks after launching the supplement, Abdel Nasser received a special thanks from the board of directors, officially delivered by the editor-in-chief. The financial report for the last three months had been presented; it showed an increase in newspaper sales on Thursdays, which the attendees attributed to the new product. The board members requested the creation of more new supplements, one for every day of the week, hoping that that would increase sales and so raise the com pany's profile.

Si Abdel Hamid rushed to hold a meeting with the editorial secretary, the section editors, and Abdel Nasser. He opened the meeting with the board members' suggestion. He also praised Abdel Nasser's work and explained his presence in the meeting as allowing them to learn from his experience with *Literary Notebooks*. He asked the attendees to present their proposals and plans for how they might be executed.

The attendees exchanged looks, hesitating. Si Abdel Hamid noticed their silence and started to call on them, one after the other. Lotfi, who was on his right side, seemed enthusiastic for the project and ready to make it happen. He was an obedient man: if he'd been asked to launch a daily newspaper with a thousand pages, he would have done it. He was an expert at being on the side of the group, whether they were right or wrong. Then the section editors spoke, expressing their willingness, but following that with a litany of excuses: they were already short of journalists, and three or four journalists would be needed for every supplement, to help the person in charge. They set impossible conditions, as if they had been asked to edit articles for *Le Monde* in half an hour.

Si Abdel Hamid was smiling in agreement, which encouraged the attendees to go on with their justifications. Abdel Nasser, sitting to the left of the editor-in-chief, was the last to speak. He decided deliberately not to answer to what the others had said, since it was not his responsibility. He suggested releasing the sports supplement on Sunday and Monday. He thought it was basically already there, it just needed to be made more visible with its own artistic personality. Tuesday could be for the economy and Wednesday for regional issues. As for Friday, Abdel Nasser thought it should be for the youth and their concerns, while Saturday would work well for a diverse cultural and artistic supplement. Since Thursday was already designated for literature, that would cover every day of the week. He added another suggestion: a monthly newspaper with a selection of in-depth articles, reports, and interviews developed from what was published in the daily newspaper and its supplements.

They looked at him as if he was from another planet. He ignored the difficulties and obstacles that they had listed and instead started laying out plans—grinding the flour of his ideas, kneading the dough, and baking bread on the spot.

Si Abdel Hamid ended the meeting abruptly, repeating his welcome to all the attendees and stating that this was only the first meeting. He asked the section editors to consult with their journalists and submit written proposals before the next meeting. They left, looking askance at Abdel Nasser.

A few days later, Si Abdel Hamid told Abdel Nasser that he was happy with the outcome of the meeting. "No one will say a word now. I gave them the opportunity to work and evolve, but they're incapable of taking advantage of it."

"The project will fall apart, then?"

"Who said there was a project?" Si Abdel Hamid replied. "Do you think the board of directors cares about supplements? I was laughing to myself when you talked about a supplement for the youth. Do our youth have concerns? Not at all, Si Abdel Nasser! You were talking about regional issues— what's wrong with our regions? Development there is good; we've brought them into modern Tunisia despite their tribalism! What do we care about art and culture? We're a serious and hard-working people. You might as well ask for a political supplement . . ."

"I almost did."

"If you had, you would have proved that you don't understand a thing. What is our fearless party doing? Well, it's working day and night for the country's politics, with the Supreme Warrior's leadership. The country's politics are explained in the editorials; what more do you want?" He added, "Anyway, none of them will present the vision that you asked for."

6

As Abdel Hamid spoke, his words dripped with bitter sarcasm. He cursed the day he chose journalism and the day he'd been appointed editor-in-chief. He told Abdel Nasser that he had received offers from Agence France-Presse to oversee its Tunis office. But accepting them might be considered a kind of treason, scorning the honor bestowed upon him by Bourguiba himself to jump into bed with foreigners. He often thought about intentionally making some mistake, something that would rid him of his shackles, but he felt he lacked the courage for that. Especially now that the political conditions and increase in Islamist violence didn't allow for any blunders.

"If you stay at the newspaper for a while, I'll suggest your name to them."

"Them who?" asked Abdel Nasser.

"Agence France-Presse, of course! Do you think they would appoint a left wing extremist as head of a government paper? Are you nuts?"

He spoke to him, one friend to another, about how difficult it had been to officially appoint him as a journalist at the paper. Abdel Nasser's folder at the interior ministry was like tar. If not for a close friend of his in the political police, it would have been difficult to convince the upper circles that he should be hired. He'd promised this friend that they would invite him to dinner with them one day, as long as Abdel Hamid promised not to reveal the secret in front of Abdel Nasser. "I know that he defended you more than you defended yourself. I didn't understand at the time why he was so enthusiastic about you the second he heard your name, but, actually, you're in his debt."

"I'm in your debt for your faith in me—"

"Forget about my faith in you; you won that the day we argued about that grammatical error. But you should know, my friend, that it was this officer's reports that were decisive. Do you understand?"

The political police officer was Si Othman. They met by coincidence a few days later, as the two journalists were leaving a restaurant. Si Othman was heading into the same restaurant, accompanied by two men wearing suits and ties. Abdel Nasser later found out that they were security office acquaintances of Si Abdel Hamid. Si Othman greeted Abdel Nasser with a "Hello, neighbor!"

He was surprised. Si Othman greeted Si Abdel Hamid with kisses on both cheeks, and Abdel Nasser realized, from the greetings, that Si Abdel Hamid knew the other two officers, as well. The four of them noticed his confusion. Then Si Othman asked him, jokingly, "How's the teacher doing?"

"She's well," Abdel Nasser responded.

"As long as you have the teacher at home and the editor-in-chief at work, I have no doubt that you'll do well. Right, Si Abdel Hamid?"

Si Abdel Hamid launched into a soliloquy of praise for Abdel Nasser. He reiterated his gratitude to Si Othman for his help, meaning his security clearance report that allowed el-Talyani to join the newspaper.

Si Othman leaned toward Abdel Nasser and said in his ear, "I only did what my conscience and duty dictated. Don't pay any attention to Si Abdel Hamid. Think of me like you do your brother Salah Eddine. Don't hesitate to ask for anything you need, no strings attached. I know your worth."

He didn't respond, but he smiled at him. He remembered all of Si Othman's favors . . . Manouba. El Gorjani. The danger of assassination facing him and Zeina. The clearance report. His exit visa for the Switzerland trip. And, now, discovering the role he'd played in getting him his job.

7

Two days before the supplement was published, an insured letter from the university administration arrived in Zeina's mailbox at the Bab Mnara post office, informing her that her thesis defense was scheduled for Wednesday, September 16, in

Salah Garmadi Hall. Initially, she was overjoyed, but she quickly sank back into her usual stress. Writing two or three pages to introduce her research to the committee, as her advisor had requested, became a crisis that required iron nerves from Abdel Nasser. She showed him a new draft every day to get his opinion. In the beginning, he would be interested in what she was saying, and then—because she insisted that he offer critiques—he would start critiquing everything. He humored her with what she wanted to hear, but she only got more anxious. Every time he sat down to listen to the oral presentation of her latest draft, it ended in a quarrel. He asked her to find someone else to listen. She got angry and said that he had never helped her, never. He reminded her of what he'd done for her. He pointed out her excessive anxiety. Finally, on the Monday two days before the defense, she invited Najla to come listen to the rehearsal. She asked Abdel Nasser to be sure and come home early on that fateful day.

The living room furniture was new. Abdel Nasser had bought it. He had started bringing something new home every month, at first just to make the house look acceptable, like other people's houses, and then later to add more style and comfort. He purposefully decided not to buy a desk, so Zeina continued to work at the kitchen table. She probably wouldn't have bought a desk anyway; she sometimes said, in moments that revealed the less practical side of her brain, "This table is good luck—I'm never getting rid of it!"

Abdel Nasser, intentionally trying to irritate her, would answer, "Unless Raeef comes to take it back, since his father's money paid for it!"

"Never!" she would answer. "I would offer him double its price for it to stay here; it's my table."

On that day, that particular day, he saw Najla as he had never seen her before. He noticed her crescent eyebrows and found himself drawn to her long, curly lashes. The blackness of her eyebrows and eyelashes contrasted pleasantly with her bright, honey-colored eyes. Clear forehead, smooth cheeks. She was tall and fit, shaped by the volleyball she played for Zitouna and that she had continued to play as a hobby, even after becoming a PE teacher at the Institut Supérieur du Sport et d'Education Physique. She was older than Zeina by six or seven years but, in contrast to her philosopher friend, dressed fashionably in her athletic clothes from the best international brands. Her hair was long and straight, shining from (as el-Talyani figured) the aromatic oils she used. She wore a distinctive perfume that filled any room she was in. Her eyebrows were carefully shaped, and her skin was luminous with creams and lotions, which no doubt preserved the youthfulness of this sculpted diamond at her brightest. In Najla, el-Talyani saw the embodiment of love of life and spontaneity.

He had seen her before, briefly, but that day Zeina allowed him to really contemplate her. Zeina read, over and over, like a bewildered schoolgirl reciting memorized poems and trying not to mess up. She read from the paper the first time without lifting her head, then the second time like a news anchor reading the news bulletin. Then she informed her audience (made up of only her husband and the colleague who had become her only friend) that she would memorize the text after it was ready. But the interesting thing about this not-so-fun reading party was that Najla's and el-Talyani's eyes met more than once. He noticed that she was looking at him admiringly, with a slight smile that she quickly hid to look back at Zeina, busy with her paper, checking to see if she had noticed her looking at him. El-Talyani, on the other hand, was familiar with Zeina and her state of mind when she played the philosopher who would save philosophy in Tunisia from sudden death, so he kept his gaze trained on Najla. Instead of looking away, he licked his lips—which flustered her—and lightly bit his lower lip, turning her confusion into complete bewilderment. Clearly he was trying to lure her into his snare. She pretended to be serious at first and stopped looking at el-Talyani, who was sitting directly across from her. He didn't care what she did, but just kept watching her while she kept her wide beautiful eyes as far away from him as possible.

When Zeina finished her first rehearsal, Abdel Nasser applauded hypocritically. He'd hardly heard a word she said. To better understand the content of her presentation, he asked her to read it again, slower, on the pretext of timing her.

He looked at Najla. He moved closer to her. He picked up her hand to look at her watch and verify that it was in sync with his. In the skillful combination of the firmness with which he grasped her hand and the tenderness when he let it go, he told her all he wanted to say. She didn't move, as if she had understood nothing.

8

When Zeina had finished, Abdel Nasser recommended adjustments to some of the long sentences to make them clearer for the listeners. Then it was time for Najla to go home. She lived nearby, on one of the small streets off of Boulevard du 20 Mars in Le Bardo. It was around seven-thirty, and Abdel Nasser insisted that she couldn't walk home alone so late. The state of the country wasn't stable. He suggested to Zeina, knowing that she wouldn't accept, that they both accompany Najla home. Strangely, Zeina actually accepted el-Talyani's proposal, but she only made it as far as the front door before remembering that she had to prepare a new lesson for the morning.

He noticed a look of relief on Najla's face and knew that she had understood what was behind his suggestion. He asked her first for her address, the address of her father's house, which she had gone back to after her divorce. When she headed for a shortcut, el-Talyani asked her to take another way. She didn't object. To make sure his intentions were perfectly clear, he said, "Unless you want to get rid of me as soon as possible, that is."

She shot him a flirtatious look and got directly to the point: "I just hope you don't get rid of *me* quickly out of fear of your wife!"

"That's an insult, but from you I'll take it with pleasure."

His hands were in his jacket pockets. He extended his arm a bit for her to take it. She understood his intention and moved closer to him. "We met months ago," he said. "Why did we waste all this time?"

"You didn't make a move. I've wanted to . . . be your friend since I first saw you. But I wasn't getting anything from you." She added, laughing, "You were a faithful husband."

She asked him to hurry a bit so they wouldn't arouse Zeina's suspicions. Then she said, with a boldness he didn't expect, "We're playing with fire. If you decide to enter the flames with me, you'd better not stop halfway."

El-Talyani tried to wax philosophical: he told her that not everything in life was mutually exclusive. To every flower its own fate and its own luck—he wouldn't confuse their colors but would instead give each one what it deserved.

She answered him with more practicality: "Think of it however you want, but I don't want any problems for either of us. Just be cautious, and I'll be even more cautious than you."

All that was left was to cross a busy street filled with careening cars and buses. She asked him to leave her there, then leaned in and kissed him on the cheek with trembling lips. He closed his eyes, feigning a sort of trance. He gave her a kiss— a better kiss—on her cheek and told her, "You smell amazing . . . And that was such a sweet kiss."

"Okay," she said. "That's enough." Then, with a final squeeze of his hand, she rushed to cross the street.

9

I'm not going to lie to you, the day Zeina defended her master's thesis, I noticed something between el-Talyani and Najla. I noticed because, to be honest, Najla was quite attractive. Once you noticed how beautiful her figure was, you couldn't take your eyes off her. El-Talyani, too, had stayed fit despite all his drinking, smoking, and staying up late. None of that had affected his attractiveness and vitality. They were like two models who'd escaped from an advertisement and were suddenly standing in front of you; you couldn't help but get lost in their charms. But the attraction between them was more than simple kindness. At least, that's what it seemed like to me. I denied it at first, even though I knew el-Talyani's recklessness. I wasn't judging them based on ethical reasons, even though my personal ethics were still deeply rooted, unaffected by the moral relativism philosophy called for. I realized, after thinking about what I'd seen, that I was caught between two fires. One was the fire of my friend, the bright philosopher who could maybe have been mine if I weren't such a coward with my family. To me, she wasn't just any woman. I was jealous. I worried about how el-Talyani's new madness might affect her. I'd always known that though she seemed strong, she was unbelievably fragile; her outward appearance of strength actually concealed ingrained weakness. The other fire was my radical rebel of a friend, who rejected all limits to his freedom, in his personal life, his views of society and its conventions, and his political choices. I had thought that his marriage to Zeina would allow him to perfect his revolution, moving away from the realm of ideas and ideals and leaving the muck of university politics behind. I'd thought that he would find his personal salvation with this exceptional woman who could guide the sweeping flood of his ideas.

The discussion that day was very articulate. The committee members praised the subject, the new approach, and Zeina's extensive knowledge of Hannah Arendt's work. They also commended the precision of the methodology and her full command of the concepts, as well as the ways she'd overcome their difficulties. One of the most memorable and influential moments in the discussion was the opening remarks of the committee chair. She was a professor known as "Thatcher the Philosopher" to her students, who also nicknamed her the Iron Lady. She mainly taught graduate students, in addition to holding some academic administrative responsibilities. No one could argue with her; everyone was impressed by her great knowledge but lived in fear of her strictness, which abolished any human aspect in the relationship between the students and professors. When the Iron Lady took the floor, she said, in her husky voice and beautiful, precise French, "I would first like to express my regret, my deep regret, because today I am sad." She paused with emotion, and the attendees in the late Salah Garmadi's namesake hall at the Faculté 9 Avril held their breath, thinking she was going to destroy Zeina's research.

She continued. "My regret is that I did not take part in mentoring you, *mademoiselle*, because you are among those students who make their teachers proud. And my sadness is because we encounter a student like you only every five or ten years. I would like to congratulate you on your work and wish you *bonne continuation* on this path. You will have great influence in the world of philosophy in our country and the world— yes, the world—provided you keep up this work."

At these emotional words, the attendees broke out in applause, and I saw Zeina's eyes welling up. But the applause angered the Iron Lady, who yelled into the microphone in front of her for the audience to keep quiet and show due respect for the committee. She reminded them that the university was not a theater or a soccer stadium and threatened to expel them. The atmosphere got tense; everyone there knew what this woman was made of.

The discussion lasted for two hours. After the committee returned from its deliberations, Zeina received her grade: passing with honors.

Abdel Nasser was in a rush. He suggested that Zeina, Najla, and I meet him at Restaurant Carthage to celebrate his brilliant wife's grand success. He asked me to accompany them home, then rushed to take a final look at the supplement that was to be published the next day. We were all meeting back up at 8:30 P.M.

10

At the restaurant, I became sure that there was something between el-Talyani and Najla. I sat on his right; Zeina was across from him on my left. So Najla was directly in front of me. Abdel Nasser nearly monopolized the conversation, talking about the supplement and the political situation. He asked about how things were at my work and told a lot of jokes whose topics varied from politics to sex. He was drinking like a sponge. Zeina, on the other hand, looked exhausted. It didn't seem like she was enjoying her success: the few words that she contributed to the conversation at the restaurant were about her concerns for her future plans, now that the research was done. Deadlines for the *agrégation* courses and exams, the delay of the new class schedule, her fear of translation from German and the mathematical logic and linguistic philosophy classes. Abdel Nasser stopped her with a firm order. "That's enough, Zeina. You're always busy with school. Today's a day off, so let's celebrate your success. Today is for drinking, tomorrow can be for philosophy."

She was obliged to stop talking. It seemed that the first two glasses of wine had had a strong effect on her, and she was dozing off. I was focused on Abdel Nasser but occasionally snuck glances at Najla. She was turned toward the star of the night, my friend el-Talyani, while he spoke. Her gaze was admiring, following his words and hand gestures. She didn't smoke or drink; Abdel Nasser tried to lure her with a drink, but she declined. He ordered her a glass of pastis, telling her that it was sweet and flavored with anise: delicious, but doesn't go to your head. In the end, she seemed to agree because she ordered a second one.

Abdel Nasser told her, "I'm responsible for the first glass, but the second is on you. Fair warning—though I would love to see you drunk."

She answered him flirtatiously, "The most important thing is that I make it home. With you." Then, as if remembering that Zeina was next to her and might understand the sentence in more than one way, she added, addressing her, "Would you mind having me as a guest tonight?"

Zeina pulled herself back from her wandering state, looking exhausted as she answered, "No . . . no, of course not."

Abdel Nasser joked that Najla would need to be ready for any emergency and not blame him if he said or did anything to her that she didn't approve of. He was a sleepwalker, see, and would walk and talk in his sleep without realizing it. Najla answered, "You don't need to worry about that; I'm a heavy sleeper. Very. You could bring in a king's choir, and I still wouldn't wake up before I got my full eight hours."

He answered, in a tone that mixed seriousness and wit, "My type of choir is different. It lifts you up to the seventh heaven and keeps you from sleeping."

The table fell silent as everyone searched for an interpretation of Abdel Nasser's words. Zeina finally said, playfully, "Behave yourself, Abdu."

I broke in with a comment addressed to Najla, "My friend is dangerous; he's his own special breed of sleepwalker."

Najla just smiled.

11

I have no doubt that Zeina slept well that night. She was reassured when Abdel Nasser insisted on sleeping in the living room, leaving his place in the bed for Najla in spite of her protests.

Abdel Nasser woke up early. He bought breakfast for them: pastries, yogurt, and juice. He got milk and fruit out of the refrigerator and boiled four eggs. He made coffee.

As their guest got ready to leave, Zeina went to grab her purse and wallet. Abdel Nasser took advantage of his wife's absence to whisper to Najla, "I'm going back to bed, to smell your scent on the sheets." He pinched her lower lip with his right hand and winked at her.

For almost two weeks, Zeina did nothing but teach and sleep, as if making up for all the late nights of fatigue and exhausting mental work. The *agrégation* courses were set to start in mid-October, but she had already begun gathering sources and making hard copies of whatever was not available in libraries or bookstores.

One Friday, she decided to go visit her family, specifically her mother. She bought a number of gifts for the family. It was a long weekend, three full days and nights that he was meant to spend alone. He took her to the minibus station at Bab Saadoun on Thursday evening. He offered the driver 20 dinars and asked him to take her all the way to her house, so she could avoid taking overcrowded rural public transport, especially since she had heavy luggage.

Abdel Nasser, meanwhile, lived the long weekend as a new groom. He rented a car and booked a room at one of the resorts in Hammamet.

12

Najla was older than Abdel Nasser by a year or two. During their discussions over the two days (Friday evening, Saturday, and Sunday morning), he learned more about her divorce. She had married one of her relatives from a rich family. Her mother had insisted that she marry him, especially because a lot of men were asking for Najla's hand, and she kept refusing them. She was the oldest daughter of parents who, unfortunately, had only had girls. Five beautiful girls that her mother, as she used to say, always feared would bring heartache. She also used to say, "It's better to be pretty than stunning; men fear true beauties as much as they want them. They are toys that they'll abandon quickly."

Najla had never been able to understand what her mother meant by that. But then she only made it through three months of bitterness before she became, in the eyes of the law, a disobedient wife because she left her house to go back to her parents'.

Her husband was a handsome man, polite and well mannered. He had two flaws, though, one clearly visible and the other hidden; she described the latter to no one except her mother and the judge. His visible flaw was his obedience to his mother that bordered on worship. He wouldn't have even threaded a needle without consulting her. She came over anytime she wanted and would start criticizing her. *Why did you leave the dishes on the counter after dinner? The floor here isn't clean. Keep an eye on the maid; open your eyes! Move this piece of art; it would look better in the office. Why are you always half-naked or wearing workout clothes? You're the wife of a respectable man. Blue eyeshadow doesn't suit your eye shape. Your mouth is too big to wear that red lipstick; it makes you look like a whore. My son has lost weight; he must not be eating well. Your future rests on the health of your husband . . .* and so on and so forth with these stupid comments.

The strangest thing was that the husband was happy around his mother; whenever Najla would argue with him, he would answer, "What do you want me to do? She's my mother, and you should consider her yours, as well."

The honeymoon passed bitterly. One beautiful summer morning, about two months after the wedding, they were sleeping in when they heard the doorbell ringing non-stop. They thought at first that it was the maid; then Najla reminded her husband that it was Sunday. He went quickly to open the door, and she heard the voice of her mother-in-law, complaining about them sleeping in. Najla decided to stay in bed, as if unaware that her mother-in-law had arrived. Her husband called her, but she didn't answer. A few minutes later, her mother-in-law invaded the room where she was practically naked. She covered up with the sheets and yelled, "What are you doing? Is not even this room private?!"

Her mother-in-law shouted at her, "The honeymoon's over, get up! We're all going to the village of Raf Raf, to my sister's house."

"I don't want to go anywhere; I want to sleep."

"What? Sleep?! We're a family that likes to spend time together."

"Then consider me *not* one of the family."

"What?" her mother-in-law exclaimed, then recited the proverb, "'He who grasps a finger gets the whole hand.' Now get up and get ready."

Her husband, the mama's boy, interfered, repeating the order his mother had just given in a firm voice.

She looked at him and scoffed, "You go—take your mother with you. I'm going to my father's house. I've been missing him and my sisters."

He told her, "You'll regret this."

She didn't comment. She pulled the sheet over her head and put a pillow on top of it. It was clear that she wasn't going to go with them. She heard him calming his mother down. Then he changed his clothes and left with his mother, slamming the door on the way out.

Najla told her mother what had happened, and she sympathized with her but told her to be wise and to have patience. The man was from a good family, but some mothers were just like that. She warned her against considering divorce and gave her advice on how to deal with such situations in the future—but to no avail. The man was truly a mama's boy.

Najla's visit to her family's house also gave her an opportunity to tell her mother about the secret she had discovered during the honeymoon and had been suffering from for the past two months. She had found out that her husband suffered from delayed ejaculation: he could only come after a long effort that brought her to climax and then left her waiting for him. Often he couldn't come at all. She didn't mind at first, but it had started to leave her with persistent soreness and burning. It felt terrible during intercourse and turned into ceaseless pain afterwards. If not for the ointment prescribed by a Spanish doctor at their Mallorca hotel during their honeymoon, the pain would have either killed her or driven her to suicide.

When she tried to talk to her husband about it, he just laughed. He told her that it was an advantage that other women liked about him—how could she complain that it was a defect? She talked to him gently, trying to convince him to see a specialist after they got back to Tunisia. He refused. The subject became a point of contention between them. It seemed to him that she was trying to avoid fulfilling her spousal duties. She tried to make him understand in every way she could think of, but the gap between them widened. Finally, she had had enough and told him, "I'm not a porn star: you are *hurting* me. Do you understand?"

"Other women wish they could have a man like me."

194 - SHUKRI MABKHOUT

"Then find another wife. Give the both of us a break."

"Are you saying you want a divorce?"

"Yes," she responded, "as long as you refuse to see a doctor."

Two weeks had passed since the honeymoon had ended. She'd seen what he was really like and was put off by both his delayed ejaculation and his mother. She turned a blind eye to his affairs. Her mother told her, before finding out the truth of the matter, "He may wander, but he'll always come home to you at night." She added, "Your father was like him, but look at him now: a pious man who comes home early, sometimes even before his daughters."

13

El-Talyani asked her why she hadn't remarried, so she talked to him at length about her opinion of marriage, even before her bitter experience with the would-be porn star. She explained that marriage, for young women, liberates them from society and its firm restrictions. She knew that. But her divorce showed her that the path to true freedom didn't have to go through a man who would enslave her. She said that a woman's freedom in Tunisia was limited to the freedom to choose your master; it didn't allow you to choose your life.

El-Talyani thought she was exaggerating when she compared herself to her mother's generation. She thought that they had freedom within their social bounds, despite their restriction to the private sphere and the apparent dominance of men. Whereas Najla and her generation were victims of a merciless society that required them to be in the public space as well as the private one, but without any real redistribution of roles. She explained it to him: "Bourguiba gave us a new sort of restriction that we thought was emancipation. But now we're stuck: we can't go back, and if we want to move forward, we're unable to. The house was a small prison, but the street is just a bigger one. One of them is run by a stupid warden with endless demands, a small child spoiled by his mother and probably not even weaned. And the other one is controlled by the assholes who harass women, using aggressive sexual language to scare them into 'behaving' and visibly undressing them with their eyes.

"You don't experience the same kind of nasty violence of eyes and tongues," she added. "It's a violence that's meant especially to destroy us."

El-Talyani provided treatment for what had been destroyed in Najla, as well as for his own neglect by Zeina. He discovered that Najla was shy and deeply modest, contrary to what he'd expected based on her appearance (especially her clothes and the way she took care of herself) and her first conversation with him. She would close her eyes, as if she didn't want to see anything, and she was quick to cover up as soon as they finished. There were no traces of passion or any extraordinary acts in her behavior in bed. She made love like someone performing a biological act: not a sound, not a word, no surprises. It bothered him their first time together that she didn't seem to react to him at all. If not for the erection of her nipples and a single moan of pleasure, he would have thought that she was completely cold.

He spoke with her on the subject and was frank and articulate. After that, her performance on Sunday morning before returning to Tunis seemed to improve quite a bit. Her tongue loosened. She started sometimes opening her eyes. She allowed his hand and his tongue to explore hidden places that were usually tucked out of sight.

"You're a book that would take months to read," he told her.

"Do you want to finish reading it quickly?" she responded. "Are there other books waiting for you?"

"I'm used to reading more than one book at a time."

14

Zeina returned home worried. When she left, her mother had been sick. Her father had gotten old and started to spend most of his time at the local shop playing cards, chatting with the farm workers, and spending his day like an old animal waiting for death. Her brother was unemployed and, if not for his savings from the harvest season, he would have died of hunger, along with his wife and four children. For the first time, she had seen the village with new eyes, how it was in reality. She was shocked: how had she managed to live with them, to grow up and become a teacher in such conditions—conditions that didn't even provide the basic necessities of life?

She came home carrying sad scenes and stories that almost drove her mad. She told him that city dwellers had no idea what the poor villagers and farmers were going through. There had been a long drought, which conspired with the country's preoccupation with the crisis at the palace to grind down the village and make them even more miserable. She felt like a stranger to her family; even the normal clothes that she wore for the trip became a source of shame: she saw them as an act of violence against her family, even though her mother was delighted to see the fruits of her labor. She was happy to see Zeina as a full-grown woman, capable of taking care of not only herself but also her mother and disabled father. She talked to her for a long time about marriage and starting a family, saying, "I want to see you married before I close my eyes forever."

Her mother didn't understand her desire to continue her studies since, in her opinion, finding a husband was the most important thing. Zeina was tongue-tied and couldn't find the words to say to her mother. When she'd been a child and a student, Zeina had been more courageous and convincing, despite the fact that her behavior went against the norms. But now, when she showed tenderness when talking to her mother, her mother decided that she'd matured and needed to get married.

Abdel Nasser, only half-jokingly, quoted the prophet's saying that "Paradise lies under the feet of mothers" and asked her, "Seriously, why don't you tell her about me, about your husband?"

That brought them back to the old discussion about the marriage certificate under duress versus marriage by choice. The game had become clear: it always started with differentiating between the two concepts and ended with an argument about sincere feelings, their visions of their future, one-sided love, and the unrestrained ambition blinding Zeina's judgement. But this time Abdel Nasser struck at the sore spot: "Your life and career are on track. And, by happy coincidence, I have become an established journalist. Why don't we reveal our marriage?"

"You're still singing that old tune," she said. "Give me one more year to finish my *agrégation*. And we're already living as a married couple, anyway."

"I don't think so," Abdel Nasser said. "You're benefiting from a married lifestyle without committing to its duties."

Zeina objected, furiously. Abdel Nasser's words were cruel, especially since she had just come back from her village heartbroken by what she saw and the deteriorating situation of her mother and father. They raised their voices; she accused him of selfishness, willfully misunderstanding her, and pushing her to commit to something she had not chosen. He was trying to crush her future and ambitions, to reduce her to a traditional, enslaved woman. Enslaved, ironically, by the revolutionary activist who left the revolution to work with the regime, acting as a watchdog in one of its ideological mouthpieces, a government newspaper that justified its oppression and exploitation.

Her words were harsh, and it was the first time Abdel Nasser had heard her say anything like that to him. He asked her, protesting, "Are you saying that I'm a traitor?"

"No. I'm saying to stop claiming revolutionary wisdom, integrity, and purity. You're a privileged petit bourgeois, looking after your own interests while being guided by your blueblood *beldi* family. Revolution for you is just a cover; peel it back, and your truth is revealed . . . your reactionary truth!"

He answered back with anger and sarcasm. He told her about her selfishness masquerading as hard work. He said that he'd never seen any of the caring, tenderness, and attention that any true woman—lover, wife, or girlfriend—would show for the person she was sharing her life with. She was too busy with her books, her future career, her research—all at his expense. He said what he didn't want to say: that there was nothing left between them, other than his support for her. He hadn't meant to say that; he felt he'd lost the best of himself and become too hard on her. He concluded, "Think about whether you want to continue living with me. I can't keep quiet anymore. I can't put up with your . . . personality . . . anymore."

She stared at him in shock, as silent and still as a statue. Then she stood quickly; she went into the bedroom and burst into tears. He chose to go outside for some air.

15

The crisis at home worsened when Zeina started attending the *agrégation* courses. She fell back into the habits of her thesis-writing period. They didn't speak to each other, aside from greeting each other like neighbors in the morning and evening and on the few occasions, like Sunday mornings, that brought them together.

Even the gift he gave her for her birthday on October 29

left no special mark in their memories, despite its value. He had received the extra bonus for the supplement he was supervising, a bonus of two months' salary. He asked Najla to choose a bracelet and a necklace for Zeina. Her choices confirmed that she had excellent, and expensive, tastes, so he gave her some extra money to cover them. Najla knew they were meant as birthday presents; she herself had bought Zeina a purse as a gift.

She brought him the bracelet and the necklace. He asked her which she thought was nicer, and she responded that the bracelet was the prettier and more eye-catching of the two. He put the necklace in his jacket pocket and asked her to close her eyes. She understood, despite some misgivings, when she felt him put the bracelet on her right wrist. She was over the moon, and she kissed him warmly, heedless of the other customers in the café. She started admiring the bracelet on her wrist. Suddenly, once she had recovered from the shock of the expensive gift, she asked him, "But didn't you buy this for Zeina? I can't accept it!"

"Who said it's for Zeina?" he replied. "I wanted to give you a gift you'd like, and I couldn't think of a better way to do it."

Najla's gift was sincere, a true gift for a generous woman who never expected anything from him, to the point that—as he recalled—she had tried to pay for the hotel room they'd shared, or at least split the cost. Zeina's gift, on the other hand, was out of duty for the neighbor he lived with.

Hesitantly, el-Talyani told Najla that Zeina had never given him a gift and that he couldn't expect any kind of tenderness or caring from her to make him feel that she loved him the way he loved her.

Najla decided to stop by their home the next day, waiting until Zeina had come back from her evening courses. She arrived while Zeina was in the kitchen preparing dinner and Abdel Nasser was watching television. He had a number of papers scattered in front of him, which he nervously cleared away when Najla arrived. Zeina welcomed her, and Abdel Nasser tried to hide his joy at seeing her.

When Najla gave her the purse, wishing her a happy birthday (followed, of course, by the usual litany of expressions wishing her a long life, et cetera), Zeina hugged her tightly in appreciation, saying that she loved the gift.

Abdel Nasser stared at her in surprise, then interrupted their friendly conversation, saying to Najla, "I'm starting to get jealous of you; my wife was happy with your gift but is never happy with mine."

Neither of them answered, as if they hadn't heard him. After a few moments of silence, Zeina went back to talking with Najla, but Najla interrupted to let her know that she had to leave, since it was getting late—she had just come to drop off the birthday present. Suddenly she asked, "And what did your lovely husband get you?"

"A necklace . . ."

"Did you like it?" Najla asked. "Can I see it?"

"Of course, of course."

Abdel Nasser asked sarcastically, "Of course you liked it? Or of course she can see it?"

She didn't answer him but went to bring the necklace from the bedroom. Abdel Nasser winked at Najla and indicated with a movement of his head that he wanted to accompany her outside.

"It's stunning, Zeina!" Najla exclaimed. To Abdel Nasser she said, "Since you've shown yourself to have such good taste, I'll take this opportunity to officially inform you that *my* birthday is on January 20. You still have plenty of time."

Najla took to examining the necklace, as if seeing it for the first time. She held it against her chest, then stood looking at it in front of the mirror hanging by the front door. She asked Zeina to put it on. She looked at it with admiration on Zeina's chest, then said to Abdel Nasser, "You have to complete your wife's set now. This necklace needs matching earrings and a bracelet!"

"Yes, indeed, Mademoiselle Najla," Abdel Nasser answered. "But after January 20. And after Zeina gets her *agrégation* diploma, so that she'll appreciate its value and enjoy it."

Zeina looked at him askance, then asked him to accompany Najla home, since it was getting quite late. Abdel Nasser jumped, as if he were waiting for that, but made a show of displeasure while putting on his shoes. Najla insisted that there was no need to bother him.

16

Najla walked arm-in-arm with el-Talyani on the road toward Boulevard du 20 Mars. He told her, "You know what? With you on my arm, I feel like I'm floating on a cloud of femininity and tenderness."

"Why?" she asked. "Am I the first woman to hold your arm?"

"You . . . you're the only one I feel this way with."

She looked at him in surprise, then suddenly smiled, saying, "That's only because I'm your new toy."

El-Talyani went on, without responding to her comment. "Seems I've gotten addicted to you . . . But how long can we go on like this? There's got to be a better option."

"You're married, but I'm free. The only restriction I have comes from my worry about you and my relationship with your wife."

"Will you marry me?" he asked.

She laughed out loud.

"I'm serious. I feel very comfortable with you . . ."

"Abdu, listen," she said. "You don't know me."

"I know you."

"I just told you that you don't. If I married every man I liked who liked me, I would've collected a tribe by now." She added, "Don't get angry: I just hate marriage."

"You can't judge things that haven't happened yet based on one bad experience."

"I feel free right now, and I wouldn't have that freedom if I married you. Also, what are you complaining about? I'm available whenever you want. And I like you . . . I'm still enjoying our last date; that kiss I stole from you yesterday at the café is still on my lips."

They arrived at her house. He wanted to kiss her, but she warned him that her sister was watching them from the window. He asked her to visit him tomorrow morning, to call off work if she had to—he missed her. She reminded him that he also had work. He told her that he was trying to finish a report and would be staying home to edit it.

17

Abdel Nasser finished writing his report. Najla came for an hour after Zeina left. Then he went to meet Si Abdel Hamid. He finished the editorial quickly; it was an easy one because the topic was the Supreme Warrior's pet demolition project. The editorial analyzed the human perspective of this decision and its role in improving citizens' living conditions. Proper housing was, after all, one of the Supreme Warrior's top priorities, and he was eager to make it a reality.

After he revised the editorial, he went back to Si Abdel Hamid's office. He proposed that they go out, but to a different restaurant that nobody knew he frequented; he needed to talk to him about a sensitive matter. Despite the professional nature of the meeting, he refused to discuss it at the office: the matter was urgent, and the walls had ears.

Si Abdel Hamid had never seen Abdel Nasser so excited about something he had written; he was clearly anxious and felt that what he was doing was important. Abdel Hamid commented on it: "You remind me of myself when I was young, and had written something I thought was exceptional!"

Abdel Nasser wasn't looking for praise so much as feedback about his writing. He took the five pages that he had written in his small, clear handwriting out of his inner jacket pocket, which was closed with a chain. Si Abdel Hamid took them, saying, "Alright, I'll have a look at them, but I have no doubt that I should send this directly to the printer."

"Slow down, Si Abdel Hamid. Read it please; don't just look at it."

Si Abdel Hamid was smiling as he unfolded the papers. He read "Exclusive," followed by the headline, "Shocking Facts Expose Conspiracy."

Si Abdel Hamid's smile got tighter and tighter until, finally, it disappeared. He looked around at the few other occupied tables at the Italian Circle on L'Avenue de La Liberté. The other customers were mostly foreigners, and his and Abdel Nasser's table, one of the few circular tables in the restaurant, was at the far end of the room.

He had been holding the papers up, but now he put them down on the table and covered them with his hand as he read, like a student hiding his test paper from a cheating classmate. His face paled as he read on. Every now and again, he would lift his head to glance quickly around the restaurant before returning his focus to the text. He read quickly and with visible apprehension. Abdel Nasser was nervous as he awaited the verdict—from the *sayyid* of journalists in Tunisia—on the article he had written.

Si Abdel Hamid then gathered the five pages, folded them, and put them in the inside pocket of his jacket. Reconsidering, he took them back out and handed them to

Abdel Nasser, telling him to put them back where he'd had them. He gulped down the glass of whiskey in front of him and ordered another while Abdel Nasser waited to hear what he had to say. Finally, he said, "Tear up those pages and don't tell anyone about this."

"What? Why?" Abdel Nasser asked. "My information is accurate and verified."

"Do what I say; it's not the time to argue."

For a moment, a heavy silence hung over the table. Si Abdel Hamid was drinking a lot and had hardly eaten anything.

Abdel Nasser wanted to break the thick wall of silence that Si Abdel Hamid had built. He seemed worried, lost in his thoughts, and Abdel Nasser couldn't guess what he was think-ing. He lit a new cigarette from the butt of the previous one. He asked him, "Would you like me to leave you alone?"

He looked at him, then shook his head no. He asked him to change seats to move closer to him. Si Abdel Hamid seemed to take mental note of the people in the restaurant, customers and staff. He asked Abdel Nasser, "Where do you think you are? America? France? Who do you think is going to protect you?"

"But there's nothing against the state in what I wrote," Abdel Nasser protested. "I got all my information from well-informed sources."

"Your sources don't matter. This information is sensitive, and you have no right to use it."

"My sources are trusted people within the security sector. Didn't you tell me that the real journalist is the one who has connections inside the interior ministry but doesn't become a snitch?"

"True," Si Abdel Hamid conceded. "But that's so you know which way the wind is blowing—not so you can stand up naked in a hurricane. There's a big difference. Who's going to protect you now?"

"The journalist tells the truth and acts as a channel for the news; it's a report, not an opinion article."

Si Abdel Hamid smiled mockingly. "Listen, son. There's only one source of truth in Tunisia: the state. And these days, the interior ministry is the state and the state is the interior ministry. No one asked you to take Minister Ben Ali's position. He has the confidence of the Great Leader and doesn't need you to tell him what he already knows. Forget about lies and truth. Also, did you ever think that your sources might be trying to trick you?"

"Impossible. The facts are corroborated from several sides."

"Don't be so sure—nothing's impossible in Tunisia when it comes to the security agencies. Facts can become lies with a single statement from the interior ministry. Quit being delusional."

"Are you saying that what I wrote is false?"

"Why are you still talking about true and false? I'm not talking about the content of what you said; I'm talking about who has the legitimacy to say it. From a professional point of view, it was great, very cautious in presenting the information available to you. Legally, nobody could sue you or the newspaper. Your information would be suitable for even the major foreign magazines and newspapers, but in Tunisia, it would expose you to risks you can't imagine. Plus, I wouldn't publish it in a government newspaper; I *can't* publish it. They don't close our newspapers, they don't confiscate them like they do the independent or opposition papers, but we don't have immunity either. They would confiscate *me*; they would come up with some accusation. And two accusations for you. That's the way it is, son."

"I understand. So we know the truth, but we're not allowed to tell it."

"Almost . . . more like there are truths that shouldn't be told, or that you don't have the right to tell. The facts in this article—*you* don't tell them yourself, but there is someone who has the right to tell them. Obviously."

"Obviously."

The journalist fell silent, as did the editor-in-chief. After a moment, Abdel Nasser resumed, "So should I send it to *Libération* or *Le Monde*?"

"They would love to have you, but I don't advise you to do that. In fact, I forbid you to."

"Why?"

"Basically, you would be accused of spying for a foreign country or selling security secrets. If you want to become a martyr to the cause of a free press—with worldwide support in exchange for a bleak prison cell—then go ahead and do it."

18

The report that el-Talyani wrote was about the arrest of a leader of the Islamic Tendency Movement on October 27, 1987. He wrote it one week after the arrest—nobody had heard about it. Abdel Nasser provided information about the precise facts of the arrest, including the time and the surrounding circumstances, though he'd left out the exact location owing to a gap in his information.

But the most important feature of the article was the clear portrait he drew of this leader: his formation and history, his role in the organization, and his alleged connection with the bombings of hotels in the coastal tourist cities of Sousse and Monastir in August of 1987.

The leader was a math teacher who'd begun reading Muslim Brotherhood texts in high school, among them books by Sayyid Qutb and Abul A'la Maududi, and he'd been the link between the civilians and the militants in the movement, especially after the movement leader's arrest in 1981.

He was a dangerous man, cloaked in mystery. He had carried out many missions through operatives deployed in Paris and Frankfurt. One of these missions was an attempt to smuggle mace bombs into the country in January 1986, to be used against the riot police and inside the universities during conflicts with the leftist students.

He had participated in the movement's secret congress in the town of Sulayman in 1984, after the historic release of their leadership in the wake of the Bread Riots. A document entitled "Intellectual Vision and the Fundamentalist System" emerged from this congress; Abdel Nasser quoted some passages from it to show the violent nature of the movement, which was based on jihad against society.

At this congress, the leader of the movement became emir of the group, as well as president of the executive and political offices, after he removed some of the founders; this dangerous man retained his position. In another special congress—held in the summer of 1986 in El Menzah, after Bourguiba had removed Prime Minister Mohammed Mzali and the Islamists felt that the moment of confrontation with the regime was near—he agreed with many of the other leading figures on a plan called the Alternatives Project.

In his article, Abdel Nasser mentioned the names of the civilians who headed the preparation and execution of the project. It wasn't entirely clear to Abdel Nasser what it involved, but he thought it likely that the explosions in Sousse and Monastir were either part of the Alternatives Project, or of another plot called Preparing the Ground that the movement president had begun working on in August of 1987.

After giving a chronological picture of the chain of events, Abdel Nasser explained that this plan was behind the agitation at universities and high schools as well as the near-daily skirmishes that erupted in multiple places at once. In this way, the arrest of the dangerous man was shown to be part of a larger detention campaign for the public leaders of the movement and the dismantling of their secret networks and sleeper cells.

This wasn't what bothered Si Abdel Hamid. It was clear that these facts were taken from intelligence and security information. He didn't ask Abdel Nasser to reveal his source. He surmised (correctly) that Si Othman had provided at least some of it. There were other facts included in the report, however, that terrified him.

In investigating the bombings of the four hotels in Sousse and Monastir (the two major cities in the coastal Sahel region), Abdel Nasser had uncovered the involvement of the son of one of the Sahel's most prominent politicians. The young man had participated, at the very least, in providing logistics information. Which meant that he was directly involved, either by knowing about the plan and not informing the police, or by actually helping to carry it out. As the son of a prominent party member, no one would ever suspect him. But Abdel Nasser had been able to get information on the existence of secret bank accounts abroad that the politician's son had used to fund the organization.

Si Abdel Hamid focused here on the fact that this accusation had nothing to support it and acquiring proof was beyond his capabilities, as long as the authorities and intelligence agencies had not—to his knowledge—arrested the man. Also, this set off a trail of assumptions whose very consideration was extremely dangerous. One, that the father was not aware of his son's affiliation and political and religious leanings: that was improbable and dangerous in and of itself. Or, that the father was aware but put his paternal instinct above the interests of the state: a catastrophe. The other assumption was that these facts, if true, meant that the regime itself was unsound: the Islamist termites had begun eating away at it from the inside. If they had infiltrated the political body, what would prevent them from next infecting the security body, or the military body? This report, then, would spread terror among people who still hadn't recovered from the unprecedented bombings the country had witnessed. The mere arrest of the Islamic Tendency leaders was not enough to reassure them. The problem, in Si Abdel Hamid's opinion, was that the regime was itself divided over Bourguiba's succession. The conflicts in the palace were at peak intensity, and the Supreme Warrior's niece appeared to be in charge of him. Even the hope of including the Islamists in the political process had evaporated with Mzali's firing.

From Si Abdel Hamid's analysis, Abdel Nasser saw that he'd been hasty regarding the politician's son's involvement in the bombings, even if he was sure there were strong suspicions. His source on that was an Islamist in Sousse with access to a large number of secrets; he wanted to leave the organization but feared for his life. He was also afraid that, because he'd witnessed the movement's violent side, he would be arrested if his name were mentioned in connection to an investigation. He had decided to leave the country, trying not to attract the attention of either the organization or the security forces.

Abdel Nasser surmised that this friend was not entirely honest with him but was actually a spy who had infiltrated the Islamist group unnoticed. He had mentioned this suspicion to Si Othman, who—quite uncharacteristically—rushed to deny that the man had any connection to the security services. In Si Othman's eyes, however, Abdel Nasser observed a kind of apprehension that was at odds with the composure and strength of personality that he'd come to expect from him.

19

Their discussion of the report was a good opportunity for Abdel Nasser to learn that Si Abdel Hamid, contrary to his multiple assurances, was among the journalists, intellectuals, and politicians that had played Mohammed Mzali's card, before his removal and humiliation. He'd heard that from several people but had refused to believe it; today he knew better.

He wanted to gather some more facts about Si Abdel Hamid's positions and so asked him, "So you're one of those people who think the Islamists should be included in the political game?"

Si Abdel Hamid paused a moment to think, then said, "It's too late now. That would require clarification of a lot of things that don't seem like they'll be clear anytime soon. We need a few years of conflict and bloodshed before the Islamists learn the meaning of the state and what it means to defy it. A lot of men will die because of this 'game.' There's no heart or soul to it; all the players want is power. And the state is stronger than any doctrine: the Constitutional Party freed the country, and it's embedded in every town and village, and inside the mind of every Tunisian. We need time for the fruit to ripen, or rot and fall of its own accord. But the state will still be here; the party has at least fifty years left in it."

"So you don't think there will be any change at all in the structure of the state?"

"Look," Si Abdel Hamid replied, "consider the country's history. France left, then Bourguiba built the state with what was left. So far, Bourguiba hasn't used weapons to legitimize his rule; he's used the power of the state and its will. He went through all those crises, starting with the Youssefists, then the Nationalist coup, the Maoists, the leftists. And now, since the Iranian revolution, we're in the Islamists' stage. They won't succeed, either: they might leave their mark, yes, but they won't take power. Change will come from within; Tunisians are not a revolutionary people. Go back to the history: the entire game has been controlled from within the state party since the Bizerte Congress in 1964, with Ben Salah and his group and Mestiri's group, and Achour and the union."

"But times have changed," Abdel Nasser protested. "The structural reform policy has led to disaster. The country's on the brink of bankruptcy, and the World Bank and the IMF are in charge of everything. Attack the union now, and the laborers—

and even the white-collar workers—won't be able to breathe. The situation's a complete catastrophe—it could explode any moment, and the Islamists will be there to ride the wave of revolution."

"Forget the university jargon. There's no revolution or any such nonsense. This is just a temporary price that has to be paid. The Islamists aren't the offspring of our society: they're branches of an international organization, backed by a lot of money to strike at the Tunisian model of government, especially Tunisian nationalism and the gains we've made since independence. They hate us; they hate Bourguiba's modernity. They hate the Code of Personal Status and the freedom that Tunisian women have won. Have you forgotten that they're the offspring of Hassan al-Banna, Sayyid Qutb, and Maududi, all foreign reactionaries? They have no connection to our home-grown Tunisian intellectuals, to Hayreddin Pasha, Tahar Haddad, Echebbi, or the Ben Achours—father or son. They came to us from abroad, just like the Maoists and Trotskyites and Nasserists and Baathists before them, a mix of Egypt's Muslim Brotherhood, the Wahhabism of Ibn Baz in Saudi Arabia, and the Iranian governance of Khomeini."

"But didn't Bourguiba himself come to us from the French models of modernity?!"

"You're comparing two totally different things," Si Abdel Hamid said. "One is an ideology that goes hand-in-hand with the progression of history and is embodied in institutions. The other one is a utopian fantasy of Arab unity or a new Islamic caliphate, embodied outside the national arena in reactionary and authoritarian institutions that oppress humanity and destroy any possibility of us catching up with the rest of the world."

Abdel Nasser gave him his analysis of the Islamist phenomena from a historical–materialist perspective. He considered the group, as he had at university, a product of Tunisia's semi-feudal, semi-capitalist mode of production and the state's inability to fight poverty. As well as, of course, the state's sur-render to international capitalism and imperialism.

He saw the Islamists as an expression of rural impoverish-ment and the ruralification of cities during the Bourguiba era. The social power they represented was a mixture of the ideo-logically conservative segment of the petite bourgeoisie and the rural poor. The former found themselves unable to climb the economic and social ladder to the upper reaches of the petite bourgeoisie. And the latter had been forgotten by the unequal distribution of development, whether in their deprived villages or in the belt of rural migrants surrounding the capital, the result of the "economic opening-up" policies and unfettered liberalism since the early seventies.

Abdel Nasser added to this analysis the political factor that a faction of the Constitutional Party wanted to hurt the Tunisian left. So they encouraged the Islamists, sponsoring them and allowing them to work in mosques and form the nucleus of a parallel society, all in the name of preaching Islam and good ethics. He mentioned the Quranic societies, the scout organizations, the preaching lessons, the sermons—not just in mosques but in university quads and dorms and in fam-ily homes—all of these divided people into believers and infi-dels, veiled and unveiled. They'd even been hostile to the syn-dicates and their leadership when they were fighting against the authorities, especially during the events of 1978. The Islamists had tried to infiltrate them in order to ruin them from within and change the direction of the social conflict.

Abdel Nasser considered the Islamists like an *afreet* egg that the Constitutional Party thought they'd imprisoned in a bottle. The egg hatched, and the *afreet* grew so large that it broke the bottle and turned on its owner. So now the conflict was taking place among the reactionary groups; the working people had no interest in it.

Abdel Nasser was full of enthusiasm as he spoke, and Si

Abdel Hamid watched him calmly, with a neutrality bordering on pity. His only comment was that it seemed that Abdel Nasser still hadn't changed out of his student activist clothes. He found what his protégé was saying strange for the intelligent person he knew he was—a precise observer who could usually analyze an issue in all its subtleties and contradictions. He told him that it was impossible to avoid the guidelines of the international financial institutions, whatever the social cost. The days of the welfare state in the world were over. He accused the Tunisian left of holding onto its dream of a dictatorship of the proletariat; they wanted to overthrow the regime just as much as the Islamic Tendency. The only differences between the two groups were in their colors (red vs. black and purple), their slogans (oppression vs. imperialism), and, of course, their goals: one sought a tyranny of bureaucracy with the leaders of the revolutionary party, while the other sought the tyranny of semi-religious scholars and those hiding behind religion in the name of God and *sharia*.

Si Abdel Hamid then shifted, reminding him of the coalition between the leftist and liberal parties to oppose Nazism and Fascism. He thought the question in Tunisia could be presented as a conflict between those who wanted to hold onto the modernist gains that the independence government had brought, and the threat of the Muslim Brotherhood, spiced up with Wahhabi and Iranian Shiite flavors. He concluded that the progressives in Tunisia should align with the party of the president, the protector of Tunisian modernity, despite all their differences with him. As for the question of democracy: it would undoubtedly come.

20

Si Abdel Hamid stopped talking, as if he had suddenly

remembered something, then told Abdel Nasser, "By the way, for Thursday's supplement, you have to delete the paragraphs you translated from al-Kawakibi's *Nature of Despotism*."

"But it's a new column—a Francophone introduction to the history of Arab enlightenment . . ."

"I know. I liked the title: 'The Memory of Arab Modernity.'"

"Then why should I delete it?"

"Because of its content. Abou Saoud H. came to talk to me today and said that you had crossed the line and that the government newspaper was starting to look like the opposition papers."

"What?! The bastard!"

"Yeah . . . He saw the text you chose as hinting at Bourguiba's tyranny and the concentration of power in his hands—or, at least, that it could be interpreted that way."

"And did he convince you? Let them ban the book, then! This is the heritage of modernity that the Tunisian state is defending against the Islamists. The text is a warning about *their* tyranny if they ever come to power."

"Don't get upset: everyone is just doing their job. That was Abou Saoud's opinion—so be it. His mission is to play the role of goalie and keep balls from entering our net. Intentions and questions of true and false have nothing to do with it."

"So I should just give in to his stupidity and crappy interpretation?"

"I'm giving in, too—to avoid headaches. They *are* bastards, and I wouldn't put anything past them. They assume they know the country's best interests better than Bourguiba and the political police themselves. Believe me, no one has ever asked me not to write about a subject. I know my limits, but I've still been able to write about a number of subjects without getting myself into trouble. But ever since he arrived, this stupid censor has been lowering the ceiling of banned subjects however he likes. He's suspicious of everything. He sees revolution in every line and instigation and slander in every word. What do you want me to do with him? He was sent officially by the information ministry to be the 'general censor' for the newspaper—a job I'd never heard of. He's the one who signs off on the newspaper and allows it to go to print, him and the editorial secretary."

Si Abdel Hamid paused, as if choosing his words carefully. "Do you know who he is?" he asked Abdel Nasser.

"Yes, I have an idea. He used to be in prison because of his activism as a student."

"Right. Now he's more dangerous to us than all the Constitutionalists put together; it's like he wants to do penance for his years of opposition to the regime. He's trying to please his superiors and taking revenge on his past self by proxy—so he's castrating the editors who remind him of himself with the same scissors he castrated himself with."

"But even when he was a member of the student movement, some of his comrades knew who he was, even though no one believed them," said Abdel Nasser. "They suspected he was a cop. And even in jail, it seems that he was informing on them to the police, disclosing their plans to go on hunger strikes or to organize a protest about the conditions in the prison."

"Forget about all that. All of you have been infiltrated—the state is the state. It has installed a policeman and an informer in every single one of us. Some of them stayed asleep, some of them wake up when it suits them, and some of them have made it a profession. Look around you at the newspapers, and you'll see informers of every stripe and color. We won't understand anything, as long as we don't understand the logic of the state."

El-Talyani launched into a philosophical argument about the state and authority, moving between Hegel, Marx, and the anarchists and referencing *The State and Revolution* in a concrete analysis of reality. Si Abdel Hamid just laughed; he summarized all the talk and enthusiasm by saying, "Bring them to Tunisia! They'll lose their minds. What will they find here? A people terrorized by their own shadow, who applaud every newcomer and agree with him no matter who he is, who not only accept their own oppression but actively participate in it, gossiping and informing on each other with relish."

Abdel Nasser realized that Si Abdel Hamid was drunk. He could always tell he'd reached that point when he got extremist in his ideas, generalizing and trying to prove his generalizations. He would disparage the common man and didn't believe in anyone but the elite. And the only people he felt sympathy for were the elite when they sank to the level of the rabble, taking up their inferior mindsets, their ambitions and dreams. One thing that Abdel Nasser liked about the editor-in-chief was that he didn't exclude himself from this harsh criticism when his brain charged forward, sweeping everything out of its way. He decided not to argue with him by reminding him of something he'd said before: "The state is the biggest lie that humanity has ever created and then believed in. The state is me. And you. And the secretary who gives me her body in the office, without me asking for it, because I represent the state in her eyes. We've known since antiquity that the state is omens and signs but is intangible. It's a hidden god: no one has ever proved its unseen existence, so they both love it and hate it."

21

Abdel Nasser went home that day with a heavy head, both from the drinking and the conversation. He was annoyed by what Si Abdel Hamid had told him about his report. He felt oppressed, but he thought about his new situation and what he would do if he left the newspaper. He blamed himself for going back to writing about national affairs with that pig around, when apparently the media was only supposed to be a propaganda machine. He decided to focus on his weekly supplement and the cultural pages; at least they were an outlet for his writing, even if he felt more drawn to politics.

Zeina was sleeping when he got home. When he woke up, he was surprised by a note that she'd taped to the bathroom mirror. In it, she greeted him, then told him that she was leaving for her village because her mother was critically ill, hovering between life and death. She said she didn't know when she'd be coming back.

Abdel Nasser's mood darkened. He didn't know what to do: should he go to the village to be with his wife? Or would that embarrass her? How would she act in such circumstances? Might she need to take her mother to the hospital? Did she have enough money? His thoughts were whirling, but he gave up after realizing that he couldn't do anything before she returned and asked him for whatever help she wanted.

He arrived at the newspaper at 11 A.M. He was preparing the content of the new issue, finalizing its design, organizing the articles, and laying them out on the four pages. One of his colleagues in the editorial room called to tell him that someone was on the phone for him. He thought it might be Zeina, but it was Najla. She told him that she had contacted Zeina to check on her by calling the owner of the food store in the village. He had told her that Zeina's mother had been taken to the regional hospital, practically paralyzed and comatose. He also conveyed Zeina's message that Abdel Nasser shouldn't worry, since she had relatives in the city of Siliana and had enough money with her. She promised to contact Najla at her home number and update her; if she wasn't home, she would leave a message with her mother or one of her sisters.

Najla did not call again that day, and Abdel Nasser did not want to call her. It was a heavy day for him, on top of his work with the supplement. He finished his work with Aamm Hassan at around 7:30 P.M. There were last-minute changes in two arti-cles, and he'd had to translate a text by Ismail Mazhar about Darwinism to replace the excerpt from *The Nature of Despotism* that the scissors-wielding Abou Saoud—that personification of the Bourguiba regime's interests—had not approved of.

He went home early. He bought some bottles of wine from a bar near the newspaper and put them in the refrigerator to cool down. He got a pizza, then sat down to watch a political interview on France 2.

He didn't feel Zeina's absence and didn't remember her until he went to the kitchen to open a new bottle. Her absence was obvious at the kitchen table, only palliated by the presence of the bag of books and notebooks that she used for studying and teaching.

It had never occurred to Abdel Nasser to go through Zeina's things. He didn't know what it was, that night, that made him decide to look in her bag. He found a philosophy textbook. Some pages with words underlined. A doodle of a laughing face by some paragraphs. Question marks next to a quote, or a ver-tical line in the left or right margins next to a passage. Short comments here and there in French, some of which he recog-nized as translations of terms, others quotes by philosophers, and the rest a criticism or opposing idea or note about another school of philosophy. The only chapters not marked up that way were the psychoanalysis and art chapters. The chapter with the most comments was the one about the notion of phi-losophy and its texts.

He opened a plastic folder. Strips of normal white paper, cut crosswise. Bullet-pointed fragments. Starred quotes in French. Bracketed paragraphs with bullet-pointed or numbered sections.

Among those strips, he found an envelope with a French stamp on it. He felt it: it was thick. He wasted no time in open-ing it. A card with a message inside:

Wishing you a successful new academic year.

*Congrats on your successful thesis defense and good luck
with the* agrégation *exam.*

Until we meet. Kisses.

Eric S.

He checked the envelope again. He looked at the address
and the addressee. It was written in French:

Zeina S.
P.O. Box 142
Bab Mnara Post Office
Tunis, Republic of Tunisia

On the back of the envelope were the French initials E.S. in
place of the sender's name. He looked at the two sides of the
card. On the front was a picture of a road and a far-off horizon; a small red flower on the horizon drew the eye, as it would
at twilight.

On the other side of the card was a verse of poetry in
French, written in a gothic font. In translation, it said:

Every man has a rose living in his heart,
the sun of his secluded soul
that he searches for all his life.
He awaits her warm rays.
If he has found her, and how difficult that is,
he should not let her wilt.
For that,
the words "I love you" are enough.
The rose will understand them in all languages,
and her scent will fill the air.

Najla immediately popped into his head. He forgot the card

and what was written on it. He forgot the sender and didn't care, at first, that this card was addressed to his wife. Legally his wife, at least; in reality, the girlfriend he lived with. Could Najla be his promised rose and warm sun? And what about Zeina?

He understood everything, or imagined he did. She was intellectually drawn to this Eric. She was a philosopher whose mind was open to the world, and now she wanted to open her legs for a man on the other shore of the sea. Who was he? What did she write back? Did she have his address? He thought the whole thing was ridiculous. The most important thing was that now he knew why she wouldn't accept the reality of their marriage, or at least one reason. Why hadn't she talked to him about it? If the card were innocent, just a card from a friend, she would've mentioned it. But who was this friend that he'd never heard of? Did she even have time for that kind of friendship, having professed unswerving dedication to her academic path?

Abdel Nasser decided to wait and see. Time would reveal the truth. But what was he going to do with it? What mattered most was that he no longer felt guilty. The playing field was wide open as he waited to see what was on the horizon. He wouldn't be a fool, cheated on while he snored away contentedly. His eyes were wide open now. She clearly thought his kindness in respecting her privacy was naivety and a lack of attention, as if she didn't know the Abdel Nasser who fought Islamists at the university in the open air, the Abdel Nasser who refused to take advantage of the female comrades who threw themselves on the altar of his good looks.

Zeina didn't know that el-Talyani had chosen her at the moment their desires got mixed up with their sacrifice under the police truncheons. It had been, in his eyes, a moment of revolutionary purity and spiritual clarity that brought their souls together, or at least that's what he'd imagined. She had forgotten all of that. She'd forgotten him. If he hadn't saved himself by finishing the requirements for his diploma and going into journalism, she would have let him starve and left him to pursue her own interest.

Was he done with Zeina, then? Abdel Nasser, lost in the thick of this inner monologue, wasn't sure. Why not give her another chance as he waited for her to realize her dreams. Then again, could someone as thirsty as she was ever actually quench their thirst? She was eating at the table of ambition—and could you ever feel satisfied when what you *really* wanted was to climb to the head of the table?

1

When Abdel Nasser met Najla Thursday evening, he didn't tell her what he'd discovered about Zeina. They were sitting in a bar at the Hotel International. She told him about the stroke that Zeina's mother had suffered: she was in the intensive care unit and in bad condition, according to the doctors. Zeina was only allowed to see her from behind glass. She also told him that Zeina had tried to call him at the newspaper but hadn't been able to get ahold of him.

Abdel Nasser quickly moved on from the story. This was his way, whenever anything was bothering him. He didn't like illness and didn't like talking about it. Najla didn't know that, so she gave in to his sweet talk and his caresses in the corner of the bar. She forgot about the smell of smoke that had been bothering her and made her cough. As usual, she was happy and smiling, making eyes at him and enjoying his conversation. She let his hands go wherever they wanted, unmindful of the other people in the bar. Abdel Nasser asked her to spend the night with him. But she asked him if they could put it off a day, since she didn't teach on Saturdays. She needed to prepare a believable lie for her mother—especially since Zeina wasn't in Tunis, which made that more difficult.

He told her, "I want you today, and tomorrow, and the day after that . . ."

She tapped his nose with her finger and told him, sweetly, "Stop acting like a child. I told you: tomorrow night. I'll check with Zeina before coming over. What if she came back tomorrow?"

"Well, then it has to be today."

"I have to work tomorrow morning at eight. If God loves us, Zeina won't come back tomorrow."

Abdel Nasser accepted her decision grudgingly; he was disconcerted, but he didn't see that he had any other choice.

After Najla left, he went to the newspaper. He quickly revised an editorial Si Abdel Hamid had written personally and sent early in the morning, contrary to his usual practice. He was scheduled to travel for twenty-four hours with the finance minister.

2

Abdel Nasser went back to the International to have a coffee with a young journalist that Si Abdel Hamid had asked him to train in cultural journalism. He was to visit every department before he decided which department to put him in. Abdel Nasser asked him to walk around the city during the Friday prayer and write a report about the religious books being sold on the sidewalks in front of mosques. He was to check out their titles, authors, and contents to determine their subjects and categorize them. In addition, he was to ask the sellers about their prices, sources, and customers to get a sense of whether the trade was lucrative. Abdel Nasser also asked him to see if they sold agarwood incense, natural perfumes, prayer beads, and prayer rugs along with the books, and what the connections were among these items.

The young man was astonished by the outpouring of questions that Abdel Nasser had come up with. He told him that he liked the subject, but asked him how to know what subjects to choose in the future—especially because he saw these vendors in front of mosques all the time, but it had never occurred to him that they were a recent phenomenon that was spreading and would be a good subject for a cultural report.

Abdel Nasser told him, "Ideas are everywhere. We just have to regain our ability to wonder and ask questions. The enemy of journalism is familiarity with the abnormal and overlooking simple things. The deepest ideas are the simplest, but we have to see them first."

They finished drinking their coffee. El-Talyani paid the bill. Then he said, "I'm going to the central souk now—come with me and look around for some cultural subjects that haven't been addressed yet. You have to find them for yourself."

The young man laughed and told him that he couldn't imagine any culture in piles of vegetables, meat, and fish, but he would accompany him anyway.

Abdel Nasser went into the fish market. He bought two large sea bass and some other seafood and left them to be cleaned at one of the small shops to the right of the entrance. Then he went back to explore the souk. He wandered around with the young man and bought some dried herrings. He stopped by a pickle vendor and bought a few different types of olives, handmade Tunisian harissa, and some ricotta and other Italian cheeses. He asked his companion to check what was being sold in the market, then stopped by some butchers' stands; from one, he bought some beef salami prepared with pistachios and, from a second, carpaccio.

They left the butcher and pickles section of the market and went back to the fish cleaning shop. Then they left the souk. Abdel Nasser asked the young journalist, whose name was Imad Eddine, about possible cultural topics from the souk.

Imad Eddine seemed to be at a loss for words. Abdel Nasser told him to think about it and respond after he'd identified an issue or two, but the young man pressed him to hear his own reaction to the market they'd just visited. Abdel Nasser, clearly proud of his own refined cultural sense, mentioned two possible topics as examples. First, he encouraged Imad to ask simple questions about the history of that market: when it was built and why, what style it was in and why the columns were distributed this way, whether it had ever been altered, and so on. A historical report like that was important for learning about the history of architecture in the modern city and the urban planning of the entire city of Tunis.

The second subject was what distinguished this market: what ingredients did it have that weren't available in most ordinary outdoor markets, and what cooking styles were they useful for? Tunisian cuisine is a mix of Berber, Andalusian, Jewish, Turkish, and Italian dishes, and maybe even others that we don't know about. El-Talyani mentioned the herrings he'd bought and asked Imad if he knew what dishes they were used in and what their origin was. He stressed to him that Tunisian cuisine was a harmonious mosaic of Mediterranean dishes: it reflected a mixture of cultures because our country, if you looked at it, was at the heart of the Mediterranean. One part of it was no more than a pigeons' flight from the north shore of the sea; the other part in the south got the *simoom* winds from Africa, as well as the winds blowing from the east and west.

Abdel Nasser bought the rest of his groceries from the Touta market in Le Bardo. When he got home, he rested for an hour, then went into the kitchen. He could cook as well as any woman: he prepared shakshuka with herring and poured it into flaky pastry crusts in oval and circular shapes. He rolled out some more dough and put it in a mold for a Tunisian tagine prepared with a mix of ricotta, tuna, melty Italian cheeses, parsley, and eggs. He prepared a Tunisian salad and added some lettuce, then decorated it with pickled lemon slices, chopped olives, and dried mint. He prepared a sauce with bay leaves, rosemary, and lots of garlic. He sautéed the seafood with onion, peppers, and thyme, then prepared an olive oil marinade, mixed with garlic and cumin, for the sea bass. He coated them with it, then put them in the refrigerator in a glass bowl covered with cling wrap.

Everything was ready; now all he had to do was wait for the queen!

3

Abdel Nasser had a headache. He took some acetaminophen and lay down on the couch in the living room. He brought his hands to his temples and rubbed them. Feeling slightly dizzy, he stood up and went to the bathroom. He washed his face, scrubbed his hair, and looked at himself in the mirror. His eyes looked red, and his face seemed yellowish and pale: he felt like he was looking at a stranger. He asked the Abdel Nasser in the mirror, "What's wrong with you? Snap out of it, would you? Today is going to be beautiful. Najla will be here any minute, and you need to be a proper host, so pull yourself together. You're going to need all your energy tonight. It's time to celebrate, not to get all queasy and anxious. Don't mess it up."

His advice to himself did not work. It was 7:45 P.M. by his watch; Najla was late. He started to feel overwhelmed by strange concerns about her and about himself. His concerns about himself stayed with him, even after Najla arrived, half an hour late.

He was agitated when he asked her why she was late and told her he'd been worried about her.

She smiled and asked, "Which is better, complaining or kissing?"

He apologized for his tactlessness. He explained it by the bad mood he was in and the discomfort he'd been feeling.

She answered him with a wicked smile. "Don't worry—all lovers feel that way before big dates."

"Stop kidding around, Najla. I'm serious," he responded.

"Then you're feeling upset because you're about to cheat on your wife with her friend—in her own home—for the first time."

She laughed, then took hold of Abdel Nasser and pushed him against the wall in one quick and graceful movement. She pinned his hands to the wall above his head and kissed him passionately. He felt his body relax and his bad mood evaporate. He asked her, "What did you do?"

"I breathed my soul into you and swallowed your bad mood."

He took hold of her and repeated what she had done to him. The kiss was longer and deeper, almost suffocating them.

He wanted to bring the food from the kitchen, but she asked him to wait. She opened her gym bag and gave him a gift-wrapped box, asking him to open it. It was a man's wristwatch. She put it around his wrist and said, "From now on, you will adjust your time to me."

He stood at attention, like a soldier in front of his commander: "Aye, aye, mistress of my soul." He pushed her down onto the couch and kissed her, the honey from their lips the perfect appetizer.

He put the marinated sea bass into the frying pan and started heating and moving the food he had prepared from the kitchen into the living room. Najla was waiting for him on the couch. She asked him if he needed any help to set the table, but he told her that everything was ready and the queen—the queen of his soul—was always served first.

She would get her turn later on—at the big feast.

4

Abdel Nasser was dazzled by what he saw when he returned to the living room. Najla was wearing a short satin nightgown that revealed her knees and part of her thighs. It was sleeveless, with a deep neckline and a low-cut back. The top and bottom were trimmed with lace and there was a slit between her breasts, held closed with a tie. Under the nightgown, she wore a white strapless push-up bra that accentuated her cleavage, and an embroidered white G-string.

As he looked at her, almost nude, he admired her abundant femininity. He saw her with new eyes, different from the way he'd seen her at the hotel in Hammamet. She was brighter and happier. Even her soft skin he felt as if he were seeing for the first time. He stared at her openly, admiringly, then asked her why this felt so new. She answered that a real woman should always look as if she'd never been seen before. He forgot the food and wanted to enjoy her instead. Taking his face in her hands and planting a long kiss on his lips, she told him there would be time for that soon—the night was still young.

Najla was impressed with the feast he had prepared for her. She asked about the different dishes she could smell and tasted what he placed in front of her, expressing her admiration for his cooking. When it came to the herring shakshuka in its pastry molds, however, she balked; its smell and taste were too strong for her. El-Talyani urged her to eat and enjoy it, but she declined.

He started telling her about it, this fish from the North Sea, where the locals used it in everything. How it came to Tunisia cured, and how his brother Salah Eddine used to love shakshuka with herring and swore that the dried herring in Tunisia was the most delicious in the world, even though it was imported from the North Sea.

Then he recounted a legend for her, though he couldn't

remember where he'd read it. The story went that the herring was originally one of the giant fish of the North Sea, feeding on the underwater grasses with the elephant seals and manatees. When the moon was full, the herring would turn an immaculate white color, but at all other times it was pitch-black, to the point that it couldn't be seen in the darkness of the North Sea. According to the legend, if someone caught a herring at the moment between the full moon and when it began to wane, he would find a small stone on the left side of its head. The stone was the size of a grain of salt; some called it "klopias" and others called it "skolobidan," and if a man sucked on it, he would gain a sexual energy that would never vanish, even in his old age. If a woman sucked on it, it would prevent her body from ever changing or aging; she would always remain as she was the moment she sucked on the herring stone. It could also remove illnesses from the body. But if the fish reached its full growth without having ever been caught, it would spoil from within and decompose into a pile of fishbones.

Abdel Nasser was telling the story about the fish with enthusiasm, and Najla looked at him fondly. He told her, "I don't know why I like the legend of the herring so much. I guess it reminds me of human beings: we either give someone else our energy and life, or we perish from within."

"Be my herring, then," said Najla, "and grant me my youth before it's eaten away from the inside. And from the outside!"

El-Talyani sensed that that night was a full moon; he was sure of it. All of this shimmer and splendor couldn't be a coincidence. He sank into Najla's seas, where the herring migrated, and found warm, refreshing waters. In these waters they laid their eggs, which hatched and nested, granting Najla the water of life to purify her sweet soul and refresh her athletic, sculpted body.

5

It was a big night, between el-Talyani's feast—with its different colors and delicious flavors—and Najla's feast, which revealed new secrets for him to discover and enjoy. She was generous and held nothing back from the Italian who had taught her to accept the strong smell of the herring and its pleasant, biting taste.

She felt like a purebred mare who had found her ideal rider. The fitness of the horseman was undeniable, as if he'd been training with her every day. He quickly learned how to control his mare when she bolted or when her neighing urged her forward; he confidently bridled her without dampening her enthusiasm or reining her in, but kept up with her until they slowed, attaining the farthest reaches of the seventh heaven.

She found him a graceful and skillful rider, combining presence of mind with physical prowess and flexibility, mastering the movement of hands and feet and the changing of positions, top and bottom. The mare could see that he was taken by her, like a bird carried by the wind wherever it pleases: eyes closed, magically attracted to the bottom of the world as if about to fall down unconscious, or else floating in the air like a pegasus penetrating the sky. But then, in the decisive moment, the moment of descent or of disappearing behind the clouds, he would awaken once more to take charge, guiding Najla where he wanted with tact and firmness.

He knew how to slacken her reins so that she could flow like a stream from the mountaintop. Then he would rein her in as they reached their goal, and she would obey his guidance, the tender and supple movements of his legs, thighs, stomach, and chest. Arms embracing chest and back in turns, torso turning to the front or back. Leaning to the right, leaving no inch of the mare's left side untouched, then to the left. Their waists met. Rider and mare tumbled over each other until the one blended into the other, caressing faces, lips, ears, temples, hair.

He took the satin nightgown off slowly. Standing behind her, he started at the base of her neck, tugging gently at the tie, then slid his hands down to the saddle restraining her chest and lifted her breasts. He took hold of the mare's mane, her plait and loose hair, then unhooked the saddle and pressed himself against her back, caressing her with both hands, from her belly button to her neck.

One of them made a slight movement on the reins. He pulled on them. Tremors of excitement. A pressure that grew, little by little. Tension and release. Light touches of the spur on the tensed body. A low sound like a camel's growl, a whinny from the mare. Balanced breathing until finally the race made the rider cry out. Her back was a pleasure, her belly a treasure. The mare was generous. As for the rider, in the words of the immortal poet, *the horse and the night and the desert knew him well.*

Her pleasure was complete; it showed in her whinnies and then her sigh, until the neighing became a thunder that left her neither worn out nor unsatisfied.

He lay down next to her, remembering her surge of passion. He had never in his life seen a mare stronger or sleeker than Najla. She was a purebred who buoyed him up with an ecstasy that lingered into the night.

She put her head on his chest, remembering how he released the reins and pulled them back, firm, but tender and supple. She thought about his fading then reviving, his movements around her and atop her like a spinning top. She loved the tenderness of his hands, his consideration and gentleness. But she also loved his prodding and swagger. She was swimming, completely free of the body's shackles.

She dozed next to him, relaxed. He drifted, eyes closed— until he awoke with a start at a mental image of Zeina in tears.

He didn't know whether it came from a feeling of guilt, or one of pity due to her mother's crisis. In either case, did she really have to come ruin his night? To clear the image from his mind, he told himself, *It's nothing but a marriage certificate, that's what she says. She should let other women have compassion for me, since she can't—or won't.*

He looked at Najla. She was sleeping, with the face of an angel. Her naked body exuded temptation. He picked her up gently and moved her to the bed in the bedroom. She stirred and smiled at him languidly, then put her hands around his neck and buried her head in his chest.

6

He went back to the living room, where he gathered the dishes and the leftover food. He tidied up the room and washed the dishes. It was 1:30 A.M. As elated and satisfied as he was, he also felt troubled and annoyed, and his head felt heavy. He didn't know what was wrong with him: he'd barely had anything to drink. He hadn't had time to drink from anything except Najla's glistening stream of life-giving water.

He wanted to go out into the street to get some fresh air. But it occurred to him that it wouldn't be right to leave Najla alone in the house; what if she woke up and couldn't find him? He tried to settle his nerves and go to bed. He closed his eyes and started counting on his fingers. He turned off the lamps, thinking that the light might be what was keeping him awake, even though it was dim. He got all the way to one hundred several times in a row, when usually he was asleep by the second hundred. He recited a prayer, tapping his right thumb along each fingertip on his right hand as if on prayer beads. He felt like he was suffocating. He took a deep breath, let it out slowly. He tossed and turned in bed. He picked up a book and read a few pages but didn't understand a word. His thoughts were scattered, wandering. Images came back to him from the university: him giving a speech or having a discussion or facing the security forces during protests. He saw Zeina again, with her sad face. She was worried and distressingly tense. He saw Lella Jnayna in front of him at her house, offering him honey mixed with sesame and pomegranate seeds in a big spoon. What brought this other woman back, too? He saw the faces of his aunt, his mother, Jweeda. His "club" meetings with friends at home, in his room on the top floor. He moved to Najm Eddine's house; he found himself with Nabeel, Jaafar, and Redha. Zeina appeared in the scene in front of El Gorjani police station, as they got out of the police van. Si Othman stood in front of him and Si Abdel Hamid by the restaurant entrance. Angelika, on the night of her birthday. Sheikh Allala Darwish in the ablution room in the mosque, then at Lella Jnayna's house when the ball fell into their courtyard. That idiot censor Abou Saoud who always knew what was best for the nation. The herring in the central market. Signing the marriage certificate with Yosser there as a witness.

The images all blended together. What was happening? *Is my life flashing before my eyes because I'm about to die?* The idea was horrifying. He remembered a poem by Nâzim Hikmet about the beaches he hadn't seen, the dodgy bars he hadn't visited, and the fine wines he hadn't tasted, or the bad ones, either. He wasn't yet thirty—but what had he done in his life?

There was something wrong. Somewhere. There was something murky. Had the herring started to rot, leaving nothing but its splintery bones? So be it! Tonight he'd seen the full moon filling the sky . . . He would swear that what he'd experienced with Najla was the essence of what had gone before and what was to come. If his time had come and he had to go in a moment . . . or an hour . . . or a few hours . . . he would go happily. They could write on his tomb in invisible ink that he had truly lived. They could write on his tombstone that he had died the day he was born in Najla's arms, during the night between the sixth and seventh of November, 1987.

Abdel Nasser didn't actually die that night—but he also didn't sleep for more than an hour or two, in spite of his exhaustion and the late night they'd had. The fear and the images that poured forth from the vault of his memory overwhelmed him and kept him in a bad mood, somewhere between sleep and wakefulness. A suffocating night of worry and distress.

7

Abdel Nasser couldn't explain the state he was in. But he wanted to connect it with his unerring intuition; he considered his state that night to be a mirror image of the state of his country. That night, Ben Ali, the prime minister and interior minister, was putting the final touches on his coup against Bourguiba. He was shining up his combat boots, getting ready to enter the presidential palace. As Abdel Nasser later told Si Abdel Hamid, laughing, the physical and psychic pain he felt that night were labor pains as a new era was born.

Calm didn't come to Abdel Nasser until he turned on the radio, shortly after 6:30 A.M. He felt lucid, despite being sleep-deprived. The cup of coffee almost fell from his hand as he listened to the brassy voice, banging in his ears like a military march:

> *Fellow citizens,*
> *The great sacrifices made by the Leader Habib Bourguiba . . . Are why we granted him our affection and regard and worked under his leadership for many*

years . . . But the onset of his senility and the deterioration of his health and the medical report made on this called us to carry out our national duty and declare him totally incapable of undertaking the tasks of the president of the republic . . . With the help of God, we take up the presidency of the republic.

We are counting on all the children of our dear country to work together in an atmosphere of confidence, security, and serenity, from which all hatred and rancor will be banished . . . Our people have reached a degree of responsibility and maturity where every individual and group is in a position to constructively contribute . . . This guarantees the conditions for a responsible democracy, fully respecting the sovereignty of the people as written into the constitution . . . The times in which we live can no longer admit life presidency or automatic succession . . . Our people deserve an advanced and institutionalized political life . . . We shall see that the law is correctly enforced in a way that will proscribe any kind of iniquity or injustice. We shall act to restore the prestige of the state and put an end to chaos and laxity. There will be no more favoritism or indifference . . .

By the grace of God, we are entering a new era of efforts and determination . . . Long live Tunisia! Long live the republic!

"Tell them, 'Do as you will. Your deeds will be observed by God, His Messenger, and the believers.'"

Abdel Nasser couldn't believe it. He immediately started to wonder what had happened. He wanted to go outside, to see the military and police tanks that he was sure must be spreading everywhere. When he woke Najla, the expression on her face switched from calm angel to an annoyed angel; he hadn't meant to wake her so rudely, of course. But she quickly forgot his brusqueness in the horror of what had happened. She ran with him into the kitchen, waiting for another broadcast of the statement. She was shocked and didn't comment, except to note in a sad tone, "Poor Bourguiba."

It was around 6:55 A.M. He told her that he was going to the newspaper. She begged him not to go; the situation was unclear, and the army must be everywhere. She said, "Don't you understand? It's a coup."

"But I'm a journalist; I have to know what's going on. Don't worry—I'll take you home, then go."

"Now? No way."

"Let me just go outside and see what's going on. Then we'll decide."

Abdel Nasser took a quick look outside. The street wasn't totally empty: he saw cautious faces, most passersby quiet or whispering. He was on Avenue Habib Bourguiba in Le Bardo; he headed toward the Parliament building. There was no sign of any coup. No security presence, no tanks or soldiers. He shared the good news with Najla. She couldn't believe it. She got dressed quickly and put her things in her gym bag. They walked quickly, and he said goodbye to her at the head of her street, so that he could go to the newspaper. She asked him to call her.

8

When he arrived at the office, he found Si Abdel Hamid there, along with the editorial secretary and some administrators. They were all quiet, waiting for news from the Tunis Afrique Presse agency. The radio was on, and the voice of Salah Jegham on the morning show was playing nationalistic songs and promises of a new era. There was the voice of Naâma singing *Zein passed by . . . Coming back from a night out . . . He just passed by.*

Abdel Nasser saw Si Abdel Hamid anxious, biting his nails like a worried child. The editorial secretary looked abashed, hiding that morning's newspaper with the picture of the Supreme Warrior on the front page and the editor-in-chief's editorial. There was a pervading feeling of shame and disgrace.

Abdel Nasser approached Si Abdel Hamid and said, "There's no point in waiting. It's obvious—a coup, with medical certification. I'm sure it will all end well; it's a weight off of everyone."

Si Abdel Hamid interrupted him. "That's enough—now leave me in peace."

Abdel Hamid asked the editorial secretary to leave the office. He hurried toward the door, obeying the order, as did Abdel Nasser. Si Abdel Hamid called Abdel Nasser back.

Once they were alone, he got up from his chair and closed the door. He moved closer to Abdel Nasser and said, "I didn't want to talk in front of him. What do you think about what's happening?"

"It's clear," Abdel Nasser responded. "It's a successful coup. Don't forget that Ben Ali is a military man and an old hand in the intelligence services: he doesn't make mistakes."

"This means that what Bourguiba has always feared has happened. He appointed Ben Ali to get rid of the Islamists— but instead he got rid of him?"

"A few days ago you were telling me about change from within, from inside the state apparatus. Bourguiba was done for a long time ago; he's no longer the right man for the times. You'll see. All of them will welcome Ben Ali. You told me that the Tunisian people follow their interests, wherever they lead, and their slogan is that God gives victory to he who wears the crown."

Si Abdel Hamid didn't answer. Abdel Nasser continued, "Personally, I've never liked the man; he's put down protests, and he's killed people. I've been telling you that ever since they appointed him prime minister. I'm against military rule, but his speech recognized the opposition's demands and reassured the ruling party members and international powers. What more are you waiting for?

"Do you think he managed the coup on his own?"

"No way. There was definitely foreign support. The coming days will show it."

"Yes, that's very likely."

Abdel Nasser advised Si Abdel Hamid to publish a special issue right away, even if only a single page front and back. He also advised him to fall in on the side of Ben Ali from now on, since Bourguiba had no future. He encouraged him to take the gamble and promised him he'd win.

At that moment, the telephone in Si Abdel Hamid's office rang. It was the handset with the special number that nobody except influential people in the government knew. Si Abdel Hamid leapt to answer the phone. Abdel Nasser couldn't hear the call but was sure that it was from someone important. He heard Si Abdel Hamid say to the caller, "Of course . . . Of course . . . We've started preparing a special issue that will be ready shortly . . . Good luck."

He found out later that the call was from the interior ministry. At the other end of the line was one of those who had planned the coup. He asked Abdel Hamid to do his duty in support of the blessed change.

Si Abdel Hamid asked Abdel Nasser to focus on writing an article welcoming the change as the most important event since independence. The constitutional nature of the power transition must be emphasized as a lesson for the Arab world. He described Ben Ali as the savior of the country, rescuing it from a quagmire of doubt and fear and inaugurating a new era of hope. He told him to sprinkle in some democratic language about participation for all, human rights, and loyalty to the country.

Abdel Nasser heard him on the phone asking the different section editors, the directors of human resources and finances, and the editorial secretary to come to his office.

He told the attendees to immediately call in the print workers, especially the technicians, even if they had to send company cars to pick them up from home.

He told the section editors to go into the streets and gather public opinion (as long as it was positive) and to prepare a report within the next hour or hour and a half. He wanted everything before 10 A.M. at the latest. He told the editorial secretary to collect whatever news Tunis Afrique Presse issued and use it as a primary source. One of them suggested interviewing the opposition leaders, but Si Abdel Hamid rebuffed him.

He gave instructions to take preparatory measures to release the issue at noon and distribute it, at least throughout the capital. This order was addressed to the editorial secretary and, more particularly, to the financial director.

Everything went well, as Si Abdel Hamid had wanted it. All the articles were ready by ten. They couldn't find the newspaper designer, so Abdel Nasser took care of the design. He started with the ad pages, since the articles weren't long enough to fill four large-format pages. Si Abdel Hamid whispered in his ear, "Do whatever you want. What I care about is the front page, and supporting Ben Ali. Do you understand? This is not an issue of the newspaper: it's a political stand."

Abdel Nasser threw himself into the work. He prepared the layout of the pages with astonishing speed, despite the news he was given in the midst of his work: Zeina's mother had died the night before, and the burial would be that afternoon at the village cemetery.

9

Shortly after 11 A.M., the newspaper was ready to be printed. It was Si Abdel Hamid who first heard the news about Zeina's mother; Najla hadn't been able to reach Abdel Nasser and instead left a message with the telephone operator. Si Abdel Hamid called Abdel Nasser to his office and offered him the use of his private phone for whatever calls he needed to make. Abdel Nasser agreed with Najla that they would go together to Zeina's house in the village.

He left Si Abdel Hamid's office in a hurry. The editor-in-chief stopped him at the door to express his condolences again. "My car and driver are waiting for you downstairs," he said. "Take care of yourself and convey my condolences to Ustada Zeina."

Abdel Nasser thanked him and left.

The trip was long. They passed through villages and rural areas they would never have imagined driving through. If not for Najla, sitting next to him in the back seat and made even more beautiful by the striking black she was wearing, the trip would have felt even longer. The driver tried to chat with Abdel Nasser about what had happened early that morning, but he had learned to be cautious of drivers in general—and of the newspaper drivers in particular.

Najla rescued him by telling him to get some rest. She claimed that the signs of sleep deprivation were clear on his face, which he justified by how hard he'd worked that morning. He closed the window blinds of the Mercedes, rested his head against the back of his seat, and slept fitfully.

They arrived after the funeral and asked where Zeina's house was. It could only just barely be called a house. He couldn't imagine how the philosopher had grown up in that hut, which seemed to spring out of the ground like a satanic plant. He noticed for the first time the stark contradiction between the residence and its resident.

Zeina seemed all right, no tears or signs of emotion. That seemed strange in itself, but they found it even stranger when she insisted on accompanying them back to Tunis, as if she had at last completed a boring duty. Najla told her, "That's not right. You should stay until the memorial on the third day, at least."

Zeina answered, "The last link between me and this village is gone now. I'm free as a breeze." Her voice was even, neutral.

Najla said, "I don't know your traditions here. Don't you visit the departed's grave the day after the funeral?"

"I don't know, either," Zeina responded. "And I don't care. Rituals, traditions, customs . . . The person I came for is gone. I don't care about the rest and their customs."

"I really think you should stay until the memorial—"

"No way. I have courses to catch up on. And I have students preparing for their baccalaureate exams."

"Your mother just died! Forget your courses!"

"My mother wanted a different life for me than the one she had. The best way I can honor her is to live that life. Don't you understand?"

Abdel Nasser didn't interfere. Zeina didn't introduce him to her elderly father or her brother. All they understood was that he was an important person from the capital. They thought the car and its driver belonged to him and that Najla was his wife. The people gathered around the house, sitting on the floor or on the few chairs, started asking him about the situation in the country. They might have thought that he was someone of influence, despite his youthful attire with his casual shoes and stubble on his face.

Najla convinced Zeina to stay in the village long enough at least to visit her mother's grave the next morning, then return to Tunis in the evening. Zeina told Abdel Nasser, and he didn't object. She asked them to take her to Siliana, to her uncle's house where she had stayed the past few days. She would spend the night there. Her uncle's wife rode with her in the car, carrying her baby. There wasn't room for the uncle and their other children to ride in the car with them. Even her aunt didn't know about Zeina's relationship to him. Abdel Nasser was waiting for her to give even the smallest hint in that direction.

When they got out of the car and while her aunt was saying goodbye to Najla, Abdel Nasser kissed Zeina, slipping some bills into her purse. He expressed his sympathy one more time and told her to be strong.

10

The driver took them to Le Bardo, to the head of Rue des Orangers facing Café El Hajj. They walked to the house. Najla noticed that el-Talyani was lost in thought. He seemed agitated, too; he had stared out the window at the passing roads, fields, and trees the entire way back, jiggling his leg distractedly. Najla did the best she could in the car, smiling at him whenever their eyes met. He tried to smile back, but he couldn't hide his anxiety.

When they had gotten as far as the pastries shop, she asked him, "What are you thinking about, my herring?"

"What? Nothing . . ."

She didn't press him. He asked if she wanted him to walk her home, and she responded that she wouldn't leave him like that, unless he wanted to get rid of her.

"You know that isn't true," he said. "If it were up to me, I would ask you to spend the whole night with me."

"I will if you ask," she responded. "I want to celebrate the new era in your arms, too. Or have you forgotten that we began the coup yesterday?"

El-Talyani smiled, a trace of happiness appearing on his face. He walked faster to close the short distance remaining between them and the house. His eyes sparkled with a light that Najla had started to recognize, a sign that betrayed his longing for her.

He didn't waste any time. As soon as the door was closed, the anxious horseman became softer, transforming the negative charge inside him into a flowing energy that excited the mare. Their sprint was smooth and harmonious, but not without some roughness, as evidenced by the blue bruise on a neck, the fall of a trouser button, the marks of nails on Abdel Nasser's back and arms.

It was a cleansing, washing away the dirt of silence, depression, and anxiety that they had picked up on the way to the village and back.

Abdel Nasser spent the evening with his head on Najla's thighs, watching the national television, even though it was only broadcasting vapid songs. During those days even the tasteless programs on the television became important, because anything could happen. People were still in shock from the sudden fall of the Supreme Warrior, whose face and activities used to dominate the news, as well as the pre-news programming that was made up of his old speeches. They were still suspicious and fearful, unable to believe that there was another powerful man in the country. Would the story—which was enlarging rapidly via gossip in the cafés—really end that easily, without bloodshed, without resistance, without calls for revenge?

Najla's comments were infuriating him. "Poor Bourguiba" . . . "I've never known any leader but him" . . . "What will he do to him? Will he kill him, or throw him in jail?"

As furious as he was, he controlled his anger. He agreed with whoever it was who said that a woman "should be beautiful—and silent." Wasn't it enough that her body spoke for her? Every part of her body was eloquent! There was nothing for it but to put his index finger on her lips as though playing with her. He was looking at her, but his ears were straining to hear every word coming from the television.

He scrutinized Ben Ali's speech, in all its denotations and connotations. He listened to the statements from Tunis Afrique Presse, the names mentioned in the news. He heard a woman, her white *safseri* wrapped around her, addressing Zine El Abidine Ben Ali in a report. She was answering a question about what she thought of this change at the top of the pyramid, saying, "May God soften his heart toward his country."

Abdel Nasser caught the sentence. He jumped off the couch, grabbed his small notebook, and wrote down what the woman had said. Two days later, a column was published under Abdel Nasser's name, analyzing the spontaneous consciousness among the people and highlighting their real demands, the ones the new leadership should consider.

That night, however, all Abdel Nasser wanted was the tenderness of Najla's beautiful and talkative body, and she showered it on him in abundance. What a woman! She was an artist, drawing the loveliest paintings with her hands, fingers, lips, breasts, and feet. She composed the most beautiful music with her voice, her moans, sighs, and breath. Her chameleon-like perfume refreshed him from the first kiss until they relaxed, exhausted; her scent stimulated his every pore and offered him her honey, distilled into pure drops to quench his endless thirst.

11

Zeina returned home around five. Sunday evening was heavy: Abdel Nasser welcomed her with kindness and sympathy and asked how she was feeling. She took off her clothes and went directly to the bathroom, spending much more time inside than usual. Abdel Nasser asked her a few times, from behind the door, if she needed anything. When she didn't respond the first time, he feared that something bad might have happened and went to check on her. He opened the door without knocking to find the bathtub filled with hot water, its thick steam filling the room. Zeina was relaxing in the water, which came up above her chest, her eyes closed and her face red from the heat.

She roused when she felt his breath in the bathroom. She looked at him, smiling, as if drunk. She rose up to her knees, revealing the upper half of her body. He saw the swell of her breasts and the almonds of her nipples. She handed him the loofah bath glove, poured soap on it, and asked him to wash her back.

The soap made the glove almost slip from his hand. He started with her neck, scrubbing down in a straight line to the middle of her back. He moved to her right shoulder, then down her arm to her side. He slid his hand deep under her arm, then gently to her shoulder and back. He handled the glove as if giving a massage, moving in between her shoulder blades and pressing on the six vertebrae. He moved to the left side of her back and repeated all the motions with precision: shoulder, arm, side, under the arm, between the shoulder blades, back.

He returned to the center of her back, following the path of her spine from between her shoulder blades down to her hips, finding the soft cheeks on the left and right of her tailbone. Abdel Nasser had always loved women's bottoms, loved touching them. She felt a tickling sensation when he began to scrub them with the glove, and he noticed goosebumps rise in her flesh. He lost control; he didn't know when or how, but suddenly he was out of his clothes and in the tub with her.

Steam was rising from her reddened body, and her curls were tousled. They sunk down into the water, which flooded out over the bathroom floor. She kissed him with the longing of a woman who was hungry, lust flooding through her as it never had before.

A little while later, as she lay on the bed in her bathrobe, he leaned next to her, asking her questions and caressing her like a faithful husband. She gently asked him to let her think, saying only, "A new chapter in my life has begun. I will never go back to the village; I've become a mother to myself."

12

He left her to rest and went and turned on the television to see if there was any breaking news. He realized, from what he was seeing, that something new had indeed happened. The country felt relieved, and so did Zeina. Zine El Abidine Ben Ali had turned the page on a faded glory that didn't want to withdraw on its own, just as Zeina had turned a page in her personal history. He thought about his relationship with her: would she really start a new chapter? He decided to see what the coming days would bring, hoping that they would be as joyful as what he had just experienced in the bathroom.

He heard her leave the bedroom and go into the kitchen. He didn't want to disturb her. He had left some food that he'd prepared on the kitchen table; he and Najla had eaten from it at noon and left enough for dinner.

When he went to the kitchen to eat dinner, he found her sitting at the table with her books and papers in front of her. He was a bit surprised by this eagerness to study, but he figured that she was probably preparing her lesson plan for the next day.

He busied himself making coffee, without interrupting her, as they had agreed on for whenever she was sitting at the table studying. But suddenly she said, "Next time tell her to collect her personal things before leaving the house."

"She who? What are you talking about?"

She didn't answer him but busied herself with her papers. He repeated the question, and finally she answered, "I don't know who. Whoever this silver bracelet belongs to."

She tossed it on the kitchen table near where Abdel Nasser was standing, without looking at him. It was a silver bracelet that he had noticed around Najla's ankle the night before, when she was resting her feet on the living room table.

"I don't know whose this is. I have no idea . . ."

It must have fallen when Najla was washing her feet before bed, or changing her clothes in the morning. He had no idea where Zeina had found the damn thing.

She looked at him, holding back her anger and trying to appear calm and wise. "I don't care what you do. I only ask for two things: Nothing happens in my bed. And don't put me into an embarrassing situation with your women."

"What bed? What women?"

She interrupted him, firmly. "I'm done discussing this. You are free, and I am free. And if you don't mind, I've turned the page."

Her words "you are free" and "I am free" were ringing in his ears. He dropped the subject, as she wished. He secretly cursed Najla, though the image of her wearing the bracelet on her ankle, in the place of a traditional *khalkhal*, was sexy as hell.

13

Zeina called him on Tuesday at the office. It was the first time she'd called him at the newspaper and gotten ahold of him. He couldn't believe his ears: there was an unusual flirtatious lilt to her voice. She asked him to come home early, around 8 P.M.

When he opened the door, he found the living room bathed in dim light. There were four or five candles on the table, and the smell of perfume. Zeina hurried to him.

He had trouble taking in what he was seeing. She had changed her hair, which was now cut in an Italian hairstyle. She seemed like a different woman, one he'd never seen before. Her face seemed clearer and more beautiful. She was even taller: he saw that she was wearing high heels. She was also wearing a light pistachio sweater and a grey mini skirt with grey stockings that he'd never seen before.

She wore green eyeshadow and a touch of green eyeliner around her lashes, as well as a subtle lipstick.

"Look at all this beauty!" he said.

She came to him and pressed up against him. She pushed him to the wall, pinning both his hands to the wall above his head, coincidentally in the exact spot where Najla had kissed him. But Zeina's kisses, movements, and lust were different from Najla's: each flower has its own distinctive nectar and scent. He didn't want to compare between them, but the identical position made it impossible not to note the differences and similarities. He became sure that it was impossible to visit the river of desire twice—unless there were two different rivers. It seemed to Abdel Nasser that Zeina had, thanks to some miracle from God, become ready to quench his thirst.

He didn't understand what had happened and didn't want to ask. This was Abdel Nasser's nature in everything: he seldom expressed surprise or vocalized what was going on in his mind.

She gave him a gift. He opened it and found a fine leather wallet, as well as a Zippo lighter that reminded him of American films. She said, "My husband is an important person now; ordinary lighters are no longer good enough for him!"

He responded with one of the smooth lines that came to

him like a revelation: "All lighters are ordinary; you're the one who really sets me on fire."

He hugged her, thanking her. He realized that it was the first gift she'd ever given him. He didn't say anything, but he suspected that something was going on. How could Zeina, who knew nothing but books and the paths to work, university, and the library, come up with these gifts? And all with the skill of a woman who's accustomed to going shopping and knows what men like?

They ate dinner together and talked. He wanted to flirt and flatter her because she really looked beautiful and he felt the heat of a vague longing for her, but he hesitated. He examined the change in her without letting her see what was going on in his head. As he sweet-talked her, she seemed to be surrendering to him, leaving her logical brain and philosophical notions behind, far from the kitchen, despite the papers piled on the chair.

After dinner, which she had brought from the market along with red apples and navel oranges, she moved her papers to the table. She gave him a long kiss, then sat down to work. He went to watch television, as usual over the past few days.

Every day, Zeina opened her bag of surprises to pull out a new treasure. On Saturday night, for example, she wore a lacy nightgown. On Thursday, it was a new perfume. In the span of a week, she had started to use three different kinds of perfume. The vanity in the bedroom and the glass shelf above the bathroom sink started to fill up with different makeup and accessories, even though Zeina did not usually wear much makeup. She bought a hair dryer for her new style, as well as hairspray.

What was more important than all that, for el-Talyani, was that she was showing her femininity, which she had long hidden behind her serious appearance, her wall of papers and books, and her determination to succeed. As she became more feminine, she seemed to be more in love with el-Talyani and more attracted to him. She started to steal time from her studies and course preparation whenever possible to flirt with him, to invite him to bed, or to make love to him on the living room couch or rug or anywhere else she wanted. She reminded him of that day in the bathtub, his invasion into her space that was imprinted on her brain, in her new memory after she had become "mother to herself," as she said.

El-Talyani started thinking about her all day long at the newspaper, arriving home longing to see her, like a lover waiting to see his beloved. The taste of life with Zeina became truly sweet and reminded him of Lella Jnayna's honey. Zeina had started feeding him real honey, from eucalyptus flowers or orange or wild thyme. She would feed him a spoonful every morning when he woke up, or after making love. She explained, "You smoke a lot. Nothing is better for the throat and chest than honey."

It was impossible for him to reject it. Honey from Zeina's hand was pure sweetness, and he had no doubt that it was a cure—for the soul, if nothing else.

14

Najla came to visit him at the newspaper a few days after the remarkable change in Zeina's lifestyle and her relationship with el-Talyani. He was sure that she was the hidden hand he was looking for. He suspected it, then ruled it out, but then couldn't find any other sound explanation.

The employee at the front desk called him, and he went down quickly. He stole a kiss, and she told him, "Out of sight, out of lips, heart, and mind!"

He started telling her, even before they arrived at the International café, about Zeina and her new style and his surprise over the change. She smiled craftily and asked him, "You like her more like this, don't you?"

He answered in the affirmative, and she expressed her happiness with that. He took her by surprise when he said, "I knew you were behind all this."

She didn't answer him but kept looking at him, as if waiting for him to finish speaking. He continued. "Why did you do that?"

Najla explained that Zeina was her friend and that she confided in her, including about the bracelet that she'd forgotten at their house. She suspected that he was having affairs. Najla didn't want to lie, but she didn't want to expose their relationship, either. So she took a different path: she helped Zeina understand that she had ignored el-Talyani and so could hardly blame him if he searched for his pleasure elsewhere. Najla discovered, contrary to what she had thought, that Zeina loved her husband and wanted him for herself, but she didn't know how to keep him; nor did she have to tools to make him attracted to her. All the changes that had happened were, in fact, under Najla's advice and guidance.

El-Talyani was incredulous. "Don't you know that you were working against yourself?"

She told him that she did it as a favor for a beautiful but ambitious friend who was so busy realizing her dreams that she ignored her beauty. And Najla loved beauty, so she had befriended her. She added that Zeina's rural roots made her inexperienced in how to highlight and elevate her beauty. It was a raw, naive beauty that could fade at any moment if she didn't take care of it.

She had avoided answering him, so he repeated his question. She asked him if he really wanted an honest-to-God answer, and he said yes. So she told him. "You men don't get it. You see nothing in women but jealousy. Yes, we get jealous. And we love the man who makes us feel that way. Jealousy among us is a source of life, a sort of clinging to life. To be honest, I consider myself the most beautiful woman. Still, I started to get annoyed, like a purebred filly running by herself on a racetrack."

Her eyes narrowed, and she added, "I know I'm the only woman who deserves you, but I want to be jealous over you. So I need a competitor, and I found one in Zeina. She was in front of me the whole time, but I didn't notice her until she started getting jealous. Does that make sense to you? You'll never find another woman who will talk to you as honestly as I just did."

She explained to him that she had found her ideal horseman, and it didn't bother her if he rode another, especially Zeina, because he would compare them and would know his mare when the time was right. If she didn't deserve him, then that was her fate and she wouldn't cry about it.

She told him that after the two days they had spent together, she'd moved from "like" to the chaotic zone called "love." She admitted that she loved him but still didn't want him—him or anyone else—as a husband. She told him, "Even in this, I want a fair fight. I don't want to steal you from my friend. I hate it when women do that to their friends."

He asked why she had stayed away all these days. She laughed and told him he'd forgotten her, so she'd looked for someone else but couldn't find anyone. Then she told him, more seriously and in French, "I was on my period and in a bad mood." Then she added, "But I'm missing you now. When can I see you?"

"Now, if you want!"

The home of one of el-Talyani's journalist friends wasn't far away. They walked there and put out the fire that was consuming Najla. They didn't have a lot of time, so everything was quick. The house was dirty: the smell of sleep was still in the air, and the bed was in bad shape. The house was a picture of the misery of bachelor journalists—and the misery of the media, in general, even many days after the "blessed change."

Abdel Nasser noticed it but didn't say anything; Najla noticed, as well, and protested to the point of suggesting that he find an apartment near the newspaper; they could split the rent. But she didn't hide how impressed she was that they'd managed to put out the fire standing up, relying on her fitness and flexibility. However bad the house smelled, she noted, this way of extinguishing fires was a great discovery.

1

Zeina, Najla, the newspaper, and the country—with its new hero who had changed its life—they were all in a state of ecstasy. There was a new hope emerging among the people, separately and together. Only two people, each in their own way, mistrusted more than they believed: Si Abdel Hamid and Abdel Nasser. There was also a third person who didn't believe at all and who persisted in what he deemed to be in the state's ultimate interest: Abou Saoud H. The censor was being undermined by some journalists, under the illusion that the media had become free.

Abou Saoud would say, whenever he clashed with a journalist, "I am doing my job as I understand it. Talk to Si Abdel Hamid if you want—I have no new instructions."

The truth was that Abou Saoud was incredibly disciplined, and he knew things that other people didn't. So when he told people that there were no new instructions to accompany the new era, he wasn't lying. Nothing had changed; only the blatant interference had disappeared. In any case, most of the articles were ploughing the ground of optimism, waiting for a miracle to sprout. No journalist found anything in Ben Ali's speeches that would arouse suspicion. What more could they want? If the people were talking about Arab-Islamic identity, well, it was clear that Ben Ali was going to reinstitute our noble religion and beloved identity. For both nationalists and Pan-Arabists, Ben Ali had added a missing flavor to Pan-Arabism: democracy. So what was next? What was left to do? Let's build things up rationally, starting with the *Maghrebi* dialogue. Now was a time of powerful blocs, interests, and economy; the slogans of Pan-Arabism had done nothing but destroy and divide us.

As for the Islamists, who Bourguiba had imprisoned and whose leader he had almost executed, they could see with their own eyes that the houses of God were now filled with people. And the call to prayer was being broadcasted on television and radio stations at every prayer time. All they had to do was comply with the law by changing their moniker and not claiming exclusive rights to Islam, the religion of the people. So why the exaggerated outcry and the skepticism? Hadn't their leader and master said, "I trust first in God, then in Ben Ali"? And how could he say differently, after Ben Ali had saved his neck from the hangman's noose?

The left, however—at least, most of the left, with the exception of the extremists like the small university groups—cast doubt on Ben Ali. They withdrew from the scene, hiding within the student body. But they were a splinter of Tunisian politics that nobody cared about, either nationally or internationally.

As for the human rights groups and liberals, there was nothing left for them to do but to help the hero savior guide the country into a new democratic era, built on respecting the people's will and human rights. Hadn't the president himself declared as much in his immortal statement that there would be "no injustice after today?"

At the same time, the crisis of the workers' union was being solved. Who could be more merciful to the workers—both blue- and white-collar—than the son of the people, who had come from among them, from a Tunisian family like thousands of others, with neither reputation nor money nor pedigree. His people and his homeland were proud of him and would never be able to pay him back.

This was the view of Abou Saoud, as he was seeing it embodied in articles and columns. As he always said, he was on the lookout for anyone who even thought of damaging the new project that had resurrected hope among the people. Like Hicham Djait, who wrote a stupid article casting doubt on the legitimacy of those who had saved the country, full of academic jargon and pseudo-intellectualism. He was deconstructing words and pontificating about the difference between the state, authority, and power, and between legitimacy, legality, and divine law, and so on and so forth with all that useless nonsense. Some people were never happy about anything—better that Djait stick to the history of Kufa and the Arabian peninsula. If Saoud had been in charge of that irresponsible journal, he would have prevented the article from being published.

This is what Abou Saoud told them all one day, but nobody knew that he was right: a prophet has no honor in his own country. People judge based on what they see, and all they could see was a vile censor.

2

Si Abdel Hamid remained doubtful, despite the fact that weeks had passed since what had become known as the "blessed change," and that Ben Ali and his government were firmly ensconced, with the blessing of the political and social elite. He was writing most of his editorials himself, with his clear and poetic style, highlighting the wide horizons that the change had opened up for Tunisians. He focused on the principles of democracy, the legitimacy of the country's rescue, the wise plans for solving problems, and the comprehensive development strategies. He recognized that many of the slogans of the period were being taken directly from international development reports and commitments by the UN and its various agencies, or from financing bureaus for the Tunisian economy. For each editorial, he would choose a new idea to explore deeply—as much as an editorial column could bear—to reveal the president's rational process, his realistic choices, the human dimensions, and his eagerness to make the country a part of the major universal issues.

Si Abdel Hamid's best days were when the president would give a speech, carry out a surprise visit to one of the impoverished "shadow areas," check on a government institution, or declare a new measure. These were lessons, giving him the opportunity to analyze the significance and perspective of the speech or action. Si Abdel Hamid was exceedingly skilled at hunting out the new ideas in every speech. His analysis was astute, focusing on the time, location, and style, as well as the particular words or phrases that were filled with meaning and significance that the people, as well as the elites, should understand. His approach to different measures, recommendations, and decisions, no matter how simple they were, was unique. He could find hidden rationality in them that no one else could see, as if Ben Ali were revealing the secrets of his strategic plan and vision to no journalist but him!

Abdel Nasser would argue with him sometimes—away from work, of course—when they were enjoying a relaxed moment while eating or drinking. Si Abdel Hamid would answer him, with sarcasm, "Why all the fuss—they're all happy. Am I Che Guevara? I am almost sixty; you all are the future."

Si Abdel Hamid would explain to him that those surprise visits were a smart piece of political messaging in the beginning, but time and repetition would expose their populist, folkloric character. The truth was: there was no meaning or significance or any of that nonsense. Nothing had really changed. The speeches that Ben Ali had learned how to read (at first with difficulty, word by word and completed only painstakingly) were nothing but rewordings of the different reports and policies produced by the ministry technocrats.

He always pointed out that Bourguiba had left a strong

administration, with a powerful administrative elite, without which the country would have long ago collapsed and fallen into the hands of any ambitious rascal or vain adventurer like the Islamists. No one can bring down a state of technocrats, who govern from behind a curtain and withdraw into themselves in times of crisis to preserve the minimum, then take off as creative innovators whenever they find strong political support. Si Abdel Hamid opined that Ben Ali needed them now, but he wouldn't let them work, and one day he would either get rid of them or would win over the best of them. At that moment, he would have begun digging his own grave.

As Si Abdel Hamid drank, lubricating his conversation and whetting his appetite for analysis, his brain and his analytical sense would sharpen. He then considered the new measures a mere advertisement campaign, a part of the daily work of the presidential institutions, ruling party, and administration. The state didn't need that whole song and dance. He added, with the air of someone who is completely confident in what they are saying, "Just wait a little while. We'll go back to daily recorded presidential addresses, just like Bourguiba's, but in a new style, without the Great Leader's charisma."

Deep down, Si Abdel Hamid did not believe in Ben Ali. Abdel Nasser thought at first that that was because of his Bourguibist upbringing and his secret support of Mzali. When he told him as much, Si Abdel Hamid became angry and offered him his own analysis of Bourguiba, who he said had been on borrowed time since the early seventies and the congress of Monastir. That was the time, in Si Abdel Hamid's opinion, that Bourguiba was finished; he didn't know how to become an eternal leader. He had been in need either of martyrdom by death in battle (which he'd missed out on before independence) or of leaving the national stage with honor. But his megalomania and image of himself as the father of the country had prevented him from doing the latter.

Abdel Nasser disagreed with Si Abdel Hamid, both in his analysis of what had happened and in the way he dealt with the new situation. He discussed it with him nicely, though. He insisted that Ben Ali's coup was a military one, no matter how much he presented the image of a civilian. He even accused him of being a spy for the Americans, inferring this from what had started to leak about Ben Ali's role when he was a military attaché at the Tunisian embassy in Poland. Furthermore, he considered what had happened to be simply a change of the chess pieces in the hands of the Sahel elite. The powerful people in that region were very rich, very well connected, and basically held the keys to the country. They had the money and the political acumen and were capable of changing the rules of the game at any time. So Ben Ali would surely protect the interests of those people above all others; he would also be a good student of the international financial institutions and apply their policies to the letter.

He also focused on the idea that Ben Ali did not have any new social or political plan. He would make do with some pro forma reforms to make the bitter pill of structural economic reforms go down more smoothly, and would tie the Tunisian economy more closely to Western interests. Politically, he was more dangerous than Bourguiba because he was able, from the first, to absorb all of his adversaries and put them in his jacket pocket with a few sweet words. So what could they ask for now?

3

While Najla didn't change along with the changing political situation, after several weeks, Zeina—despite the differences in career, interests, and the way they moved—seemed to have much in common with Zine El Abidine Ben Ali.

Najla continued to be beautiful and generous. She knew what she wanted from el-Talyani; she gave him everything he needed and more but without disrupting his life. She knew when to appear and when to disappear. She was always fresh: the passing of days didn't seem to affect her or to touch her sweet, cheerful spirit. She was a thing of beauty that God had sent to el-Talyani as if to prove to him that, despite everything, life was worth living. She was an image of the best face of life, a delicious wine that he enjoyed, a warm beach for him to rest on, and an athletic body that he squeezed like an orange to get to the refreshing pleasure within. She did not ask for anything but to be with him, whenever possible. She required nothing but to be guided by her rider toward the finish line. She was at his beck and call whenever he wanted her, and if she wanted him, she knew how to make him hers without pressure or coercion. She wasn't a philosopher in her ideas but was the product of a philosophy of intelligence, devotion, and pleasure. A practical, sensual philosophy that exuded a special spirituality.

As for Zeina, she had tried to become a woman fighting for her husband, but she couldn't keep up the pace she had started at. It was hard for her to combine her studies, her career, and the work needed to defend the lion in her den. That goal required the time, creativity, and resourcefulness of an experienced woman; how could Zeina do that when she hadn't given up her ambitions or naivety and so had no time to acquire the needed expertise of hard experience that Najla had pushed her into?

If it had just been a matter of ambitions and naivety, it would have been easy. But, instead, something unexpected happened to Zeina, in which she was complicit with Najla. El-Talyani considered that complicity to be what ruined his relationship with Najla and started to signal his break with Zeina.

Najla told him that she had acted with Zeina as her conscience demanded, as her friend and a fellow woman. Zeina was still young, only twenty-four years old; plenty of people her age hadn't even graduated from college yet. It wasn't possible for a woman to open up to her desire, for that miraculous feeling to stir inside her, if her body didn't ask for it and she herself didn't want it. What had happened was an ordinary car wreck that needed to be cleared away for her to continue on the road she had chosen.

She accused him of being like all other men, not seeing anything but his own interests and desires, even at the expense of the woman he shared his bed with. She was a bully in her defense of Zeina in a way that el-Talyani couldn't have expected. She cheats with her husband and then *defends* her? Defends her mistakes with that husband in addition to her selfishness? He swore to Najla, with God as his witness, that he didn't understand a thing she was saying. And she swore, with God as her witness, that Abdel Nasser was incapable of understanding anything about women except their genitals. She sensed that she had perhaps gone too far and belatedly added the word "almost."

He reminded her that he was a defender of women, but he still couldn't accept what Zeina had done. She had disappointed him and had crushed a hope that he had hidden inside. No justification was acceptable, in his opinion, not studies and not desire. She should have at least told him about it and asked him what he thought. They might have disagreed; they might have appealed to Najla or someone else for mediation. But he couldn't accept being treated like a stranger, a blind fool, a deceived husband who was blissfully unaware of what was going on until it was too late.

4

Zeina returned home exhausted one day, when he thought she'd gone to the National Library. It was 11 A.M. and el-Talyani had not yet left for the newspaper. Najla was with her. He saw something in their eyes, as if they were hiding something embarrassing or some news.

Najla simply informed Abdel Nasser that Zeina was sick, and she had just come back from the doctor. He asked what was wrong; Zeina told him it was a female issue that required a day or two of rest and that she just wanted to sleep.

Abdel Nasser opened the window to let in some fresh air. He got the bed ready for Zeina and brought her pajamas as she sat with Najla in the kitchen. He heard Najla begging her to eat something, juice or bread and butter. He heard her say that she was weak and needed to eat.

Abdel Nasser went back to check on her. She looked pale and fragile. She had overexerted herself; Najla helped her change her clothes and get in bed. She gave her a pill.

Abdel Nasser signaled to Najla to join him in the living room. He asked her what had happened to Zeina. But she didn't tell him anything new, just repeated that it was a female issue and that she would feel better by the end of the day or the next. He shouldn't worry.

Najla sat on Abdel Nasser's side of the bed and conferred with Zeina. She agreed to make Zeina vegetable soup for lunch and to barbecue some lamb liver from the neighborhood butcher. Abdel Nasser heard the conversation between them and hurried to get the soup ingredients and the meat. When he came back with the groceries, Najla told him to go ahead and go to work; she would stay with Zeina. This was during the last week of their winter break.

He thought, on that first day, that it was her illness that had made her anxious and worried, making her normally sunny face cloudy. She seemed sad. He asked her several times if she was all right, but she would just give him a strained smile that seemed forcefully pulled from her lips.

From time to time he noticed that she was trying to hide

her tears. Sometimes he found her eyes red from crying. But she would keep herself under control, pretending to be studying or busying herself reading. She began to avoid him and reject him on the pretext of fatigue or headache, or being in a bad mood.

He tried to gain some understanding of Zeina's problem from Najla, but with no luck. Najla would skillfully turn the question around on him, accusing him of no longer desiring her or wanting to be with her. He would fall right into the trap, justifying himself and making excuses and promising to spend some quality time with her.

Abdel Nasser got to where he could no longer bear Zeina's mood. He sometimes thought that perhaps her grieving for her mother had not run its course as it should have. She was no longer sick, but her mood was still murky. He had a feeling that something had happened but that Zeina and Najla were hiding it from him. He couldn't figure it out . . . Had Najla talked to her about their relationship? Had he maybe gotten a venereal disease from Najla and given it to Zeina, causing the "female issues" they'd talked about?

5

El-Talyani went back to his old habit of staying out late with Si Abdel Hamid or his other friends: journalists, artists, and intellectuals. He was fond of these meetings, as they gave him the chance to meet people who thought differently from him. Each of them had a story, a path and style that made them distinctive. But their society's misery had turned them into albatrosses that couldn't fly, impeded by wings that had been made for that purpose. The art and culture in this country caused a lot of problems: they started with heavy drinking and ended in insanity. In between were depression, frustration, ennui, and a range of uncreative forms of nihilism. Neurotics each channeled their neurosis in their own way.

Sometimes, he would stumble upon a beauty among them, drowning in alcohol or hiding an embarrassment or a psychological complex that would wax and wane with circumstance. He could always tell when a woman was being eaten away by some tragedy. His charm and silver tongue were enough for him to get any of these beauties that he came across. Many of them would hit on him at the restaurants or bars, even in front of their female friends.

He met many people—men and women—during the period when Zeina was secluding herself, sometimes with her books and papers and other times alone with the stories she was hiding.

When he came home, he could see the signs of fatigue and insomnia on her face. He would ask her about it, but she would just sigh and hide her face. He could sometimes hear a stifled sob, or see her wiping her tears with her hands. She slept fitfully.

From what he could tell, she was suffering from depression. At the very least, it was clear that she was tired and her body was weak, but she fought to sit at the table and study anyway.

During the first few days after her unexpected return home with Najla, she suffered from a fever that she treated with medicine. She complained of pain in the left side of her back, severe pain that made her writhe like a chicken being strangled. Acetaminophen wasn't enough to get rid of the pain. After almost four days, she complained of stomach cramps and spasms. Abdel Nasser's concern increased dramatically when she told him, her face yellow and contorted by pain, that she felt shooting pains in her vagina: exactly in the vaginal opening, as if nails were being driven into the flesh. He insisted on taking her to the doctor. This was around 10 A.M., but she insisted that he call Najla and have Najla take her; she refused to let him come with her.

Najla prepared a hot cup of verbena tea for her and agreed that she would stay with her for the last few days of the break.

The atmosphere in the house changed completely. Najla filled the house with her overflowing femininity and joy. She started taking care of Zeina as if she were her daughter and el-Talyani as if he were her husband. He didn't know where she was getting all that energy, that generous energy that transformed misery into joy. She was truly comforting. Zeina started getting better and recovering from her illness, with the exception of a trace of sadness that lingered on her face.

6

The most important task that Najla undertook, when she became the lady of the house, was to plan the New Year's party herself. She decided that it would be at home, since she said she didn't feel like going out to a restaurant or hotel. The party, however, turned out to be a miserable start to 1988.

Abdel Nasser brought the cake, which wasn't easy to find. He nearly gave up, finding everywhere crowded and noisy, but he finally found a small cake at Pâtisserie Ben Yedder in Le Bardo. He thought to pick up a ready-made *vacherin* cake from the Touta supermarket, then added an ice cream cake, as well.

Two days before, he'd bought a good quantity of beer and wine; he also had a bottle of whiskey that a friend of his had brought from France.

Najla didn't prepare anything but instead brought everything from her father's house. Her mother, Khala Naima, was a talented cook who could make great dishes out of almost nothing. Najla told Abdel Nasser that all the tagines, salads, and roasted chicken were prepared by her middle sister, but under Najla's personal instructions and recommendations. He thought to himself that she seemed to be from a family of women who were skilled at everything and wanted to share the joke with Najla, but then remembered that Zeina was with them, trying to overcome her misery to welcome in the new year.

The conversation, like most conversations on such occasions, was meandering and spontaneous. It covered everything with no plan. Abdel Nasser brought all of his jokes out of storage, dirty and non-dirty. Najla shared her jokes, which she had memorized from the routines and the plays of the Egyptian comedian Adel Emam, especially the play *School of Rascals*. They laughed heartily. They changed the subject to what their wishes were for the new year. The three of them agreed on wishing Zeina success in becoming a university professor: Zeina by saying that it was her dream that she wanted to make a reality, Najla by saying that Zeina had worked so hard for it and deserved the best. El-Talyani, however, expressed his wish in a way that Zeina didn't like; he embarrassed her, leaving her feeling resentful and leaving Najla smiling but a bit unsettled.

Zeina's success, in his opinion, was the beginning of his real life because there would be no more difference between the marriage certificate and the marriage, and she would be ready to have a beautiful, brilliant baby girl like her. He said that he preferred to have a girl because he thought, like the song said, that women were the future of Tunisia and our top source of pride. But if the baby was a boy, then he would be an activist like his father.

Najla quickly changed the subject, saying, "And me? Did you forget about me? I want to find a wonderful, loyal husband, who will be a friend to Abdel Nasser and be like him— so I don't get jealous of Zeina!"

Zeina laughed and agreed, adding, "You have a big heart, and you will find someone who deserves you."

Abdel Nasser said, jokingly, "I am the last of my species. Zeinab's factory closed its doors years ago."

Then he added, "Your only solution is for the Islamists to take power, by the grace of God. They'll let us marry four women like good Muslims: you'll be my second wife—plus all my concubines, of course."

Najla laughed out loud, saying, "I hereby testify that I will be the first to believe in the Islamists. I'll vote for them in the election!"

Zeina came out of her sad mood for a short moment and pinched Abdel Nasser's thigh, saying, "I will only agree on Najla. But can you take care of two women?"

Abdel Nasser answered her, continuing the joke on the surface, with some hidden meaning for Najla. "We have a long weekend coming up, Thursday through Sunday. I'll try you out as a companion over the weekend, then we'll decide when the Islamists take power." He looked at Zeina. "What do you say?"

Zeina didn't know how to answer. He turned to Najla to ask her, and she answered slyly, "When we have our old Zeina back and she's happily recovered from her illness, we'll see."

As soon as she mentioned the illness, Abdel Nasser insisted on knowing the truth about what had happened. He pressed the issue. He told them he felt there was something secret in their conversations, and he didn't understand why they were hiding whatever it was from him. Especially seeing as Zeina was his wife and he'd noticed for a while that something was wrong; she'd been dealing with nightmares, tears, insomnia, and pain. He stressed that he had a right to know: he loved Zeina and couldn't bear to see her in that state and just keep quiet, as if he were a neighbor or something. He hinted that he'd seen some private "women's things," as they called them, that he hadn't seen before. He said that Zeina's period had lasted for too long, and he saw some blood once when he was helping her out of the bathroom.

He confessed that he'd read the insert for the antibiotics

she was taking, and the medication that was prescribed to stop the bleeding. He was no doctor, but he knew it was a medication for sepsis. He added that he had some suspicions but didn't want to shock them.

Zeina and Najla kept exchanging glances. They knew how intelligent Abdel Nasser was but still found it hard to believe that he'd been able to connect all of these clues. They saw him starting to get upset. Najla shook her head at Zeina slightly, *don't tell him*. She tried to change the subject, but he became stubborn and refused to back down.

Najla went to bring another dish from the kitchen. When she came back, she found Zeina finishing the story she had started:

". . . so I had no choice but to get an abortion."

7

Najla was rooted to the spot in surprise. She looked back and forth between Zeina, broken down sobbing with her head in her hands, and Abdel Nasser, pressing his hands against his jaws and rubbing his nose and beard. His silence was terrifying, her tears bitter.

Najla tried to repair the situation. She sat next to Zeina and pulled her toward her. She started wiping away the tears and enjoining her to stop crying. She asked Abdel Nasser to leave the subject alone until tomorrow, so as not to spoil the night.

He smiled sarcastically, then started pouring out his vitriol. He accused Zeina of thinking only of her personal interests without ever giving a thought to his feelings or opinions. "It was *my* child as well as yours; why did you make this decision alone? What makes your ambition more important than my desire to have a child?"

When Najla asked him to try and understand Zeina's motives,

he accused her of being complicit with her and even encouraging her to get the abortion. Najla answered calmly, "You know that Zeina is independent; it's an insult for you to insinuate that I control what she does."

He didn't know how to answer her. There was a precarious balance in the situation; any disruption would make them team up against him. He decided not to play the game of divide and conquer: what had happened, happened, and there was no use in opening up new wounds.

Najla asked him to respect Zeina's feelings. She was already full of guilt and regret; she was confused, not to mention exhausted and suffering from a nervous breakdown. Najla reminded him that she could understand the feelings of emptiness and guilt that were eating Zeina up better than he could.

Abdel Nasser started applauding sarcastically. "What a great lawyer! Bravo!"

She pleaded with him to stop being sarcastic; the matter was more serious than he could imagine. After a long silence, Zeina interjected, "Let's assume that I'm selfish, like you say: I made a decision about my body freely, without asking you. Now, since you know everything, you can do whatever you want. Issue your ruling, Your Honor, and command me. I will obey your orders."

She explained to him, with great emotion, the feelings of motherhood that had stirred inside her. She said that he would never understand her pleasure in the milk dripping from her breasts, or what a strong feeling of regret and horrific feeling of guilt it had left behind. She told him that she'd never grieved properly for her mother, and here was a second grief, for her possible daughter, or for a son who looked like Abdel Nasser. She shouted at him, "I have enough to deal with already: mourning twice over, plus the regret, pain, and self-loathing! And I feel it in my body; it's not just some idea in my mind! Do you have any idea what it means to have a pain like this hollowing out your insides? Or to have your spirit torn apart like this? Do you have any idea?!"

Zeina collapsed as if dizzy and lost consciousness. Abdel Nasser rushed to her and sprinkled some water on her. He brought a perfume bottle and put it next to her nose for her to smell. He sprayed some of it on her face and below her nose. Najla took her to bed.

After he was reassured that Zeina was all right, he turned on the television and started watching a singing show on the Italian station. He drank a lot, alone. He started his new year drunk. After an hour, Najla joined him. She wished him a happy new year, wished him all the good wishes her sweet tongue could lavish on him. He embraced her and gave her a long kiss. He asked about Zeina. He went into the bedroom to wish her a happy new year, but she was sleeping deeply. He then sank with Najla into her honeyed sweetness; they didn't sleep until four hours into the new year.

Najla blamed him for being harsh with Zeina, but in her own style that left no room for reply or discussion. Her blame and reproach were like flirting, making him weak and making him forget his anger. The wine had almost taken his senses, but Najla's wine finished the job. He was tense, but she sucked all his tension away the same way she had his anger. He forgot about Zeina sleeping in the next room, and about the news of the abortion that had ruined his night. How could this charming woman not leave him senseless?

She wanted to sleep, unlike the other nights, in the living room, but el-Talyani insisted that she sleep in his place so that her scent would linger on the sheets and pillow. She was about to go to bed when he suddenly remembered, at that late hour and despite being exhausted, the day they went to his journalist friend's house. He suggested that they relive that encounter in Raeef's empty room. She didn't know about it; she'd never been in there. El-Talyani opened it up, and she lit up the dark room with her beauty and flooded its humid air with her sweet scent as she exclaimed, "This is perfect for working each other out and learning new tricks!"

8

That night marked the end of his emotional relationship with Zeina. She recovered fully and returned to her work and studies. She herself understood that something had been broken, but she didn't have the time, peace of mind, or means to gather it up—whether to throw it away outside, to fix it as much as possible, or to live with it as it was. At other times, her ambitions to teach at university abandoned her; she couldn't find the time to take care of her life and her relationship with Abdel Nasser, much less her future. Abdel Nasser didn't even see much of Najla in the new year. He had started leading a hedonistic kind of life, spent between bars, restaurants, and at the houses of his friends, mistresses, and fans. A life filled with conversation, discussion, drinking, having fun, and promiscuity. He was no longer the choosy aristocrat, carefully selecting his prey. He had entered a new era; women became an addiction just like his addiction to alcohol. It was a style of life that seemed like all fun from the outside but in reality was a frantic attempt to forget something. But the good part, for el-Talyani, was that—although he was giving the rope of his desires some slack, letting out his animal instincts, his whims and craziness— he remained awake; he never lost consciousness. He was like someone enjoying their descent into the swamp. He gave the illusion of identifying himself with it. He rediscovered some of the criminals and thugs in his neighborhood, despite their intellectual and artistic cover. He was in a downward spiral, at any moment liable to totter and stumble into the abyss, but he always righted himself at the last moment.

Some of these stories I heard directly from Abdel Nasser, some I heard about him from trusted sources, and others I learned about by coincidence. During this time, I was in my village in Kairouan, teaching philosophy and wisdom to the children of our people. If I were going to tell all of what I heard, I would need hundreds of pages to copy it down accurately, and I'd never finish editing them all. I don't want to do that; these are digressions that might make me lose the thread of this story, of what led to the scandal involving Abdel Nasser at the cemetery. The truth is that many of these stories don't tell us anything about Abdel Nasser's life or his motives for beating Imam Sheikh Allala on the day Si Mahmoud was buried.

Other stories, however, show us what Abdel Nasser suffered when torn between his submission to the miserable milieu of Tunisian intellectuals and media and his sharp awareness that it wasn't enriching him or contributing any meaning to his life. It was an ennui that fed off of ennui and a disgust that was born of disgust. Abdel Nasser had a passion for self-reinvention and personal development; he was always on the lookout for things that could enrich his feelings, knowledge, sensitivity, and outlook on life. So, based on what I know about him, I can say that he was almost certainly forced into that environment; it wasn't a choice. That environment breeds futility and nonsense; Abdel Nasser was and is a serious man, even in his jokes: he has always searched for significance, even at the height of his hedonism.

1

The year of 1988, for Abdel Nasser, was a year of futility and nonsense. It was also the year he first noticed in that futility a likeness to the neighborhood he'd grown up in, among a different crowd.

People had changed in his old neighborhood and so had the place itself. Some people from affluent families, and even from poor ones, started to move away. New dialects appeared and new residents, who acted differently from what the people there were used to. You started to see young men harassing the neighborhood girls just as often and just as obscenely as strange girls passing on the street. Nothing could stop them from using profane, explicit language, even with girls from respectable families. The original residents of the neighborhood also learned of repeated home burglaries and started locking their doors, which they had always left open for their neighbors, no matter how far from home they were.

At the end of the street, young men started gathering to smoke and talk loudly about everything, embellishing their conversations with profanity. Then, over time, the residents started seeing them opening up beer bottles or sometimes cheap wine. They would drink in the open, within sight of the elderly. The neighborhood sheikhs felt frustrated and asked for God's protection and cursed them, but they couldn't talk to the newcomers or ask them to respect the neighborhood and its traditions. One day Aamm Bashir, the baker, dared to talk to them, and in response, he heard words the likes of which he'd never heard in his life. If not for his age, they would've beaten him instead of just threatening him.

On summer evenings, after the worst of the heat had abated, Aamm Bashir would spray down the street in front of his shop, put out his big terracotta pot of basil, then sit on his rocking chair. How the kids used to envy him that chair! He would take small sticks and arrange jasmine buds on them in a small, fragrant bouquet, threading them with mulberry leaves and then wrapping white thread around them. Then he would put the *machmoum* he had made behind his ear. His friends would come over and spend the evening chatting with him. Aamm Bashir would smoke a hookah (the only thing he smoked), which he shared with his visitors.

One day the previous summer, he'd seen some young men gathered in the street speaking as they always did in vulgarities, in whose invention and embellishment they displayed a great deal of creativity. He asked them to respect the passersby and keep their voices down. After that day, the residents no longer saw Aamm Bashir, nor his basil pot or hookah, in front of the shop door. That was a sign that the strangers' and thugs' domination of the neighborhood was total. The neighborhood embarked on a new era, bereft of blessings or goodness.

The situation eventually evolved into gangs and networks that secretly traded in alcohol and sold all different kinds of hashish, cannabis, and pills. These men scared the girls so much that they stopped going outside after dark, either in summer or winter. The neighborhood had new masters now. Their ranks were soon joined by a group of bearded men who occupied the neighborhood mosque and kept it full all day long. Many of the new delinquents who had seen the light of God became the strong arms protecting their religious brethren from the new masters' violence. There were also a lot of new faces wandering around the neighborhood like they owned it. A finely balanced division of power was established between the bearded men of faith and the group selling alcohol and drugs on the sly. The rest, however, the ordinary people and original residents, were disturbed and angry at the state of the neighborhood. But they were helpless.

El-Talyani, on the other hand, was living in another world, a dream-world envisioning a better society, where social classes would disappear and the revolution would come to life. He considered these new groups to be victims of the unchecked liberal development and policies that pushed people to emigrate. He called them the "ragged proletariat" and said that they would be the most dangerous people in the coming revolution: any of the revolution's enemies could employ them against the people who had a genuine interest in change. They were victims who could become victimizers-on-order serving the counter-revolution. They had already established relationships with the police—who, in exchange for their share of free wine and beer, turned a blind eye to their dealings. They never enforced the law unless they disagreed with the thugs about their requisite quantity of beer or wine, or when they disrespected or attacked them. Abdel Nasser remembered many events that he had witnessed: a late-night fight between one of the sellers and a police car; chases on the roofs and knives being drawn (or daggers, or even swords); blackmail attempts; the kidnapping of a lost girl; a group of them ganging up on a new prostitute to take turns with her, then beating her until she ran for her life.

If not for Abdel Nasser's physical strength and fitness, which allowed him to challenge anyone who dared approach him, they would have stolen his money or stabbed him in the back. But he taught one of them a lesson that put fear into these new masters and kept them away from him.

That day, he was going to his parents' house for a short visit, to maintain the family ties. One of the neighborhood's new heroes stopped him to ask for money. Abdel Nasser refused.

The boy, who was not even twenty years old and barely reached Abdel Nasser's chest, threatened him with a straight razor. Abdel Nasser put his hand in the back pocket of his jeans, as if to take out money, then kicked the hand wielding the razor in one graceful movement of his military boots. He restrained him and took him to the police station, the kid begging him for forgiveness the whole way. The others heard about this. The young miscreant was new and unsupported by the neighborhood masters, who came to Abdel Nasser to distance themselves from the young bastard and what he had done.

2

Abdel Nasser realized that what he saw in his neighborhood looked a lot like the world of journalists and intellectuals he spent time with. They worked under the logic of gangs and networks, too, fighting amongst themselves with words (and sometimes with fists). It was a world of gossip, hate, slander, lying, hypocrisy, and dangerously wounded egos. A world with neither the old inherited morals, nor the new journalistic and literary morals. They acted like the neighborhood thugs; most of them didn't even read the newspaper they wrote for. As for books and keeping up with new ideas in literature and culture, that was far too much to ask. El-Talyani would wonder, incredulously, *How can someone who doesn't read, write?* He had learned that reading and writing were two sides of the same coin. You would see the journalists wearing ragged second-hand clothes, bought from the *frip*, with a pound of filth on the collar, food stains on the vest, and the trousers unironed. They'd never once polished their shoes.

They were garrulous when discussing big names they'd heard. They would catch a word from intellectuals' or academics' mouths, then inject it into sentences where it did not fit. They used words from the philosopher's lexicon without knowing what they meant, or what the people who had coined them intended by them. They talked about films they'd never seen and books they'd never read. Their conversations were part and parcel of the appetizers and mixed nuts placed in front of them, used to lessen the bitterness of the beer or the sourness of the cheap wine.

Abdel Nasser, in the beginning, was not one to accept this shameless attack on ideas, so he didn't hesitate to debate, discuss, and correct. He didn't understand that there was an implicit rule among the group. They all knew that everyone was lying, but they conspired to believe each other, without defamation or doubt. At first they would seem pleased with Abdel Nasser's comments and corrections. They had a way of bragging that allowed them to accept him in the beginning, but then they started to find him annoying. He persisted so often that soon no one wanted to sit with him, and they avoided him like a mangy dog. As soon as he understood the rules of the game, he started to enjoy their conversations and their lying to themselves. He even fabricated theoretical notions, which quickly became a frequent part of the conversation, attributed to fake philosophers. He would also tell them made-up plots from movies that he said he'd watched, which would then come back to him in different versions. He would pretend to be interested and ask about the director and actors or the screenwriter. But he wouldn't get an answer; the person would always "not remember" or change the subject.

Gossip about female journalists and their secrets, as well as the liaisons and adventures of actresses and artists, were the main dish of these meetings. So-and-so is intimate with her editor-in-chief or the manager; that journalist over there has an open marriage and sleeps around; this one harasses her colleagues constantly, even in the bathroom; another woman made their colleague divorce his gorgeous wife (even though she's not half as good-looking); and yet another is an expert at seducing famous politicians and powerful men, and then bragging about it . . . Stories like that, all from the bottom of the barrel. They would act surprised when Abdel Nasser would ask them about their motives for this behavior, or when he mocked them, suggesting that they were just jealous. They claimed to be morally upstanding and eager to protect good ethics by exposing the story, but really they were fantasizing about sleeping with this one or that one. This was obvious when a female intellectual or journalist would sit with them: you could see their penises stand to attention and lust practically shoot from their eyes like magma.

The world of the media and intelligentsia revealed all its secrets to Abdel Nasser. He started to see it as a huge lunatic asylum that destroyed its patients with lies, illusions, wine, deprivation, and sometimes cannabis. The qualitative difference between the writers and intellectuals on one hand and the criminals and drug dealers on the other was non-existent.

3

Si Abdel Hamid used to say, in some of the late meetings on days when he had written an article or editorial praising Ben Ali as a savior and change-bringer, "The common people see him as a savior. Conservative, poor, illiterate—they all see him that way. And the intellectuals try to outdo the people in formulating futility and stupidity with flowery words."

Once, Abdel Nasser looked down, hiding a smile. Si Abdel Hamid knew what he was thinking and continued, "Of course, we're all just cogs in this great machine, the machine of spreading futility and lies. My whole life, I've never known any job but this one. What do you want me to do? Life is difficult. It's a schizophrenia I just have to deal with; otherwise I would go crazy, and they would haul me off to the Razi asylum, or I would commit suicide or join the opposition. Each one is a form of insanity I can't handle. That train whistled and departed the station at full speed a long time ago."

That day, Si Abdel Hamid began suggesting to Abdel Nasser that he find a way out of the situation, worried that he would end up sinking in the mud. He thought that, without a doubt, the real dictatorship was coming, one that would make the people miss Bourguiba. He didn't trust Ben Ali's intentions: he was a dangerous man trying to win over and please everybody. He was willing to become an Islamic leader or a Pan-Arab leader or even a Marxist–Leninist leader. The only thing that mattered was that he held onto his stolen throne. He hadn't spilled a drop of blood, but that wasn't the good thing that people thought it was—it was more dangerous than bloodshed. The country was no stranger to being conquered: Carthaginians, Vandals, Romans, Shiites, Kharijites, Banu Hilal, Turks, Spaniards, French—they all subjugated it. It experienced some pain but embraced them with a welcoming heart. Despite the veneer of conservatism and religion, it kept up its prostitution and asked for nothing but protection. Ben Ali understood all this and had learned the lesson well: he would not leave the country without spilling blood.

Si Abdel Hamid would say, with a touch of prophecy, "Just wait. From the beginning, he's pulled the rug out from under all of us. He'll get rid of the Islamists; then, he'll take care of the rest of the opposition; after that he'll be able to devote himself to killing—his favorite pastime."

He promised to help Abdel Nasser meet Western journalists and contacts at Francophone news organizations so that he could get a job as a correspondent. He was sure that Abdel Nasser would become a world-class journalist. He fulfilled his promise, and Abdel Nasser got an offer to join Agence France-Presse, with the help of Si Abdel Hamid.

Si Abdel Hamid would say, "This country is a blind machine, and it crushes the intelligent."

He didn't respond when Abdel Nasser added that intelligent people sometimes crushed themselves, if their ego was big and their ambitions bigger. The editor-in-chief didn't understand him because Abdel Nasser was talking about Zeina. He was leaving her alone to focus on her *agrégation* exam the same way he'd left her the previous year to focus on her master's research.

4

Zeina acquired new habits two or three months after the start of the new year. She was practically living at the National Library. She would go there right after teaching her courses at the high school. Najla told el-Talyani that she would eat lunch at a small *kafteji* restaurant in the old city. Najla had bought a small car, which liberated her from waking up early and liberated Zeina from the pain and crowds of public transport. She would walk from the National Library with some of her colleagues to the Faculté 9 Avril to attend her courses; then she would return home. Abdel Nasser didn't know what she did after she got home, but he noticed leftover sandwiches, pizza, Coke, bread with Gruyère or ricotta cheese, and sometimes some leftover olive oil in a small dish. She would be fast asleep when he got home, and he wouldn't see her in the mornings because he always woke up late.

He found, on a few occasions, slips of paper with notes that she wrote for him while he was sleeping. He would read "I miss you" and understand that she wanted him. He would often take a break from his new lifestyle and go home early to put out that fire—first out of a sense of duty and secondly out of a small hope that a normal relationship was possible, after she finished the *agrégation* that had destroyed his nerves.

Sometimes he would find a slip saying, "How are you doing? I worry about you lately. You're up so late, and your snoring at night is scary strong." He would write back on the other side of the paper. "Don't worry, I'm fine. Work is hard, but it's fun."

One time, he found a note that ruined his day. He went home early to explain himself, to discuss the matter and try to absorb her anger with his eloquence, which often betrayed him on occasions like this. The note said: "I know you don't like condoms, but if you're going to sleep around, you need to get over it. Please at least respect me enough to be careful about your health—and mine. Use a condom. There are plenty of STDs that you don't notice because they don't affect you—but they do affect me. At the very least, you should be worried about AIDS. I can't deal with the repeated infections anymore just because you lack awareness of basic hygiene. *Bisous*."

Najla had noted the same thing once, telling him that he'd given her an infectious disease. She said it was a sensitive issue for women: it had nothing to do with whether a woman was "clean" or "unclean," like people said. Rather, every woman was susceptible to these problems because men could be infectious even if they had no symptoms.

Apart from these slips of paper, which Abdel Nasser called "talismans," and some occasions where he copulated with her on demand, there was virtually nothing left between them. Even breakfast on Sundays became curtailed, for two reasons. The first was that Zeina no longer celebrated it the way she had before; she'd changed since the abortion, becoming irritated and worried. The second reason was that Abdel Nasser had started going into the newspaper to prepare his supplement peacefully, in the absence of the other editors, three days before submitting it for print. The supplement was what's considered "dead" pages in the jargon of journalism, pages that rarely needed to be updated; if something urgent happened, he would simply change the editorial and include that event in it. He often had enough content on hand to cover his supplements for two months, or more.

As the *agrégation* exam approached in the second half of May, the house became a satellite office of the National Library. Zeina brought two of her classmates home with her. They would come early in the morning and leave late at night. Zeina finished the program with her baccalaureate students, who were starting to take their practice exams. She increased the pace of her preparations. She bought another coffee machine. The refrigerator became full of drinks and fruit. Abdel Nasser learned that one of her classmates lived in Le Bardo, as well, and every day her young brother would come at lunchtime with a basket full of delicious food, so that the three of them could focus on their studying. Abdel Nasser ate with them once or twice, when he woke up late after staying out till dawn.

The presence of Zeina's classmates served to decrease the stress in the house, as it gave her new energy to work peacefully and quietly. Perhaps the approach of the big match, after which she would be crowned champion of the *agrégation*, led to a reversal: her weakness became a strength; her stress became peace and calm; her ambition became a sparkling glow.

5

Zeina came home after every exam of the four-day *agrégation* examinations jumping with joy over what she'd written and putting the final touches on her preparations for the next day's exam. And while her female colleague seemed less optimistic, her male colleague was outright preparing himself for failure, as much as anyone can prepare for such a thing.

She would come back home with her papers, happy, and give Abdel Nasser a big hug. She would hug him like a child hugging her father; she would take him by the hand and talk to him about what she wrote, showing him her draft and reciting her text. She was saying difficult words that he didn't fully understand, though he found it coherent. He was sure that she would be the best, as usual. He told her, sarcastically, "What a weird world! On the Day of Knowledge, a leftist activist will receive the President of the Republic prize from the murderer Ben Ali!"

There was a delay between the end of the exams and the announcement of the results, and Zeina spent those days sleeping, trying to regain some of the energy she had expended in her year of non-stop hard work. There was no source she hadn't read. Her German had improved greatly. She had prepared oral and written presentations, text analysis, and translations that made her colleagues who had already passed the exams jealous and all of her professors proud. All signs pointed to her being at the top of the list.

She didn't get anxious until the day the results came out. She asked Abdel Nasser to come with her to the university in the afternoon to wait for the results to be posted. It was a Tuesday in June, and the heat was suffocating. He'd reserved a table at Dar El Jeld to celebrate her success in the written examinations, in anticipation of the final success after the oral exams.

They saw her classmates running toward the administration staff as they opened the board where the examination results were hung in the graduate hall. They all craned their necks to see the results. Abdel Nasser looked over the heads of the three or four students in front of him at the list; Zeina was next to him, waiting to double check. He didn't see her name. It was a short list, with only five names. He scanned it again: Zeina's name wasn't on it. He moved closer. He verified. He read again. He was sure that she hadn't passed. In that brief moment, he tried to figure out how to tell her.

He looked behind him and found Zeina's friend who had prepared with her, hugging her tightly and crying. Zeina asked about the results. The faces around her, those who had passed and those who had not, stared at Zeina in disbelief and astonishment. Silence prevailed.

At first, Zeina didn't react. She held it together. She went to verify for herself. She was about to leave the hall when suddenly she saw the chair of the committee coming from the professors' offices, accompanied by the "Iron Lady" who had praised her so strongly at her thesis defense. She headed toward him, and Abdel Nasser followed her. She stopped both professors and asked them, her voice chilly, "Why didn't I pass?"

"We're all terribly sorry," he said. "You're the best student, but you failed the essay. Your grade was 2 out of 20."

"You mean for the course that you taught?"

"Unfortunately, yes. Though the papers were anonymous, to protect the secrecy of the exam."

To everybody's shock, Zeina pulled her shirt open, exposing her breasts, and shrieked at the professor: "Anonymous, you motherfucker? I wouldn't give you a taste of *this*, so you destroyed my paper with the all the objectivity of your dick!"

She spat on him. She raised her hand and slapped him so hard they heard the sound echo. She broke out cursing him with vulgar words Abdel Nasser had never heard from her before. She was a lioness in a state of frenzy. Abdel Nasser grabbed her from behind and pulled her away from the professor, who lowered his head and left the university quickly. The Iron Lady stood staring at Zeina, astonished at the state

she was in. She was pulling her hair and sobbing, then collapsed on the floor, pulling at her clothes. Her friend helped
Abdel Nasser calm her down. The students and some of the
staff gathered around them, but luckily the university wasn't
too crowded on that June evening; exams had ended, and the
staff were on single shift.

6

Zeina was sick all night. Abdel Nasser fetched the night
doctor when her condition worsened. The doctor gave her an
injection to help her sleep. After that, she didn't wake at all
until 10 A.M. Abdel Nasser asked Najla to stay with her; new
procedures in book publishing and distribution had just been
announced, so he had to rewrite the editorial for Thursday's
supplement.

Zeina insisted that she would meet with the dean and the
university president—with the higher education minister, if
that's what it took. Abdel Nasser asked her to take care of her
health. She had time to appeal, even to take the case to court
if she wanted to, but she had to avoid making mistakes that
might cause her harm, as she did yesterday. No matter how
despicable the professor was, what she did put her in the place
of the offender rather than the victim.

Zeina didn't know how she made it through that second
night. The next day Abdel Nasser went with her to meet the
dean, who expressed his sympathy for her failure. He knew
how exceptional she was, and he blamed the results on bad
luck in the game of examinations. She explained to him that
she wanted a second grading for her paper because she
doubted the validity of the grade she'd received. He explained
to her that there was no such thing as a "second grading" in the
rules because to require one cast doubt on the integrity of the

professor, who was considered an expert in his field; no other expert could review his academic evaluation. Academic traditions allowed only for verifying against a manual error, which meant checking to make sure the declared grade was identical to the one on the examination paper. He explained to her the required procedure, which involved submitting a request through the registrar's office and inviting the chair of the examination committee to examine the paper. He promised her to verify it himself with the committee chair, independently of her right to request it.

He began to blame her for what she had said to the professor and her behavior with him. The professor had submitted a report requesting to refer her to the disciplinary council for her behavior, for attacking a professor and falsely accusing him, and he was reserving his personal right to sue her. He suggested that she contact the professor to apologize in hopes that he would withdraw his report. As dean, he was required by the administration bylaws to convene the disciplinary council, but he would guarantee her right to defend herself.

The dean spoke calmly, with his scholar's seriousness and administrator's diligence, but he didn't hide his sympathy with Zeina, the exceptional student. But when he presented his proposal, she exploded. Abdel Nasser calmed her down, out of respect for the setting. She held herself together and recounted how the professor had harassed her. He'd assigned her, and only her, three presentations since the semester began, and would invite her to his office on the pretext of discussing them and supervising her. He would close the door and start to come on to her, but she would pretend not to understand his intentions. In the beginning, he would speak to her affectionately, but she would always try to lead him back to the discussion, often successfully. But when he persisted in making passes at her and she persisted in rebuffing them, he started threatening her, telling her that he would fail her and warning her of the disastrous outcome of her behavior with him. She explained to him that she had nothing against him, but that she was a married woman. (Abdel Nasser here was surprised; this was the first time he'd heard her say the word and sound convinced about it—if only in her own interest!) She told him she wasn't going to cheat on her husband (this word pleased Abdel Nasser, as well, since Zeina said it with such confidence!) But these polite justifications didn't stop him from abusing her. He pushed her against the wall in his office and started kissing her mouth and cheeks and neck, while she tried to duck him and push him away. When she felt his arousal against her leg, she slapped him. That was the last time she had ever gone to his office.

"Why didn't you make a complaint immediately?" he asked.

"I wasn't eager to disparage a professor; I'm here to study and succeed, not to have to deal with this kind of nonsense."

"But you ended up having to deal with it anyway. I can't do anything with a mere accusation; I have to have a written complaint to take administrative action. You should have at least contacted me to let me know."

The dean was obviously sorry and embarrassed, but he didn't want to show his emotions to Zeina any more than necessary. He asked her, "Did you let your classmates know at the time? Did you tell your husband?"

"No," she replied. "I didn't want to disparage the professor. As for my husband, I wanted to keep my personal life separate from my studies. But you can verify the professor's reputation: he's doing the same thing with other students."

"I have no problem believing you, but me believing you has no meaning from an administrative point of view. Anyone hearing about this would say that it was virtue after the fact, and coming too late. Unfortunately."

Abdel Nasser had kept silent throughout the meeting but here interjected, "What should we do, then, *sayyid* dean?"

"Unfortunately . . . there's not much you can do. We have to verify the grade first; I hope it's not the same as the one on the list. The oral exams start tomorrow, so I'll do my best to find out the truth today."

Zeina interrupted, sharply, "You won't find anything. He knew the grade and was sure of it. And when the results were announced, the other professor was with him."

"I know you won't like what I'm saying, but I don't want to give you false hope." He looked down for a moment, then said, "You have no option but to retake the entire year."

Zeina lowered her head for a moment, then stood up, angry. "I won't let that snake bite me twice. He'll never get as much as a kiss. I will become a professor in spite of him."

The dean sat looking at her, without any comment, then stood as a signal that the meeting was over. He shook Abdel Nasser's hand, then told Zeina, "I admire your courage and perseverance, but don't be reckless."

She walked out the door without saying goodbye. That was the last time she set foot in that prestigious university.

7

Zeina started smoking more than two packs of cigarettes a day. In just a few days, she'd finished the expensive bottles of liquor that Abdel Nasser had in the cabinet for special occasions. She didn't seem to be in a bad mood; rather, she was impassively traversing a peaceful phase where she seemed to be doing a lot of thinking. She was filling up blank pages with scrawled symbols, signs, and words that were difficult to read.

He tried to be with her, to think with her, but she politely asked him to leave her alone. He tried multiple times to take her out for a walk or to a restaurant, or to spend the weekend at a hotel. She refused all his offers nicely, with a politeness that surprised him in her. He tried, with Najla's help, to figure out what she was thinking but failed.

8

At the end of July, Zeina informed el-Talyani that she was going to Paris. He thought she just wanted a change of scenery. He asked her where she would stay and whether she knew people there, but she told him not to worry about all that. He asked to go with her, but she refused. She said, "I want to go on my own. I want to face my fate on my own."

Abdel Nasser didn't understand that she wasn't talking about going as a tourist. She just said that she was going to check on something over there, but didn't want to tell him what. She had to be alone. He thought a lot about the matter and concluded that she must be going to ask about studying at one of the French universities and trying to find out if she could do the *agrégation* there or remotely. He thought this was a good idea, especially since that damn professor wasn't going to let her pass except over his dead body.

She came back to him after a week, asking about a divorce because she was going to move to France. El-Talyani laughed at first and told her she was being crazy. He joked, "So you'll be one of our migrant workers abroad! Let's stay married just in case I need French citizenship after you get it."

He recognized that Zeina was dead serious. She was annoyed by what he was saying but calmly reiterated that she wanted a divorce as soon as possible. She went on to say that she no longer loved him and couldn't see him as a husband who she could build a future with. Their paths were going in different directions, and there was no horizon that could bring them together. El-Talyani couldn't believe what she was saying. He thought it was a mere whim, that she was just trying to find a way to gather up the broken pieces of her ambition after failing the *agrégation*.

Her insistence on divorce was so strong that she threatened to cheat on him with another man, as he had done with other women. She saw no need to aggravate the situation and resort to extreme solutions: their relationship began with mutual consent, and it should end with mutual consent. She tried to convince him that she wouldn't change her mind: she knew what she was doing, and, in any case, she wasn't going to stay in Tunisia, divorced or not. She would leave everything—the house, the job, the husband—and start a new life from scratch. In a moment of clarity and frankness, she told him that she'd lost her desire to live in Tunisia and that she had started relishing her freedom since her mother passed away. She reminded him of when she said she'd become "mother to herself" and told him that she hadn't been joking: it wasn't a metaphor so much as the essence of a real feeling.

She spoke to him with a calm that he hadn't seen in her before. Finally, he became convinced that she was serious about what she wanted and that nobody could stop her. She would travel her path with all the force and momentum of a hurricane.

After many long discussions, he agreed to what she wanted. He would let her go, but he promised, with the narcissism of a man who doesn't understand the anger of a broken woman, that she would regret it one day and that, when she did, he wouldn't take her back. Her response: "The stage I'm living in now is post-desire, post-regret, post-hope, post-despair, and post-good-and-evil . . ."

His conscious mind woke up. He thought about it then said to himself that their relationship had ended a long time ago, so why was he insisting on making her stay? They hadn't really lived except for a few months before signing the marriage certificate. After that, they'd been like two lines, one convex and one concave, that as soon as they met, diverged.

The probability of the lines meeting had ended when she chose the abortion and so erased the only tangible trace that might have remained of their life together. She hadn't been wrong, then, to consider what was between them merely a marriage certificate and not a real marriage. Maybe this was what she'd been planning all along, even before the abortion. But he had also passed the stage of regret, despair, and pessimism. Ethics and principles aside, Najla had taught him—as had Lella Jnayna before her—to think outside of the fatal dualism of faithfulness and cheating, good and evil, justice and injustice, love and hate.

9

By coincidence, the case was given to a judge who was one of Si Abdel Hamid's relatives. Abdel Nasser had the option of prolonging the procedures; he thought that was for the best, to give her enough time to rethink her decision, especially because failing her exam had been so painful. Zeina did not hide her displeasure with that: she left the high school, the divorce case, and the country.

It wasn't until November of 1989 that a mutual consent divorce ruling was issued. It was almost a full year prior that Zeina had become the mother of herself. She was a free woman, making her own way in the world alone—almost alone—in one of the suburbs of Paris . . . with Eric S.

1

I maintained my friendship with Zeina, who sent me a letter with her phone number. We met when she visited Tunisia as a tourist with her French husband; they lived together without a marriage certificate from the Tunisian courts, because he hadn't converted to Islam as Tunisian law required.

I met Eric S. at the beginning of 1990 and spoke with him. He was a researcher at the Centre National de la Recherche Scientifique in France, specializing in sociology. He was a cultured man, proud to be a child of the May 1968 revolution, leftist in heart and mind. He'd been associated with the researchers who followed in the steps of Pierre Bourdieu and published in the famous journal that he had founded. He specialized in the sociology of media and was also interested in Islamic movements in the Maghreb.

Zeina had met him for the first time alongside Abdel Nasser but didn't care for him. Then she got to know him, a few days later, at a conference organized by the Institut de Recherche sur le Maghreb Contemporain in Tunis when she was a senior student. He saw how smart, knowledgeable, and enthusiastic she was. She listened to his presentation about the relationship between religion and politics in the *manaqib* genre and found depth, novelty, and vision in his speech. He invited her to have dinner with him, and she accepted. They spoke at length about thought, philosophy, and culture, which made them like each other more.

Eric was a supporter of Arab issues, particularly the

Palestinian cause. His opinions about it seemed to me to combine a romantic vision of Arabs and the East with the leftist ideology in support of oppressed peoples. It seems most likely, in my opinion, that he saw Zeina—with her sharp mind and the Berber beauty that made her look Caucasian in terms of eye and skin color—as a way of combining the romantic image of the East and the rational and modern image of the West.

I might be wrong in my description, but there is another factor. In 1990, Zeina was twenty-six years old; when Eric met her, she was twenty-two. Whereas he appeared to be about sixty, give or take a few years, with his thick white beard and salt-and-pepper hair. He was elegant, the way French academics are, despite his ordinary clothes. Truth be told, he had an extraordinary personality: he would speak about such engaging and interesting topics but was, at the same time, considerate in his interaction with others. He would get excited as he spoke, as if he were a politician giving a speech in public, but when he stopped to listen, he was quiet and attentive.

Based on my knowledge of Zeina, this kind of man would seduce her with his knowledge and make her feel secure and protected. It was clear that he was her father's age; in addition, he was a distinguished researcher.

She revealed to me that, after that dinner with him at the restaurant and their mutual attraction, she'd spent the night with him in his hotel room. He'd embraced her with a gentleness she hadn't experienced before, kissing her in a way that electrified her and made her melt. She told me that if she hadn't been on her period that day, they would have kept on till dawn, especially since he was leaving early that morning.

This was a few days before the start of her relationship with el-Talyani, shortly before the incident at the Faculté des Lettres de la Manouba. They kept up a correspondence after that. He congratulated her on her success with her master's thesis. Though she refused many times to meet him, he didn't cut ties with her. He returned to Tunisia around the time that she had had the abortion but wasn't able to see her. He had come specifically to meet with her, but she broke her promise to see him because of her poor physical and mental state.

2

I should admit that Eric, based on what I know of him, loved Zeina dearly and treated her as if she were a precious pearl cradled in his hands that he was afraid of dropping. He would gaze at her fondly while she spoke, and if she asked for something, he would rush to get it for her without argument. And if she spoke to him harshly or recklessly—a habit she hadn't yet ridden herself of—he would overlook it and simply smile. He looked at her as if praising God for creating the master-piece in front of him.

As for Zeina, she hadn't really changed. She had become somewhat more confident and firm in her interactions with people. She'd also become more abrasive (a kind of rudeness we called *tjelteem* in our neighborhood); she hadn't acquired the French sense of etiquette or gentility. It wasn't my business, in any case: the man was satisfied with his companion, so who was I to judge?

I strongly suspect, based on my little experience with women and their moods, that she wasn't sexually satisfied. She was, no doubt, comparing him and el-Talyani in this arena because of the age difference. Perhaps this was why Eric accepted the way Zeina sometimes insulted him when he spoke about his field of research. This was something she would do even in front of me, during the few occasions that I met with them. She wouldn't hesitate to say things like: "No, that's not true . . ." or "A naive analysis of the phenomena" or "You keep saying that; forget that nonsense." Eric would stay silent, answering her only with a fond smile. He once salvaged the conversation after one of these insults by saying, "You see? This great mind in front of you"—meaning Zeina—"has corrected some conceptual and methodological errors of mine that I'd never noticed. What brilliance!"

I don't know whether he was just flattering her or if he really meant what he said. But I do believe that he considered himself a student and her his professor, mixing the objectivity of science with the complex relationship between them.

Men who marry girls half their age (or sometimes one-third their age) are like this. They start to lose their brightness and their virility and believe that a young woman will bring back their youth, when in reality she turns them into comical dolls, bowing down before their maker and obeying her the way an impoverished believer does their God.

The reality is that the small amount of information I gathered about Zeina and her life in Paris with Eric—both from the news she shared and from what I gathered from some Tunisian acquaintances of his in France—allows me to imagine the tragic path that Zeina was walking, and the horrible end it led her to. It's a sad story that confirms that this country—as Abdel Nasser and Si Abdel Hamid always used to say—pushes its children toward destruction and loss; it eliminates the brightest among them or grinds them down until they're just like everyone else, or worse. Zeina left the country to get a PhD and become a college professor, but she wasn't able to realize either of those dreams. Instead, she lived under Eric's care: a naughty girl who'd become a plaything for (by our Tunisian standards) a dirty old man. So she unleashed her madness and unsated desires until she made him completely lose his dignity. Anyway . . . I wasn't happy about Zeina's fate. If she'd stayed with Abdel Nasser, things would have been different.

3

Abdel Nasser's life after Zeina was spent between the newspaper—where he'd redoubled his efforts—and the hunt for beautiful women in bars and restaurants. He would scheme to get them into bed, which sometimes required no effort at all. The only difference was that now he had a house to lead his prey to, one that he didn't have to share with anyone: the apartment that Salah Eddine had bought in the Ennasr district and asked his brother to live in and take care of as if it were his own.

El-Talyani would have a woman stay over, sometimes for a few days, but then they would part. He no longer had any illusions about women. He was living by the logic of self-interest, but he was still good company. He detested women during that period of his life. He thought about going back to Najla, who had visited him at his house on Rue des Orangers to comfort him and show her support for him during his crisis. But after a short while, he added her to his scrapbook of romantic failures.

Abdel Nasser mentioned that, after that visit, he'd started spending a lot of time with Najla. After getting her new car, she became freer in terms of moving around and staying up late. And she no longer had the burden of Zeina. But the real reason was a friend of hers, a hairdresser she'd gotten close to a few months before. They met at the gym, and Najla wound up being a good and happy customer of hers. As is always the case with hairdressers, she became her confidante. Najla told her about el-Talyani after the hairdresser had confided in her about some relationships she had with influential men of the new Tunisia, rising politicians and businessmen.

The hairdresser insisted on inviting Najla to a party at her house. El-Talyani understood that it was a party to recruit beautiful women for the pleasure of influential men. Najla was naive and believed that she'd invited her out of friendship; he warned her about the reality of the situation a few hours before the party. She found herself in a dilemma: if she canceled, it would be bad manners, but if she went, she didn't know what might happen or what trap she could fall into. El-Talyani urged her not to go, saying that she should avoid that kind of diseased environment. In reality, as he told me later, he was feeling a little bit jealous and worried about her.

Najla vacillated but then, as usual, she found a solution: el-Talyani would go with her as her boyfriend or fiancé, especially since the hairdresser had heard of him. To convince him to go with her, she promised him that if he saw a woman more beautiful than her, she would play matchmaker herself! The important thing was to save her from this dilemma.

The house was a large villa surrounded by a high wall on one of the back streets in El Menzah 9. Najla wore a cocktail dress that showed off all her beauty, and el-Talyani wore a brown Italian suit over a sky blue shirt, without a tie. He looked Italian; anyone who saw him would doubt that he had Arab blood in his veins. His agreement with Najla to speak only in French during the evening added fuel to the speculation among the other attendees. As everyone could attest, they were the most beautiful couple there. Women outnumbered men at the party: single women, divorced women, artists, hairdressers. As for the men, some of them had big bellies and held cigars. Others were pretending to be poised and sophisticated, but by the time they finished their third glass, they shattered the illusion with dancing and singing.

All eyes were on el-Talyani and Najla when they entered the room. The men undressed Najla piece by piece with their eyes, which were filled with wolf-like hunger. The women devoured Abdel Nasser with their smiles, their tongues wetting their lips. He felt a few exciting caresses when he was shaking hands with some of them and received flirtatious winks from others. He noticed some pressure on his arm, almost a pinch, when they greeted him, or on his thigh as he sat chatting with them.

From the hairdresser, he got the trifecta—winks, licking her lips, and pinching—until it was obvious to Najla that she was trying to seduce him. She looked at Abdel Nasser, with her skill and experience, and asked whether he liked her. He whispered in her ear, "Her lips look like an Indian elephant's ear."

Throughout the night, she asked his opinion about each woman, and every time he found a defect. He made sure not to leave her side, so that she wouldn't be attacked by the birds of prey circling the room. The hairdresser asked her into the hall near the kitchen, but el-Talyani joined them. He understood that she was planning something, so he decided to go for it and tear down all the barriers. He approached the hairdresser and said, "Thank you, Madame, for inviting us. Do you have a room for us?"

The hairdresser was surprised by his request, but, seemingly being an expert in men, she answered him without hesitation. "Najla's like my sister. I'll take you to a room—it's yours whenever you want it."

She led them upstairs and showed them the room and bathroom. She closed the hall door leading to the stairs and left. When they returned downstairs, she told them, "I hope you liked the room. Don't forget, it's yours whenever you want it."

The general impression was that el-Talyani's presence had annoyed the male attendees as much as Najla's presence annoyed the women who were hoping to devour him. But, as the saying goes, the ship can wish for a path, but the wind blows as it will.

During the party, Abdel Nasser met the attendees one by one, each of the businessmen and high-ranking officials. The highest of them was a young undersecretary of state who displayed his stupidity by dancing and allowing one of the attendees to photograph him. But Abdel Nasser's greatest discovery was an old woman, an activist in a society advocating for mothers' rights. He became certain, after a while, that Si Abdel Hamid knew her; she was a specialist in bringing women—married, single, or divorced—to the beds of ministers, thereby relieving the stress and tension caused by working in the government of his excellency the Change Maker, the man who worked so hard and gave tirelessly to the homeland. Si Abdel Hamid had shared with him, in a rare confidential talk, that he himself had enjoyed what her generous hands bestowed. In any case, she was a woman of public relations and communications. Abdel Hamid told him that she had come into favor with his excellency and that she had a large network, nationally and internationally. This had allowed her to gain the trust of the president, who appointed her (in spite of his instinctual caution) to carry out difficult missions. She was able to quickly and flawlessly execute these missions, thanks to her worldly knowledge and planning skills. Si Abdel Hamid told him, with the prophetic tone he put on whenever he thought he was betting on something other people didn't expect, "The woman is ugly, but she's very knowledgeable about life. She'll be an important figure."

That night with Najla took el-Talyani away from the restaurants and trashy bars where he hung out with those media people and their ilk. It also removed him from Najla's life permanently.

He didn't know how Najla fell in with the hairdresser and her crowd, or what kind of pleasure she found in it. Once he finally noticed, it was too late. Najla had become melancholy and lost the ready smile and energy she always brought when she entered a room. She became a body without a soul, an instrument of pleasure for those who requested it. The few times they met before parting forever, Abdel Nasser noticed that her mannerisms had become affected and insincere.

She basically became a card-carrying professional prostitute, playing in open fields with the big sharks in money and politics. She became the favorite of the mothers' society activist, who pushed her to mother every one of Ben Ali's orphans. She would help him carry out his glorious mission for the homeland, the country of the blessed change and the happy new era.

Everything between Abdel Nasser and Najla quietly ended. He began to detest her and could no longer stand the rotten scent of men that clung to her body no matter how many liters of perfume she bathed in. Her splendor in his eyes was gone, despite the fact that he remained the only man who could excite her physically or mentally. She told him as much, but he told her that he couldn't lie to her anymore. She tried to rekindle their romance multiple times, but finally she understood that it was over.

4

After the 1989 elections, Abdel Nasser joined Agence France-Presse and spent more than a year in their Tunisia office after the death of Hajj Mahmoud. Then he traveled to other places—I heard Cyprus, Sudan, Somalia, Lebanon, and Iraq—before coming back to Tunisia in 1994 to found a marketing company called Oyoun. At which point, he started living a life that was even stranger than what I can narrate.

As for the circumstances of this migration, I'll come back to them. But regarding the reasons for his return, I have no definitive answer. I've tried to get to the bottom of the matter directly with Abdel Nasser, but he made it clear, by the way he was talking and evading the matter, that he didn't want to discuss it.

All of the malicious gossipers, however, agreed that he'd been fired from AFP, though the purported grounds for his dismissal varied from one telling to the next. Some people said

that the intelligence agencies in Lebanon or Iraq had bought
Abdel Nasser and that when the AFP administration found
out, they fired him. In my opinion, that's unlikely. I don't
believe that Abdel Nasser's political consciousness would
allow him to fall into such despicable activities. He spent his
university years recruiting people—it wouldn't be that easy for
someone to recruit him.

There was other gossip not worth mentioning. Many journalists claimed that, without Si Abdel Hamid, Abdel Nasser
was nothing. They couldn't understand the relationship
between the editor-in-chief and the proofreader who'd
become, in such a short period of time, a brilliant journalist.
Some of the kindest gossip, though simultaneously the filthiest
(with a filth that reached the level of slander for the sake of
revenge), claimed that Si Abdel Hamid had homosexual ten-
dencies. But no rational person could pay attention to that
kind of talk. I don't buy it at all; based on everything I've seen
and heard since el-Talyani and I were kids together, he's never
been like that, either as penetrator or penetrated.

These accusations came only from low-class people, not
from those who measure their words and think before they
speak. They may have been the result of hateful slurs during
one of those drinking parties where our journalists, intellectuals, and artists lose all their inhibitions, giving free rein to their
sick imaginations and miserable illusions.

I personally consider this nonsense that no one with a brain
would believe. The gossip that was closest to reality—because
it was at least reasonable—was what circulated about the role
of Si Abdel Hamid in Abdel Nasser's hiring at AFP. It was one
of the pieces of gossip that (despite the fact that it was highly
probable) was rarely mentioned in connection with Abdel
Nasser. But whether it spread or not meant nothing because
the journalist community was marked by petty hatreds and
envy. Si Abdel Hamid was well known among journalists and

international correspondents in Tunisia. He had connections with French journalists who respected his writing and considered him, just as Tunisians did, one of the authorities of Tunisian journalism in both French and Arabic. Moreover, they respected his position as a president and editor-in-chief of a government newspaper that was not only best-selling but also the most expressive of the country's policies.

I imagine that the person in charge of AFP's Tunisia office needed to add some new members to the team, given that the country had witnessed an important change and a new era was visible on the horizon. This new era promised political pluralism and democracy, a political thaw of the union issue, the release of Islamists from prison. This detente was called the "national approach" and was based on the National Pact of 1988 and Islamists' participation in the April 1989 elections, on the independent ticket. Their strong showing in the elections horrified the political elite and modernizers. The latter, which included leftist leaders of secret organizations in Tunisia and France, then joined the governing Constitutional Socialist Party, which changed its name to the Democratic Constitutional Rally. With the speed of events and decisions and the nascent change in the political and social equation, no one knew where the situation might lead.

What's most likely is that Si Abdel Hamid was asked to nominate a few outstanding journalists who could keep pace with the professional workload at a high-credibility agency like AFP. He gave them the name of the best journalist on his team, who he knew very well, and that was Abdel Nasser.

I don't see any problem with that; on the contrary, I think it was a great choice, especially after Abdel Nasser's great success with the *Literary Notebooks* supplement. What was the problem, if you put envy aside? If you're talking about experience, that's relative: a smart journalist with great talent and vast knowledge like Abdel Nasser can learn in a short period of time what might take someone else years. Experience is a qualitative, too; it can't be measured just in months and years. There are plenty of journalists who've spent years in the fourth estate and yet still can't (even after ten years!) interview a politician or writer—or even an ordinary citizen.

5

The story began when Si Abdel Hamid asked Abdel Nasser, shortly after his divorce, to prepare a special supplement celebrating the first anniversary of the blessed change. Abdel Nasser hesitated at first, then accepted under the condition that his name would not be listed in the production team and that he wouldn't have a byline on any article. They disagreed—practically for the first time—on the matter, but Abdel Nasser convinced him that if he was going to write the supplement, he would go back and analyze the events from his point of view. Si Abdel Hamid would need to guarantee that Abou Saoud wouldn't interfere. He also stipulated that he be allowed to choose the journalists who would be working with him on the supplement.

That was too much for Si Abdel Hamid, who said sarcastically, "Is that all? Or would you like to be made president and editor-in-chief while you're at it?"

Abdel Nasser reminded Si Abdel Hamid of a previous conversation they'd had, in which he'd expressed his fear that Abdel Nasser would get trapped and that this would lead to his downfall. He urged Si Abdel Hamid to fulfill his promise to get him out of the mud.

The deal was clear: Abdel Nasser would prepare everything, including selecting the photos and writing up the narrative of the coup in an exciting way. He would introduce the government's most important accomplishments; the national, Arab, and international reactions; and the development progress and economic indices. And Si Abdel Hamid's name would be on everything. Abdel Nasser assured him that the elegant supplement he was going to prepare would put Si Abdel Hamid on the throne of Tunisian media; it would please Ben Ali so much that it would make him the most important journalist in the country.

Abdel Nasser was as good as his word: the supplement was truly exceptional. Si Abdel Hamid opened the door for him to become a correspondent with a Belgian francophone newspaper, covering the situation in Tunisia and especially the Islamist issue, and mediated a good connection between him and Agence France-Presse. But the Tunisian information ministry's elevator was out of order, and Si Abdel Hamid was unable to use it to reach the minister's office.

6

Abdel Nasser had gotten a foothold in international journalism. He came to it through the door of the Belgian newspaper but made it to the real press arena through AFP. Owing to his extensive networks, he was an important source of many reports and precise coverage for the fierce struggle taking place in the countryside between the ballots of Ben Ali's Democratic Constitutional Rally (the heir of Bourguiba's Constitutional Socialist Party)—which had spread its tentacles throughout the country—and the independent ballot. Though "independent" in name, the ballot actually belonged to the Ennahda Movement, the heir of the Islamic Tendency, which remained unrecognized by Ben Ali's government even after its name change in 1988.

Abdel Nasser traveled to the villages of various governorates, covering people's opinions and the competitive atmosphere. The Ennahda Movement showed a remarkable ability to mobilize people, a strong indication of its popularity. But it also showed a superficiality in its candidates, who held hostile opinions of the Code of Personal Status and so threatened the advancement of Tunisian women's rights under Bourguiba, as well as individual freedom and human rights in general.

The month of April 1989 was a difficult month for Abdel Nasser because he was constantly traveling between different cities and villages, but it was also an important time for him. He was able to get to know the conservative and religious depths of Tunisia, which were often invisible from the vantage point of the capital. Half of the people in this Tunisia saw in the Islamist movement's leader a new prophet; the other half saw Ben Ali as a savior and liberator.

Abdel Nasser learned during this period how to introduce the news by trimming and condensing, or by lengthening and elaborating, organizing his words with care until he was able to express his position and his personal opinion in a subtle way.

He felt that his time at the Tunis office, in addition to doing his job, was a training period that would allow him to benefit from the French office director's guidance, as well as the help of his Tunisian and French colleagues. But they didn't have enough time to train him—and he didn't have time to be trained—so they threw him into the turbulent river of the elections. He felt like he was practicing journalism for the first time in his life; what he'd been writing in the paper was mere literature. Even his style of expression changed: it became simpler, more precise, and more readable, but without giving up the magic touch of his pen.

7

Abdel Nasser, after the end of the elections and his relationship with Najla, went back to his hedonistic lifestyle with a vengeance. Although more than a year and a half had passed since his divorce from Zeina, he was still speaking of her with a mixture of sarcasm and bitterness that he tried—unsuccessfully—to use as a mask for the still-raw pain. When I listened to him, I could see his resentment, anger, and desire for revenge. Who did she think she was, leaving *him*? She had gravely wounded his ego when she flung him aside without so much as a backward glance.

This probably explains his rush to gather the broken pieces of his soul as soon as he met Reem. He was determined, in his own fashion, to pick himself up and resume his path. But he tried to do it too quickly and took a blind leap that landed him in a deep, abandoned well. This resulted in his hysteria at the cemetery on the day of Hajj Mahmoud's funeral. Or, at least, it was decisive in leading him to that state.

My personal opinion is that el-Talyani had completely lost his bearings after his divorce from Zeina, but he hadn't completely lost his mind. He began hunting for new prey every day, without caring about her age or beauty or personality. I think Salah Eddine's apartment in the Ennasr district became a brothel and a bar. Until he met Reem and she, for whatever reason, made him lose his mind completely.

1

A bdel Nasser prepared everything with great attention to detail, as he always did when hosting. More than usual this time, though. He'd managed to get a date with her only after great effort, which was unlike him when it came to beautiful women. Reem S. was reluctant in the beginning, and he didn't understand the reason for her aversion. He attributed it to how young she was; he imagined that she was scared. But then he ruled out this possibility; most girls these days wanted to harvest the sweetness of the date without the hardships of love or having to commit to a young man their own age.

He assumed that her self-confidence made her arrogant and determined to maintain the thick barrier she'd put up. But he considered this assumption contrary to everything he knew about beautiful women. First of all, his stature and Italian good looks held a strong charm that essentially brought beautiful women to their knees—as many women, both friends and lovers, had told him. Second, all belles, no matter how beautiful they were, had at least a small inferiority complex. They didn't like their nose; their eyebrows were too thin; their lips were too thin (or too thick). Women weren't satisfied with themselves, no matter how harmonious their features were. There's a black spot on even the most beautiful painting: this is what they believed. Reem could not possibly deviate from this rule, no matter how confident she was.

During his surveillance of her (inside the apartment from

the window, or from a corner on the street, or from the court-yard in the center of the five buildings of Résidence Les Princesses), el-Talyani studied the smallest details of her life. He knew what time she left her apartment every day and what time she came back. He followed her on the bus and in taxis. He knew the name of the university she attended, the tea salons where she would meet her friends (both male and female). It was a surveillance that was practically a siege, in which el-Talyani used all the techniques he'd learned during his work as a journalist, as well as before that during his clandestine work with the organization at the university. To this extreme caution, which had become second nature, he added the experience he'd gained over time in reading someone's personality from their face, body movement, behavior, and their way of standing and speaking. Reem was a favorite subject of his, during the final few days before Hajj Mahmoud's passing, and he poured into it all of his experience with humanity, his social knowledge, and his analysis of personalities.

El-Talyani was seriously invested in his new adventure; he left behind everything, almost, to catch his Reem, to the point that it became a kind of personal challenge for him. *She'll be mine, or else I'll hang up my shoes like one of the old soccer players*, he told himself. He had stopped searching for a woman who would make him forget Zeina. After a humiliating divorce and the woman he'd placed all his bets on running away, what was left for him? He'd started to believe something he'd heard from one of the employees at the newspaper, when they were discussing Hammadi, the designer. The general opinion was that he was getting on in years and should find a good woman to take care of him in his old age. The employee responded, "Why buy a cow when milk is sold at market?"

After his failure with the philosopher, el-Talyani decided not to bother with buying milk in bulk, but rather to make do with the individual retail cartons. He would remain a bull, choosing the most beautiful cows in the field.

2

He bought the best pastries, both sweet and savory. He prepared a pot of coffee and a selection of juices. He took out the silver plates and crystal glasses that his sister Yosser had bought (over his objections) as a gift for him because they suited the new house. He sprayed the living room, the foyer, and the hall with lavender. He didn't forget to put a fresh piece of soap and a clean bath towel in the bathroom—Reem might need them if everything went to plan. He put out a second pair of wooden bath clogs, as well. Although he had given up the habit of going to the public hammam with his father many years before, he couldn't imagine leaving the bath without clogs. Perhaps it was a memory that remained dear to him.

The bell rang at around 6:15 P.M. That was all right; fifteen minutes late wouldn't annoy him. Reem entered, tall, with her honey hair falling over her shoulders. She was wearing blue jeans with tennis shoes and a greenish sweater. She wasn't wearing any makeup, other than a light touch of eyeshadow and some eyeliner. Her skin was a dewy rose. He made a point to kiss her cheeks as he was greeting her at the door; it was like pressing his lips against fine cotton, or against the cotton candy his father bought him as a child from the vendors near the Belvédère Zoo.

He'd seen her for the first time from his balcony, in mid-March 1990. The early signs of spring were spreading a feeling of warmth in the air. He stood on the balcony, overlooking the courtyard at the center of the Résidence Les Princesses towers. A luxury car stopped; the driver got out, then two young men from the back seat, followed by a girl. It was not only the color of her dress that was attractive, nor was it just her slender body. From his third-floor vantage point, he could see the open top of her red dress, which showed her neck and shoulders, as well as part of her back and chest. The neckline emphasized her cleavage. He couldn't see her face well; he was focused on the breasts that had so suddenly appeared in his crosshairs. He watched as the two young men took some belongings out of the car. He assumed she must be a bride getting ready to furnish her home; perhaps one of the two men was her future husband. It would have never occurred to him that she was a student, coming to live with her sister on the fifth floor. The high-end apartment building was relatively far away from the universities, and the rent would be expensive for a student her age.

He hurried to the elevator, determined to get a good look at her. She didn't seem interested in him, but at least he found her face acceptable. If he hadn't had plans with his friends, he would have pursued the situation at close quarters. But at least he knew which floor she lived on—as for the apartment, he would find that out later.

3

After that, he only saw her once or twice. He almost forgot about the whole thing at first because he was busy for several weeks with his disparate adventures. But then he met her again by chance, at the end of June. He saw her entering the building and hurried to catch up, making it to the elevator just before the door closed. He couldn't stop gasping for breath, though he tried. He greeted her, and she answered with an abbreviated greeting. He welcomed her to the building, but she didn't answer, just stared at the floor of the elevator. He got out on the third floor and wished her a good evening, without knowing if she responded or not.

He kept wondering about this coldness and arrogance. He might even call it insolence, or contempt. She hadn't even looked at him. She didn't raise her eyes from the floor of the elevator once in the whole time it took for him to get in, for the door to open, and for it to close again. She didn't even try to sneak a glance at him in one of the mirrors that covered three walls of the elevator. Reem took up residence in el-Talyani's head.

After that, he went up to the fifth floor. He hesitated between two apartments. He went back down to the interphone and pressed the speaker button for apartment 11; a young boy answered, so he knew that was wrong. He tried the button for apartment 12. No one answered. He repeated this process several times. Later, he tried again at different times of the day, with no luck. Maybe it was broken. He attributed the matter, in the beginning, to coincidence.

He saw her again in the elevator, with another girl who was more beautiful and was acting much differently. She seemed to be a social girl, brimming with vitality. El-Talyani felt that she liked him, but he decided to leave that for later. Reem was the goal now. That was the day he decided to stalk her.

He rented a car. He got up at 7 A.M. He saw her leaving the apartment building around 7:30. The next day, she hailed a taxi. The driver drove toward El Menzah 6, then passed it and turned right. Traffic was at its worst around a quarter to eight, and he didn't get to Bab Saadoun until 8:20 A.M. The car stopped next to a sidewalk across from the Bab Sidi Abdessalem souk. Reem got out and crossed the street in the other direction. She passed the metro light rail tracks and headed toward the Institut Supérieur des Beaux-Arts. He watched her until she disappeared inside the building.

He kept this up for a whole week, waking up at the same time every day, until he had memorized her morning routine. But her times coming home from school were irregular. He devoted himself to it and was eventually able to discover a number of things:

On Monday, she left school at 2:30 P.M. She rode the metro with other students. They stopped at the Ibn Rachiq station, then wandered around Avenue Bourguiba until 5 P.M.

On Tuesday, she left school shortly after 4:30 P.M. She took a taxi with two female friends. They headed to a tea salon at El Menzah 6 near the Monoprix supermarket and the Fifty Boutiques shopping mall. She returned home around 7:30 P.M.

On Wednesday, she got out of school at 5:30 P.M. and went directly home.

On Thursday, she left school at around 1 P.M. She went directly home.

On Friday, she left school at 4:30 P.M. with two other girls (Abdel Nasser thought they were probably students) and a male student and walked toward the Espace El Teatro next to Hôtel Abou Nawas near Bab El Khadra. He saw them look-ing at an art exhibit; then they went into the theater to watch the Taoufik Jebali play *Things Said at Night*. He concluded that the male student with them was dating one of the other girls: he sat behind them during the play and saw them acting like a couple.

As for Saturday, he waited until 10 A.M. but Reem never came down. He assumed that exams were probably over. He became certain of that when, around noon, he saw her take a taxi to the Moncef Bey station. He followed her to the shared *louage*; "Tunis–Sousse" was written on the outside of the minibus.

He wished he could take her to her destination in his car! He would drive as slowly as possible. They would stop at rest areas to eat sandwiches; he would buy her good chocolate and fresh juice; they would drink coffee. He would pretend that he needed to fill the car with gas, while really he was filling his eyes with her beauty and listening to her stories and memorizing the tone of her voice. Her voice was doubtless tender music . . . But his precise, rigid plan didn't allow him to act on that desire yet; he had to be patient and persevere. His desire to know everything about Reem almost made him follow the *louage*, and why not? But no—the future would be better, sweeter. He'd planned it all out: his ears would be filled with the music of her voice in a day or two, or a week, or a month. He must have Reem, however long it took.

4

In the end, all of el-Talyani's carefully laid plans were for naught. He had tired himself out with the patience and waiting, the stalking and surveillance, for no reason at all. The matter ended up being much simpler than he'd imagined: luck always trumps meticulous planning. It comes to you out of the blue, no matter how strong your imagination is or how bright you may be.

El-Talyani was a regular customer at La Maison Blanche on Friday nights. He never got a table, but would just sit on a stool at the circular bar. He liked to sit by himself to eat dinner and drink peacefully. He started with two bottles of the local beer, then a bottle of red wine, then would cap off his weekly solo on the strings of loneliness and contemplation with a glass of Thibarine. It was a habit he'd instituted for himself since he started his job with AFP; he considered it his day off from friends and women. It was an enjoyable evening for him. He would spend it watching the other customers as they came and went. He was trying to train his brain to imagine what was going on inside their heads: their confusions and complexes, their happiness and depravity, their failures and their glories. He saw some of himself in them, especially in their longing for life, even a life crowned with pain and deceit. It was an evening to become drunk with contemplation and to think about writing a novel drawn from his imaginings. Or even better—a screenplay for a long film, his first film. He'd found himself unable to write this script, despite the advice of his friend Hedi K. and the books he'd given him to read about screenwriting. Despite, as well, all the films that Hedi had made him watch and analyze and the visual scenes he'd trained him multiple times to create.

El-Talyani's dream was to leave an artistic trace. Zeina had deprived him of the chance to make a beautiful creature of flesh and blood with her, to prove that he'd passed through the world and left something wonderful behind. If he wasn't going to leave children to prove his existence, then let the film be his legitimate heir and the witness to his life. That day, the opportunity presented itself: he found the beginning of a story that he wanted to tell.

He was paging through the June issue of *Studio* magazine. He'd found it at the newspaper stand when he went to buy a pack of cigarettes. He finished his two beers, then occupied himself with the magazine, then tossed it aside. He raised his head to start the people-watching party—and saw Reem. It was definitely her, sitting at a table with a middle-aged woman and three men. He didn't recognize any of them except Mounir, one of the technicians at an advertising agency who would sometimes come by the newspaper to follow up on the printing of their advertisements. Reem seemed happy. They were drinking white wine; the woman was sipping on a glass of liquor that, from its color, he guessed was vodka.

He called over the waiter and ordered the table a round of drinks on him: a cocktail for the girl, a glass of vodka for the woman, and white wine for the three men.

They all looked toward the sender of the gift. Mounir didn't recognize him, and one of the other two men came over. He thanked Abdel Nasser and asked, embarrassed, whether any of them knew him. He told him, "It's a gift from me to my friend and his friends at the table." He didn't understand, but went to tell the group. Mounir stood up and rushed to embrace Abdel Nasser, welcoming him in a way he never had in the past. He saw that they were talking about him and pretended not to notice.

After fifteen minutes, Mounir came over to thank him again on behalf of the group and invited him to drink a glass with them at the table. He demurred at first, until one of the other two men came over and urged him to join them. "Don't deprive us of the company of such a great journalist."

One of the men was a friend of Mounir: he was a single schoolteacher who was also active in one of the movie clubs of the Association for Film Critics. The other man was a bank executive and a cousin of the film-critic-slash-teacher; he was also the middle-aged woman's husband. She was an ordinary woman and a bit heavy; like her husband, she pronounced "I" as *ani*, instead of *ana* like the people of Tunis. She was introduced as Reem's aunt. Abdel Nasser greeted Reem without showing that he knew her. But he said to her, "Your face is familiar . . . Where do I know you from? You . . . and the gentleman?" He indicated the cinema-loving teacher.

El-Talyani had roped him in, so he assented: he knew him, as well. El-Talyani told them all, and with a special emphasis to Reem as a hint that he meant her specifically, that they had probably met in one of the cinematic events organized by the association. As the coordinator of the most popular cultural supplement in Tunisia, he covered such things.

Reem was looking at him with admiration. She seemed about to devour him with her eyes, all while he pretended to be busy looking at the others and not seeing her.

As soon as he had finished his conversation with the film critic teacher, Reem jumped in, "I remember where I've seen you! Don't you live in Building D in Résidence Les Princesses?"

He feigned surprise, "You're dangerous; you know where I live. Even Mounir doesn't know that!"

She seemed flustered. "Just a coincidence, Si Abdel Nasser."

"I'm just kidding," he said. "Do you have some family or friends you visit there?"

"No, I live there. In the same apartment building, at my sister's."

"Then we're neighbors, and I didn't even know it! What a happy coincidence . . . It was nice meeting you all. Enjoy your time with Mounir—his friends are my friends, if that's alright with you."

They all answered that they were honored to meet a man like him, an intellectual with a successful career, prominent in the world of media and culture. He excused himself, saying that he had an appointment the next day with a director who was working with him on his first film. He stood, but the teacher stopped him, asking about the film. El-Talyani told them he wouldn't spoil their pleasant evening with such a long discussion, but promised to speak with him about it another time. Reem's aunt asked him to find a role for her niece, who was dying to become a film star. El-Talyani didn't answer at first. He looked at the aunt and then at Reem and said, jokingly, "Well, the prophet did call on us to take care of our neighbors. I promise to look into the matter with the director tomorrow."

Reem's aunt asked, with an audacity he hadn't expected, for his phone number at home or at work. He dictated both numbers to them. He told them that if they couldn't get ahold of him, because of his busy schedule at work or time away from home, they could leave a message on his answering machine with their phone number, and he would call them back.

5

On Saturday at noon, he found a message from Reem, who was clearly eager. He let almost two hours go by before he called her: he'd wanted to return the call right away, but instead gave her some time to get more anxious. He decided to be patient; he had to see his plan all the way through. This coincidence had presented him with something he hadn't expected. The road was paved now, but he needed to slow down. The level of his calm must match that of his desire; his execution had to be as deliberate as his lust was intense.

He knew that her aunt and uncle had spent the night in the apartment in the same building and that they had gone to take care of some errands and visit friends of theirs in Tunis. Abdel Nasser asked Reem to invite all of them to come over for dinner that night, but she quickly refused and said over the phone, "I want to see you alone."

He could tell that she'd said more than she meant to, and he smiled. She tried to backtrack. "What I mean is that we can't see you together because they already have plans tonight."

"Will you be with them, then?"

"Yes, unfortunately."

"Don't worry; another time is better. When can we meet, then? I spoke with the director, and I have a new film project for you!"

He could tell that she was jumping for joy; she was pretending to be unperturbed, but the excited edge in her voice gave her away.

"They'll be going back to Sousse tomorrow. Can we meet around six? I'll be done with everything by then."

"Whenever you wish. I live on the third floor, Apartment 7. I'll be waiting for you."

"Okay, see you tomorrow."

"Goodbye, Zeina."

"You mean Reem?"

"No—from now on, you're Zeina. Zeina's the main character of the film."

He laughed, so she did, too. He continued, with a note of flirtation, "I see Zeina in you. You'll understand tomorrow when I tell you the plot."

6

Around six-fifteen, when Reem entered the apartment, the sun broke through the gloomy Sunday evening. Her presence set off a wave of temptation in the apartment. He chose a place for her next to the lamp. The lights were dim, and the scent of lavender filled the room. He could see her admiration and approval of the apartment. He excused himself, then came back after a moment with a small bouquet of three red roses. She was pleased with them and apologized for coming empty-handed. He told her that her presence was the best gift. He said, "You can give me a kiss as a gift."

She seemed both daring and submissive, contrary to how she had appeared. She kissed him. He wanted to embrace her, but the voice in his head told him to be patient once more. He felt a need to pull her close to him because the way she smelled reminded him of Lella Jnayna. True, she didn't decorate her body with *harkous* and she did not chew on *miswak* like Lella Jnayna—they were definitely from two different eras—but he could detect a scent that he knew well. It was Lella Jnayna's scent when she came back from the hammam. How had this scent come back to him? Lella Jnayna's scent that he'd known since he was a child and that he'd come to know even better—filled his nostrils with it—once he turned fifteen. Reem had undoubtedly just come from the hammam.

He intuitively knew that she would do whatever he asked her. He was sure that her outward, uptight appearance didn't match her real self or her age. He guessed that she was twenty-two, at most. She was in her third year of college. She asked directly about the role that she would be playing, not giving him the chance to get to know her more.

He thought about telling her that they would write the script together; she would have to tell him about her life in detail—to be the hero of the story and the hero of the film—and he would write the events that she was narrating in a creative way. He considered talking to her about cowriting the film: instead of giving her a fish, he would teach her how to fish and enjoy it. He realized that this proposal might scare her and push her away from him: it required her to trust him, and to have some life experience. Also, what if her life was ordinary and uneventful, with the exception of some childhood and high school adventures?

He also considered doing the opposite. He would tell her the story of his life, or parts of it. It would be an occasion to reorganize things in his memory, to look for a meaning in his life among all the disintegration, failures, petty cheating, and despicable justifications. But how could he put all his cards on the table? Would someone of her age and experience understand him? Yes. He was desperate after his breakup with Zeina. He really needed to sit in front of someone who could help him figure out the past and the present, and to look forward to the future with its ambiguity and confusion. He felt that was a risky strategy, too, though: if she found out about all of (what he considered) the vileness and filth in his life, she would run away like a would-be inmate from a probable tormenter. She was also so young; she might not understand these things. He put the idea aside, despite its temptation.

Instead, he invented a story for the screenplay he hadn't written. In it, he gathered together the crumbs of the stories of women he'd known. He named the protagonist Zeina. He described her appearance as if he were describing Reem; he convinced her that Zeina was Reem, copied and pasted. That reassured her and whetted her appetite.

He warned her from the start that cinema doesn't countenance fake ethics. He talked to her about Tunisian cinema and its boldness. He told her that Nouri Bouzid, for instance, had doubled his audacity, and so Abdel Nasser could not be less daring than he. He told her not to worry about what people said, about Tunisian cinema being all homosexuality and nudity. Reality—as he knew, and he was sure she knew, as well—was more terrible than anything you could see in Tunisian movies. She agreed with what he was saying. He moved on to a criticism of society, accusing it of hypocrisy, lies, and the suppression of individual freedom. She agreed with him again.

As he was speaking, he saw that she was impressed by his rhetoric and couldn't add even a single word. She just nodded. What could this girl, with dreams of the silver screen, do in the presence of the person who would open the doors of stardom to her?

He summarized the script. "The story of Zeina is the story of a girl from Sahel; her father is a prominent member of society, and her mother is foreign. She's the victim of two cultures: one—open and liberal—that she learned from her mother and the other eastern—conservative and closed—that she got from her father. Zeina experiences a shock in college, where she finds a bigger world than the one her father imprisoned her in. It resembles the world of novels she's read and movies she's watched. She lives torn between two cultures: what her father wants from her and the new reality she has found. While she's still a student, she marries a man her father doesn't approve of; she marries him without her family's blessing. This is her way of rebelling against her father. Her marriage fails after a year because her husband becomes violent, and turns out to be more psychologically complex than even her father. He would get jealous if a bird flew in her direction or if a breeze caressed her skin. After her divorce, she starts a journey of searching for her future, her freedom, and herself. She sees her life as a series of failures with men and adventures that have done nothing but make it even more difficult for her to adapt to society's constrictions. She has built herself an illusion: on the one hand, combatting the society that she wants to challenge, and on the other, waiting for a Prince Charming who—because she no longer believes in love—will never come."

He explained that the tension in the plot comes from Zeina's sense that she's failing to reach her goals and failing to control her love–hate relationship with her father, combined with the knowledge she's gained on her meandering road about her society, her body, and her mind. It becomes clear from the film, which combines both social and psychological perspectives, that she's telling the story to a psychoanalyst. He helps her to realize that she's suffering from a complex that has pushed her to torture herself and to take revenge on her own body in the stead of her father and society. In all of this, the film seeks to dissect the state of Tunisian women, their contradictions, their struggles, and the severe pain they suffer.

El-Talyani spoke slowly; he wanted to draw out the conversation, and she was listening like a good student, absorbing her teacher's words with admiration and fascination.

When he asked her to come sit next to him, she didn't mind. He put his hand on her thigh while talking, and she didn't stop him. He turned halfway toward her to caress her face and run his fingers through her hair, and she smiled, satisfied. When he kissed her on the cheek, her smile widened. He kissed her lightly on the lips, and she closed her eyes. He descended to her neck, and she moaned with pleasure. When he touched her breast, she relaxed her head back against the couch. Abdel

Nasser had never seen easier than this girl, who in the beginning had seemed so arrogant and vain.

He started getting ready for the most important part. He
wanted to celebrate her in a special way. He opened a bottle of
vodka in her honor and asked if she wanted a drink. She'd told
him before that she loved vodka. In fact, she'd hoped, the
night they met at La Maison Blanche, that he would offer her
a glass, surreptitiously since she didn't drink in front of her
uncle. They both relaxed. They drank their first glass in
between kisses, which melted her like butter and inflamed him
like a bull.

As soon as he finished pouring the second round, the
phone rang. He didn't pick up, but it kept ringing. He thought
it must be something serious. Yosser was on the line, crying.
"Father died . . . Hajj died . . ."

7

Abdel Nasser's face blanched. His mood darkened, and he
inhaled sharply. Reem asked him what was going on. He didn't
tell her. He went back and embraced her forcefully. He
downed the glass of vodka. His body was with her, but his
mind was at his family's house in Bab Jedid. The image of Hajj
Mahmoud in a shroud came to his mind. He kept trying to get
rid of it, to focus on Reem's face in front of him. She could tell
that something had happened, but under the onslaught of his
kisses, she just kept her head back on the couch, her eyes
closed. Her only reactions were fake moans that she didn't
realize made Abdel Nasser more excited. He carried her to the
bedroom. She had her hands around his neck like earth
preparing to be tilled. He took off his clothes quickly while she
lay on the bed, awaiting whatever he was going to do to her. He
took her clothes off quickly, as well. She put her hands over the

secret place, as if to cover herself with them. She let him wander in her tender meadows even though what he was doing had more than a touch of roughness and violence. She wasn't reacting with him.

When he approached the secret place, she firmly put her hand at the level of her pubis and said, "No. I'm a virgin!"

She turned over. He understood that she was offering something else. He went crazy but didn't move. She wasn't looking at him; she didn't understand what had happened. She looked back at him and found him staring into space, as if remembering something. She asked him, "What's the matter?"

He didn't answer. She saw his length of rope slacken. He was frowning, kneeling on the bed. His handsome face warped into something almost demonic. He was shaking, staring blankly, and suddenly collapsed onto the bed. She didn't dare ask him what was going on and didn't know what to do. She was horrified. She dressed quickly, got her purse from the living room, and left the apartment. The closing door cut off the terrifying sounds of muttering and whimpering that emanated from the bedroom.

1

A bdel Nasser called me in a state of total breakdown. He asked me to get ready to go out with him. He picked me up, and we went to his family home. He cried in front of his father's shrouded corpse like a little girl terrified of being orphaned. I accompanied him, not knowing what to do. Then he abruptly washed his face in the bathroom and asked me to leave with him.

It was around ten-thirty. We went to La Goulette. The beach was full of people who had come to stroll, and the restaurants were overflowing. We secluded ourselves next to El Karaka fortress, on the sea side. Abdel Nasser stood on the beach, talking and crying. The humidity of the sea was unbearable for me; I've had severe allergies in my ears and nose ever since I was a child. But I didn't care about that: at a time like this, I could ignore the salt-drenched breezes—my friend needed me.

He didn't talk to me about Hajj Mahmoud, God rest his soul. He talked about Reem. Reem, who I've still never met to this day. He told me everything that had happened in detail. He was feeling horribly emasculated. He said it was like his stomach had swallowed his tool—he put his hand down there and couldn't find anything. He was talking and crying, and I didn't know what to do. It wouldn't have been appropriate to contradict him. Yes, I'm his friend, but I'm not a doctor. I tried to explain to him that it was just a feeling and that he needed to see a doctor: it might be a mental disorder, resulting from his inability to have sex with Reem.

He insisted that he was only a memory of a man, no longer able to excite a woman. He was adamant that what was hanging between his legs was a slack rope, at best.

I kept trying to calm him down until finally he sat on the sand, sitting cross-legged like we used to sit in the old days. I squatted next to him. He wouldn't look me in the eye.

He started telling me about what the imam had done to him, when he was between eight and ten years old. When Reem gave him her back (the way many girls who want to remain virgins do) he was overrun with scenes of his abuse at the hands of Allala, the caretaker of the neighborhood mosque who was working for Si Shadhli, Lella Jnayna's father.

2

One scorching Tunisian summer day, during *qailulah*, Hajj Mahmoud had sent his son out to buy him a pack of cigarettes. Allala—who we used to call "the *darwish*" because he looked like a dirty vagabond—called from the mosque door. When Abdel Nasser went over, he forced him inside and into the ablution room, and the boy quickly understood that what was happening wasn't normal. Allala put his hand over his mouth. He would have almost suffocated if not for breathing through his nose. Allala pulled down his trousers and the boy's shorts. El-Talyani tried to escape from his grip. He felt the man's saliva, and a small, loose piece of flesh. He didn't know how Allala let him get away.

He bought the cigarettes and went back home quickly, confused. He gave the pack to his father and ran to the bathroom to wash. He immersed his cotton underwear in water, then started tearing it apart. He remembered that part clearly because Jweeda gave him hell (at his mother's instructions) when she saw the ripped underwear. She had no idea of the more dangerous rip in the boy's soul.

Abdel Nasser told me that, after that, he thought of committing suicide. During *qailulah* the next day, after a long night spent in pain, he took a knife from the kitchen. No one had felt his pain. He took it with him to the bathroom and started trying to push it into his stomach. He wanted to slice open his stomach, but his fear of the pain and the blood that would result changed his mind. He used to hate Eid al-Adha because he couldn't bear to see the blood, even though Hajj Mahmoud—who sacrificed the Eid lamb himself—would invite him to watch the sacrifice rituals so that he could perform them when he grew up. Ever since he was small, he hated the whole process and would hide to escape seeing the slaughter. But they insisted that he watch anyway. Those scenes of slaughter later saved him from killing himself.

3

Allala Darwish, before becoming an imam and Lella Jnayna's husband, almost cornered him again when he was nine or ten years old. A group of four of us was playing together in the alley. *Qailulah* had ended, but the weather was still hot. We were known in our families as the *qailulah* devils who refused to sleep and threatened to disturb everyone else's rest with our chaos.

I remembered, after el-Talyani reminded me, that I had kicked the ball so hard it had gone over the wall and into the courtyard of Lella Jnayna's house. It was Abdel Nasser's ball. We all ran away, afraid of Si Shadhli, Jnayna's father. But Abdel Nasser knocked on the door. He knew the house; they were his neighbors, with only a courtyard wall between their house and his. The door opened, and he ran inside to retrieve the ball.

When he was about to go back into the alley to continue the game, he found Allala Darwish with his arms spread, waiting for him and laughing evilly. El-Talyani remembered that he was wearing a dirty *jebba* with gray and white stripes. He darted away from him through the house, and Allala followed, trying to catch him. Abdel Nasser was terrified: the memory of the ablution room was still fresh in his mind. He started crying, and when Allala caught him, he collapsed, shaking and sobbing. Suddenly he heard the joyful trills of women approaching the house and a loud knock on the courtyard door. Allala became flustered and released the boy without doing anything. Abdel Nasser rushed to the door and opened it. Jnayna took him into her arms, kissing him and playing with him. She was accompanied by two maids. He could smell the scent of the hammam on her; later, he heard his sisters chatting and discovered that they were at the hammam preparing for the wedding of a neighbor girl who lived on a different alley off the same street. The important thing was that they'd come back just in time. Abdel Nasser forgot his horror; he was entranced by the perfume of the hammam and *harkous*, by the smell of the *miswak* on her breath when she gave him kisses on his mouth and neck. It was the same scent he'd caught from Reem when she entered his apartment, the smell of the hammam. So why hadn't Reem given him what Lella Jnayna used to give him? Why had she given him her back, like what had happened to him that day in the ablution room with that goddamned son of a bitch Allala?

Lella Jnayna's fresh scent emanated from Reem when she was on the couch in the living room. But when she'd turned and given him her back on the bed, the smell of the ablution room and that impotent fudge-packer Allala's saliva filled his nose.

I tried to help el-Talyani numb the ragged edges of this memory. Imam Allala's tool was broken—everyone in the neighborhood knew that (Lella Jnayna made sure they did, after she was falsely accused of being barren). He should be thanking God that Allala never penetrated him. The neighborhood was full of stories about boys who were forced to inherit this habit, to the point that it became an addiction they never got over. I reminded him that even some of the neighborhood thugs were bisexual. I recited that ancient proverb that "he who is forced does not become a catamite." Nothing worked. The force of el-Talyani's feelings was terrible to watch. He sobbed like a young widow as he told me his secrets, snot dripping from his nose. There was nothing I could do but bring more tissues from the car.

Since my reassuring comments weren't helping, el-Talyani continued to remember more details. He seemed awake. There were no more tears, though his eyes were red and swollen. He thought that Allala was trying to use him to train himself to get erect. He was undoubtedly impotent. If his penis ever started to stiffen, it would immediately go limp again; it was like a tatty hose, inflated when the water was on full, but as soon as you turned off the faucet it would fall to the ground like the tail of an emaciated dog. El-Talyani recalled the madness that would come over him and the way he exhaled with a hiss like a lick of fire. He looked like a demon: eyes closed, nostrils flared, the veins in his fat neck bulging.

The boy remembered that, about two weeks after the incident in the courtyard of Si Shadhli's house, Sheikh Allala again took him by surprise. He was playing on the roof, on the side next to the neighbor's, setting traps for warblers. We used to love this game in the summer. Like most of the neighborhood kids, he never actually caught a bird, but lived in the hopes of catching one, just one.

He grabbed him from behind while he was kneeling to set the trap. A heavy hand, holding his neck. He couldn't get away. He turned the struggling boy toward him and started licking his neck with his rough tongue. He put one hand on the fragile parts of his body and held his backside with the other hand.

He slapped his penis painfully. El-Talyani was fighting back, trying to run away. He didn't scream, terrified of the scandal he was sure would result if someone saw. Allala made a quick movement, trying to take off el-Talyani's shorts. He escaped from him, almost falling, and ran toward the ladder on the top floor next to Salah Eddine's room. He scrambled down the ladder two rungs at a time. His small heart was beating hard, and he was panting. He remembered that the bastard's hands were shaking. He felt drops of sweat running down his naked back (he wasn't wearing an undershirt) like drops of burning fire, stinging wounds. Even now, he remembered them as if they had just fallen.

As Abdel Nasser remembered, only a striking coincidence had saved him that day in the courtyard. The house had been empty. In addition to Jnayna and the two maids who'd gone to the hammam with her, he later found out that Hajj Shadhli, Jnayna's father, had gone to Bizerte to attend an old friend's funeral. So that day he hadn't followed his daily ritual of coming home at noon, reading *Assabah* newspaper after lunch (served punctually), and drinking a cup of tea (green with mint in the summer, black in the winter). Hajj Shadhli, unintentionally, had almost destroyed the boy and done away with the rest of his soul.

4

We sat on the beach in La Goulette for a long time. I didn't dare ask Abdel Nasser to get back in the car or go back home. He'd chosen me to confide in, and I didn't know what to do. That night his memory chest had burst open, and el-Talyani took out the ones he thought were dirty and shameful for me to see. Though, in comparison with what I know about other people, they seemed to me simple stumbling blocks that didn't deserve all of this pain and tears and snot. As I thought about it (keeping my thoughts to myself, as usual), I no longer knew if the state he was in was caused by a mix of the shadows of failure after his divorce from Zeina, the impact of the news of Hajj Mahmoud's passing, and the interference of all that with his plan to sleep with Reem no matter the price. Why had he insisted on continuing his cuddling and caresses with the young student despite Yosser's call and the painful news? How could he continue what he was doing? In what state of mind? Wasn't he himself destroying the possibility of enjoying the encounter, owing to his eagerness to finish the mission instead of postponing it? Wasn't all of this far removed from the solution that Reem had offered to him to quench his desire? I knew I was rambling mentally while Abdel Nasser was contemplating the night and the sea and the sand. And I was filling up with the deadly humidity.

I was thinking about how I had to wake up early to help grade the second-round baccalaureate exams. The funeral would also be tomorrow. I needed to go home to shower and rest.

Nothing saved me until Abdel Nasser suddenly and laboriously stood up. I thought he wanted to walk on the sand, so I was happy to see him heading toward the car. I asked him what he wanted to do, but he didn't know where he was going or why. I took advantage of the opportunity to remind him of his duty the next day: he would need all his strength for attending the funeral, supporting the family, and accepting condolences. He needed to get some rest. I suggested that he spend the night at my place, since it was late, almost 2 A.M.

If I'm honest with you, I should confess that I was thinking of myself as much as him. It seemed to me that while we were in the car—going back to Le Bardo on the road connecting La Goulette with the capital—he seemed to revive and get his second wind, while I fought the fatigue weighing down my eyelids.

I had to stay awake to make sure that he didn't get distracted or wander and miss seeing a car or a cart in front of him, even though he wasn't speeding.

Abdel Nasser was revived and refreshed and went back to opening his reservoir of memories. He asked me, after a long silence, "Do you know what Lella Jnayna smells like?"

"What? How could I know that?"

I noticed that his eyes widened and his smile was nostalgic, shaped to the leftover pleasure that he sipped when he talked about Lella Jnayna.

5

He said, "Do you know the smell of *miswak* and bitter Arabic chewing gum? Do you know the smell of mint, thyme, rosemary, lavender, and marjoram? Do you know the smell of henna and *harkous*? Do you know how incense smells when it mixes with citron? Do you know the smell of Turkish coffee, mixed with ground sun-dried orange peel? Or the smell of pear or apple seeds, burning on the charcoal of a clay *kanoun*? Gather all of these smells if you can, mix them well, and spray it on Lella Jnayna—I would still be able to distinguish them on her body, her things, her clothes, her scarf, smell by smell. Her body was a filter that extracted the essence of these scents while discarding the cloying excess. Every time, she had a scent that overcame everything else."

I woke up to the scents of these memories, which came back to me that night to refresh my soul. All of us boys in the neighborhood, we would all stand up and try to steal a glimpse of Jnayna, the daughter of Imam Hajj Shadhli, when she passed by. She wore her *safseri* differently and walked enticingly to the rhythm of her wedge sandals, revealing her calves.

She was the first woman to wear a golden bracelet around

her ankle (her right ankle, to be exact), and we were amazed by that. We had seen the thick silver *khalkhal* on the ankles of some of the new neighbor women, who flocked together in their peasant costumes with the traditional marks tattooed on their foreheads, noses, and cheeks (and sometimes on their hands and feet, as well). But the golden anklet was an innovation created by Jnayna, and we never saw anyone who imitated her in that.

I still remember the sound of her smacking her Arabic gum, which she would chew while walking, her shoulders swaying as she looked around her. Her *safseri* kept trying to slip down to her shoulders, and she kept pulling it back up.

She turned heads with her wide eyes, her blushing complexion, and her dark black hair. I don't remember a single man who ever dared to harass her, though. Not even the group of thugs—they would look down, avoiding her, or look at her after she'd already passed. The truth was that we'd never seen her walking by herself. She was always accompanied by Allala Darwish or one of the two maids.

Everyone in the neighborhood knew that she lived without her mother, who had died after hearing her first cry. People explained it as God's will, but I once heard my mother blame the midwife for enlarging the birth canal more than necessary with her forceps. She had probably perforated one of the membranes; Jnayna's mother bled so much that the midwife wasn't able to stop it. She was a new midwife who had learned the fundamentals of the job from Yina the Jew (who they say was Italian), but the difference between them was night and day.

Perhaps this was the reason for the neighborhood men's reticence (even among the worst fornicators and adulterers) to go after Jnayna, despite her flirtatious ways.

Everyone in the neighborhood knew that Lella Jnayna was brought up like a princess. Two maids at her service, Allala

Darwish who took care of everything, and a loving father who stayed faithful to the memory of his wife. He refused to remarry after her passing and devoted himself, as he said, to taking care of Jnayna. He chose that name for her after her maternal grandmother, hoping that she would be like her: intelligent, composed, tactful, polite, and organized.

The daughter grew up spoiled by her father, who was trying to make up for her deprivation of a mother. He wanted to be both father and mother in his own way. He used to say to people, "God—may He be glorified and exalted—has made up for the loss of my late wife. When Jnayna was born, she brought good luck and fortune with her. Glory to God, He only takes away that which He returns to us two-fold."

Indeed, Jnayna's birth coincided with Si Shadhli—who hadn't gone on the pilgrimage, so wasn't yet a *hajj*—obtaining a great fortune: several properties in the old city (shops and both medium-sized and large houses); vast tracts of land in the suburbs of Manouba and Mornag; as well as an olive press that was in addition to the Cape Bon orange orchards that he already owned. He was originally from Nabeul but had settled in Tunis after he finished his studies at the Great Mosque and married Jnayna's mother, who came from a Bizerte family. It was kind of a strange marriage for that time, but its fruit was good. Jnayna the daughter combined the warmth of the women of Nabeul (which comes, they claim, from the city's spicy red peppers) with the coquettish nature of the Bizertine women, which itself was enhanced in terms of charm and politeness by its mix of French, Italian, and Maltese people.

Jnayna's late mother had inherited some real estate, land, and fishing boats from her father. Si Shadhli had appointed one of his acquaintances to harvest the income from these on his behalf every month.

6

Everyone would attest that Si Shadhli and his wife were never greedy with beggars, passersby, or the less fortunate in the neighborhood. They would give generously but silently, without embarrassing the people in need. Everything went through the small mosque at the end of the street. Si Shadhli devoted himself to it. He repaired it and renovated it and completely changed its *mihrab*. He rebuilt it, relying on the expertise of craftsmen from Nabeul who specialized in embellishment and decoration, as well as the expertise of the remaining tilers at Souk El Kallaline to redo the entire floor. The mosque became "the little Zaytuna Mosque," as the residents liked to call it, considering it their pride and blessing. It was natural for Si Shadhli to become imam of the five prayers at the mosque after the aging sheikh became unable to carry out his role in the neighborhood. In addition to contributing a lot of money, Si Shadhli's piety was indisputable: he was always present at the prayers, totally devoting himself with constant readiness and continuous attendance.

One of the people saved from destitution was Allala Darwish. He was a short, heavy man. One who saw signs of sloth and stupidity on his face would not be mistaken, but he was an easy, obedient person from whom you never heard anything but *yes* and *thank you*. Some of the adults who mocked him told us his story: even Allala himself didn't know where he came from. He was found during the first years of independence in the fifties, a homeless child dressed in dirty rags. In the beginning, the owner of the hammam looked after him: he allowed him to bathe after the customers left, put some old clothes on him, and let him sleep on straw mats. Allala would wake up early to bring wood, heat the hammam, keep the fire stoked, and open the hammam for the customers. All of that he did in return for room and board.

However, the first real change in Allala's life was with Si Shadhli. He took advantage of the hammam owner's anger with Allala (over some problem I never heard the details of) to recruit him to come work for him. Allala was given a room with a luxurious bed and wardrobe in Si Shadhli's big house.

His meals were served to him—morning, noon, and night—in his room. The two maids treated him like anyone else in the house and took care of his needs, including cleaning his room and washing his clothes. Though there was the occasional outburst when he would throw his cheap RT cigarette butts on the floor, or put his dirty clothes back in the wardrobe instead of in the laundry basket they'd supplied for him in his room. Allala would look at the two maids blankly, as if he didn't understand what they were saying or exactly what they wanted from him.

His life became organized around the rhythm of Si Shadhli's. He attended the five daily prayers with him. He cleaned the mosque every day and supervised the weekly cleanup campaign on Friday mornings. Si Shadhli taught him to do the call to prayer. (Luckily, his voice was not bad.) He became like a Swiss watch: he knew when to go to the mosque and when to come back and when it was time for the *adhan* and what he had to do before and after. He knew when it was time to go to the souk, what to buy from the grocer, the butcher, the fishmonger, and the corner store. But he would always forget something that Si Shadhli's wife had asked him to buy, so he would go back at least once to bring this or that thing that he forgot.

During this new stage of Allala's life, the epithet *darwish* kept chasing him, even though he was no longer homeless and did not beg. Although his appearance was not very different from that of the other neighborhood men, he had acquired—with age and experience in life—some tricky maliciousness and a big mouth. He would no longer take an insult lying down, and he started to refuse some people's requests when they asked him to bring them something from the market.

7

Gradually, Si Shadhli started to take Allala to people's houses when he was invited to perform at *soulamia* gatherings. Si Shadhli was also a Sufi singer: he had memorized religious songs based on the Qadiriyya and Shadhiliyya orders, and he had developed new approaches to religious song. Owing to his pure instinct and Sufi enculturation, he could put new lyrics on well-known songs of praise for the prophet and supplications to God. Many Sufi songs that you still hear at *soulamia* gatherings today have lyrics by Hajj Shadhli, but people didn't document that kind of thing, and copyrights didn't mean anything to him. It never even occurred to anyone. But the older people in the neighborhood still talk about his powerful and moving voice, the attention he commanded when he started playing on the tambourine among the singers and reached the refrain *"ya Bel-Hassan Shadhli . . ."* They also said that they'd never heard a voice more beautiful or pure than Hajj Shadhli's voice when he sang Al-Busiri's poem "Al-Burda":

My master, peace and blessings upon you always and evermore, your beloved, the greatest of all creation . . .

And when he finished it, he would add a touch that was uniquely his, with the Ahmed Shawki poem:

A white gazelle fawn on the plain, between the moringa tree and the mountain.

Over time, Allala became specialized in warming up the tambourines. People who know little about this might assume it's a simple task—just a matter of putting the tambourine next to the small clay *kanoun*—but in fact it's an art in and of itself. The tambourine skin needs to be heated slowly, like food that must be cooked on low heat, so the fire can be neither too strong nor too weak. There is a precise balance that gives the skin the perfect tension, like when you tune the strings of an *oud* or adjust the pegs of a *qanun*. The former furnace boy at the hammam learned this fine art. God opened his heart to that mission, so he renounced his rudeness and became soft with the tambourine skin. He was able to estimate the temperature without a thermometer, and as soon as he held his hand over the *kanoun*, he knew just how close to put the tambourine, without needing a measuring stick.

Hajj Shadhli was completely satisfied with Allala's performance, whether in taking care of the household business or caring for and cleaning the mosque or preparing the tambourines for singing.

8

Then came the big surprise: the surprise of the century, as far as the neighborhood residents—men and women, old and young—were concerned. The news of Allala's marriage to Lella Jnayna spread. No one believed it in the beginning. They considered it a rumor or a tasteless joke. People laughed and wondered at this strange nonsense. No one dared to ask Hajj Shadhli about the potentially offensive rumor. They were sure it would make him angry; such talk was insulting and clearly a big mistake. How could the ravishingly beautiful daughter of Hajj Shadhli, who he had sacrificed his life for, be married off to a person with no name, a bit of flotsam carried by the current, the loyal servant and former furnace boy? The distinguished daughter and sole heir of Hajj Shadhli's immense fortune, marry a servant, a tambourine boy? Why? Was she one-eyed? Crippled? Defiled? What was wrong with her? If the *hajj* had asked any of the young men in the neighborhood to marry her, they would have knelt out of obedience and gratitude, kissing his hands and feet. If he'd seen fit to arrange a marriage for his daughter with any scion of the wealthy families in Tunis—or Nabeul or Bizerte or anywhere from the north of the country to the south—the chosen one would have been happy and grateful, thanking God for the many blessings this marriage would offer. It's true that the girl was spoiled, but she was entitled to that as an only child. It's true that she dropped out of school early, but the girl's future was to be under the protection of a man. A real man—not a shadow of a man, like Allala Darwish. Would Hajj Shadhli give his daughter and half of his fortune and kingdom to Allala? That mentally retarded *darwish*, a son-in-law to Hajj Shadhli? Ha! What rubbish! The neighborhood assholes must have sharp tongues to spread such vile rumors.

Despite all that, the vile-tongued were right. What's more, the wedding was fit for a girl from a big wealthy family marrying the son of big shots. Seven full days and seven nights. A different dress for the bride every night and every night a party with drinks, bowls piled high with food, tables for people to sit at, and live music. For the first time, the neighborhood residents saw some of the shining stars of the Tunisian music universe: Safia Chamia, Ali Riahi, Hédi Jouini, Raoul Journo, Hedi Kallal, Mohammed Sassi, Ahmed Hamza, Choubeila Rached, as well as the singers Oulaya and Naâma at the beginning of their careers and Taher Gharsa in his youth. This was in addition to the king of the violin, Ridha Kalai, and many others who were not famous—Hajj Shadhli's house was packed.

The neighborhood had become the heart of the shining stars of Tunisia. If he'd had more time, Hajj Shadhli would have brought Mohammed Abdel Wahab, Oum Kalthoum, Karem Mahmoud, Souad Mohammed, Fayza Ahmed . . . and Scheherazade herself, if necessary.

It was a real wedding and an immortal music festival that

the remaining old people in our neighborhood still reminisce about, lamenting the fact that they haven't seen anything like it since.

The wedding week passed quickly amidst of the joy of the guests—who, for the whole seven nights, never stopped whispering. The neighbors and people of the quartier smelled something fishy in the story. But they couldn't get to the bottom of it, and they had no evidence for anything they imagined. But after spending a lot of time and effort speculating and imagining, they started to show sympathy to the motherless girl and her respected father. They remembered his generosity to all of them: families who borrowed money but without a doubt didn't pay it back, or those asking him to mediate in a family dispute or to hold a *soulamia* gathering (for which he refused to accept payment and paid his assistants out of his own pocket). There was no family in the neighborhood that Hajj Shadhli hadn't helped as if they were his own. When they celebrated the marriage of a son or daughter, he would give money without counting, paying for bags and boxes full of fruits and vegetables, as well as lambs (slaughtered and live), without forgetting the gifts for the bride and groom, which were generally expensive and made of heavy pure gold.

Whatever they did, they'd been unable to pay him back for what he'd done for them, and they would never be able to. It was enough for them to see how happy he was those nights. He was so excited that he took off his *jebba* and danced in front of everyone. He put aside his poise to express his joy at his daughter's marriage. There was nothing at all that seemed to spoil his joy. He welcomed them all, thanked them for their attendance, and invited them to dance or sit or eat more of this food or that. He served with his own hands the fresh almond *rosata*, or pieces of baklava, or of *baklawa el-bey*, or *bjawia sfaxia*, or *kaak al-warka* with its fragrance of sweetbriar rose.

Despite the many strange aspects of this irrational marriage, all wished lasting happiness and joy for Hajj Shadhli, both out loud and in their hearts. What did it matter what they thought of Allala, whether they had contempt for him or didn't consider him good enough to marry that sweet-smelling flower— or even the whole sweet-smelling garden? What did their reservations matter at all, as long as the judge that mattered was this happy with his daughter and son-in-law?

But the wishes of all the neighbors and others in the quartier ended up being in vain. Hajj Shadhli's happiness didn't last, and nor did his joy: he didn't live long enough after choosing a husband for his only daughter to enjoy his enormous fortune. One month after Allala and Jnayna's marriage, the Merciful One took to himself what was his. As if Hajj Shadhli had accomplished the mission he was born to fulfill. Perhaps he died content and his soul went to its creator reassured about his daughter's future, both with her husband Allala and with her large fortune. But most likely—and as the neighbors and people of the quartier believed—was that he died of grief, having accidentally buried his daughter when trying to give her a happy life under a man's protection. But since when was Allala a suitable man to indulge in Jnayna's garden?

I knew this story in general, as well as some of its details. Abdel Nasser and I were small when we attended Jnayna's wedding festivities with our families. We didn't care what the grown-ups around us were up to, and we didn't know what was on their minds. It was an opportunity for us to enjoy sweets and juice and to play with our friends. The events themselves I remembered only vaguely, but who in the quartier didn't know the story of Jnayna and Allala? We used to hear the women in our families bring up the story from time to time, whenever they heard about something strange happening in the cursed house, the house of Hajj Shadhli, may God have mercy on him. The story circles back around because our women like to repeat it whenever Allala's name or news of Jnayna are mentioned in front of them.

9

That night, on the way back from La Goulette, Abdel Nasser told me some secrets I hadn't known before. We were from the same quartier but didn't live in the same alley; I had never visited Hajj Shadhli's house, as Abdel Nasser had done his whole life. The truth I discovered was that Hajja Zeinab treated Jnayna like one of her daughters, especially after she dropped out of school in the fifth or sixth grade. The day she decided to quit school, she made quite a scene: she put all of her textbooks and notebooks in a large copper wash bowl, poured alcohol all over them, and lit them on fire, reducing them all to ashes. Hajja Zeinab chided her; her father did not, though he didn't like what she'd done.

Jnayna started spending all day at el-Talyani's house, doing everything his sisters did, especially the older sister Jweeda. Jweeda taught her how to cook, wash clothes, and clean the house. She was lazy and refused to do such things—which she considered maids' activities—unless Hajja Zeinab or Jweeda asked her to. Jweeda taught her embroidery on summer evenings and crochet in the winter. Jnayna seemed to be very skillful in handicrafts. She was also fast: she would finish her embroidery hoop or doily or sweater before even Jweeda, with all her skill. Jnayna's hands could spin silk into gold with just a touch.

When Hajja Zeinab found out how skillful she was, she taught her to design and make clothes, and she excelled in this, as well. She didn't use paperboard to design a pattern and cut the cloth. She used to look at the person, take the scissors, and gauge by sight without using a tape measure. She would make do with some pins to hold parts of the dress or trousers, and it would come out as if she had made it with a tried-and-true template. But she remained lazy; she did that (if she did it) as a way of killing time, nothing more.

Jnayna was a dexterous woman; she knew everything that was needed to manage a house and performed all the tasks that women do to perfection. But after her father passed away, Hajja Zeinab and her husband no longer heard anything but Jnayna's yelling, day and night. She would curse Allala and call him names that made you feel sorry for him. She fired the two maids after a few weeks. She stayed isolated in the house all day; she didn't go out, and no one knew what she was doing.

Allala came to Hajj Mahmoud and asked him to have Hajja Zeinab talk to Jnayna and make her come to her senses. She had started to see him as a devil. She would scream at him whenever she saw him, and would hit him with whatever she found at hand. He started staying at the mosque all day, from the *fajr* prayer at dawn until the late-night *'isha* prayer (he had become the imam of the five prayers, inheriting the position from his father-in-law without hearing any protests), but that didn't help. His stomach was no longer full, and he wasn't getting good sleep. She'd forced him to sleep in his old room and wouldn't let him sleep before she had lit into him with a long list of curses, expressing her discontent and anger at he didn't know what.

He swore that he hadn't once touched her since their marriage. She sentenced him to sleep on the rug for many days. He would wake up to find her spitting in his face and kicking him; sometimes she would pour a glass of water on him while he slept. He started to lock the door to his room; no one cleaned his room or washed his clothes anymore. He would buy plenty of groceries, thanks to what Hajj Shadhli had left to him: he'd given him two estates that brought in a good amount of money every month; he also bequeathed him the Sufi singing group, which gave him the largest portion of the income compared to the other members. He would buy the usual and more: vegetables, fruit, meat, and fish. He didn't remember ever shirking his duty; he had learned many years ago exactly what the household needed. But since Jnayna fired the two maids, the meat would rot, the vegetables wilted, the fruit filled with worms, and the fish decomposed and stank. All of this without anyone opening the bags or checking what was in the baskets. He didn't know what Jnayna was doing in the house, which had become like a stable. What was she eating? How was she spending her days? All that could be heard was the radio, broadcasting talk shows and songs day and night, from the moment it began transmitting early in the morning until it stopped late at night.

During one September *qailulah*, the *qailulah* devil Abdel Nasser saw a scene he'd never witnessed before, even though his mother Zeinab, who was in charge of the house, could sometimes be harsh and cruel. They heard screaming from Lella Jnayna (or "Nana," as el-Talyani used to call her as a child, the same name he gave his older sister Jweeda) coming from her house. They heard the loud noises of things hitting the marble floor, the shatter of glass and the clatter of copper dishes, the smashing of the small wooden chairs that were used for sitting around the low table. This is what the almost-thirteen-year-old boy heard. But everyone in Hajj Mahmoud's house heard Allala Darwish pleading with Jnayna to let him go.

Hajj Mahmoud woke up annoyed because they had disturbed his nap; Hajja Zeinab started wailing about what kind of annoying neighbors would disturb the peace at this time of day. Hajj Mahmoud shouted at his wife, "Why is God tormenting us like this?!"

"What have I got to do with it? It's as bad for me as it is for you! The girl has lost her mind since her father passed."

10

Hajj Mahmoud headed out the front door, muttering a frustrated, "*Astaghfirullah!*" Hajja Zeinab followed him out the door, and neither of them realized the boy was behind them.

In the courtyard of the neighbor's house, they saw Lella Jnayna, next to naked and sitting on top of Allala. She tore at his *jebba*. She dug her nails into his face, leaving bloody scratches. She had bashed his head, and blood was trickling from that wound, as well. Allala was trying to cover his head with his hands to stop her slapping and punching.

Hajj Mahmoud turned his face away. El-Talyani stood in the far corner of the covered entryway, spellbound by her nude back and thighs. She was wearing nothing but shiny white underwear decorated with lace. He found out later that that kind of fabric was called satin and that it was soft and slippery. He was laughing at the state of Allala Darwish. *Just what that son of a bitch deserves*, the boy thought to himself. Lella Jnayna rose in his esteem. She was getting some of his revenge on that wretched rat. If he'd been as tall and strong as she was, he'd have done that and more.

Hajja Zeinab admonished Lella Jnayna, pulling her off of Allala with difficulty. She took her into her bedroom. Allala rushed toward Si Mahmoud, crying and complaining about what Lella Jnayna had done to him. He showed him the bite marks on both hands—she'd almost taken off some of his flesh. She had sunk her teeth in deep. Meanwhile, the scratches and red mark above his eyebrow and the bruise above the other eyebrow were all obvious to the naked eye, as was the blood dripping from the open wound. Hajj Mahmoud told him to go to the mosque and promised to join him later. As he left, Allala didn't notice the boy hiding next to the storage room in the covered entryway.

He heard Hajja Zeinab calling the *hajj*, who rushed to the

room she was calling from. El-Talyani snuck up to eavesdrop. The rooms surrounding the courtyard had curtains hanging in front of the doors to protect the wood from rain in winter and the harsh rays of the sun in summer; el-Talyani spied on the three of them from behind the curtain as they became engrossed in their conversation.

Hajja Zeinab started scolding Lella Jnayna about the state of the room. "What happened to you? Is this what I taught you? This is a pigsty, not a bedroom!"

Lella Jnayna's head was bowed; she would sometimes lift her eyes, embarrassed, without saying anything. The *hajja* reminded her that she'd become a wife and lady of the house and so must act accordingly. She was the daughter of a noble family, the daughter of Hajj Shadhli, who was a great man; she must honor her late father and let her mother rest easy. She told her, "Do you know that your father is rolling over in his grave? Have some mercy on him, at least."

Tears rolled down Jnayna's cheeks. The *hajja* dried them with a tissue from the table. She added, "Crying doesn't help—it just tortures our loved ones in their graves. You should be looking after yourself, not to mention your house and your husband. What would people say about us? Stop acting like this so people stop gossiping. Please, my daughter—in the neighbors' eyes, you're Zeinab's daughter."

Hajj Mahmoud interjected, "What you're doing, my daughter, pleases neither God nor his prophet. Before he died, your father asked me to take care of you. You're a debt that your late father put around my neck, so don't make things difficult for me. Tell me what's wrong with you: what do you want?"

Lella Jnayna broke down crying. She moved next to Tata Zeinab, as she used to call her; she hugged her and put her head on her shoulder. El-Talyani's mother stroked her hair and told her to stop crying. She told her, "You're the most beautiful girl in the neighborhood; you have everything. Aamm

Mahmoud and I are here to help if you need anything. Tell us. Did Allala beat you? Did he insult you? Did he deprive you of anything? It looks to me like the poor man is at your service."

Hajj Mahmoud clearly wanted to end the conversation and get back to his *qailulah* that Jnayna had spoiled. He said, "Come on, daughter, bless us with a little boy."

Hajja Zeinab rebuked him with her eyes and ordered him out with a sign of her eyebrows, without Lella Jnayna noticing anything. Abdel Nasser ran toward the main door, but his father saw him before he got out. He said, "What are you doing here? Spying on the adults as usual?"

The boy swore to God that he was just waiting for him and hadn't heard anything they'd said. He expected his father to punish him by taking him with him to the bedroom to make him sleep. It's what he always did when he was angry or afraid that Abdel Nasser would cause chaos at that time of the day. But Hajj Mahmoud did not.

After almost an hour, Hajja Zeinab came back home, accompanied by Lella Jnayna. She prepared some hot water so she could bathe and put on clean clothes. From that day on, Lella Jnayna did not leave their house except to sleep. Over the days, she recovered her charming smile, her seductive laugh, and the secret way she smacked her chewing gum that no one but her knew. It was, without a doubt, a deal suggested by Zeinab and executed by Si Mahmoud. El-Talyani found himself the greatest beneficiary. Jnayna was now very close to him. In that room on the upper floor of Hajj Mahmoud's house, she would play with him, spoil him, and take care of him—even wash him!

11

For three or four years, he remained fond of what Salah Eddine had left him: the records, the books, the rocking chair . . . and Lella Jnayna. But his room was no longer a safe place to be alone with her. He heard Hajja Zeinab talking to her about it one day in the kitchen: "The boy has grown up, Jnayna, and you're in my care here."

"What do you mean, Tata Zeinab? Abdel Nasser was raised at my hands."

"I don't mean you, you know that. But the boy's eyes are no longer innocent."

"What are you talking about? He's like my son or my brother!"

"Even so, we must be cautious. Hajj Mahmoud pointed it out to me."

Lella Jnayna didn't comment. She started to spend more time in her own home. She didn't cut ties altogether, but she started claiming that she was busy supervising the two maids in some projects. She started cooking a lot of food that she would send to Hajj Mahmoud's house out of gratitude and affection. She didn't cut her ties with the boy who had grown up, either. Sometimes, one of the two maids would be at the main door, waiting for him to secretly invite him into the house: Lella Jnayna needed him for something urgent. He understood that the two maids were in on it with her. He didn't ask, but all evidence pointed to it. What did a young man of his age, burning with desire for a lush body like Lella Jnayna's, care about these deliberations? Yes, she was the wife of a man (an impotent man, no doubt) and she was satisfied with what they had, so why shouldn't he be?

And since a secret known by a third person is no longer a secret, shortly after Abdel Nasser turned eighteen he decided to stop playing with fire. His game with Lella Jnayna had become too serious. She had started to ask for him too often; one of the maids waiting in front of the door was calling him multiple times a day, especially during school breaks. He noticed that Lella Jnayna had become addicted to the boy's body. (And was he Salah Eddine or Abdel Nasser?) She was no longer satisfied with the minutes needed for reconnecting and putting out the burning fire. She started wishing that he could spend the night with her and she could tell him stories, sing for him, dance for him, and offer him tea and seasonal fruits. She started making *crème kordiène* (with eggs yolks and sugar) and prepared quince jelly mixed with halvah. She would also mix honey with almonds, pine nuts, and pistachio and give it to him before and after having sex. Sometimes she would offer him queen's honey mixed with some yellow grains, dissolved in a glass of milk. She would tell him, "Drink this, it's good for virility."

All of this, with the passing of months, made him feel like a prisoner of Lella Jnayna's desires. But the straw that broke the camel's back was when his little sister, Yosser, informed him about the conversations that were taking place at home: conversations about a relationship between him and Lella Jnayna. She warned him of a plan, put in place by the women of the house and led by the absolute evil of his mother Zeinab, to catch him in the act. At that time, the matter was mere rumors and whispers; Hajj Mahmoud hadn't yet heard about it, so Abdel Nasser needed to be cautious.

It wasn't easy for him to leave Jnayna and her charms—but having their secret exposed, with proof, wouldn't have been easy for him, either. He didn't tell Jnayna, but he no longer accepted the maids' invitations. He started making up a new excuse for them every time.

12

Once, he found Lella Jnayna herself waiting for him at the door. The door was closed, and she appeared so suddenly he didn't know where she came from. Clearly flustered, he looked around in all directions to make sure no one would see them, then asked her to go into the entryway with him. He was truly missing her; he hadn't touched her for more than two weeks. She started reproaching him for abandoning her all that time. He tried to come up with different random reasons and justifications. It came into his head to tell her that he was busy preparing for exams for the "big degree" the next year. He told her in detail about everything the degree required in terms of hard work. But she wasn't convinced.

She waxed poetic in expressing her attachment to him. She told him that she was ready to divorce Allala and marry him to give him all of her fortune. She didn't want anything else from life, just him. Him and nothing else. She didn't give him a chance to speak. She pulled him to her with force. It was like she'd gone crazy; she entered a strange state, kissing him, hugging him, and taking off his clothes. He didn't know what to do. She put out her fire in the flame of his body. He gagged on the spoon of honey that she shoved in his mouth and almost choked to death while she patted his back and poured him a glass of water. She kept repeating Salah Eddine's name. He fell silent, and she did as well. He took advantage of the opportunity, telling her, "You don't want me. You imagine Salah Eddine when you're with me."

She looked at him, surprised by what he'd said. He could tell that the words had had an impact and continued, "I don't like it. I'm me, I'm not Salah Eddine, and you're still living in the past. Wake up: I'm not Salah Eddine. Do you understand? Understand?"

He left her staggered. She put her head in her hands and became a lifeless corpse. He left her in bed, naked, and left the house quickly. That was his last time with her.

Sometimes he would long for her, but his mind would respond, reminding him of the risks that Yosser had warned him of. It wasn't easy, but Abdel Nasser's will was strong. Even stronger was that he overcame his jealousy when he saw her sometimes receive boys who were younger than him and less handsome. They would come and go, carrying candies and fruit. He understood that she had found replacements for him. He couldn't do a thing about it: sometimes he felt like the guilt was killing him and sometimes like jealousy was, but he just kept himself busy.

13

Other foul smells came from the house of the impotent Sheikh Allala the imam. But the official story in the neighborhood, the story that satisfied everybody, was that Lella Jnayna was infertile and that she loved children and young boys. She made up for her dry well with them; that's why her house became a sort of sanctuary for many of the neighborhood boys.

As for Sheikh Allala, he said that his wife was crazy and not fit to be the wife of a pious man like him. She smoked and didn't perform her religious duties and didn't want to be reminded of the *Hajj* pilgrimage or the *Umrah*. She would openly eat and drink during Ramadan in the presence of the maids and visitors. He kept asking God to guide her to the right path and praying for her. She was, after all, his wife that God was trying him with; he must be patient because God guides whomever he wills and leads astray whomever he wills.

As for the house of Hajj Mahmoud, the conversation ended quickly any time Lella Jnayna's name was mentioned, as if her name were a mangy camel or a vulgar word being said in that noble and virtuous house: the house of Hajja Zeinab and Hajj Mahmoud, may the scale of God's mercy equal the scale of his magnificent funeral on that great day, which nothing spoiled but Abdel Nasser's attack on Sheikh Allala, the neighborhood imam.

GLOSSARY

'ilm al-kalam: Literally, "the science of discourse." The study of the fundamental beliefs and doctrines of Islam.

'isha: Dinner; dinnertime. Also refers to the prayer at this time, which is the last of the five daily prayers in Islam.

Aamm: A title meaning "paternal uncle" which may be applied to any older man as a show of respect.

adhan: The Muslim call to prayer, sung or chanted from the minaret of a mosque at each of the five daily prayer times. Pronounced *a-DHAAN*, with the *dh* digraph representing the *th* sound in *the*.

Astaghfirullah: "God forgive me." Commonly used to express disapproval or frustration.

ayah: A verse of the Quran.

baklawa el-bey: "The bey's baklava." A tri-colored triangular sweet made from white, green, and pink layers of almond paste.

beldi: An adjective and noun referring to the old Tunisian economic elite, many of whom were of Andalusian or Turkish descent and used to live in the old medina of Tunis.

bjawia sfaxia: A cube-shaped candy (originally from the city of Sfax) composed of chopped dried fruit and nuts bound together in hardened syrup.

darwish: In Tunisian Arabic, a *darwish* (pronounced *der-WEESH*) is a dirty vagabond or homeless person. This term comes from the Arabic word for an ascetic Sufi wanderer, from which the English word *dervish* is also derived.

deglet nour: A variety of date grown in the south of Tunisia, characterized by its translucent, golden color.

fajr: Dawn. Also refers to the prayer at this time, which is the first of the five daily prayers in Islam.

Fatiha: The short surah which opens the Quran. (The word means "opening.") It is an essential element of the required prayers; it can also form a minimal prayer on its own.

frip: An open-air market where used clothing (often imported in bulk from abroad) is displayed and sold. Pronounced *freep*.

Hajj: The pilgrimage to Mecca; one of the five obligatory practices ("the five pillars") of Islam. Also the title given to a person who has performed the pilgrimage. (The feminine form of the title is *Hajja*.)

halal: Permissible in Islam. Opposite of *haram*.

hammam: Public bathhouse; also used to refer to the bathing act itself. Men and women bathe separately, though young boys accompany their mothers to the women's *hammam* prior to puberty.

haram: Forbidden by Islam. Also used to refer to something unacceptable in society, or colloquially for anything negative or regrettable. Opposite of *halal.*

harkous: A substance used for decorating the skin in intricate patterns; similar to henna except that *harkous* is black and sits on top of the skin rather than staining it. Like henna, it is only used by women and is often applied before weddings and other special occasions.

harissa: A ubiquitous Tunisian condiment made of hot peppers, garlic, and spices. Pronounced *ha-REE-suh.*

hawzas: Seminary centers for the education of Shi'ite scholars in Iran.

hijab: A headscarf worn by some Muslim women for modesty. The modern *hijab* is a cultural import from the Middle East and differs from the head coverings traditionally worn by Tunisian women.

jebba: A long, sleeveless tunic traditionally worn by Tunisian men, often paired with a red fez. Can be any color but is most commonly cream-colored with gold embroidery running down the front.

kaak al-warka: Donut-shaped cookies made by wrapping several layers of paper-thin pastry (*warka,* "paper") around an almond-paste and rosewater center before shaping into a ring and baking.

kafteji: A vegetarian dish made with a mixture of vegetables (including potatoes, bell peppers, squash, tomatoes, and olives), served with either a fried egg on top or scrambled eggs mixed throughout. Spices used and optional meat accompaniments (like liver or *merguez* sausage) vary by region and recipe. Was originally peasant food but is now common in fast-food restaurants. Pronounced *kef-TA-jee*.

kanoun: A clay charcoal-burning stove, usually six to nine inches tall. The *kanoun* has a fluted base, a bowl holding the charcoal, and three points protruding upward from the bowl on which a small pot or teapot can rest.

khala: Maternal aunt.

khalkhal: A heavy gold or silver ankle bracelet worn by Tunisian women, especially in rural areas.

khwanji: A disparaging name for members of the Muslim Brotherhood (or Islamists in general) in Tunisian Arabic. Derived from the word *ikhwan* ("brothers,") combined with the Turkish suffix *–jee*, denoting a profession or habitual occupation.

Lella: A title sometimes used for women in Tunisia.

louage: A variety of shared minibus taxi that travels between cities in Tunisia. (From the French word *louage,* meaning "rental.") They are boarded at designated stations and depart when they are full rather than by any set schedule. Pronounced *lou-WAAJ*.

machmoum: A small bouquet of jasmine buds, traditionally worn by Tunisian men behind the ear or by women like a corsage. Sold widely (especially to tourists) in the summer.

mehrasse: A mortar and pestle, usually made of brass or olive wood.

makroud: A rhombus-shaped cookie, often prepared for Eid al-Fitr (the holiday that marks the end of the Ramadan fast). Consists of a date-paste filling wrapped in a semolina crust, deep fried, and coated in honey (or syrup) and rose-water.

manaqib: A traditional genre of biography in Arabic, Turkish, and Persian literature.

mashrabiya: A type of projecting oriel window enclosed with carved wood latticework located on the upper floors of a building.

merguez: A spicy lamb sausage common in Tunisian cuisine.

mihrab: A semicircular niche in the wall of a mosque that indicates the direction of Mecca and hence the direction to face when praying.

miswak: A tooth-cleaning twig made from the *Salvadora persica* tree.

oud: A short-necked string instrument that is played like a guitar but has a distinctive sound.

qailulah: A nap taken during the hottest part of the day, similar to the Spanish *siesta*.

qanun: A flat string instrument that is held on the lap while played.

rosata: A milky-colored drink that is made from almond syrup and served cold.

safseri: A traditional Tunisian women's garment, composed of a single long piece of white or cream-colored fabric and wrapped around to cover the body, including the hair. In the past, most urban women would wear a *safseri* over their clothing when they were walking in public; today it is only worn by old women and is rarely seen.

sayyid: Literally, "master." Can also be used as a title ("mister,") though is often shortened to *Si* in Tunisian Arabic.

shakshuka: A North African dish of eggs poached in a sauce of tomatoes, olive oil, peppers, onion, and garlic, and commonly spiced with cumin, paprika, and cayenne pepper. It is eaten with bread and may include *merguez* sausage or other meat. Also called *ojja*.

Si (or *Sidi*): A personal title used in Tunisia, derived from *sayyid* ("mister," "master"). Often used as a sign of deference to a socially higher-ranking person, such as a boss or an older brother. The variant *Sidi* ("my master") is also used as a title for saints and is a common component of place names in Tunisia (like the city Sidi Bou Said).

soulamia: A gathering at which Sufi music is played. Also used for the genre of music played at such gatherings.

Standard Arabic: The modern written language of the Arab world, which is closely related to the Classical Arabic of the Quran. Standard Arabic is not the native language of any group of speakers but is the language of education, broadcast news media, government, and writing in general throughout the Arab world. *The Italian*'s Arabic original was written in Standard Arabic.

tagine: A baked-egg dish, similar to a quiche, though often without a crust. Also the name of the clay pot with a conical lid in which the dish was traditionally cooked. It is different from the Moroccan *tagine* (which is like a stew), but they share the same name because they were both traditionally cooked in a *tagine* dish.

Tata: French for "Aunt"—can be used literally or as a respectful title for an older woman.

Tunisian Arabic: The vernacular varieties of Arabic spoken in Tunisia; in particular, the prestige spoken standard of the capital Tunis. Tunisian Arabic shares many similarities with the vernaculars spoken in Libya and in Eastern Algeria but differs markedly from those of the Middle East and Egypt. Tunisian Arabic is not traditionally used in writing (though this has begun to change since the spread of internet access and the 2011 revolution).

Umrah: A pilgrimage to Mecca, often called the "lesser pilgrimage." Differs from the full pilgrimage (the *Hajj*) in that it can be performed at any time of the year, whereas the *Hajj* must be performed on specific dates.

Ustad: A title given to a teacher or highly educated person. Feminine form is *Ustada*.